The Search for Universal Consciousness

Adventure of Consciousness

- Analytical Ayurveda/ DR. K.A. LATHEEF
- Upaniṣads and Edith Stein: *A Dialogue on Models of The Person*/ THOMAS MAROTTIPPARYAIL
- Tirthaṅkarāsana: *A Work on Jaina Yoga*/ SHANTILAL D. PARAKH
- Aparokṣānubhūti: *The Essence of Self Realization*/ DR. SHRIKRISHN DESHMUKH
- A Critical Study in the Schism in Early Buddhist Monastic Tradition: *Dasavatthu and Pañcavatthu*/ LOKANANDA C. BHIKKHU
- Mystical Poems of Jnaneshwar: *Original Translations from the Marathi*/ ANAND MUNDRA
- Exclusion of Śūdras From Brahmajijñāsā: *Re-Reading Apaśūdrādhikaraṇam of Brahmasūtra Śāṅkara Bhāṣya*/ JAISON VADAKKAN
- The Search for Universal Consciousness : JULIO OZAN LAVOISIER

The Search for Universal Consciousness

Julio Ozán Lavoisier

MLBD
PUBLICATIONS

The Search for Universal Conciousness/Julio Ozán Lavoisier

First Edition: Delhi, 2021

ISBN : 978 81 9481 58 6 0

Published by
Motilal Banarsidass Publications
93, Shyam Lal Marg, Daryaganj,
New Delhi-110002 (India)
mlbd@mlbd.com

MLBD Cataloguing-in-Publication Data
The Search for Universal Conciousness
by Julio Ozán Lavoisier
ISBN : 978 81 9481 58 6 0
I. Prologue, II. Preface, III. Premises of the Method, IV. What I Understand by Philosophy of History, V. On the Quest, VI. Universal Conciousness

Printed by : Repro Books

In memory of my parents,
my first teachers.

Original title in Spanish: La Búsqueda de la Conciencia
Translation to English: Minni Sawhney,
University of Delhi, India
Revision of the English translation: Sydna Younson,
English Professor, Salta, Argentina
Dirección Nacional de Derechos de Autor, Argentina.
Expediente N° 5306983

Prologue by Côme Carpentier de Gourdon

Consciousness is now acknowledged by an increasing number of scientists, whether physicists, biologists or neuro-psychiatrists as the ultimate enigma as well as the key to understanding reality in all its aspects, physical and not. The word itself poses a challenge as its current scientific definition (everything that is of a mental nature) is rather new. Traditionally it was regarded as a solely human attribute and often equally with conscience which lent it a moral, ethical significance. A conscious being may be said metaphorically to have no conscience; yet, in Latin languages, there is only one word, 'conciencia', alluding to both, in Spanish which may account for the fact that the author of this book, eminent Argentinian philosopher and prolific writer Julio Ozan Lavoisier did not use it in the original title, 'The Quest for the Spirit', much better understood in his native tongue. However 'spirit' has a strong religious connotation ('the Holy Spirit" or Ghost) and is also associated with controversial practices such as spiritualism that rest on a particular concept of individual animal and human spirits. The blurry line between the spirit and the soul in many philosophical and 'spiritual' texts can also breed misunderstandings. The spirit is etymologically associated with air and the wind, which gives it a very 'naturalistic' resonance in the context of the ancient cosmologies based on four or five elements and in many theological and mystical scriptures, the biblical, hermetic, Christian and Islamic contexts among others, it is described as fire, whether literally or by analogy.

Consciousness, more culturally neutral is now the term of choice to refer to everything that makes us aware and self-aware and mediates all reality for us, both outer (the world) and inner (the self). Scientists all have to eventually come around to the conclusion that anything perceived is mediated by the mind or consciousness which we cannot bypass as nothing can be apprehended unless it is observed, thought about or imagined as Bertrand Russell concluded. Beginning with what the neurobiologists of the Santiago School, Maturana and Varela defined as 'sentience', which is perceptible in the simplest microscopic vegetal and animal organisms and reaching up to the loftiest human intellectual exercises, consciousness is at some level inseparable from life since its rudiments appear in the earliest known biotic forms.

Ozan Lavoisier's books all have ambitious agendas and the present one is no exception. He draws a summary history of Western philosophy in six eras: the Hellenic, the Latin, the Medieval, the Renaissance, Enlightenment and the Romantic with regard to what he understands as its idealistic mainstream, which is far wider than the Hegelian tradition as it is both moral and philosophical and not speculatively subjective. This succinct recapitulation leads to the final part which lays out the author's version of idealism, defined by him as the realization of universal or cosmic Consciousness. He adds a summary depiction of the eastern perspectives on consciousness, mainly in the Indic philosophical traditions but clarifies that he mostly dwells in this volume on the European legacy in view of the latter's centrality now that the world shares a common intellectual heritage mostly derived from the Greco-Roman past and from western 18th century political and epistemic concepts .

Ozan Lavoisier acknowledges his intellectual debt to South Asia and the Far East but he situates the oriental contribution to mankind's spiritual capital beyond history as it is timeless in its formulations (*nirguna brahman, nitya, rita, sanatana, akaliko, Tien, tao*), contrary to the chronologically defined and personalized genealogy of thought which characterizes Western civilization. Yet our philosopher also warns that all his system is based on experience and intended for individual and collective liberation, a characteristically 'eastern' trope which accounts for his explicit emphasis on contemplation, a definitely 'spiritual' practice and not a mere intellectual exercise based on reading about the theories of other thinkers. The book restores philosophy's original meaning as love and search for wisdom.

Ozan L. explains the longing for freedom as an inkling of the thirst for transcendence which is 'where the search for universal consciousness begins' since the mere conquest of physical freedom is quickly found to be insufficient and reveals the limited and somewhat fictitious character of socio-political and economic liberty.

In spite of this strong 'spiritual' bend, the *'Search for Universal Consciousness'* is not a mystical treatise or a theosophical sum. The author does not join the endless battle between religious believers and atheists and points out that believing or not believing in God only denotes a difference in one's position without indicating knowledge or lack of knowledge about God nor obviously affecting divine ontology. He focuses his attention on man's perception and on his biological, geo-historical and socio-cultural conditioning that affects the two components of his identity: *homo sapiens* and *homo habilis or faber* (crafty or handiworking man). The former factor goads man to reflect, develop ideas and achieve greater understanding of the higher, more permanent aspects of reality while the latter pushes him towards the satisfaction of his immediate needs and desires. His analysis of the great intellectual families which thinkers of all countries throughout the centuries have claimed for themselves: polytheism and monotheism, rationalism and spiritualism, materialism and mysticism is concise, yet deep and sharp. The author's conclusions lead one to realize that those ideologies are all points of view which correspond to diverse levels of understanding, themselves determined by personal experiences and degrees of introspection. None of them is objectively real or comprehensive.

Ozan Lavoisier states early in the book that in this age dominated by the pursuit of factual knowledge, religions based on belief, tending to become dogmatic and unthinking, may not survive as they cannot demonstrate their fundamental affirmations by any hard logical or historical proof and must rely on textual apologetics. The West has a particularly acute problem as the notion of God is so closely bound with Christian theology that anyone reluctant to embrace the biblical concept of a personalized God who allegedly loves people and yet lets manifest injustice take place in the world is categorized and usually seems himself as an atheist.

On the other hand religions or rather spiritual traditions that have remained dynamic and open, such as Hinduism, Buddhism and Taoism evolve with the times as they are rooted in the individual experience of transcendence and the contemplation of nature; they are hence paradoxically better able to inspire the new science-based technocratic civilization that has been taking shape during the last three centuries. However one can doubt whether human beings in general are changing or will change to the extent of no longer needing the moral and emotional support that a personal objective God provides, even if philosophers regard him or her as a mere symbol created by our minds.

Recent times have seen, perhaps in reaction to rampant techno-scientific materialism the revival of many rigidly defined and expansionistic religious creeds which reject any possibility for critical examination or even for a diversity of interpretations. For better or worse the success of those old or new belief systems invoking the authority of one or several dead or living human figures or allegedly divinely dictated texts shows that many if not most men (and women, since it has now become necessary to explicitly refer to both genders) are not ready to embrace the *unitive idealism* which the author champions in contradistinction with its subjective homonym. His early reference to Aldous Huxley's account of the perennial philosophy makes it clear that he has independently come to adopt the same perspective.

In the end Ozan Lavoisier's main message is a call for and an evocation of the 'unitive knowledge' that may reconcile the many, often conflicting worldviews developed by cultures and nations the world over. A pressing need for such a new convergence has arisen between contemporary scientific research and the age-old philosophical reflection on 'mind and matter' that arguably produced during the centuries the highest achievements in art, wisdom and moral excellence. *The search for universal consciousness* is particularly needed now that life is commonly described by authoritative sources as a chemico-physical phenomenon and man, like all creatures as a material body equipped with sophisticated software and nothing more. Yet Ozan L. is not alone in pointing out that such seductive and apparently rigorous scientific theories cannot explain what lies behind the phenomena they seek to account for. Consciousness cannot be reduced to the effect of neuronal chain reactions mediated by electrical currents and can be demonstrated to precede physical systems as various peer-reviewed research papers persuasively agree.

Without following scientific specialists in their ever more sophisticated probing of the 'quale of consciousness' (Visan) and its necessary but arcane relation with Space-Time, aware as he is that science and philosophy belong to two different categories and that the latter can therefore never wholly follow the methodology of the former, Ozan Lavoisier as a true cosmopolitan sage from the Andes shares with us once more in the following pages the essence of his intellectual intuitions, supported by an erudite survey of mankind's pursuit of its highest aspirations since the dawn of recorded history.

Côme Carpentier de Gourdon is a writer and lecturer. Convener of the Editorial Board of World Affairs, the *Journal of International Issues*, New Delhi. He has lectured in more than a hundred universities. Carpentier is one of the main commentators in the documentary film *The Hindu Tradition*. (Note by the author)

Preface

In this work I want to show that in human history there has been a constant search of the same objective and the same Reality. Since the realization of this objective is the highest human aspiration, I have deemed my work necessary. My commentaries on these authors have (as is usually the case in my works) sought to delineate the contours of my own thought. This quest is not exclusive to some thinkers, it is humanity's quest, it is the spirit that animates our consciousness, and we are all partners in this search. If the reader is drawn to this work, I will have fulfilled my objective.

Here and in all my work the reader will see the development of two projects: that of fulfillment or personal liberation, which is feasible, and that of the collective liberation, which is an impractical project, ideal and utopian, but as long as it is realized and the external favorable conditions are available, all levels of society will reach a higher level. Hence my parallel preoccupation for social especially cultural matters: the situation of the spirit in time and space, *The Evolution of the Spirit* and the *Origin and Destiny of Man*, I am convinced that with this knowledge individuals and societies will be able to follow a process of *natural evolution*; which has been heretofore unrealizable due to the simple but grave reason that the human being is alienated from his Nature.

My purpose is to elevate the level of consciousness exempt from all belief till it reaches a perspective from which the spiritual panorama is shown to be clear and cleansed of all doubt. It is from this *essential perspective* that we will compare our vision with others whom we consider more representatives in order to follow the trajectory of the spirit in the West. Suffice to say that if I have not followed any belief, I am not trying to make the reader the authority of the said perspective. In earlier works, especially in *Psychosophy*, I have laid out the necessary mediums and requisites to achieve it; that has been the primary purpose that I continue to hold on to, as only by acquiring this vision can one have the certitude that what is explained here has a solid basis. All my philosophy is based on experience, and at no time do I ask the reader to believe in it, i.e. in my authority. For this reason before expounding my philosophy in my early works, I showed the path that leads to this experience and this present work has no other purpose apart from this.

I should again warn the reader that a spiritual praxis is necessary for understanding the essentials of my work, i.e. a *primarily contemplative life* that allows the spirit to observe the beauty and order of Nature, in relation to the beauty and order of the mind. Philosophy is not born of too much thought but of an awakening, an opening of the eyes, and an opening of the mind towards another reality which is the one that is revealed by this order and beauty in all life. Reflection without contemplation is like making a leap over the reality that we are trying to understand; one has to first see what one wants to understand. There is a natural time that the spirit needs for the impurities of the mind to be flushed out so that they can allow clarity just as the rain purifies the air and allows one to perceive with clarity not only things but also the transparency of the air, without which there is no clear perception. The impurities that disturb the mind are always greater than what man might imagine: Inherited beliefs, unfiltered education, ideas that are preconceived or conceived to enrich the ego, constantly perturb the understanding. It is this cleansing of the spiritual atmosphere that gives birth to philosophy. Later, of course there comes growth which should be realized in the same atmosphere of calm and creative contemplation so that it produces flowers and fruits in keeping with the Nature of things.

I must insist on the need for self–knowledge, since one of the main functions of reason has always been that of justifying our vices and mistakes; if it were not so, history would have been very different. All knowledge should begin with the knowledge of oneself, but it is evident that man tends to invert this order, leaving the most crucial for the end. There are many complex reasons for this (see *Why Man Remains in Ignorance*, in *Origin and Destiny of Man*). What has happened in general is that the ego has taken hold of the center of consciousness and it suspects or intuits that if it induces the spirit to be aware of the meanderings of consciousness, it would begin to attack the clearly selfish desires that make up its personality and, in the final instance, could put into question its own existence. There is thus an ontological problem that is found at the root of all human knowledge, which precedes the multitude of psychological problems facing man: *the desire of being and the fear of not being* lead him to postpone and indefinitely derive his own knowledge. This being the case, it is easier and more convenient for man to have ideas about himself and have beliefs about reality, rather than knowing himself, and as he keeps identifying with his ideas and beliefs, he goes on molding his personality which is what keeps his ego alive; his first great wrong identification, on which many others will accumulate, a multitude of opinions which will keep him ignorant.

I start from a basic scientific principle that unfortunately has not been taken into account by millions of believers and by thinkers who are believers: *no belief generates an existence.* For example, my belief in God or lack of it only changes my position not my knowledge of God and naturally does not ever change the ontological situation of the latter.

Throughout this work we will be seeing the various shifts of the spirit, in the psyche and in history, as it searches for its transcendent destiny, at other times we will see it attend to the material needs that animal nature requires; the *homo sapiens* and the *homo habilis,* have alternated their primacy since the time of the origin of our species, it is part of the human condition, it is and will be part of our history (See *Origin and Destiny of Man*). To reach the present we have to make a review of the history of the spirit, and in this review I will apply the same theories to throw light on the state of the spirit in each age, its location under the influence the most eminent thinkers, and creative and inspired men.

The Manifestations of the Spirit are inexhaustible and for this reason in various works I have dwelt on this matter. In principle they will be divided in four for the following reasons: The human being has four specific faculties for perceiving the manifestations of the Spirit: the moral, the artistic, the religious and the philosophic; the four configure a consciousness that envelops them, which I have called *unitive,* because all of them tend to unify the mind and integrate it in the Spirit. By expressing this perception, man, especially in the West has been developing different disciplines that, though they might clear his understanding on a rational plane, tend to disarticulate his primary unity. My intention is to reintegrate the human spirit in this primary unity therefore the direction I will follow is ascendant and convergent. Nevertheless for this purpose and due to reasons of space and method I have to make use of the division established. For this reason this attempt has to be spread out in various essays: the present work will attend to the manifestations of the Spirit perceived and expressed by philosophical and religious consciousness, which will be followed by *The Roots of Moral and The Roots of Art*.

The fact that this work is limited to the Western framework does not mean that we should remain cloistered within it. In an age of globalization this attitude signifies a provincial spirit and would put us at the opposite pole of my proposed universal projection. My own life can serve as a point of reference: I have devoted half of it to the West, the other half to the East, especially to India.

We can learn a lot from Asian cultures and especially in what is most decisive in the field of the spirit. We should not forget that of the three great civilizations made by man, two are a legacy of the Far East. Of course, we do not have sufficient experience of this spirit, but the same history has made us converge in it and sooner or later we will have to assimilate this experience. Conscious of this need, I have written commentaries on Hinduism and in greater detail on Buddhism - from its origin till *Zen* in *The Evolution of the Spirit*- as I consider these doctrines outstanding expressions of idealism. I have also been working for a long time on *The Spirit in India* that I have made into an extensive documentary film (a serial in 25 episodes) called *The Hindu Tradition,* which aspires to be a kind of abbreviated visual encyclopedia of Hinduism.

These works are based on my conviction that the Indic civilization, a product of Hinduism and Buddhism, has kept itself closer to the *Sources of the Spirit*, and thus its search has been more constant, systematic and coherent. But this does not mean that Western thought has distanced itself from the said *Sources*, rather as I have shown in this work, idealism constitutes the main current in its philosophy. But beyond this endeavour I am interested in showing that there is a *universal idealism* that transcends geographic and cultural boundaries that I have tried to bring together in my philosophy. My book *Parallel Civilizations* has the same objective of showing a parallel between the Hellenic and Indic civilizations.

Moreover, the limitations of the *Philosophy of History,* which due to reasons of space is based only on Western thought, are apparent as what is important therein is the perspective or the general vision is applied to history. The philosophies of the Far East take hold of my thought; they are part of my organ of sight and are useful for universal perspective. This means that even if I have not followed Eastern thought in its particular trajectory, it is not lacking in my vision of the unfolding of Western culture. In other words, in my *Philosophy of History*, only the historical part is Western, as the East is omnipresent in my thought and inserts itself in all the ages of Western civilization. It is thus a universal philosophy applied to the development of a single culture. On the other hand till the XXIst century, and only till then, the West has not received any significant cultural and spiritual influence from the Far East, henceforth our Planet will have only one history; hence the importance of a cosmopolitan philosophy.

I think this is sufficient for the purpose of this book. The objective is not just to explain history, I do not know if this would be of any use to anyone at this point, instead of compiling facts, the objective is philosophical in the original meaning of the term: to make men happier and wiser.

A lot remains to be said, as life has been too short to cover such broad subjects, but I hope that someone will take this up and extend it; as long as he does not believe that he can end it, as the framework of this task is infinity itself. No one must believe that these theories are sufficient, as it would still be necessary to live them in order to experience and understand them. The time that I have spent in clarifying these ideas (surpassing my own desires to do so), has the sole aim of giving others more time to live them, which could generate a mankind of the type I would have liked to have known and lived with.

Table of Contents

Premises of the Method

The reader will find the theoretical explanation of this critical vision of history in my earlier works, especially in *The Spirit in History*, where I develop the basis for this and for the entire philosophy of history. I therefore consider this reference as indispensable for the understanding of this work. For the reader who have not consult my earlier works, I will try to make a synthesis of my *theory of knowledge*, intimately linked to my *transcendental psychology* that can be found in my *Psychosophy*, in order to familiarize him with a terminology that he will see spread throughout this book. These are my psychological and epistemic premises which will be the instruments of my work:

The concepts of discernment, intellect, reason and understanding have been indiscriminately used and this has caused great confusion. Some thinkers have given them a specific meaning to clarify their own philosophies, but these differ so much from mine that I will not borrow their concepts and I will redefine them. The understanding will cover all the cognitive faculties, including those that transcend reason. I have differentiated five planes of understanding and the levels of consciousness within them; knowledge will depend on the plane and level used. These are: 1) The plane of external *representations or discernment*; 2) the *intellectual or that of the intuitions*; 3) *the central or vital*, that we can also call *unitive* due to its path of knowledge; 4) the animate or that of the *sentiments and emotions*; 5) the plane of *internal representations*, which would correspond to what has been called "unconscious".

Reason occupies two planes of the five in understanding, one is the intellect, and the other is discernment. Discernment has the capacity of unifying, separating, comparing and establishing relations; its specific instrument is logic. *Discernment* is born (on this genesis see *Origin and Destiny of Man*), as something separated from the surrounding matter, duality is implicit in its origin. This duality implies a spatial and temporal distance, and thus, its knowledge is external and mediate. As the *I or Ego* is identified with discernment, this faculty has been taken since time immemorial as the "consciousness" of man as it is nothing more than a relative and incipient faculty. Through this identification man sees, thinks, believe and acts in keeping with these characteristics; the history of thought and human actions confirm this. *The I* is not stable nor is it a reality as man wants to believe, but an idea that keeps making itself, which makes it look like a series of scaffolds in which he never stops fitting in. This *I* is settling itself in a place in the mind from a vantage point from which it usually looks towards the world; but the living, creative and real part of the mind is the *spirit,* thanks to which it knows and is known. The *I* is reflected in the spirit, and it thus makes ideas, *a posteriori*, from which the spirit sees or directly experiences. Man does not know himself, as he believes, observing his mind from his *I,* but as he observes his *I* from the spirit. In reality the *I* does not exist but as an identification with the belief of its own existence.

What really exists, given its indispensable and constant presence is the *spirit*. I refer in this way to the reference that we always find in all knowledge in all planes and at all levels. This spirit or constant reference or center of consciousness is not based in any of the said planes or levels; it frequents them but shifts itself in them, and this is what makes knowledge possible. The spirit moves through the different planes of understanding and levels of consciousness which keeps giving it different perspectives. In spite of common experience, of Descartes and in general of Western psychology, the real center of consciousness of man is not the *I* or a supposed fixed entity in the mind, but the same spirit that permanently fluctuates. I could have used another term to designate the concept of *spirit,* as *the self,* or *the observer,* since it is he who observes, not only the motions of the *I* or ego, but the reasons its adduces, and, even beyond, his intentions. The *spirit,* then, in my terminology, is the one who knows, is the true self of the human being and acts as an intermediary between the individual consciousness and the universal Consciousness, and knows because it has the latter as a reference and not the habitual self. The universal Consciousness is not, as we shall see, heteronomous, it is the very apex of our consciousness. Henceforward the reader should remember that the subject of unitive consciousness is the human spirit, not the *I*; these concepts will be clarified later.

From *the perspective of discernment, that I have called individual perspective,* the *I* looks at the world and its peers in a distorted and egocentric way. The *I* is installed in the external faculties because from there it can attend to its material necessities, but as it attends to them it is distracted from its spiritual necessities and in this way it has become alienated from its spirit and separated from its medium, the Nature, to which *it looks objectively in order to use it subjectively.* Its accumulative knowledge is derived from this way of thinking and feeling and this has given so many material advantages to man.

The intellect is the internal part of reason in which the spirit has access to the intuitions and which discernment generally uses for its utilitarian purposes. *Intuitions,* that have always been a mystery for man, are explained by the aforesaid reflection of reason by way of the intellect, in the universal Spirit. When the reason is very elevated, and it is so due to its closeness to the Spirit, the Soul of the World, it comes into contact with the Transcendent; these are the *transcendental or intellectual intuitions.* These provide a perspective to knowledge that illuminates reason in its path; as we will see, all the great philosophies emanate from it. The mistakes and disagreements between them are due to the fact that they do not necessarily produce a radical and intrinsic change in the subject, as the spirit is still linked to the *I* and to its individual perspective, which makes it usually accept inherited cultural or subjective beliefs or give in to particular interests. Overcoming this perspective is not easy but it is viable; my work is directed towards this objective.

The internal plane, called the unconscious, also has its peculiar way of instructing us with its knowledge as it has the capacity of establishing partial and at times universal relations, with the facts that it takes from other planes, although these relations may seem to be irrational and even crazy to discernment, which is in no position or too prejudiced to understand it. *The animate plane* houses the feelings. These can be low like fear or elevated like love. On all planes the spirit can take an ascending or descending direction, but especially on this plane it is exposed to the winds of desire that can transport it in all directions; for this reason I have called it animate.

In my conception there are no planes that are objectively superior to others, thus for example, I do not believe that the intellect is superior to feelings or vice versa; even if there are more suitable planes for determinate objectives. What gives greater clarity of vision are the *levels of consciousness,* i.e. the perspective gained in any of the planes of understanding, even though I consider that the most direct path for the knowledge of the spirit is the *vital or central plane,* which is not discernible from the external plane; for this reason it remains unconscious in common man. In this plane the spirit is not found separated from its internal, psychic nor external circumstances, and thus his knowledge is not mediate, as in discernment, but immediate. From this central plane the spirit, far from seeing an opposition between the different planes of the understanding or mental faculties feels the need to integrate them. Their harmonious integration constitutes the *unitive knowledge*, which allows the progressive ascent of the spirit. Due to the aforesaid characteristics, the vital plane is the centre of the human consciousness, and is the real path of access towards the highest levels of the consciousness: the *altruist* consciousness, the *unitive*, and the *pure or unified consciousness*. The correct consciousness of man is the *unitive consciousness*, which is the zone of equilibrium of the spirit between his animal and divine condition. It is also the home of the aesthetic, moral, religious and philosophical consciousness.

The displacements of the spirit and its rest in the different levels take place through *realizations of the consciousness*. The ideas that result are eventually propagated in societies through mimesis, contagion or fashion; these expressions will define the spirit of the age. If they reach an elevated level of consciousness they will generate *ages of growth*, if not they will produce *ages of perigee*, as the spirit will be more distanced from the Spirit. (See *The Spirit in History*) The highs and lows suffered by societies result in the predominance of the *I* that enslaves the spirit and applies its knowledge to its utilitarian requirements, or the progressive discovery of its identity with the spirit. This struggle between the *homo faber* and the *homo sapiens* is the very motor of a human history. When the spirit nears the *I*, utilitarianism prevails, when the *I* assimilates to the spirit then spiritualism prevails; *The Quest for Consciousness* develops in this process.

The majority of human beings are attracted by material advantages, and they are clueless about this attraction that keeps them in a *state of survival.* In fact in the developed countries our species has overcome this stage, but human consciousness is stuck in this external sector of the mind that prevails through ignorance and greed. Superior men are aware of this, and are not happy just being comfortable, they feel that there is something beyond because they are closer to the spirit; they are aware that the freedom of physical action will always be insufficient because it is not the freedom that they long for; *it is in this longing for freedom that the Quest for Consciousness begins.*

What I Understand by Philosophy of History

Experience has instilled in me the conviction that the best and most direct way of knowing peoples is by discovering their spirit. We find their roots in the spirit in which cultures have grown and given root to civilizations. This spirit is defined by their desires, their searches, their aspiration, their conscious or unconscious transcending of themselves. By knowing these motivations we will be able to cover different historical periods, to investigate them from within, and to recognize the spirit of the age better as we identify with it; in this way history reveals itself.

If there is a "true history" it is that which was lived in during the time of those who made it, and it becomes real as we continue experiencing, reliving and making it our own, and the most effective way of doing so is by placing our spirit, not only in the age that we want to understand, but also on *the same plane of understanding and level of consciousness of the most representative and creative of men*. Thus we could say that *the true history is the present*; paradoxical as it may sound, as we would be bad mariners indeed if we read all the histories of navigation without leaving the coast. We can speak of the storms that befell Ulysses, Cook or Drake, but if we have never been in a storm we will never have a clear idea of them. And the "clear idea" comes from our experience. My objective thus is to "navigate" through history without preconceived ideas, without the baggage of our beliefs, our faith, our age, and finally our personal perspective. Because otherwise this would be to determine history *a priori*, and besides not being very "scientific" is of no more use to us than to prove our ideas and beliefs to ourselves. There are, basically, two ways of traveling: one, the usual, that entails carrying heavy suitcases full of prejudices passing judgments on the countries that we visit and returning home with our load of criticism, the other is travelling with empty suitcases in order to fill them with what we have to learn, and with the ability to find a home in each place that we visit. It is this ability that we need if we want to learn from our journey through history. My intention in any case is to make the past and present circumstances of man reflect in his soul for the latter to be illuminated, as the study of history becomes useless if man does not manage to know himself in his present; if he does not look directly in the mirror of his conscience, his past errors will not serve him as examples.

All *Philosophy of History* that tries to be such, i.e., express the most essential and truthful of events, cannot disregard the perspective that governs the age from which it will be studied, as it is the latter which determines the comprehension of past facts, as the present will also become the past, and its perspective will become obsolete. This is one of the most common errors made by the researchers of history: that of applying the perspective and beliefs in which they live to the past, thus we encounter the same history recounted in different ways in each age, and we never know which is the real one.

Thus just as there is no single way to philosophize, there is more than just one way of devising a philosophy of history. A philosophy of history, in keeping with the Hegelian model, that has unfortunately often become an exemplar, would be the development of one single idea that weaves the whole fabric of history. This idea is so broad that though it might pretend to incorporate the multitude of different ideas of mankind, ends up discarding them by simultaneously justifying its mistakes and denying its wrong moves. In this way, the fabric spun with all the thoughts and human acts that covers all of history is simply as it should have been. But it turns out that when we see, not only the past, but also the result of this development, we are left with the inevitable impression of the history of mankind being written by a demented person with some brief moments of lucidity.

Since this is my impression, my project of a philosophy of history would consist of: firstly, in developing its theoretical bases, already demonstrated in *The Spirit in History*; secondly, in discovering and highlighting the causes of madness that have destroyed our history when it is not material or spiritual, and that have deviated from the course of healthier, elevated and more intelligent projects; and thirdly, in discovering and highlighting the moments of lucidity that have resulted in more creative periods and the greatest plenitude of man and to draw connections between them.

I am not trying to connect facts, ages or civilizations as if they were grids of an inevitable logic. I do not believe that logic has this supernatural power, nor that there is any supernatural factor that decides the action of men and that they respond like robots to some external stimulus. Neither do I believe that philosophy has to be "scientific," least of all when dealing with something as contingent as history. The common sense that derives from historical experience and daily life, much before logic, tells us that history is a result of passions and human aspirations that vary in keeping with circumstances that are also variable. Of course there are constants, but these are more a part of the animal nature of man. As we will see (and we have seen in *The Spirit of History*), *it is man who repeats himself when he returns to the same mental mechanisms* (planes of understanding, or levels of consciousness); it is in this way that history repeats itself, that the spirit awakens or again falls asleep. And it is in this way that a more realistic and possibly edifying philosophy of history can be proposed.

As is evident, the psychological aspect plays as important a role as the philosophical in its descending function, revealing the madness of men paving the road to their destiny as a transcendental psychology. In this way, this project can also be called a *Psychosophy of History*, as it never loses sight of the psychological factors that motivate man, even if it is not limited to them, as it knows that behind them there are impulses that transcend them. We will see that what is decisive is the *position* of the spirit in the mind that generates a *disposition* in individuals and in peoples that determines its sympathies and beliefs during a time and place in history. The reader will find the elements that constitute my transcendental psychology in *Psychosophy.*

I believe that philosophers and historians can agree on this: history can help us a great deal in knowing ourselves, it is part of our circumstances, and not just those of the past, as our present earthly circumstances are derived from historic ones. Finally, I believe that the main task of the *philosophy of history* is not to explain the happenings of the past, but rather the revelatory ideas, the creative works, *the sources of inspiration,* if possible, that have influenced individuals and exemplary societies so that by elevating the spirit we can reproduce these states of the soul. History is the experience of humanity; if it is not useful to us as a personal experience; it becomes a dead letter, a useless story.

What Aristotle said of history being inferior to literature because it concerns itself with particulars, is true from his perspective, but there are other ways of seeing the matter.

Human beings are not simple figures but spirits with ideals and beliefs, with moral, social, artistic, religious and even philosophical principles. In history we find characters who since they are real affect us more deeply than those that are found in literature. The historical event that took place in Thermopiles clearly illustrate what has been said. It was a very particular event, being, one of the smallest battles recorded in history and yet, the whole world knows about it. Is it for its particularities that it is remembered or for its moral and social exemplarity? Who knows Nimitz (outside U.S.A.) the admiral of the greatest sea battle? The Kamikazes (a Japanese word incorporated into all languages) who took part in this battle were more famous than him. And why? Because of their exemplarity, much like those Spartans two thousand five hundred years before. *Particular acts are universal if they have become exemplary,* that is to say, ideal.

This work should not be read as a *history of Idealism,* but as the development of the spirit in the West, whose protagonists are the spirits who have been able to transcend their individual consciousness to be able to intuit another more elevated, more universal consciousness. It is not about the evolution of man in general as man cannot leave his own perspective although he might sense another consciousness. This happens to man as well as to other animals, who have no other remedy but to repeat for themselves what is always essentially the same; for this reason we see him repeating the same vices over and again. He is aware of them, and tries, of course, through laws and other practical recourses to regulate them, but nothing more; he will continue to commit them. Just as the deer and dolphin will continue to be deer and dolphin, so will man continue to be man; unless... he changes his perspective: hence the importance of these idealists who have glimpsed another way of seeing. Although this, as we will see, is not enough, the purpose of this and all my work is more ambitious: to realize another way of being.

I hope with my theory of perspectives to present a *Philosophy of History*, of the equilibrium between extremes and others, that would contribute to transforming the reader and that will try somehow and in some way to change the course of history. I would not write without these ambitious pretentions, although I do not ignore their measure of utopia, because I have sacrificed a significant part of my life for the future, revising the work of those who have come before me. I have seen too much ruin and blood in the road of history and feel obliged to propose some solutions that I consider reasonable and viable.

Of course my philosophy does not explain particular historical facts, but is concerned with the essential current of history and the underlying spirit, man's constant search to animate and feed his daily activities. History can be understood as a succession of concrete facts, but this aspect only shows what man has constructed (and destroyed) the material and external aspect of his activity and does not reveal to us the human being. Of course, historical facts are not only explained by the drives of the spirit, they are definitely the result of its interrelation with matter which generates its struggle for survival, that in turn awakens the ever present passion that lead man on unforeseen paths distant far from his destiny; it is this human condition that history is weaving. And this framework is so compact, multiple and complex that it covers the fundamental threads that go from its origin to its destiny. Rediscovering them and exposing them under the light of the eternal Conscience of the world is the work of philosophy; and in my understanding it is the function of a *philosophy of history*.

I repeatedly turn to history because each time I observe a culture and a society I come to the conclusion that they are products of the past, even though fortunately, they are a result of something more. History appears to me as a current that flows, like water, filling first the spirit of men, in order to later, drag them along by apparently following a natural course, partly in conformity with them, partly in spite of them. This wave is made up by the majority, which allows itself to be filled and dragged along; its force lies in quantity and not in quality. This principal current receives tributaries, the origins of which lie not in history but in the Transcendent; they are the ideas of a few which by influencing this current manage to change its course in some way, but they soon lose their force and are incorporated in the great torrent that ends up dragging them too along. We can speak then of a natural tide that our species follows, against which luminous ideas are shown to be impotent. In other words, history continues to be a failure, or, in the best of cases, the evolution of humanity is exasperatedly slow. Is undeniable that technology advances rapidly and in a progressive manner, but all the apparatus created are like ships that float on the current of history, and unsurprisingly since it is made by them and for them is borne along like the spirit of men. History, in any case, is presented as a vicious circle.

Such being the state of affairs, the only way to effectively change the course of history is by changing the nature of man. This, at first, is presented as utopian idealism, and, of course, as an attack on nature. But it is actually the opposite, based as it is on the premise that man has developed on the margins of his real nature, he is alienated from it, i.e., from himself, his spirit is decentred and, as a result his vision, his projects, his desires, finally his history, is diverted, or, more precisely, flows at the margin of his correct path. This does not only mean that the human is not led towards his destiny, but that all his labour and effort lacks value, and even his life lacks meaning. All this is not entirely absolute, as we all intuit at times that these are luminous ideas and we all sporadically feel that there is something more than this present state that we passively accept, we all have a foreboding that something is amiss. We all have these ideas, feelings and presentiments because our true nature warns us, it beckons us towards reflection. My work only aims to help us to reflect on these matters on which our life depends and which can help us avoid history passing us by.

On the Quest

The human being finds himself faced with two kinds of fundamental circumstances: some are infinite and permanent, others are temporal and local. The latter depend on social, technological and cultural progress. Permanent circumstances underlie these: the same sun, the same firmament, the same infinite, the same death, the same uncertainty follows. Both circumstances are presented to him as external and internal, although he does not always discern them as such, as they converge in the centre of his consciousness. This centre of consciousness, the spirit itself, that he takes as fixed and permanent, is not so, it is changing, dynamic, and moves through the different planes of understanding and the different levels of consciousness, attending to its physical or spiritual needs; the first ones project it towards the impermanent, the latter towards the permanent. It is easy to infer that everything is part of a single consciousness, nevertheless only some have had isolated intuitions of that unity.

I believe that what has been defined as idealism has been a more consistent quest within this converging objective, for this reason I will follow it in history, albeit in a synoptic way, in its more prominent manifestations, until I reach the realization of its objective. I clarify that I am far from believing that "the latest philosophy is the result of all preceding philosophies and that it should contain the principles of all these philosophies" (Hegel. *Encicl.*), as I am talking of a line or school that does not comprise of those that might have been, or have in fact been, wrong paths or fruitless meanders to the said realization. I am not ready to justify all the roads of history, the majority of which are covered with blood, nor the periods during which injustice has reigned through terror. Happiness has only been glimpsed by man for brief moments like a tenuous light in the horizon between dark clouds; and the sky continues to be overcast.

My thought has ended up being structured like a system, but this does not mean that it is enough to believe in the solidity of that structure in order to be in "the truth." My conclusions are nothing more than beacon lights towards which each one should navigate in the immense ocean of the spirit, navigating through one's own experience, taking charge of external circumstances: the political regional and historical currents etc., and the internal ones: the divergences, delays and dismasting that can cause the storms of passions. My proposal is, basically Socratic-Platonic: to make of philosophy a systematic method of spiritual life, inclining towards wisdom.

I think it is in the interest of all to discover and follow the spirit that has been generating the clearest waters, the most favourable currents, that have made the fields of the soul more fertile, in short, the spirit best directed towards the realization of man. It goes without saying that here we are not dealing with an intellectual historical curiosity, but expressing the virtues of that spirit that are and will always be valid and exemplary, so that we can emulate them in order to perfect ourselves as individuals and social beings. We should look for a spirit that is ideal in some sense, but I will not propose an unrealizable ideal, but that which in good measure has been fulfilled in periods of apogee (in *The Spirit of History* you will see my understanding of this), which is in keeping with the most prominent profiles of our character and idiosyncrasy, with the virtues that continue to awaken our admiration. Because we are dealing with this: of bringing clarity to the most adequate paradigms in order to awaken our present spirit.

As will be seen, the guiding thread of this work will be the manifestations of the spirit as idealism. This is not, as the dictionaries show, a philosophical current that the aspirant can choose amongst many others, but a paradigm to which he should aspire as it is the highest that can be reached by man, the widest all-encompassing and integrative perspective that can be obtained. It is true that idealism has been expressed by a few philosophers and even amongst them the manifestations have been varied; they have the same common inspiration, but not all have been entirely imbued with its essence, their intuitions have reached their waters, rich in knowledge, but remain distant from the spring of wisdom, the final objective of philosophy. Since this is a source of transcendent and entirely spiritual nature, it becomes difficult to explain it in terms that are amenable to reason. Because of this, even if I have to use idealism as a guiding thread, I do not have to reduce the manifestations of the spirit to philosophy in the restricted sense that the West has given it. I should speak of a philosophy of life, in which morality is indispensable as without it all ideas, however elevated they might be, are like leaves in the wind; art is also a medium, the most beautiful undoubtedly, and perhaps the most effective for those gifted with aesthetic sense.

Four basic abstractions have made human understanding possible: time and space (Kant), a nucleus of consciousness, and unity; the four, in themselves, are elusive. Man has developed four specific consciousnesses to perceive the Spirit: the moral, the aesthetic, the religious and the philosophical; and he needs other faculties for their expression, the external ones, like the intellect, discernment and memory. Thanks to them it keeps enclosing in its microcosms what it intuits of an order that transcends it or a macrocosm; in keeping with its understanding continues expressing it's perceived manifestations of the said order.

We know that in general the human being has little of the spiritual and much of the animal, due to which the history that he has been making has a base level of spirituality. However, if we investigate underneath the ashes and cadavers that he has left behind in his struggle for survival, we will see a constant force that pushes him forward. This impulse is also deviated by his passions or is applied in utilitarian occupations, in his need that keep him distracted from the essential. But at times he intuits that there is something more and this impulse incites a search for an expression of a reality other than the quotidian, to transcend himself in some way.

The pretention of monopolizing the spirit has caused a lot of misunderstanding; one has to go no farther than to see in history the disputes between philosophers and religious men, scientists and artists, all against each other. All express the spirit, except that each one believes more in his own because it is from him, from his perspective, his reality is shown to be clearer. From here it becomes clear that the spirit has diversified, but we can easily infer that the more we approach the angle from where the spirits converge, we will not just have a more universal but also more impartial vision, through which we will better be able to come to an agreement. It is one of my more vehement objectives to put an end to the misunderstanding between men, and I believe that the most effective means is the aforesaid: to bring the spirits closer to their point of convergence.

About the Origin of Ideas

When we read not just the philosophers, but what has been written about them in posterity, we find that they have invariably been influenced by others; this commentary is normal amongst those scholars who learn philosophy from books. But this is not always the case amongst the philosophers themselves because they take their knowledge not from books but from the surrounding world and from their own minds, i.e. from their own experience. This is very important not just to understand the philosophers but also a part of philosophy which is the human mind and the theory of knowledge that derives from it.

I am referring here strictly to the philosophers who are capable of thinking for themselves and of having their own ideas, i.e. of seeing their external and internal circumstances (psychic) through a *tabula rasa*, without inherited beliefs, and when these are accepted they are a *continuation* of the same, as is the case of Christian thought which is called Apologetic and not a *ratification*. For this to be so, one should start from *free* and *original spirits*, not in the sense of "novel" but spirits inspired by an origin that they have discovered and developed in keeping with their personal experience. There can of course be certain minor influences and some inherited ideas, but apart from not being central within the system or the totality of the work, they are inevitably noticed by other philosophers and given importance.

In this work I have followed idealist thought with wide

brush strokes, from the Pre Socratics to my own idealism following the aforesaid premise: the philosophers do not *take* their ideas from those who preceded them, rather that when face to face with the same universal circumstances and similar *internal circumstances* or mental composition, they arrive at similar conclusions. In other words more than a *cultural legacy* there is a *superposition* of ideas. The importance of this manner of seeing the history of thought is that where there is a *superposition of ideas* there occurs a *ratification* of demonstrated truths, which constitutes a *statistic*, a factor that is taken very seriously in scientific knowledge.

The next step in the sciences is that of *proving* if the statistic refers to a certain fact, if it exists objectively; which is plausible because in matter it can work till it collides with experience. But here lies the radical difference: philosophy (when it is so, I am not talking of materialism which is not so), concerns itself primarily with the spirit and explains matter in connection with it; matter is not enough and it tries to always transcend it. And it so happens that in the kingdom of the spirit there is no objective proof, or experimentation like there is in the sciences. Philosophy's attempt to be "scientific" has been and continues to be fruitless because these disciplines belong to two different natures.

A philosopher is one who has their own ideas; otherwise they are nothing more than a disciple. And the ideas of the philosopher have their origin in experience and not in the influence of others. If the philosopher adopts an alien idea it is because it coincides with their own. The academic who lacks their own ideas does not know where the philosopher gets their ideas from and it is precisely for this reason they search for its origin in a concrete source where they have already been written and they believe that they have discovered the origin when a similarity is found in another author. And due to this ignorance of the origin of ideas, the academic needs logical demonstrations, and is thus inclined to accept as true the ideas that are best demonstrated; it is not enough that they merely be shown.

I personally realized what I have just commented on when I asked an academic what he thought of one of my books. He answered: "Everything seems all right, but where do you get your ideas from?" He thought, of course, that he would get the references of some author or another. I told him that not just that book but my entire work tries to explain *the origin of ideas*. The book the reader holds in his hands reiterates the same subject but it has already been clarified that he will not find logical demonstrations because there can always be a contrary demonstration as in the world of ideas. Besides, if the reader remains on the plane of reason he will never find the origin of my ideas or that of ideas in general. My method takes another route and consists of trying to take the reader to the origin of ideas; showing them but not demonstrating them. The proofs of reason never reach the centre of consciousness; they remain on the plane of beliefs. When one sees, one gets the proof and knows.

In keeping with what has been said, my project has taken a different path separating the methods from the objectives. The method in the sciences is *objective and accumulative* and concerns itself with the material world while philosophy would adopt the *unitive method* in order to attend to the kingdom of the spirit whose objective is the Transcendent (to reason and to the sciences). He who does not perceive spiritual reality or achieve the Transcendent can use the *statistic* provided by the philosophers, which is derived from the superposition of ideas mentioned, and *believe* in them given the authority of those who have had fortunate intuitions and the capacity and patience to use them in an ordered and systematic manner. It is necessary to remind the reader that many scientific theories that are not entirely fool-proof are accepted as truths in the name of scientific authority and because most of us mortals do not have the means to prove them.

Now this is just a proposal that seems edifying to me, as my philosophy, of course, does not end there. The given statistic would be, as in the sciences, an incentive to induce the one interested party to take one more step directed towards experience. This means that the work that I have done in following the history of idealist thought has the double purpose of convincing the reader of the existence of spiritual reality on the one hand and on the other of incentivising him or more correctly *animating him*, as one is giving life to the spirit and thus obtaining experience; the one side would be a means, the other an end. The whole of my philosophy, my system, is directed towards this end which is *the experience of the spiritual reality*, or as a better expression, in keeping with the method and objective that I propose: *the unitive experience of universal Consciousness.*

Platonists and Aristotelians

We could call them idealists and realists, but there have been various idealisms and a multitude of realisms, which would require too many explanations and take us to the limits of our project. Besides, realism borders on positivism and later on materialism, and here we would be on the margins of philosophy.

Both tend to postulate a unique cause. Some like Aristotle start from matter from which they induce the origin and they conclude that there has to be a first motor, a God, a Spirit or universal Soul, the Infinite, the One, the Idea, etc., others start from these ideas, essence or substance and from this deduce the finite, the multiple, nature.

Both believe, intuit or glimpse the two realities, but the Aristotelians have not had the experience of spiritual reality, they can firmly believe in it, they can philosophize about it, they can even demonstrate it, but they can only transmit to us the reasons that bequeath us a belief; and the latter, as Plato rightly said, is very retrogressive in the order of knowledge. For this reason in the spiritual order we have to follow the Platonists, not as disciples but trying to experience as they do and thus obtain the perspective that allows us to see the reality in which we live from its Essence; which is really the correct mode of understanding it and of understanding ourselves.

The Aristotelians, and this includes all the Scholastics and their greatest representative Thomas Aquinas, start from two beliefs: one, that the human mind begins its knowledge from the experience of material reality, the other, the existence of a personal God; they do not take into account that both beliefs are the consequence of an individual perspective, that makes them see the reality of the senses directly and that of the spiritual indirectly; hence its dualism. What the Platonist, the idealist does is to invert this order by means of a change of perspective; and this change takes place thanks to an intuition. Here lies the key to the knowledge of the Transcendent; hence my plan to end the belief that the ideas of reason are more philosophical than the ideas of intuition.

Platonists and Aristotelians have been spoken about for more than twenty three centuries, as if all we needed to do was depending on what Plato and Aristotle said. Nobody can deny their genius, which was the expression of *a perspective of the spirit from two different faculties.* When we think philosophically "we fall" into one or the other faculty before we think about Plato or Aristotle; not only do we think like them, but also they thought like us, although they had done so before us. The difference is that between those who intuit and those who speculate, and this depends on the place where we might have placed the centre of the mind.

The same error of seeing us as Platonists or Aristotelians leads us to another: that of seeing the history of thought as a succession of cultural legacies, as the result of a clash of influences, which sounds like a mechanical interpretation that leads to an erudite and sterile search for predecessors, as if these were the only source. The source lies in the spirit of man, in his homogenous mental composition, and in his circumstances that are essentially the same, which leads one to find the same problems and resolve them in a similar manner. What continues changing is a perspective in keeping with the plane of understanding adopted and the level of consciousness reached.

In fact the distinction between discernment and intellect, attributing to the latter the capacity to intuit is what differentiates Aristotle from Plato, with all that this signifies, as from them one philosophy starts differentiating itself from other philosophy due to its inclination towards one or the other, i.e. towards the speculative faculty or towards the faculty that through intuitions discovers and provides material for speculation. For this reason I have said that discernment is not creative, and its method is inductive, while that of the intellect is deductive. Of course these are not static compartments, there is permanent interaction between them, and this is what makes a good philosopher. Speculating on the Transcendent without having had an intuition is like trying to perceive the lay of the land with the white cane of a blind man.

Universal Idealism

"One should look for the God of the Greeks not in the Olympus but in the thought of the One."

Ortega y Gasset (El Espectador, I, 38)

For Aristotle, the ideal of knowledge, the perfect science, is achieved when the subject becomes one with the object. The search for this unity or totality is one of the most revelatory characteristics of the Greek spirit. Since then this search has been the motor of idealism.

Idealism is a way of seeing reality from a universal dimension, due to which it responds to the highest aspirations of the spirit. Unfortunately its comprehension is only attainable for a few because the spirit needs a prior elevation that allows it to achieve a perspective that determines it. It has been achieved before and after Plato, but it is to his genius that we should attribute the capacity to formulate it in a comprehensible manner using reason and later myths to their ultimate limits, and other revelatory suggestions. It is not that he has "created" some Ideas that his followers have just imitated, as he and all the idealists must have earlier reached this level and perspective, otherwise there is no real understanding of this reality. Plato's great discovery is that of "ideas in themselves", the reality of the concept that is before the object, what becomes the essence of idealism. But therein lays its difficulty, as the immense majority of mankind is incapable of seeing and appreciating these ideas, only seeing objects to which names are given, which are confused with the ideas of the same. For this reason man will not be able to understand the World of Ideas of Plato with which it will try to negate its objective existence, without observing that he is inverting the idealist vision and denying that world in order to fit it in with his myopia. He will also tend to believe that the world of ideas is the product of a subjective vision; a grave error because the Ideas in themselves are Real and universal, it is like this so that all who reach it see it in this way. For this reason the tradition that I refer to differs radically from what has been called subjective idealism, and it would be correct to call it unitive and transcendental idealism. In summary, what constitute idealism is the priority of the Transcendent and this can only be seen when the human spirit has surpassed the limits that the *I* imposes on it, and these are great and varied: moral, psychological, epistemological, etc., when has transcended the individual perspective (see my *Psychosophy*).

The highest peaks of universal thought, Platonism, Neo-Platonism, German idealism, Indian Mahayana Buddhism and Shankara's Vedanta undoubtedly have common traits and if they are reduced to a single word they can be called idealism. But it is indispensable to accept that with this concept we barely have an idea of the Idea that inspires them, as the latter is the fruit of a higher level of the spirit that has allowed them to contemplate these heights. This means that he who has not reached these peaks, does not see and is in no condition to judge these philosophies and compare them with others of lesser scope, towards which they will incline because they are within their reach, and for this reason they will take them as "more real" or "veracious". Of course, I am not proposing that they be accepted as dogma rather that these philosophies due to their great scope do not need dogmas, but a certain spiritual and intellectual training. And this brings us face to face with a great mountainous division, the lowest ones need dogmas due to their insufficiency, and the highest need freedom as they obey an anti-dogmatic tradition because they can only be really reached with the free rein of the spirit; freedom here is the means and the end.

Now it is necessary that it be at least rationally understood that it is not essentially an inheritance but an experience that allows the transmission of the Ideas. Each one has to discover this treasure for himself, and as he find it he become aware that his predecessors also found it. The present is retraced to the past. This knowledge is not accumulative but *unitive*; it is not distant but as intimate as the niche of the soul; it is the product of a realization in the highest plane of the spirit; philosophy and religion converge on these high peaks in their most elevated expressions; finally, and this cannot be understood by reason, it is not the product of any subject or *I*; and for this reason it is transcendent. Universal idealism has not only been present in Hinduism and Buddhism, but it also has been more constant and secure than in the West. Furthermore, idealism has been so inconstant in Western culture that there has even been a thinker, who I think has a too large following, and who has accused all European philosophers after the Pre Socratics of having forgotten the Being. As the reader will see, the Being has been present in all the authors that I will comment on. One of the fundamental objectives of this work is to make more coherent the erratic trajectory of idealism in the West. I believe that this objective can be an efficient way of restructuring the Western thought.

Types of Idealism

There are fundamentally two types of idealism, one is philosophical, that looks for an absolute idea, the other, that believes in an ideal and comports itself in keeping with the same, and I think it is right to call it moral. One immediately recognizes that both should go together, as the first searches for a perfect, firm and trustworthy reference through knowledge, and the second has the urge to see it through. But the human being is a very special kind of animal for reasons that I intend to elucidate, and these two idealisms belong to two kinds of personalities as they have the spirit located in different places.

We could say that the first is of an intellectual kind and the second of a sentimental, although of course both use either faculty in variable degrees. But the most commonly the intellectual tries to resolve everything with reasons, and does not get involved body and soul with their ideas, whereas the sentimental gets involved with an idea without having investigated deeply either its content or its scope and the consequences of their actions. My idealism tries to unify both positions. This might appear at first sight to be a utopian ideal, but I have reasons as well as feelings that lead me to believe that it is entirely feasible. My theory of knowledge, based on an integral knowledge of the human psyche tends precisely to integrate the latter in a harmonic unity through a progressive *unitive knowledge*, thanks to which the mind and heart relate to and complement each other. I am trying to clarify as far as possible once and for all the guiding idea that will serve as a reference for the human being, and for this I will follow the trajectory of philosophical idealism, however always viewing it from the *unitive perspective* which includes moral idealism. From what I have said it can be gathered that *my philosophy of history obeys an integral, unitive or vital idealism.*

But, I should confess to the reader that personally I do not believe much in the reasons of men if they are not substantiated by elevated sentiments and the latter in turn by a real desire to know, by a real love for philosophy. I do not consider to be great those philosophers who resolve everything only with reasons, "from the eyebrows up", as is rightly said. Besides, I must confess, I am tired of this recourse, as it is the most commonly used by man "to have his own way", ignoring moral consciousness, on which it is based, especially moral idealism. Now, it is comprehensible for the common man to slip up like this, as there are few idealists under the sun, but for thinking professionals to do so is serious, because they teach us to think without the heart, without the love of truth in itself, that is to say, erroneously.

My philosophy does not obey an abstract ideal, but the reality itself of man; for this reason I have called it vital. It is from the perspective of an integrated mind that it observes individuals and societies. I clarify that it is not my desire to present something new, I detest that aspiration linked to the most serious disease of the West, that of the cult of personality, which leads one on the path opposite to the one that I propose. In the XXth century we have seen the appearance of more idealisms (not to mention the theories of knowledge), than in all the past centuries; the quantity has increased, the quality has diminished, as in all matters of the spirit; the reader will see why.

We can take, for example, the three periods that I will draw attention to in which we see the birth and rebirth of the West: Athens in the golden age, the Renaissance in

Italy and Romanticism in Europe, including Russia. None of them could ever be explained by their philosophies, but by their moral idealism and by their art; not just reason was put into play but above all, vital and unitive forces that impelled their spirits; these are the forces that make for the periods of apogee. In these we find men of State who understood the need to put matter at the service of the spirit; this application and inversion of the habitual is characteristic of these periods. It is not a coincidence, Pericles was the disciple of Anaxagoras and his minister of culture was Phidias; Lorenzo the Magnificent had Ficino at his court, and Frederick II of Prussia had Voltaire.

The understanding of these *unitive forces* that generate *unitive men* and periods of apogee is the objective of this and of all my work. There should be no contradictions between the ideal and experience, nor any need to take recourse to faith, nor to explanations of the absurd, nor the adjustment of reality to reason, but a natural search for and encounter of the spirit within itself in a framework of infinite freedom.

Mystics and Philosophers

Neither a mystic nor a philosopher, Aldous Huxley has left us one of the most edifying and necessary works ever written, *The Perennial Philosophy,* in which he has chosen and commented with excellent criteria and impartiality on the mystics of the East and West. The human genius invariably inclines towards particular branches of knowledge and it is almost always propelled by some belief through which it works out its trajectory, but fortunately there appear from time to time as if responding to the need of the times, redemptive geniuses of common sense, who again put things in their place. This is the case of Voltaire in the XVIIIth century and of Huxley in the XXth century.

Although not inspired by Huxley, I am trying in this work, like him with respect to the mystics, to put the thought of the philosophers in order, and as my vision is essentially in keeping with that of Huxley and the mystics, I consider these works to be complementary. Besides, if his work had not existed, I would have felt the need to write a similar work.

Huxley clarifies that he has chosen "the first hand exponents of perennial philosophy, those who knew them called them saints, prophets, wise men or enlightened. And I have selected them and not philosophers and professional scholars because there are good reasons to suppose that they knew what they were talking about." I believe that his choice is entirely legitimate. However the language of the mystics is in general obscure, sometimes obeys doctrinal beliefs and at other times using inadequate and even contradictory terminology, as they are not precisely professionals of thought. Even if it is true that philosophers do not always have direct knowledge, I am convinced that they have had some intuitions of the first principle and are inspired by them, despite sometimes getting lost, even to the extreme of disconnecting themselves from the sources. A correct discrimination, only possible from a correct perspective, is what is required.

Essentially there is no contradiction between the philosophers that I have chosen and the mystics selected by Huxley, both intuit or experience a unity beyond multiplicity, that Huxley calls unitive knowledge. Without knowing this antecedent, I have come to use this same concept, but applying it to a theory of knowledge and of the mind that Huxley does not develop. For him it means only a "unitive knowledge of the Base," but there is no contradiction; for this reason I insist on the complementarity of these two works.

I will now clarify what I understand by perennial philosophy: It is not that which is established once and for all by a text or philosopher, a static and dogmatic view and, thus, destined for obsolescence. A philosophy is perennial when it is open and dynamic and allows for permanent renovation, as it is the same essential inspiration that is manifested in isolated experiences of different subjects of elevated spirituality that are assimilated and ratified; it is the progeny of free interpretation and expresses the same spirit that allows for the elevation of eternal inspiration.

Since I have to speak about the God of the philosophers, but also of the importance of experience, prevalent amongst mystics, I should clarify this apparent contradiction. This opposition, that ought not to exist, exists when the religious person is dogmatic and both is pre-disposed to and limits himself to the "revealed truth" of the clergy. This kind of religious person does not use experience but belief and for this reason is even farther away from the truth than the philosopher. The philosopher actually is inspired by some intuition which is his baggage of personal experience; I am not referring to the apologetic thinker who clings to his belief, who is actually a dogmatic religious person and cannot be a philosopher.

There are fundamentally two legitimate paths of access to the Transcendent: that of rational knowledge which characterizes the Western philosopher and that of the mystic who uses his direct experience. The latter is found in the strange position of being a third party in the discord, as he is disdained by the philosopher and pursued by the dogmatic religious person.

My proposal and position, as is evident from my work, is the balanced interaction between philosophical speculation and the experience of the mystic, as the practices destined to purify the spirit and elevate the level of consciousness, far from being negligible are indispensable for knowledge of the Transcendent.

The mystic on his part being endowed with philosophical tools, could bring clarity to his experience which is so often confusing not only for himself, but also for those to whom he directs his message, and thus he could avoid the falsification of his message that often takes place. If the mystic does not think through his ideas well, he simply adheres to the religion that he has inherited, without noticing that his "heresies" could improve the doctrine and give it the dynamic that all life is in need of. I have said it: the mystic–philosopher is a rare pearl in the ocean of knowledge, and there is nothing more beneficial for a society than to produce these pearls.

Monotheism and Polytheism

At the base of all religions and perhaps all philosophies there can be found concepts that strictly obey perspectives adopted by the spirit which, when ignore its adoption, end up believing that only its vision is correct; for this reason I think it is instructive to compare these perspectives. My intention as usual is to direct the spirits towards the highest perspective.

All the gods, be they one, a few or many, female or male represented one way or another, are paths to transcendental knowledge. But these are nothing more than "paths", and this must be understood: none of them are really true or really false. The only true one is he who is One with my spirit, and I will do well in adopting gods and doctrines conducive to this end since I still do not have this experience. As we understand what is expressed, our spirit will be better placed to understand not only the function of each one of the gods, but also highly refined doctrines, like Buddhism, that never pretended to be the only truth but only the most conducive path.

For the perceptive, the affirmation that "my God is the only true one", is a simplification almost devoid of sense, because he knows that any god who has made him better, more comprehensible, more human and more divine is "true." And, on the other hand, that god who he serves, even if he pretends to be unique, kind and all powerful, has taken him towards evil, violence and the incomprehension of the others, is false; there is no "objectively true" God. I am not saying that God's truth is subjective; the matter is much more complex as we will see. It is enough to say that it is neither objective nor subjective, but unitive; I have been very concerned about liberating the spirit from the "objective truths" as well as the subjective ones in the path towards the Transcendent.

The concept of polytheism, when used by the monotheist, especially when it is applied to Buddhism or Hinduism, is either tendentiously disqualifying or a product of ignorance. It is fundamentally this, because the dualist, the Christian or the Muslim, cannot understand the monism that underlies polytheism, he does not have experience of the unity; if he did he would *ipso facto* stop being dualist.

In reality, monotheism is born of polytheism through a process of forsaking all other gods to impose only one of them. In the Old Testament this procedure was repeated time and again, and we know that in the Kaaba there were 200 gods and Mohammed brought out 199 (he left a meteorite that was the ancient cult of the desert nomads). Of course, in order to impose his God (now in capital letters), he had to subjugate the other tribes who believed in forsaken gods. The tribal mentality that governed these Semitic religions will now be understood.

So Christianity followed the same tribal tradition: When the prophet Jesus appeared, he became the only begotten son of God that Moses had imposed on the others; although Moses would not have agreed to this adoption, as the general consensus of his descendants shows. And since the Church had the economic, military and political power, it began to put into effect the same tribal, disqualifying and eliminatory policy until it wiped out all the gods from Europe; it did not get farther towards the East because it encountered the armies of the other "sole" God sustained by the nomad tribes who had also spread through middle Asia. Later, as Americans know well, it extended towards the West, where it continued with its campaign of the elimination of the gods and their faithful.

Monotheism sustains the existence of a single God, but which one? The Jews do not believe that Jesus is the son of Jehovah nor do the Muslims that he is of Allah, and the Christians do not believe that their God led them to Mohammad. The ferocious religious wars are proof of these divergences and the aforementioned exclusion of other gods, without counting the ignorance of the religious matter that this attitude implies. And all this is in the name of this diverse personal God and this practice of exclusivism of the vaunted "superiority" of monotheism.

There has been an insidious emphasis on the difference between monotheism and polytheism being that there are doctrines that do not respond to either the one or the other, but to the concept of monism, as in the case of Vedanta and Buddhism, where there is a difference of inclusivity and permissiveness, the freedom of believing in lesser gods with an underlying basis in God or universal Spirit; which clearly shows the understanding of the principle of nonviolence, something basic in religious, moral and philosophical matters. Monotheism as well as polytheism achieve their excellence in monism, where there is experience and not the limitation of belief that inevitably implies the dualism defined by Semitic doctrines.

As polytheism has been more conducive for the production of religious experience, I incline towards it, I mean; it seems more plausible for those who need to represent Divinity. The plurality of gods means the plurality of viewpoints, i.e. the opening of the spirit towards multiple possibilities. Each god represents an aspect of the mind, it obeys a particular need of the consciousness, for this reason I maintain that polytheism possesses a psychology that is much more profound than monotheism; in fact in the latter there are grave faults in the knowledge of the psyche. If for some people, God or the gods exist objectively it is because they live in their spirit. What is important is their relevance in the consciousness of the aspirant, i.e., if the function of god (if he is charitable or just or benevolent) is assimilated and manifested by the believer. It is not important that God be one with all his virtues or that these be distributed among many gods. He who worships one god is not nearer to the truth than the one who believes in many, or vice versa, only the one who has assimilated the greatest number of his virtues, because in this way he becomes more knowledgeable and more divine. He who assimilates the virtues of the gods assimilates to them. Then, and only then, once he has become like the gods, will he be able to judge if God is one or many; these final questions irrelevant earlier, because if one is nothing more than human there is but one road to traverse, and this is the road of understanding.

In any case, there are no false or true gods in my philosophy, there are only levels of consciousness, greater clarity, better vision in keeping with the perspective adopted. The problem of beliefs is that we use ideas, fixed concepts that create obstacles along the way. By now it would be clear that my proposal is the experience of the Transcendent, where there are no things, nor ideas nor beliefs and thus no divinities. And it appears to me to be legitimate and even necessary that men express the marvels of Nature through religious art, creating myths, celebrating them and interpreting the world in a religious manner, making it sacred, because in this way they integrate their spirits into Reality.

Monism and Dualism

This subject of monism and dualism is of the first order in the field of knowledge, and for this reason it should be well understood. To start with, it is not limited to the religious field, but extends itself to all orders of spiritual knowledge. These are not just two ways of knowing God, but also the *Universus*, i.e. the internal and external reality, there are two perspectives that determine our vision, our understanding and our action.

Reason, dual by nature, and the sentiments, applied from the same dualistic perspective, need a Divinity as an object onto which they can project their reason and invest their sentiments. For this they try to give it a concrete form in a certain manner: the result is God as a Person. These faculties, however, are not inspired by themselves but by ones who are more elevated; their knowledge is indirect and more or less distorted. Thus it is not that God does not exist, but that he exists in another form. He does not exist; it is true, as an object for a subject, as his reality is One. But in order to experience this Unity the subject should disappear, and when it disappears, the object does so as well. The whole play of morality and religion in the final instance consists of the disappearance of the subject and of the appearance of the pure Spirit; in other words, in the return or reabsorption of the spirit in its Essence. When this reabsorption takes place, the spirit changes its perspective and from this *essential perspective* which is of the same Essence, the object of devotion and reason not only becomes unnecessary but disappears, it does not exist as such. Monism absorbs dualism.

God as object is an idol, a substitute of the real God; not a false but an erroneous idol. This optical error of the spirit is a consequence of our individual perspective that has led the monotheist religions to declare dualism as the final reality, as all religion points to monism or the Unity of the spirit with the Spirit. It will be understood that the difference between polytheism and monotheism is only one of degree and insignificant in comparison with what exists between dualism and monism. Polytheism as well as dualist monotheism are means, links, approaches, beliefs, premises, not true knowledge even though they have fundamentaly a life giving truth.

But they are not homologous. Every sincere and objective scholar of the history of religion knows that polytheism in its most exalted forms, like that of India, have been more edifying for the spirit. This is so in various senses: by populating the World with gods; by making the mountains, rivers, trees and other forms that we live with into objects of veneration, and making us participate in an Order which we are all part of, creating in this way optimum conditions for the growth of the spirit, conducive to a healthy pantheism founded in monism, which is the ultimate religious and vital experience. If one thinks deeply about the matter, one will be able to evaluate the damage that negation of monism can signify. Individuals and civilizations on which dualism has been imposed have suffered this damage for centuries. For aesthetic reasons we will not speak here of the means used by their representatives of making their predominance effective, but I am interested in highlighting this doctrinal aspect: Dualism dogmatically rejects the knowledge of the *Absolute*, in the name of a *relative* "truth" that it has established as "absolute".

Polytheism, correctly understood, is an extension of

monism; monotheism is a consequence of the dualist vision. The plurality of beings and spirits who become gods in keeping with human interpretation is derived from monism. The dualist finds himself in a ready-made world and thus apart from his self; he is alienated from the world and from God. An aesthetic, moral, religious, social, ecological and literally infinite list of differences, derive from these two visions. The monist sees, or tries to see from the perspective of God. The dualist sees God and all beings from his individuality; the exacerbated selfishness that today rules in the West and from which issues the general destruction of Nature, the merciless treatment suffered by other animals etc., it is a product of the dualist and egocentric vision, of the alienation of man from his Unity.

My philosophy, of course, is not against any religious belief, but it warns that the religions that are sustained by a belief system will tend to disappear if man follows an ascendant path. The restoration of the Spirit will take place in the most effective manner through knowledge; it is the latter that corresponds to the new millennium. I believe this because one can only contrast the growing scientific and technological knowledge, which has awoken faith in material development and which has substituted religious faith and it can only be compared with a knowledge capable of revealing spiritual reality. It has been five centuries since the material as compared to the spiritual started becoming more real and tangible to Western eyes, an evident sign that the system of religious belief that was imposed on Western civilization has ceased to be relevant. For this reason *my objective is to contribute to the supersession of the era of faith, in order to bring about the era of knowledge in the matters of the spirit.* Early man naturally sustained the geocentric vision of the World, today he sustains without questioning its anthropocentric vision too much. And as happened with the former, he ought to abandon the latter.

And the same has to happen with his anthropomorphic vision of God.

In synthesis this is what the reader has to remember: The mystic experience, in its pure and pristine state is monist, as the union between the individual and universal Spirit takes place there. This enables the mystic to have their own vision of the Transcendent, and even if it does not essentially differ from the experience of other mystics, it can differ in the interpretation of the doctrine established in their culture. For this reason the monist doctrines are open and dynamic, and are renewed with the experience of each mystic, as happens with Buddhism and Hinduism, which have always respected and venerated mystics. Whereas the dualist religions, being dogmatic and static, have systematically persecuted those mystics who did not adapt to the doctrine because of their own vision, as only the founder of the doctrine could have the said experience,

In other words, the experience of Unity is incompatible with dualist doctrines, it is for this reason that in the West religion and philosophy have not been able to reach an agreement, while in the monist vision both disciplines tend to converge in the same reality; this has been the rule in India and in the idealisms that we will see later. In fact, the experience that we call "mystic" in the religious order, is, in its essence, the same as that of the philosopher who has known the Transcendent, the difference lies in the amount of religious sentiment in some, and of intellect in others, in the means not in the end. Dualism cannot overcome the religious sphere, while monism not only transcends it but constitutes the very centre of philosophy.

The superiority of monism over dualism can be synthesized like this: Firstly it is the ultimate religious experience. Secondly the entire subject of religion derives from it. Thirdly it comprises of dualism. Fourthly, it has shown its wisdom with the numerous wise men it has produced. Fifthly its tolerance is a product of wisdom. Sixthly, with its all-encompassing vision it has a natural policy of inclusion and not an artificial one of exclusion. Seventhly it is an experience, not a belief; actually no one can have an experience of duality. It is in fact illogical to compare them, it would be like comparing a spring with a stream, they are the same substance, but without the former the latter does not exist, and thus to deny the spring in the name of the stream is absurd. It is for this reason that the monist understands the dualist, which does not happen in reverse. All religions are born of a monist experience, but later those of a lesser understanding make them dualist.

The God of Philosophers, Mystics, Artists and of Folklore

The first principle has been called the Absolute, the First motor, Divinity, God, Nature, etc. which are not the same as we will see. We could begin by distinguishing between the God of philosophers from that of mystics and the gods of folklore. Of course since the demarcations are not well defined, these gods are interrelated; but I believe that the differentiation is illuminating. The gods of folklore are found in all religions. Plato calls them the poets, those of Homer and Hesiod, those of the Hindu epics, those of the Old Testament, the son of this god, his mother, etc. The common man identifies with them because they are more accessible and they are part of the folklore in which they live.

The God of philosophers, as we will see, varies in keeping with the thinker, although we find common characteristics which I will draw attention to. The God of the philosophers in general is found by having a high level of consciousness that allows one to intuit the first principle; it is in this intuition that inspiration is found. The God of the mystics bears striking similarities, although they might belong to different religions. All refer to the first principle, as it is the position of the spirit within the mentioned planes and levels which establishes the level of knowledge. The God of the mystics is born of a *unitive experience* of the first principle, even if it is sporadic. The plane used by the philosopher is that of the intellect, the mystic uses the plane of the sentiments; this makes the God of some more abstract and that of others more personal. Nevertheless, those who have had a total *unitive experience*, transcend all personal interpretation. Among the gods of folklore, the spirit barely senses a higher spirit, and due to this, takes the form of a father, a creator of the world, who decides on the fate of mortals and to whom they ask favours and as folklore behaves, participates in daily affairs.

In the West, philosophers and religious men have not been able to agree, while in India agreement has been possible due to important reasons: Indian religions are not dogmatic, therefore philosophers are not forced to adapt to any doctrine. This allows them to adhere to their experience, and, since this constitutes their search and they have the means for this (the yoga), it often happens that the mystic and the philosopher become one. Besides this, traditional tolerance has allowed for an integration of folklore, mysticism and philosophy as the latter establishes the orthodox reference.

In Christianity, this has not been possible because the order of priorities has been inverted. In fact, religion has been dogmatically imposed as "truth" in the guise of folklore, the thinker should adapt to the latter, which makes it impossible for him to adhere to experience because this is categorical, no one has the experience of the gods of folklore; one can only have one's beliefs, and with these one can write good literature, but not philosophy. For this same reason apologists cannot be philosophers. This also explains why in Islam and in Christianity the mystics who have clung to their experience have been persecuted for transgressing the doctrine.

I often see that when Orientalists want to find common roots between Hinduism or Buddhism and Christianity, they take recourse to mystics, forgetting that the Church considers most of them as heretics. This means, they equate Oriental orthodox people with the Christian heterodox. They do not seem to realize that the benefits of these similarities invariably accrue to the Church, which condemns these mystics for the same sentences quoted by the Orientalists. There is an obvious reason for this discrepancy: the Church clings to dogma, the mystic to experience; for this reason there are more similarities between the mystics of the East and West than between them and the Catholic Church.

As there has been so much insistence on belief and faith in the West, it would seem that there are only two positions: that of those who believe in God and of those who don't, and it is thus usual to hear with astonishing ingenuity the question: Do you believe in God or not?, as if this could define the situation. As the Buddhists do not have a personal god but a complex divinity that escapes the understanding of the average Westerner, they are also posed the same question. This was expressed to me by Karma G. Kuthok, Minister of Education of Tibet, who always responded in the most obvious manner: "It depends what you understand by God". In fact there are as many gods as there are people as each one feels or imagines him in his own way, for this reason the Hindus in their habitual wisdom say that they have 333 million gods.

The mystics seem to agree on this: the Divinity that is experienced transcends all personal, mythic or folkloric ideas. A single example is enough: For Eckhart, the most outstanding mystic in the West, "God and Divinity are as distinct from each other as the earth and the sky. The sky is a thousand miles above the earth and so is the Divinity over God". Of course, since he is not a philosopher he does not tell us the ontological situation of Divinity but there is no doubt that He has a superior status. This was enough for the Inquisition to start investigating him; luckily he died before he could be ensnared.

The gods in mythology express the basic forces and human tendencies, the fears and desires, the virtues and vices that govern nature. These expressions are not rational but belong to other mental mechanisms that open the door to the Transcendent; I am referring to the *unitive faculties* that connect these forces in a symbolic, artistic and psychological manner. We can take the classic example of the moon. For reason it is just matter for man to conquer and tread upon, but all those who are in love know that it is propitious for love, that it has a magic and beauty that only the artist can express, as they know that it has a meaning that greatly transcends matter. There is a *unitive* factor, not in the moon, i.e. in the thing or the object, but in its magic and beauty that links all reality, its multiple reflections in the hearts of lovers who open themselves up to the world.

In the West, even in Greece, where an open spirit prevailed a grave error was committed when the gods of the poets opposed the God of the philosophers, as there are different ways of expressing the same spirit that animates the different centres or sectors of the mind, which distances the artist from the philosopher. Even Plato did not understand this and he is shown to be contradictory, on the one hand following the wise men of Antiquity, he does not conceive of reality if it is not full of gods, but on the other hand wanting to banish the poets from his Republic, as the differences are only apparent. The poet talks of appearances, he does not even try to speak of a complete round and immutable absolute, as Parmenides does, he wants to see what is living in nature, the turbulent or benevolent waters, the beauty of the world, the agility of the elements, the surprise element of events, in sum, the subjective aspects of the mind. The philosopher tries to have an objective vision of spiritual reality, he wants to be a scientist of the spirit; he thus sorely feels the difference. But before criticizing, condemning and philosophizing if he were to bring his spirit closer to the *unitive faculties*, he would see with greater proximity the poet's perspective and he would understand that the politics to be followed is that of *laissez faire* thought as it is only in freedom that the spirit of the people is nurtured and evolves.

Plato had his doubts and contradictions, Christianity did not, moreover the latter eliminated the gods from the Greek poets and also their believers, not in order to impose the God of the philosophers but that of mythic tradition. In India, where the unitive faculties have been more alert, tradition has found its equilibrium and has accorded a place to each God, so that all the gods survive, but the constant reference, the final decision is that of Brahman, the God of the philosophers who has had a spiritual experience. It is this inclusive, tolerant and differential line that I will follow in this work.

The Quest in Greece

Given the outline of this work it would be necessary to speak about the manifestations of the spirit in Greece, but for the fact that the Hellenic spirit is too broad for just one chapter, its manifestations are multiple. I will devote the time and space it deserves in the works that complement this text. I will do the same with the Greek religion because its mythic and folkloric aspects connect it more to literature and art in general. But this clarification is necessary: The systematic, arbitrary and tendentious disqualification that the Greek religion and also the Greek spirit has suffered at the hands of Christianity, has been highly prejudiced because it is impossible to understand the Greek spirit without its religion as it is more than just a vital and indispensable organ, it is an inseparable part of the Greek soul and culture. The excellence of other manifestations of this spirit cannot be denied, and they have thus been incorporated in the Western culture and become examples, but all Greek art was imbued with religion and inspired by it; the very Muses were part of it; the creation, history and destiny of men were decided by the gods; daily ritual and religious festivals took place ceaselessly; the Acropolis was full of gods and the great monuments were dedicated to them. We cannot divide the Hellenic spirit by stating that it was genial on the one hand and innocent on the other; this shows our own ingenuousness and demonstrates our ignorance. If the genius venerates some gods that we do not understand, it is reasonable not to doubt its beliefs but our own understanding. And we are not speaking of an isolated intelligence, but of the wise men of Antiquity, of the epic and tragic poets, the famous sculptors who define that culture. I will only attend to their idealist thinkers from whom I do not expect to usurp the said spirit, but only give an idea of them.

It is right to call Greece the "cradle of Western culture and civilization". But a clarification is necessary here, as this expression can be erroneous. This does not mean that there was an infantile stage and that adolescence and adulthood would correspond to later periods, because what really happened was that all the arts and thought in general reached maturity and excellence, as happens during periods of great spiritual growth. A learned man (Vara Donado, *Sophocles, Tragedies*) rightly says: "Tragedy was born perfect just like the epic during the Homeric period, like Athena from the head of Zeus". I think the same could have been said of philosophy if only the pre Socratic texts, the solid thought of which reveals the said maturity, had been preserved. And even so, in spite of this loss, the consequences of which we cannot fathom, only one century separates these geniuses from the consummate labours of Plato and Aristotle.

The Pre-Socratics

All philosophy, properly speaking, begins with the perception of the Transcendent. This implies a surpassing of the habitual, individual or egocentric perspective, which gives the spirit a new and more universal perspective, from which reality is presented in another way; this vision is what leads to philosophizing, i.e. to thinking by oneself in keeping with this experience. This experience cannot be transmitted, only the reflections that are derived from it are transmitted; to rationally understand these reflection is as if seeing a map of an unknown country. This together with the difficult fact that experience happens sporadically in isolated individuals, makes this knowledge non-accumulative and non-progressive and for this reason is forgotten and lost in time and it reappears when it is rediscovered. This philosophy begins in the West in the -VIth century, barely a century before the great Athenian apogee to which it undoubtedly contributed. Unfortunately there are barely a few conserved fragments from these philosophers, who were not really systematic thinkers, and thus we have limited samples on which not much can be inferred without risking the falsification of its meaning.

Xenophanes

The first one we know of is Xenophanes, famous for the phrase "If oxen and horses had hands and could draw like men, the horses would draw images of gods similar to horses and oxen similar to oxen." (*Frag. 15*) This statement as clear as day does not seem to have influenced any number of thinkers, who have imagined and continue to imagine God anthropomorphically, to reflect mankind himself. Another intuition from Xenophanes reveals that beyond this anthropomorphic perspective, reality is shown to be a unity. "Considering the entire universe, he affirmed that Unity is God himself (Arist. *Met. 986 b*). This has to be remembered: *Monism lies at the very root of Western thought.* It is this same idea that will underlie the work of the thinkers gathered here including that of the author himself. The later visionaries, who are curiously born in the same year in the two extremes of the Greek world, are Heraclitus and Parmenides, a disciple of Xenophanes.

Heraclitus

If his contemporaries called Heraclitus "the dark one," he will be much more so for us, and thus I have to comment with *moderation,* that this is this philosopher's "greatest virtue". Heraclitus is better known for his theory of becoming: "It is not possible to bathe twice in the same river." (*Plut. de E. 392 b*). This becoming is caused by the clash between opposites: "All things are produced through struggle and necessity." However, it is usually forgotten that behind this struggle of opposites there is an agreement: "They do not understand how what is fought about can agree with itself, there is a harmony with opposing movements of direction, like the bow and the harp" (Hippól. *Refut. IX, 9*). They do not understand the other side of Heraclitus and of reality because they do not perceive that "invisible harmony is more important than the visible." They do not perceive the Unity that underlies them, for this reason "it is wise to listen to the Logos, and not to me, and to recognize that all things are one." (*Op. cit.*) "This Logos is the one that men are incapable of understanding" as "even though things are happening according to this Logos, they do not seem to have any experience of it." (*Sext. VII, 132*). "Being this Logos common (to all) the majority lives as if it had a particular intelligence." (*VII, 133*). On this last fragment I will risk an explanation, as Heraclitus announces two fundamental points of my vision, that give witness to similar experiences that took place in dissimilar points of time and space, and this is proof of their reality. The logos is a *common intelligence* for all, but it is not perceived because it is seen from a *particular intelligence*, i.e. from an *individual perspective* in my language. Following this line of thought Heraclitus insists elsewhere: "For those who have awakened there is only one and the same world" (*Plut. Sup. 166 c*). Thus, I have reason to believe that the fundamental intuition of Heraclitus is that of the Unity that underlies all things, in whose context becoming is obvious and even vertiginous. Since we are used to living in the current of the becoming this seems natural to us, but if we leave the current and reach the "other bank," and if we contemplate how beings and things evolve, we feel the said vertigo. Heraclitus observed this from this perspective, for this reason he believes that "the soul is immortal, as when it leaves it goes towards what is of its own nature, towards the Soul of all," (*Aecio IV, 7.2*) and with this a *universal Soul* is announced. Unsurprisingly he affirms, like Thales and Plato, that "Everything is full of souls and divinities."

From this angle it will be understood that material things of this world mattered little to him and so he delegated the governing of the city, that was under him, to his brother, and rejected Dario's offer, the richest and most powerful king of that time, who offered him "all kinds of privileges," to which he replied "I am horrified at the splendour, just a few things are enough for me, those that are sufficient for my purpose." This is not a simple anecdote; I bring it up because as we will see it is this perspective that gives stability and firmness to moral consciousness. He simply deposited his book *On Nature,* in the temple of Artemis and retired to lead a life of contemplation. This attitude reminds one of another contemporary but distant wise man: Lao Tse who left his *Tao Te King* in the hands of a frontier officer and was never seen again; both men had sufficient reasons to do so.

Parmenides

Parmenides intuits a transcendent reality that tries to explain, literally, to make round, to make perfect. His vision is the most concise that can be found in the history of thought. In this way he says: "The Being is", "It is integral, immobile and infinite, and it is now at the same time a continuous one." "It is entirely full of being and is all continuous." "It is completely finished." In the West it is the first time that Being is expressed as it is, in its essence, based on direct experience, without creeds or concessions to any tradition. Philosophy, in the West starts with Parmenides; idealism begins here.

Parmenides' error, partial and relative, very common amongst philosophers, is that of ending up *constructing* its philosophy with its discernment its initial vision, because it inevitably ends up by materializing the concept, the Idea, as discernment is not made in order to be navigated at these levels, nor to express that which precisely transcends it. On deducing its Being, it puts on the same plane both what is and what should be, a distinction that those who have not transcended reason, i.e., the immense majority of scholars, cannot see. Parmenides deduces that "the Being has always existed, otherwise there would have been nothing before, and from nothing, nothing comes forth"; which seems right to me. And likewise he affirms "if something exists besides the being, that is not being, and the non being does not exist." To which a dogma is added: "It is a divine law that the Being cannot be imperfect." And as he imagines a perfect sphere, he assigns it that form. He is also concise about the attributes of the Being: "*Dike* (wisdom) that of many punishments, like Destiny, resides in this sphere." Punishment and destiny for whom? We can ask, but it is useless, Parmenides seems to be enclosed in an ontological solipsism, and so the ontological status of all living beings remains a big question mark. The same occurs with Shankara, the most influential Indian philosopher, whose thought revolves around the same absolute Being as Parmenides. I leave commentary on this author for another occasion.

Burnet "opines" that Parmenides cannot be defined as an idealist because his *Being* is material, and he will think the same of the *Nous* of Anaxagoras, inferring the matter from the affirmation: "The being is completely finished, *similar* on all sides (emphasis mine) to the mass of a round sphere." I believe that his error lies in being a prisoner of the terms, taking the images as concepts, to the point of losing sight of the philosopher's intention. This is serious because by minimising its *legacy* it provokes us to leave it fallen and valueless. My intention while citing these philosophers is, on the contrary, to revive our interest in these visions. Our error would be if we followed the opinion of the erudite and not that of Heraclitus: "Great erudition does not make a wise man."'

Anaxagoras

It is one of the merits of Anaxagoras, the last of this group of thinkers, to have specified the concept of Idea. He visualizes this as *Nous*, Mind or Intelligence: "It is the *Nous* that has ordered things as they should be, how they are and how they will be, and also the revolution of the stars, the sun, the moon and the air and the earth that are now separated." "This same revolution separated the dense from the light, the warm from the cold, the light from the dark and the dry from the wet" (*Frag. 13*). We see now that it is an Intelligence that governs the elements; he is prudent to not talk of a Creator, God or demiurge in order to not go beyond its experience. We will return later to the finer points.

It has been averred that Anaxagoras is not clear about the concept of the spirit because he does not completely separate *Nous* from matter, as if duality were a more advanced step than unity; this implies a lack of understanding of the circular, global, integrated, *pantheist unitive vision.* In my understanding Anaxagoras conserves a relation with equilibrium, "The *Nous* is infinite and autonomous and is mixed with nothing, and he is himself by himself." (*Frag. 15*).

And here we leave the pioneers of the spirit, as I consider it more edifying to persevere on the search within this perspective than in the analysis of the fragments left behind. Their legacy is immense. The two great springs of the spirit were discovered by Parmenides and Heraclitus:

the Immutable Absolute and changeable reality, what it Is and what it becomes; from then onwards we drink from one spring or the other. It depends on where we have shifted the spirit from for us to drink from one perspective or the other. The error, more than usual, reiterative, has been a negation or minimising of the importance of the opposing perspective. My philosophy does not just drink from both sources, but also finds its common origin; it is from this perspective that both realities are contemplated. These springs will irrigate wide cultivated fields and these perspectives will become clear as this work progresses.

The physics of the pre-Socratics

What is most remembered about these wise men is what I have left out: their conception of matter, their physics, because as this knowledge is accumulative, we have improved it considerably in 25 centuries, so that we have little or nothing to learn from them. Undoubtedly they were concerned about finding a primordial mass, an element from which other things were derived. For one it was fire, for the other it was its opposite, water, for another it was air, and finally Empedocles incorporated the four elements that have been used as reference even by modern chemistry. Of course, if we had followed these reflections instead of incorporating later beliefs that were uncommon in our culture, our science would have advanced many centuries. Thus, for example, Anaximander, the first of these thinkers stated that life had begun in the sea, and living beings were a result of their environmental adaptation. Furthermore, "he affirmed that in the beginning man was born from another species of animal" (Plut. *Strom. 2*); with which he announces the three basic principles of Darwinian Theory. And Anaxagoras by affirming that "nothing is created nor destroyed, there is just a separation or mixing of existing things" (Frag. 1-3 D.), anticipates Lavoisier, the father of modern chemistry, who would confirm: “Nothing is lost, everything is recovered.” And Empedocles: “Really the nature of none being exists, only the mix or change of mixed elements” (Arist. *Met. V, 4*); which is what the Buddha said more or less at the same time: “Nothing is permanent, there is only permanent change”, which would be endorsed by modern physics. But Anaximander had already stated the essential: The primordial element, “is neither the water nor any of the other elements, but a different and infinite Nature, from which emanate the skies and the worlds enclosed in them,” it is “eternal and ageless and covers all worlds” (Frag. 1-3). It seems that we are reading the Upanishads, but unfortunately we barely know anything more about him.

What is important here is the appearance in man of an ideal immaterial concept, product of an ascent of the human spirit through transcendental intuition. By being of a different, purely spiritual nature, this knowledge is not accumulative but *unitive*, it cannot be transmitted, it only remains as an idea that can attract elevated spirits and it can only take root with the existence of the moral, aesthetic, religious, philosophical and psychic conditions which I have referred to (*Psychosophy*) and to which I will later return.

Plato

In order to discern, humanity needed the faculty to produce concepts that would correspond to the objects of their senses, but this still did not give them knowledge. They had to develop and so they did, a more elaborate faculty of greater magnitude, intellect, capable of creating concepts not of things but about things and applicable to them: universal general syntheses, mathematical and geometric realities. Since these are permanent and universal, they transcend the mutable world. This fact must have impressed the

Greeks and it did so when they acquired full consciousness of this phenomenon (Pythagoras, Plato) corresponding to another perception of reality. But on projecting themselves on this world of Ideas, they intuited the same essence in them. Plato defines it thus: "That reality lacks colour and form, it is impalpable and only visible for the pilot of the soul, the understanding; that reality that is real in a way constitutes the object of true knowledge" (*Phaedrus 247*).

In spite of its ethereal nature, completely strange for the discernment of common mortals, this spiritual reality has reappeared time and again in the minds of philosophers, and it has done so with so much evidence that, contrary to popular understanding, it has been called *intelligible,* because what seems less real to the idealist is that which permanently changes condition: the tangible world. One constant aspect of idealism, although usually unconscious or latent in the West, is the overcoming of the perspective of the *I*, implicit in the search for transcendence. It is my conviction that idealism has contributed more than any other thought to the realization of this purpose; it is for this reason that I will follow it through history.

On Plato I will write little. Firstly because I have already dealt with him in my *Psychosophy,* from where I will extract a few paragraphs, adapting them to this exposition, in order to emphasize points of special interest, in particular those that seem to me to have been badly understood, secondly, because I believe that his idealism will become clearer as we advance in the history of this ideology.

Plato, as is evident from his description of that spiritual reality, found out how difficult it was for reason to express or accept it. The reader of his dialogues, who is not face to face with this reality but is recounted by it, also discovers this when he can easily ride in the safe chariot of dialectics, but if before having finished the journey the philosopher replaces the horses of discernment by other winged ones and invites him to explore the world of mythology, he finds himself very disconcerted, and if he is a dogmatic believer in reason (as modern man is in general), he will not be inclined to follow him. But Plato had his reasons that normal reason does not discern. (Pascal rightly talked about reasons of the heart, *raisons du côeur*).

Just as we can represent ourselves on an *external plane* (discernment) with what our senses have seen externally, we can represent what our spirit has perceived in the interior, as we know artists do. And this is the process followed by Plato, however, he did not extract these representations from the tangible world but from a separate world that he populated with unchangeable Forms. This world was his work of art.

Plato purposely ended his dialogues in the form of suggestive myths, clouded in an indiscernible fog, thus creating the need for an intuition to penetrate it, inviting in this way the vital experience of the unchangeable, wich he knew, was unexpressed in theory. For this reason, reducing Plato's idealism to his theory of Ideas is to make even hazier the fog that he left us in while still needing to transcend it.

Plato undoubtedly reached the highest levels of consciousness. Proof of that is the constant contact that he maintained with ideas of moral and aesthetic perfection, the Good and the Beautiful, which would guide his thoughts and be constant sources of inspiration. The fact that he maintained a dualist relation with Divinity, leads one to think that he did not manage to unify his spirit. This was not of course due to lack of talent but I daresay due to a lack of knowledge of the techniques directed to this end, and of doctrines in which he could have oriented himself. We know that the *Upanishads* as well the original Buddhism that preached a monist vision already existed; but in all probability they were unknown in Greece. In the West the most elevated doctrine was that of Plato.

In Plato's case these ideas are the result of *unitive intuitions*, as everything seems to indicate that the contact that he had with the Essence of the World, was indirect, sporadic, and at times vague, rather than direct, clear and constant as would correspond to a *total unitive experience.* Proof of this is also the fact that the link that he established between these first realities and the phenomenal world was also indirect. This mode of perception made him often recur to the *theory of reminiscence*: "According to this argument, Socrates, whom you hear repeated so frequently, that learning is nothing but remembering" (*Phaedo 73*). Although I cannot be very precise due to the nature of the subject, I would like to throw some light on it, not only in relation to this theory in particular, but because I believe that by doing so, other related points of significant importance will become clear:

When the Essence is perceived, only by intuition, the link established between the spirit and matter is the result of a particular contemplative state thanks to which even if time regresses, though not decidedly transcended it moves farther away in the horizon to the point when the reality that we contemplate seems linked to a far off time, to which the spirit is transported. This means that it has the impression that it is remembering. But in reality this distance is not due to a distant time but out of time, to the Eternal, only perceptible in itself in the absolute present (unified consciousness). Plato warned that his perception was not a result of reflection, but on the contrary, that one should stop thought in order to give way to images seemingly coming from a remote place and time. It is this kind of understanding that allowed him to visualize a permanent unchangeable reality that illuminated his soul as well as the object of his senses. Hence his obsession in explaining the link between the two realities, but when trying to rationalize it his spirit was transported to a past time and an imprecise place that decisively transcended concrete reality. The framework within which he found himself was that of myth which he rightly took recourse to as the latter gave him greater freedom of expression and allowed him to imagine an ideal situation for his Ideas.

Plato kept within the limits of dualist conception, but there is no doubt that he tended towards Unity, and he was well-disposed to it, as he repeatedly lays down the correct path: the necessary purification of the soul for every lover of knowledge, an indispensable condition for liberation. It should be clarified that this liberation is not the same as in my philosophy and the monist doctrines of India: during this life and unconditionally. Plato refers to "pure dwelling *post mortem.*" However, this is not his definitive theory of reincarnation, as happens in the doctrines of India; it gives to it an incessant dynamic. This dwelling is that of pure ideas in which the souls who visit it are inspired, but that while passing through the Lethe river, according to one of his myths, dissolve in its waters and are forgotten; and hence his theory of re-memorization.

Correctly he proposes another essential practice to follow the *unitive path*, the "imitation of Divinity" (*Phaedro 253*), a typically Greek idea, and the progressive identification of the soul with it; although it does not speak of a total identification. The limits of its initial dualism, however, in its long search and evolution eventually disappear and in his final dialogues he prefers to speak of the One instead of the multiplicity of absolutes, in such a way that the two realities tend to unify. In any case it is in this concrete world that the Creator "puts intelligence in the soul and the soul in the body" in such a way that "we can say that the world became a live creature endowed with soul and intelligence" (*Timaeus).* This is almost a definition of p*antheism,* a related idea of idealism which will continue to be structured and to which the spirit in the West will return.

Plato's mistake was to create, through undoubtedly correct intuitions, an absolute Reality "composed", or, better, a Reality composed of absolutes, in such a way that in its attempt to assimilate concrete particulars into the unchangeable, he was creating a static and even phantasmagorical world, similar to an immense wax museum of perfect Forms and thus an intermediate world which was neither an (absolute) Reality nor another (a tangible reality), but a world of representations. This was unnecessary, as each thing does not need a perfect and particular prototype for the spirit to have of it an idea of perfection, *the conscious or latent intuition of the One is enough for the individual spirits to have ideas of perfection about particular objects*. The Essence of the world penetrates and illuminates all things that participate in this manner of its perfection. The ideas of perfection in their moral *form*, the Good, and in their aesthetic *form* the Beautiful are *primary manifestations of the Essence*. We will return to them because they are amongst the most revelatory ideas that man has intuited.

Aristotle

If we read Aristotle, we can conclude that after him there is nothing more to talk about on the subject of idealism. In Aristotle however I see a typical case of the rebellious disciple who desires to exaggerate the differences between himself and his teacher, when in reality the differences are not so profound. If the world of ideas is entirely separated from the world of the senses I would agree with Aristotle. In this case "The ideas (in the Platonic sense), do not contribute anything to the knowledge of other beings, as they are not the essence of the same, since are not in them. Neither are they a cause of its existence as they are not found in the beings that participate in them." (*Met.* I, 9) But in Plato the Ideas are not entirely separated, as things *participate* in them and they are a model to which they aspire. For Aristotle the ideas are immanent to things, and this concept of immanence is close at times to that of participation and for both they constitute the essence of things: "By form (a concept that is the same as the Idea in Plato), I understand the essence of each thing." (*Met.* VII, 7) And also in its epistemological aspect: "the science of each being is the knowledge of its substantial form." (*Met.* VII, 6)

In the *Eudemian Ethics* (I, 8) Aristotle deals with the problem of Good in itself with his usual clarity, which as it enshrines the key of idealism will be useful for us to explain. Even Aristotle, one of the most intelligent men that humanity has produced and who had been a direct disciple of the creator of the Ideas, could not overcome this obstacle,; and the difficulty of this matter will thus be understood. "It is said (by Plato) that the best of all things is the absolute Good which has the attributes of being the first of the goods and of being the cause of the other goods to be good". "The other goods are so because of their participation in the idea of good and because of their similarity to it". "However –Aristotle refutes – affirming the existence of an idea, not just of the good, is a simple empty abstraction" as "even if we concede that the ideas and the idea of the good exist in their full sense, surely this lacks practical value for a good life or for conduct". For him "there does not exist a single science that has the real as its object (in keeping curiously with Platonic terminology it calls "real" what he considers an abstraction), or the good". Aristotle attends to "another class of studies that as being connected by necessity are found preferably in the field of logic." (*Op. cit.*) "It is evident –he concludes- that the absolute good that we seek is not the idea of neither the good nor the good considered as a universal, because the idea is unchangeable and unrealizable". "In this way the absolute good would be this: the end of realizable goods for man". "This is the good that constitutes the objective of the most important practical sciences." (*Op. cit.*)

Various explanations and rectifications are necessary. To start with it is surprising that someone so careful with terminology terms as "absolute" what is inevitably relative: what is realizable by man. These clarifications are very important because even today scientists erroneously judge ideal reality by inadvertently using the same perspective. In order to overcome this mistake and understand idealism from within, one has to use a method other than the "objective", that is the *unitive*, which is susceptible to shifting the spirit towards a transcendental perspective. This should be clear: without a change of perspective, which implies both an internal and external change of vision, i.e. an intrinsic transformation, intelligible reality will become unintelligible.

Aristotle says however: "Sophocles said that he represented how men should be, while Euripides represented them as they were". (*Poetics,* 1460 b) By the way, his judgment inclines towards the former, as, he later adds, "what should serve as an example is above what is." (*1461 b*) It should be pointed out that Aristotle is very consistent with this *priority of the ideal over the real,* which is typically Greek, Platonic and idealist; while judging him we should not forget this priority.

In my opinion, the misunderstanding to which scientists from Aristotle until today are prone to, is due to incomprehension of the true nature of ideas, their particular way of being, and their ontological *status.* If ideas are taken as simple abstractions (as is usual today), "created" by man, they will never be understood. Neither Plato nor Plotinus, nor the one who writes these lines perceives them in this way. Of course, I am not referring to all the ideas that inhabit the ideal world of Plato. In this I completely agree with Aristotle: "As regards those who consider the ideas as causes, one has to observe that (in this attempt) they have created many more beings, equal in number to the tangible world." (*Met.*) However, there remain some essential Ideas like the Good and the Beautiful, that are not only still existent, but, as we will see, continue to sustain the Universe. Plato expresses it thus: "In the farthest limits of the intelligible world is the idea of the Good, that is perceived with difficulty, but when perceived, one can only conclude that it is the primary cause of all that is good and beautiful in the universe; and in this visible world, it is that which produces the light, and engenders truth and intelligence in the intelligible world." (*Rep.* 517 b) But in order to understand this idea one has to perceive that "in itself", that is, from it, from a *perspective*, that as we will see, transcends the tangible world; this perception, this transcendence is what has given rise to the "world of Ideas".

With the Good and the Beautiful, Plato constructed a beacon that would guide the West towards the Transcendent. Whenever we have followed it we have gone in a straight line towards our destiny. Aristotle for his part constructed the fundamentals of a knowledge of phenomenal reality. It has been the great privilege of Western civilization to have received this rich double legacy. The error, already made by Aristotle, is that of trying to cover the two realities from a relative perspective, whereas in covering it from a *unitive perspective* there is no exclusion nor contradiction but rather convergence. These two points of view obey two different faculties, two positions of the spirit in the mind that determine two kinds of knowledge.

The Quest in Rome

Rome and Alexandria

In the first and second centuries A.D. there was a great intellectual effervescence in the two cities which had a monopoly over knowledge: Rome and Alexandria. Perhaps, genius and creativity were scarce, perhaps the spirit had become distanced from *the Creative*, but not to such an extent as to be alienated from it; it was intuited and sought through diverse means, always harking back to Hellenic sources from which various schools were derived. In spite of the disputes amongst them, points of common and generally morality can be discerned in the means and objectives. Happiness is the point of convergence, the Epicureans, Stoics and Platonists as well as the sceptics procured this. The latter had cause to disconnect from the reasons that yoked together the members of other schools; their detachment kept them in a state of serenity which is the *ataraxia* that the Stoic looks for; as Seneca expressed in *On the Tranquility of the Mind.*

Within this search Neo-Platonism emerged in the most enlightened sections. The Platonic wise man also searches for happiness which he puts on a par with the *liberation of the soul* through the knowledge of the *intelligible or the true beings*. (Albino, *Manual of Platonic Philosophy*). Note that Platonism always looks for a transformation produced by another intelligence that contemplates another order. For Numenius, there exists a *first intelligence*, which is the Goodness in itself, creator of the intelligible world; below it is the demiurge or creator of the tangible world; and later, this tangible world which is another god. Notice the sacred nature of this world, the pantheism.

Platonism never died, it has continually nurtured enlightened spirits, which have updated and given it new life with a Hellenic spirit. Plutarch is a good example, as he insists in his prolific work that he will re-establish the values of the classical age. In his *Parallel Lives* he lays down a paragon between the Greeks and the enlightened Romans with the express purpose of exalting the said moral and religious values; Plutarch belonged to the priestly college of Delphos and he was the eponymous archon in Queronea, his native city. He devoted his long life to the revival of the spirit of antiquity exalting its virtues and its glory. The reader, who feels the need to be imbued with this spirit in order to understand it better, will take recourse to its moral treatises.

Stoicism in Rome

Many historians have been struck by the fact that the predominant philosophy in Roman culture is stoicism, and that a huge civilization had as its basis a philosophy that was neither excellent nor well structured. Nevertheless it proved to be very effective and this fact should be pragmatically and seriously considered. My explanation is that, apart from the fortitude, strength and resistance that necessarily produce a stoic life, vital for the great project of this stern people, an intuition or experience of a natural Order lay beneath the various facets of this school which the Stoics sometimes call Nature, and at other times God. It was not detached from the natural order, it was rather a pantheist vision, that kept them integrated and in harmony with themselves, with society and albeit variable circumstances. This explains a good part of the matter, as the periods of creativity in all cultures have taken place when the spirit approaches Unity, and in the West it has been expressed as a manifest tendency towards pantheism. Conjoined with this ideal and practice, as stoicism was an applied philosophy, were measure and equilibrium, which were the essence of the Greek spirit. The Romans, a practical people *par excellence*, needed a practical and useful philosophy, not abstract ideas outside the context of life.

Stoicism is undoubtedly the product of that practical spirit whose objective is survival in the midst of the tribulations generated during periods of disorder; as was the case with Greece from the death of Alexander until its definite collapse under Rome. Stoicism was born in this chaotic period. It is this philosophy that Rome imports; Greek thinkers having brought it with them when they found themselves in the paradoxical situation of being both the slaves and the educators of patrician Roman families. But in certain aspects this spirit generally opposed to the rulers and Romans in general, who were essentially active as behaves a young and ascending civilization. Nothing was further away from the optimistic warrior spirit of conquest and surging power of Rome, than this spirit that brought out its essence of resignation.

All philosophy of history should heed this interesting fact: That when a young civilization incorporates a superior but older civilization, it finds it has different and even opposing objectives, to which to apply its optimism. This phenomenon takes place in both younger and older generations; in fact it is one of the causes of the usual clash that takes place between them. Given well-known human injustice, the balance made by old men is almost always pessimistic, as they have suffered the effects of all the passions that accompany foolishness; young men, fool themselves and full of passion, are generally optimists. This means that entire civilizations as well as generations find themselves in this different way of being. So even if youth uses the cultural baggage of the old, they apply to it another spirit.

It should be remembered that the Stoics maintained that the degree of reality of a being was in direct relation with the degree of the union of its parts, i.e. they intuited a superior primary Unity, which links them with the idealist tradition. It was this intuition that would inspire Plotinus.

Rome and Virgil

The reader by now knows that my vision of history is not reduced to philosophy. Poets have the virtue of naturally descending to the depths of the soul. Not so philosophers; they tend to look out, towards the distance, like astronomers, and forget the inner world. If philosophy tries to understand the Soul of the world, a philosophy of history should cover the most relevant *manifestations of the spirit*, and should be careful not to exclude the arts and religious expressions; it would have to be an integral and integrating history. Of course the task is huge but I cannot be blamed if the *Universus* is infinite.

The genius of Virgil goes beyond the excellence of his literature, one of the most precious jewels of humanity, it is revealed in his capacity to revive the Hellenic spirit, and he does so in a classic way: the Iliad and the Odyssey are renewed and with remarkable sagacity he connects them to the Latin tradition. For this reason the *Aeneid* is a classic amongst classics. Aeneas travels within this spirit, he navigates it, and he breathes and lives it. Unfortunately I cannot follow him now, but the reader is invited to embark with this Trojan hero who saves the Penates of his city in order to found the New Ilion in Latin lands; the rich treasure of the Hellenic spirit is incorporated into the shores of the new-born civilization. In this narrative voyage Virgil takes literature to its highest expression. Virgil's achievement is without doubt in every sense, including the historical and political. It is exactly what the cultured Romans had been hoping for, and Octavio perceived this at once; it was the spiritual tool that he needed to make a Renaissance of his age, a clear example that emerges from the convergence and amalgam of artistic genius with the talent of a practical spirit. These two great men clearly saw the historical moment which they were living and lost no opportunity to use the rich Greek legacy.

Here we will only accompany Aeneas on the most mysterious of journeys, in which he descends to Hades to visit his father Anchises, because in it he describes the vision that the Romans had of the cycle of life and death and the cosmos, not alien to the Hellenic idealism. "Do you know –Anchises says to his son– firstly that the Earth, the sky, the oceans, the moon and the stars enshrine a divine Spirit that animates them. Extended through the veins of the world that Spirit moves all matter and makes its immense body vibrate. Through it come the races of men, those of the beasts, the birds and the monsters that inhabit the land beneath the waves. In all beings there is a living flame, a celestial principle; but the miseries of the earthly body will not linger in altering it and hindering its efficiency. Hence the fear and desires, souls do not see light when they are enclosed by shadows. When death frees them from their shackles, they conserve all their impurities". "It is necessary that they purify themselves from the roots (...) that they expiate their old mistakes". "Later we are sent to the vast Elysian, although there are few of us who finally inhabit these fields. Here we remain till the course of time has extinguished our old vices and returned to us the said breath, that spark of celestial fire to its pristine purity. After the completion of a cycle of a thousand years, a god calls all the souls to the banks of the (river) Lethe, so that forgetting its past it returns to the higher regions (of Nature) with the desire of animating new bodies".

Virgil clearly announces the belief in a universal Spirit that penetrates Nature and gives it permanent life. That Spirit is pure and all beings participate in it. That purity is stained by man by his identification with his body, that light is obscured by fear and desire. Once purified the souls reincarnate again. The similarity with Hinduism and Buddhism is evident, and this essentially coincides with my own philosophy. We find in it another link in the chain of Western thinkers who maintain an *idealist pantheism,* i.e. a Nature imbued with the immanent but still transcendent Spirit.

The second Renaissance of Hellenic spirit takes place in the period of the Antonin's, particularly during the reign of Adrian, who deserves much more praise and commentary than I can make here. It is enough however to visually reconstruct the Rome of that age not forgetting the magnificent Villa Adriana, as well as the monuments and temples that he constructed in Athens, to show his clear intention of reliving and shaping the Hellenic spirit.

Plotinus

From the age of Parmenides to the time of the writer of these lines, Idealism has revolved around the experience of Unity and the inspiration that it generates. Later I will clarify my vision on this matter, which is the central theme of philosophy. A bird's eye view of the world of Plotinus is enough to fly with it through his transcendental reality as his knowledge is one of the most lucid in Western history.

Myths and Reality

The question whether Plotinus also tries to teach a religion has preoccupied many scholars who face the same problem with Plato, yet the question seems fruitless if we ignore the fact that the elements considered "religious" by these authors are also indispensable to the philosopher. Neither Plato nor Plotinus suggest that religious techniques are the legacy of one discipline or another, they simply put them into effect and with excellent results as emerge from their doctrines. The matter is of such extreme and decisive importance that my own philosophy depends on these techniques. Moreover, I believe that they are also indispensable in order to fully understand the said philosophers, the Pre-Socratics, the Hellenic spirit in general and, here lies the key and nucleus of the matter: in order to know ourselves.

Plotinus notes the difference of the state of the soul when it is in the Intelligence and when it is in "reflexive thought", in my terminology, between unified consciousness and discernment; he calls the first "divine", like Plato, the other, human. This *descent of the soul* has been intuited by man in various cultures and expressed in myths that have commonalities, which are dramatically visualized as a fall. It is instructive to take Plotinus who had a more direct experience of the descent as a reference, in order to understand that these myths are not simple fantasies, but the product of the intuitions of a spiritual reality; to which naturally are added elements of the unconscious and of popular imagination. Plotinus has the particularity of being in an intermediate sector: his experience is mystic, his reason philosophical, and his imagination mythic. If we can understand his way of visualizing his ideas, the reality that he wants to express will become clearer.

In his excellent work on Plotinus, E. Brehier reminds us that he lived in an age in which initiatory cults proliferated, and influenced by them he "establishes an intimate relation between inner life, the idea of the universe and purification practices". Thus, for example, in the field of Mars in Rome, the mysteries of Isis consisting of a purification of the spirit, and ending "as in Plotinus, not with the vision of a divine image, but of light" were also practiced. Once more we lament the lack of data on these secret cults, these initiatory rites, discredited and finally abolished by the Church a century after our philosopher.

In his myths, Plato made the souls travel towards other celestial regions where they were instructed and purified to later descend to this world, but his intention by all accounts was not to create concrete places in the cosmos for these phenomena, but to exemplify through parables, what I would call in my language the displacements, that the soul needs to elevate itself through virtues until it reaches the Goodness in itself. His interest was in illustrating what I understand by *levels of consciousness*, but without descending into a mere psychology bereft of a universal dimension; hence the use of the myth.

In the IIIrd century, the situation was very different, it was not Athens now that exported its philosophy to the barbarians but the Roman Empire that imported the religion of the barbarians and this changed the trend of Western history. Plotinus finds himself at the confluence of these two currents and even if he is faithful to the Hellenic tradition, the influence of these religions on the margins of the Empire is observed, not so much in what is substantial in his philosophy as in the tendency to map the cosmos in keeping with the movement of the soul, attempting to make real that which for Plato was an allegorical myth. For this reason we have to exclude the cosmologic–religious aspect of his thought as far as possible. This will not be easy as each stage of the soul corresponds to a station of the universe, but what is particularly interesting is his vision of spiritual reality, probably the clearest in the West up until now. And this is due to a decisive factor; it is because Plotinus is a mystic philosopher, which is not the same as being a religious mystic, as the latter has a commitment to his creed, making him accommodate his reason with a doctrine, while the former only has to accommodate his reason with his experience. In both there is an adaptation, but in the latter the relation is more direct, while the former carries out an extra step leaves the limits of the rational. A mystic philosopher is a rare gem found in the ocean of thought, and it is thus worthwhile to submerge oneself in it.

What makes Plotinus' thought difficult to comprehend is that that four planes are on top of each other: the psychological, the philosophic, the religious and the scientific, disciplines that have been thoroughly differentiated by contemporary man. This is not sufficient reason for man to believe without consideration of the matter, because on the whole he is in a situation higher than that of Plotinus, even if today it is a puerile thought in the scientific order, in the others it deserves to be taken into account, as in the others contemporary man finds himself in an infantile stage, far from reaching the level that our philosopher reached one thousand seven hundred years ago. The rights and wrongs of Plotinus should be attributed to a decisive factor: that he sees, thinks and feels from a (relatively) unified consciousness. This is what makes him identify the Universe with his mind, see the shifts of the soul as inter galactic journeys, see reality as a circular Whole, the processes as cyclical, with Unity at the beginning and the end of the road.

We have to remember this because the characteristics that conform all pantheisms are born of an *intuition of the original Unity*. I am not trying to justify Plotinus' errors of interpretation, but to explain them so as to approach his thought more precisely. Plotinus' fundamental error consists in explaining psychic content cosmologically, creating myths with a pseudo-scientific character. We have already emphasized how the religions of the Near East that had invaded the Empire influenced him; they suffered from the common mistake of taking myths as objective reality.. The Christian doctrine, for example that had begun to take shape, is based on the supposed "truth" of certain myths that go back to the creation of the world and man. The originality of Plotinus was that like Plato he created his own myths based on his own experience and in this he shows himself to be more a philosopher than a religious man.

Plotinus and Plato

Plotinus probably did not have the dialectical capacity and versatility of Plato, but everything seems to indicate that he had had an *experience of the First Principle* that Plato only intuited. Thus even if the major characteristics of Plato's philosophy do not improve with Plotinus, in reference to this First Principle, Plotinus places us much closer thanks to a higher level of consciousness and he perfects idealism in some essential points which I have highlighted. In my commentaries on Plato (see my *Psychosophy*) I insist on his correct intuition that always leads him on the correct path, without more divergences than those posed by the doubts of his reason. But in the great Athenian we observe the lack of *direct perception* of the First Principle, something that does not happen with Plotinus. The latter, without doubt, has had what is called "mystic union", which I prefer to call *total unitive experience* in order to clarify the concept well.

If we take this *experience* as a reference, we will easily notice the difference in the aforementioned essential points among the philosophers. All that Plato can do is postulate a World of Ideas of perfect Forms from which human intelligence is inspired, and from which he extracts his ideas of perfection. Plotinus on this point takes us to a higher level of consciousness, placing us in the One itself. From here the first emanation would be the *Nous* or Intelligence that would cover the multitude of Ideas intuited by Plato. The difference is subtle, but Plotinus would come closer, as we will see, to my conception.

Plotinus unlike Plato does not imagine a Soul of the World but something superior, in direct contact with the *Nous,* or Intelligence, but in indirect contact with matter, and another that would be the Soul of the material World, which he also calls Nature. As can be seen, Plotinus also observes a distance, and even other spaces that he tries to fill with an additional kind of soul: the individual. There would thus be three kinds of souls: the higher or purely spiritual, the lower which is the soul of the World, and the individual; each one proceeds from the other. The individual soul that precedes birth, returns on the death of the subject to its original Unity. Like Plato, Plotinus calls this joint Reality intelligible, but he divides it in three substances: the One, the Nous or Intelligence and the Soul of the World, that are derived or engendered from one to the other through emanation, although they "remain immobile (i.e., changeless) on engendering these hypostasis" (*Ennead III, 4, 1*).

Plotinus' whole theory comes from the experience of this Unity. His moral theory, following an inverse path also ascends. The practice of development of virtue, which implies the control of the passions, is the basic mechanism of self-knowledge and the real path towards the perfection of man. Since this is the Greek ideal *par excellence,* it is natural that these people knew like no others all mechanisms and realisations of these practices; their physical and spiritual excellence cannot be explained outside these stimuli of the soul. The spirit of Plotinus is immersed in that tradition.

As in Plato, reason has its limits. Plotinus finds his *Nous* beyond this, in a state of ecstasy he achieves the One who is God himself, and his consciousness becomes divine. Besides, he does not ignore the difficulty of expressing this state of total identity. Happiness is then ineffable. From his mystic experience derive his ethics, his cosmology, his metaphysics, his religion and his theory of knowledge. And the same can be said of all the Far Easter philosophies-religions and of my philosophy that confirms its knowledge at least in its essential aspects.

Plotinus in the light of my experience

My theory of perspectives can help to understand Plotinus and the idealists in general. The common mortal finds himself faced with a multiple world which he tries to understand. Curiously he does not ask himself why he feels motivated to integrate it, when he conceptualizes, relates or reflects, and in this way to reintegrate in the original Unity. The difficulty in understanding Plotinus comes from his perspective which makes him look at the world from the diametrically opposed position of the multiple, i.e. from Unity: from the order the disorder, from the mutable the immutable, finally from the spirit at its highest level (as we are not dealing here with subjectivism or psychologism), matter. The world, for the idealist, is ordered from there to here. This perspective is not the product of an arbitrary choice but a vision obtained thanks to an immense leap of the spirit that very few can make. Unfortunately there are many specialists of idealism who have not managed to make this leap.

The concept of *hypostasis,* fundamental in Plotinus' thought is a new attempt by idealism to express that *first Reality* which because it is invisible and intangible, becomes unreal in the eyes of contemporary man, who for this reason tends to believe that it is no more than an idea or concept "created" by the individual, or subjective mind, and not an objective reality. But these concepts of the subjective and the objective, valid for other knowledge's do not respond to that transcendental Reality, to which we idealists refer. This Reality as I have been pointing out since my earliest writings is *Unitive* and presents itself a *priori* to all discursive thought, to all reality seen subjectively or objectively.

Plotinus is right in his apperception of Unity that for him is the "force of all things". He is also right in his theory of emanation that completely responds to the experience of the One flowing over the World. However for him as for Plato, the said emanation flows into the world of ideas, an intelligible but multiple reality made up of perfect beings. This is very difficult to sustain and to believe, however if we remain with what is essential of that reality, as an inexhaustible source of life and whith the Good, that we can interpret as a *universal moral Order,* then I am in agreement with him.

I agree with Plotinus that Nature is ordered in the Unity. This is very difficult to explain because it transcends reason, I will try to do so with the rational mediums that we have with which to communicate: When consciousness is unified, Order reigns; the spirit finds itself integrated, and sees that when the universal Spirit pours on Nature it integrates it in that Order. This happens before the spirit penetrates time and space and finds itself with the multiple in the becoming. This leads me to explain the intelligible world of Plato and Plotinus as a result of that transcendental experience, the moment when the spirit integrates, unifies and immobilizes Nature. It is the experience of that moment in which reality is seen from an absolute Order, which has led them to postulate the existence of a world of stable ideas.

Plato suspects a mistake in his theory due to which he expresses it as a myth, Plotinus, who belongs to an age when myths were taken for reality, does not doubt the myth. However that reality as I experience it is a moment of the spirit in transit between the pure Spirit and the becoming, where there exists an absolute Order, but not a separated world, only Nature seen from this absolute perspective. What is decisive here is this perspective, and so by taking out the world of ideas from this medium, I am only discarding an unnecessary postulate, but the origin of the ideas, the Source of the spirit, the matrix of the world continues reflecting there the ideal world conceived by Plato and Plotinus.

Plotinus is faithful to his experience when he expresses the relation between the One and Nature, not mechanically but as an intangible, subtle extension, as an emanation that he compares with smell (E. V, 1,6); which seems very correct to me. Now, as this emanation becomes matter, I have here a question of weight that I have tried to respond to in *Origin and Destiny of Man.*

To ask why the One creates, is to go beyond experience. Surely conscious of this, Plotinus does not postulate a will behind the One. Nevertheless, Plotinus' answer comes from an inference: "from the moment that a being reaches its state of perfection, it engenders." While this is very reasonable, by the same logic it fall into a trap: "How does the most perfect being, the Good, remain immobile in itself?", "perhaps through impotence; he who is the force of all things?" (E. V, 4,1). The experience does not show us a moving being, neither does logic demand that it be so. His error comes because of the lack of attention to the mental mechanism used at that time, it is inferring, not perceiving. The idealists of Romanticism will commit this same error and due to the same reasons.

If we change a few concepts and adjust a few others, we will see to what point my conception overlaps with that of Plotinus. It should be clear, I repeat, that there is no cultural transmission here. I have known Plotinus since I started tracing the history of idealism to write this book and the superimpositions are thus revelatory. Thirty years ago, when I wrote my first book, *The Return to Sources*, I said that "the Sources are like a calm lake that flows over the world without reducing its content". Plotinus says, with regard to experience: "Imagine a source that has no origin. Give all its water to the rivers, but it still does not get exhausted for this reason; it remains calm at the same level" (*E. III, 8, 10*). I could not agree more with him on the path of the return of the spirit. I had said: "The individual spirits are inspired and aspired by the Consciousness." Plotinus says: "the multiple searches itself; it aspires to concentrate itself and to take consciousness of itself". "The intellectual act takes place because the Good exists and moves intelligence towards itself". "To think is to move towards the Good and desire it; desire engenders Intelligence" (*E. V, 6, 5*). Although here he refers to Intelligence, the latter is assimilated into the human consciousness and vice versa. But the superimposition is not gratuitous as: "Each one of us is an intelligible world; connected to inferior things through the body, we touch the higher things through the intelligible essence of our being" (*E. III, 4, 3*). If we understand this well we can leave out the cosmology of Plotinus, as we did with the intelligible world, in order to remain with a mental reality, whenever we give this mind a transcendent character and a universal dimension and validity. It could seem as if we have devastated Plotinus' system by taking out the two realities that mattered to him, but actually we have only dispossessed it of an unnecessary façade to leaving it naked; in this way we recover the substance of his philosophy, we stay with the soul of Plotinus. And this is no small thing as "the soul is a multiplicity and is also all things, those from above as well as those from below, in the whole extension of life" (*E. III, 4, 3*)

What interests us is demonstrating, as far as possible, what I would call the *unified consciousness* of Plotinus, as this is what makes us see the All in each and every one of us: "We remain on high through our completely intelligible side, but on the other hand, from the side that takes the last place, we chain ourselves to the things of this world, as if we would impart to them an emanation, and even better, an activity of the intelligible part" (*E. III, 4, 3*). The action of man, when we understand is the universal dimension of Plotinus; it is an expression of the Intelligence that derives from Unity.

For Plotinus the soul is made up of two parts, one that is in contact with the Intelligible, the other with the material world; to act on the latter it is inspired by the former. Up to here, we are in agreement, although we must clarify that only one who knows the Unity is conscious of this and is inspired by it, man in general ignores it; the concept of alienation seems to explain this fact. A product of this alienation is the identification with his I, which leads him to believe that he creates his ideas and does not borrow them from an ignored higher consciousness. Plotinus, like all those who have reached a high level of consciousness, contemplates Unity, the intelligible reality by which it is inspired.

While the common man sees only a multiplicity and a becoming, Plotinus from the perspective of the Soul of the world, that he identifies with Zeus, "sees that this infinite is one and that there one unique science and life" (*E. IV, 4, 9*); this would correspond completely to my idea of a *universal Consciousness*. Order is derived from this *Consciousness*; it is the very Order that according to Plotinus is spread throughout Nature. He says with precision: "The order of the world is the act of a soul that depends on a permanent knowledge, whose image is the interior order of that soul" (*E. IV, 4, 9*). Nevertheless, while in my view this order attracts or inclines to the natural order, for Plotinus it is established, which leads him to clash with the disorder of the world. His theory becomes more tangled when it takes on a determinist hue: "The guiding principle of the world knows the future" "if he didn't know it... his production would be accidental and at random", which brings him closer to a anthropomorphic vision although he does not fall into it, as there is no creative will "like a worker" (*E. IV, 4, 12*). It is very reasonable that from the experience of Unity it can be inferred that the universe be a spiritual "phenomenon", and following this sequence it can be deduced that the different celestial spheres are equivalent to the stages of the soul in its ascent. But the experience is only from Unity and the rest is inference, and here begins the mistake.

Plotinus has the experience of the purity of the soul, "but after this repose in the divine being, in Intelligence, I descend to the reflexive thought, and I ask myself how this descent of the soul in the body took place" (*E. I, 8,14*), which is very correct, but instead of explaining it as in our *Psychosophy*, as a shift of our focus of consciousness, from the pure Consciousness to the external plane or that of discernment, he imagines the soul travelling through celestial strata like the fall of a meteor. He imagines that the drama of the soul has as its background the universe, and that this immense theatre is also a temple, as all that occurs is religious. Thus builds up a graduated pantheism on the last step of which is Intelligence. This cosmological representation is a step behind Plato who with the prudence so characteristic of his time, alluded to myths with which he did not try to create objective realities but allusive images in order to awaken a rare knowledge, in order to approach or *shift*, I would say in my vision, the spirits to that Reality. I think that these celestial journeys of the soul distract the spirit from its immediate Reality where the said Reality reveals itself, to project it into a later time and space created by reason.

Brehier teaches us that the relation which Plotinus establishes between inner life and the idea of the universe is identical to the mystic religions of his time; this appropriation of Plotinus was his mistake. But this appropriation of Plotinus does not annul nor even diminish his experience; his whole philosophy is inspired and directed to the same ends. Discovering this principle is "the end of the journey" it is the realization of its destiny. In *Origin and Destiny of Man* I have said the same thing in order to express the same experience.

Even if I agree with Plotinus that there is a universal Soul in which all beings participate, I do not share his opinion that this universe is perfect and not even like Leibnitz that it is the most perfect within what is possible. I believe in the independence of Nature, in particular that of the living beings, and progressively as concerns its spiritual and intellectual evolution. In Plato and Plotinus there is a trace of determinism, absent in my vision of the world. Even if in Plotinus Providence does not find a place, as the One like Brahman or like my *universal Consciousness*, does not want anything; it is logical that if a finished and perfect Being desired something he would stop being so. A God busy with human concerns will be able to satisfy the wishful thinking of the common herd, but he will seem more like a ruler than a divinity.

When Plotinus says that the *Nous* is Beauty, I would completely agree with him. Nevertheless, Plotinus identifies it also with the Demiurge of Plato and here there will be no parallel. Even if I identify that which is Creative with universal Consciousness, I do not believe that the distance between the latter and the World can be filled with something other than hypothesis. The two realities, the supra sensible and the sensible can be the objective of knowledge, but not the union between the two; this generates a dilemma that has been resolved in a different way. The Samkhya philosophy of India has made of this distance an abyss that leaves both realities completely separated; I quote this vision as the most extreme. In my vision the connection would be Life Itself, the Spirit that inserts itself in matter, although due to the love of the truth, I admit that there is no experience of the moment of insertion of the spirit in matter; even if I know that the latter will not live without the former, even as I perceive the *vital élan* that it injects life into it and the attraction that it exercises.

The universal projection of Plotinus

Precisely in the age of Plotinus, Christianity started growing and would progressively block all openings towards other thoughts and cultures. Plotinus does not concern himself with Christianity, but Porphyry writes fifteen books against the Christians that obviously were later burnt by the new powers. It is legitimate to suppose that he must have been writting along the lines of Celsius, who was also Platonic, with the wide panorama that the astronomical vision of Plotinus provided him with. Porphyry, who knew the works of Plotinus like none other, having compiled them, must have had powerful arguments to refute those of the new faith and, he had many, as can be surmised from the size of his work. Regarding Porphyry it can be said that like his master and Plato, he lays special emphasis on virtues and on ascetic life as a means of purification of the soul and its ascent, which allows him to come closer to the intelligible world and the contemplation of Unity. So then for Porphyry the virtues have this ascendant function of the soul, starting with civil or social virtues; followed by purifying virtues destined to control the passions; and thus in ascending fashion to the virtues directed towards intelligible reality; till one reaches the most elevated and paradigmatic that are a legacy of the Intelligible, of the *Nous*. It is not clear if, as in my philosophy, from Unity the virtues of the world come forth, but if we relate this ascendant path of the virtues and descending emanations of the Good of Plotinus, we will see that they are similar ideas, similar experiences.

Copleston says in his *History of Philosophy*: "In the system of Plotinus they acquire their most polished and systematic expression the Orphic–Platonic–Pythagoric tendencies, while considering above all (...) the intellectual ascent of the soul, salvation through the affinity with God and the knowledge of the Divine". Thus in Plotinus we find not only the refined Greek tradition, but also a parallel with the elevated philosophies of the other great civilizations produced by humanity, that of China and of India, towards which he had inadvertently made a bridge that Western culture could have used. Coincidentally, at the end of his *Prologue to Plotinus*, Brehier says: "We believed that it was legitimate and even necessary, to make a hypothesis on the relations of Plotinus with India, that perhaps others who are more competent, can propose to verify". This hypothesis is very important because although the connection established is brief (he barely devotes half a page to the matter), he sees a bridge between the East and the West which I have tried to pave the way from the beginning of my work; hence the importance and scope of the matter. The said bridge was not finished by Plotinus but I beleave that from the perspective that I show, which is what has been achieved by the West after its long, painful and interrupted ascent on the path of idealism, this task can be completed.

The Spirit in the Medieval Age

Since I am interested in following the path of idealism, I cannot really devote myself to Christianity, as it presents itself as an obstacle, not just for this ideology, but also for the free evolution of the spirit, and for the natural growth of Western civilization. This being the case, the reader who might want to uninterruptedly follow the flow of idealism, can skip this period and pass directly to the Renaissance. In my view, the development of Western civilization can be represented by a huge tree that has been brutally pruned by Christianity that has used the roots and sap of the Greco Roman tree and has transported its branches to other destinations in order to harvest fruits alien to our idiosyncrasy, race and culture. What is more, the most interesting Christian writings are inspired by Platonism; but I will not linger here on vain scholastic discussions, which do not search for truth in itself, but are bent on proving the supposed truths that are revealed, established *a priori*, using borrowed philosophies; something that is completely sterile from a philosophical point of view. Rather, as we will see in reverse, on how the Western spirit was beginning to awaken as it returned to its Hellenic roots and freed itself from the tentacles of this imported religion imposed by the ecclesiastical powers.

From the beginning Christian thinkers have felt the need to bolster their doctrine through borrowings from Plato, Aristotle, Plotinus and Stoicism, but this has never been successful from the philosophical point of view. Ortega y Gasset expresses it with clarity: "Christianity has had a tragic destiny in this order. It has never managed to speak its language: in its theo-logy – its talk of God – the theo is Christian and the logos is predominantly from Greece. And seeing things with a bit of rigor, one observes that the Greek logos constantly and inevitably betrays the Christian intuition" (Man and Crisis or About Galileo). Émile Brehier, in his monumental History of Philosophy, does not find philosophical arguments that have validated Christianity. I have not found them either, not even in the Summa Theologica (or the Martyrdom of Aristotle), in which Tomas Aquinas, tortures the Stagirite until he gets his way, i.e. with his belief, but in spite of this inquisitorial method, so fashionable in that age, he only manages to convince the believers, not the philosophers. The reason is simple: as soon as the premise of faith is advanced, all philosophy disappears. As Kant has unequivocally shown, the proofs of the existence of God given by Christian theologians are untenable within a rational framework.

Although I have to sometimes had to diverge from the philosophical current inherent in this work, it is important to highlight certain essential points of Christianity. I will also refer to certain falsified facts that have been imposed as historical truths and which need to be rectified, as we can hardly build a philosophy of history with false histories. For these reasons I will not elaborate on this doctrine here. Christianity should be treated as a religion and like a moral idealism, for this reason I will comment on it in *The Root of Morality*.

Stoicism and Christianity

How a Roman can become a Christian is a not an easy matter to explain if we are dealing with such disparate spirits. I think that the question could be better formulated as this: Were those who were converted still Roman? It is not as the Christian wants to believe that they changed their false gods for one true god; not when they had been true gods for ten centuries. There are no false or true gods, but different perspectives and ways of seeing and believing. I have said that Stoicism was undoubtedly the product of a practical spirit whose objective was survival in the midst of the tribulations generated during periods of disorder; Rome lives through what Greece lived through then. Stoicism would be the philosophy of Rome until its fall, nevertheless it was precisely that which had given life to Stoicism that now caused its death, as it was replaced by a similar doctrine and then forgotten. We can concede that the conversion of the Romans to Christianity, when voluntary, could have been a reaction to the earthly and practical extreme that Rome had arrived at, and that this together with the fall of the Empire demonstrated that this ideology was not sufficient to sustain it, as we should not forget the identification of the Romans with Rome and with its limitless civilizational project. The fall of Rome was a fall for the Romans, not an external fact, just a change of circumstances; it was a catastrophe for the Romans and for the West.

There are certain aspects of the Stoic spirit that assimilate it with the Christian spirit, the fundamental one is that Stoicism is not strictly a philosophy, but a belief system, i.e. a dogmatic idea of the universe, on which human conduct is based. Brehier (*Stoicism*) reminds us that Arcesilaus, who headed the New Academy and upheld the Attica tradition, while rejecting Stoicism points out that all philosophers before this school, from Xenophanes to Plato, show a marked hostility to dogmatism. We know that none of these Stoics were born on the Greek continent, and that in the disastrous period following the death of Alexander, they showed more sympathy for Macedonia than for Athens. What is decisive is that they did not have a genuine Athenian spirit. And this is very important because what has been called Hellenism is not pure Hellenic spirit. The spirit of the Stoic has degenerated and had become so alienated that it does not perceive great truths in themselves and thus has to fill the emptiness with suppositions, with hypotheses that try to "prove" with reason. And since it can not do this, it postulates incontrovertible beliefs or rather dogmas. Christianity works within this same framework of beliefs. Hence both doctrines should formulate a whole code of actions, an ethics of particulars, as they do not perceive Goodness in itself.

Another characteristic of Stoicism, common to Christianity, and which paved the way for the latter, is the existence of God as a Father and Judge, who is witness to our actions. We find this belief in Seneca, who, however, conserves the Hellenic ideal of Divinity as an ideal of perfection to which we should aspire; although not to solicit favours in the Judeo–Christian mode; this vision establishes a duality that tends to disarticulate the Stoic pantheism. It is through these channels that the branches of Stoicism are introduced in Christianity. These similarities were also noticed by the Christians, to the extent that there were many who could create an epistolary correspondence between Seneca and Paul of Tarsus; and it has been taken as authentic for centuries.

The new religion grew not only through its politics, but also because there had been a general decay of the spirit. This happened not only amongst the Romans, but also and especially amongst the new converts to Christianity. This idea of the world was much easier to assimilate than Neo-Platonism and the Greek tradition in general. The resurgence of Platonism was focused and tardy, while stoicism had infused Roman intellectuals ever since Greece fell into their hands. And, as I said, there were decadent aspects that Gnosticism, Stoicism and Christianity had in common, such as disdain for the world and indifference to life. A God that creates the World out of nothing, as if he were a Person (as he was taken to be), and immediately after creates living beings, whose function is to serve us humans, is simple and also very convenient. And as these beliefs spread amongst the "internal proletariat", as Toynbee observed, they were used as an instrument of power, and they were used to the letter.

The Christianity that we inherited

Those who want to know about Christianity should not forget that the doctrine was never made by Jesus but by subsequent priests, first by Paul of Tarsus, a Pharisee priest, and centuries later by the Church that incorporated Paul into the New Testament, and consequently the Old Testament. With the latter it annuls the new law of Jesus and re-establishes the old law with all its defects: the jealous and vengeful God, the closed and exclusive dogmatism, an infantile cosmogony that Jesus does not even mention, etc. In other words, what should not be forgotten is that Church policies have decided the doctrine, and have accommodated it to their interests twisting Jesus message in theory and, above all, in practice. In this way we have two types of Christianity, that of Jesus and that laid down by Paul and the Church. Now, this duality persists in the Gospels, as it is known that it was the Church who selected them disqualifying those that qualified as apocryphal, and besides we do not know to what extent the message of Jesus was modified, as other Gospels confirm.

This situation demands to be judged with good criteria, that (unfortunately for the lover of knowledge and fortunately for the Church), is not an attribute of the majority of mortals. This duality has also existed within and without the Church: there are those who are interested in power, who have occupied and continue to occupy the highest positions, whom we can call the Paulists, and there are those who follow the teachings of Jesus, (not Jesuits, of course). The former have used the good works of the latter to justify and extend their power; nevertheless good Christians have always known and put up with the excesses of the higher clergy, which morally cannot be justified, even within Christian morality. For this reason, there have been many dissidents inside and outside the Church who, of course, have been persecuted collectively or as individuals. This vital nihilism, camouflaged with high ideals, dressed in promises, this life travestied by another which seemingly more real and eternal, was the corrosive element that was inserted in the Hellenic civilization. It attracted a huge mass of the dispossessed and – as always happens when where there are many faithful – it served as an instrument of power; and as we know, a love for thy neighbour means making of him a convert. This means that the ecclesiastical politics not only tried as far as possible to eliminate the Greco Roman tradition, but also twisted the message of Jesus to adjust it to its political interests.

The point is that Western civilization did not follow a *natural process* in which the morality of Jesus was slowly expanding. In the IVth century, as soon as the Church took power, a vertical and violent imposition occurred directed to eliminating all opposition in order to achieve absolute power and the establishment of a single way of thinking and believing; of the dozens of religions that peacefully lived within the Empire only one remained. A centralization of power in all orders was established; Western civilization was finished, a century later the temples and theatres would be used as stables by the barbarians and the libraries would be abandoned. Only nine centuries later would begin the task of recovering the texts and the works of art that had survived.

The Medieval Age in the three great civilizations

We will never know what the West would have been if the Church had allowed the religious traditions in particular and all manifestations of the spirit in general to take their natural course, but we can infer that instead of losing so many centuries we would have gained in all fields. It is enough to compare the elementary theatre of the Medieval Age which was limited to *autos sacramentales* in which the life of the holy family is represented (and not the *autos da fe*, in which the heretics were burnt) with the Greek theatre to realize the abysmal fall of the spirit; the miserable life of medieval man compared with the plenitude of life of the Hellenic; and we will not repeat what we all know: the stagnation of the sciences.

Historical facts speak for themselves: until the Vth Century the West competed well with the great civilizations of the Far East, India and China. Greek genius had even surpassed these civilizations. In these three civilizations there was an awakening of the spirit in the VIth and Vth century B.C. but in order to develop a similar civilization, India had to wait a few centuries and China even longer. These three civilizations are comparable until the Vth century; after that there is a marked difference: while the West regressed into barbarism, India proudly bore the fruits of a mature civilization. The barbarians were not only responsible for ravages in Europe, as India had also suffered them, but the latter could quickly re-establish itself with pertinent religions, philosophies, industries and the freedom to be creative. On the other hand, China, from the VIIIth century, i.e. during the darkest period of the West, developed one of the most refined civilizations in the history of man. Western civilization had to wait seven centuries to reach this level. There can be no clearer proof of our decadence: the most memorable periods took place in the East in the Medieval Age, in the Vth Century with the Guptas in India, and in the VIIIth Century during the Tang dynasty in China. In this way the period that in the West was called the Dark Ages, would correspond in the Far East with the Age of Light or Enlightenment. This comparison has not really been taken into account due to the all-knowing egocentric Western vision that has arbitrarily and systematically disdained other cultures, but it is unavoidable when judging the history of civilizations.

Civilizations decay when they are shorn of their spiritual premises, as happened in Rome when it was worn away by Christianity, and they flourish when they are fertilized like India during the same period. In Rome idealism was truncated by the axe of the Church, while in India idealism achieved its most genuine and elevated forms: Mahayana Buddhism would grow to such an extent that it would cross its borders and spread to the whole Far East, and Hinduism would experience a genuine Renaissance, while Rome, corroded from within, would fall into the hands of barbarians.

If we view history pragmatically and go beyond all doctrinaire discussions that with dogmatists are always fruitless, we will see that Christianity has been a failure. Firstly, because it alienated us from Hellenic civilization; secondly, because when it had more power than it needed to prove its efficiency, there ensued the most gloomy period of Western history; thirdly, because it has not even managed to imbue our society with sufficient spirit, and now, that the very history has removed it from the scene, we are spiritless and sceptical about all religions. In fact, the reigning materialism is not so much a consequence of the industrial revolution as much as it is of a lack of spirit. In this way we see ourselves faced with the need of re-establishing the spirit in a hostile environment where materialism reigns supreme.

Platonism and civilization

There are many who identify *a priori* in their defence of Christianity when they evaluate or compare it with other doctrines, only because they are part of it, of "us", i.e. out of mere egocentrism or chauvinism, out of sympathy or identification, without having thought through its attitude, without having considered its indoctrination and history, without having reflected that whatever is substantial and decisive in our civilization is that which we owe to the Hellenic tradition.

Neo-Platonism was the correct answer for our civilization but Plotinus who lived in Rome for about thirty years, was perhaps not aware of his historic circumstances (we saw that he did not occupy himself with Christianity), although he intended to found *Platonopolis,* in order to better realize the dream of the Republic. It is not possible to imagine how this project might have functioned, but it would have undoubtedly imbued the high spirit of Athens, the beacon that Rome and the West should have followed. Neo-Platonism, like all higher philosophies appealed to the cultured and privileged minorities and could not be assimilated during that period; it came a little late. Plotinus was born just after the end of Antonin's age, during which he could have grown and given marvellous fruits. If that had been the case the gloomy middle Ages might have been avoided and perhaps a Renaissance could have happened. And although different from the Florentine we can imagine it could have been more vigorous and with more solid premises. There would have been no need then to recover the old texts; the numerous libraries of Rome were replete with classics. There would have been no need then to dig through the ruins left by the catastrophe in order to discover the old wisdom; for the Greco–Roman culture was fresh and at hand.

The reader might well ask of what use are these speculations on an irreversible past? The answer is: We agree that the past is irreversible, but the history that we are constructing is reversible if we are clear about the historical process that we have followed and the destiny we have to follow. This is one of the objectives that underlie this work. And in this process Plotinus' thought is an indispensable link: Plotinus ratifies and seals the tradition that goes back to Parmenides, Xenophanes and Plato, revealing with greater penetration, the psychic, philosophical and religious Essence of man and the Reality in which he is immersed. The essential had already been said, *the quest*, from then onwards, should have revolved around this essential Truth: the Unity of man with the universal Spirit.

What can we glean from these events? A question: If from the ruins of the Hellenic civilization we have rescued perhaps five per cent and with it we have found the scientific, philosophical, juridical and artistic premise to construct our present civilization, where would we be if we had inherited all the Hellenic tradition contained in the library of Alexandria? I. Asimov affirmed that we would be on the other stars; I believe that our civilization would be living in the Spirit that I am trying to awaken.

The Quest in the Renaissance

Byzantium and Florence

What we are observing in the Byzantine evolution is a gradual shift of the spirit towards its creative faculties, that is, towards Platonism. Due to the destructive and systematic intervention of the Inquisition, this fact is still unclear in the West, but in Byzantium, where the spirit could follow a relatively natural process (as there also heretics were persecuted, albeit not as forcefully as in the West), we can follow this trend. I have no doubt that something very similar to the Renaissance would have taken place in Constantinople if it had not been for the disastrous Ottoman invasion. An assassination can not only truncate the life of a person but that of an entire people. We will never know what Byzantium could have been without this massive and definitive crime; I say *definitively* because it had already been mortally wounded by the Christians of the West.

All historians tend to agree that Byzantium would not have fallen into the hands of the Turks had it not been for its earlier devastation by the Latin Christians. In fact, the politically induced religious rancour of the Latin people for the Eastern Empire became manifest on the occasion of the 4th Crusade that directed its energies, not against the enemy of Christianity, the Muslims, but against the orthodox capital.

The fall of Constantinople to the Ottomans that sounded the death knell for the Hellenic spirit, which a long tradition of historians has called the beginning of the Modern Age, indicates the beginning of the Renaissance spirit; because, even if it is true that this spirit was born in Italy, its Greek seed came from Byzantium. It is impossible to follow here the evolution of Byzantine thought during eleven centuries of slow growth. But yes it is necessary to be aware that the Hellenic spirit was being rediscovered in that process. For information the reader is invited to follow the work of Basilio Tatakis, collected by Brehier in the wide coverage devoted to Byzantium. I borrow from there the minimum that is indispensable.

As soon as Rome fell, Byzantium, as if by natural inclination, began to look for its sources in Hellenic culture, making Greek its daily language of use; this created a spirit different from that in the West. "For example in Byzantium there are deep differences of spirit between the university scholars and the monasteries, without anything similar taking place in the Western universities, which were founded much later and put under the tutelage of the Popes, with professors recruited from the monastic orders". This situation will not change until the Renaissance. Swietlinski says: "In the West, the term Catholic has a quantitative significance, which means: universal diffusion; in the East, on the contrary, catholicity is understood in a qualitative sense and means union with all" (cit. Brehier); we cannot but see Platonic influence in this. There takes place in Byzantium a permanent interaction between Platonism and Christianity that had begun with pseudo-Dionysius, disciple of Proclus, the Neo -Platonist; not through a rational but through a dogmatic criterion, as for centuries he was taken to be a disciple of Paul of Tarsus. The elevated mysticism, the peace seeking life of seclusion that comes from contemplation, a positive result of Christianity, was of Neo-Platonist influence. We know that Plato refers to the divine part of the soul that can reach contemplation of God through purification consisting of the domination of the passions (*Phaedo*). Even though Plato believes that passion can be dominated by reason, the Byzantine mystic did not trust this faculty.

A secluded life devoted to contemplation, in an environment free from the fear of torture, and inspired by the Platonic tradition, could only produce spiritual fruit. Of course, freedom in Byzantium was relative: there were external pressures that could cost a free thinker his office and even drive him into exile, and internal pressures, like the adoption of the dogma, the limitations of a creed showing itself to be incompatible with Platonic doctrine and needing an atmosphere of freedom for its comprehension and development. In any case, heresy was tolerated in Byzantium or rather it had wider margin of action than in the West. Nevertheless, the genius, the visionary, can overcome these limitations and instead of adapting to the creed, can adapt the latter to his vision; this is the case with Meister Eckhart, one of the few exceptions I have found in the medieval West that we can cite as an antecedent in this *quest of Consciousness*. Of course, in this personal adaptation he broke the established norm. The reader will understand better by reading *Meister Eckhart and Zen Buddhism*, by the illustrious D. T. Suzuki.

In Byzantium this Consciousness was not a strange thing. Calixto Kataphisiotis who I unfortunately have to cite second hand as I have not had direct access to his work, is an example. Calixto is "the direct inheritor of the pseudo Dionysus and the Neo-Platonism of Plotinus" (Tatakis, *op. cit.*). But, I must insist on this, what is important is not that he is a passive inheritor, a "follower", but that he is one more testimony of the *unitive consciousness*. For Calixto "the One is God of gods" (*Op. cit.*) Man, as a species, and because he is the son of God, seeks to ascend in order to recover his divine nature (as in Plato), for this reason he has to overcome a diversity of concepts, which he sees as the principle of chaos, to which man is brought by his relation with the multiplicity of things, for which he proposes the contrary road towards the "One, that is the Infinite and the Eternal", where he finds repose and joy. Calixto seems to be talking of a movement of intelligence, with which he will advance my theory of the shifts of the spirit. In clearly Plotinian language he tells us that through a prolonged ascetic life intelligence ascends from the world of the senses to that of the intelligible beings and finally to the One; these are levels of philosophical contemplation. Once the last level is reached, the subject is trained to philosophize and theologize. (This advice that in the Far East is a *conditio sine qua non*, is generally demeaned in the West) It is not man who arrives but the soul (or intelligence) as in Plato, which "arrives at the truth, the true freedom and eternity". This state of absolute contemplation, represented for those who ignore it (although they still have opinions on it) as a nothingness or a faintness, says Calixto with a surety gained by experience: it is the "supreme state of the activity of intelligence." This state, one must say in his case, he achieved in his lifetime.

The first antecedent in Italy of a continuous Greek current, particularly platonic, that would flow for centuries, was the arrival of Manuel Chrysiloras in 1397 under the auspices of Coluccio Salutati who was then the Chancellor of the city of Florence. Chrysiloras, an academic of Byzantium devoted himself mainly to the teaching of Greek; with this language he would import Greek tradition especially Platonic philosophy and classical arts that would have been well preserved in his own country.

In the court of the Este, in Ferrara, Lionello d'Este was one of the examples of enlightened humanist princes. The court sheltered Ariosto and Tasso (for whom no introduction is necessary), whose master Guarino, was the disciple and companion of Crhysoloras, with whom he even travelled to Constantinople. Guarino, who under the auspices of the East would have his residence in Ferrara, was famous in Venice, Florence and Verona. His teaching was directed towards moral and physical education with the Greek and Latin classics as teachers.

The first humanist pope was Nicholas V (1447-1455) "His pontificate was a golden age in the culture of Rome. His kindness, charity and generosity have earned him the epithet of "the noblest Papal figure of the entire Renaissance" (Cecil Grayson, *La Renaisaince en Italie en dehors de Florence*). Nicolas V would help Cosme de Medici and Federico de Urbino constructing their libraries, since he was the founder of the Vatican library. These three libraries would end up collecting the classic material on which the Renaissance would be based.

Pío II (1458-64) continued the humanist spirit since he himself was a writer. One should remember the attempt of this Pope to organize a crusade against the Turks, for which he called for a Council in Mantua; unfortunately he would die when the expedition began, and this would be the last serious attempt to liberate Constantinople which had fallen eleven years before.

Federico Montefeltro, duke of Urbino, with his qualities of integrity, affability and patronage which would make him the incarnation of a "Gentiluomo," was part of Guarino's audience. Federico, in addition to the art works with which he knew how to surround himself, employed around 30 to 40 copyists who collected the most beautiful manuscripts of the classical works. (*Op. cit.*)

The most outstanding representative from Byzantium, who arrived in Italy just before the fall of the Eastern Empire, was George G. Plethon.

George Gemistus Plethon

The first thinker of note to recognize the influence of Plethon, was Ficino, who in the preface of his translation of Plotinus remembers how Cosimo de Medici after attentively listening to the conferences of Plethon on "the mysteries of Platonism," was so impressed that he resolved there and then to create the Academy. This took place in the council of Ferrara-Florence, among Greeks and Latins in 1438/9, i.e., 20 years before Cosimo would give the Villa Carreggi to Ficino for this purpose. Plethon was more than 80 years old at that time and he would die a few months before the fall of Constantinople, at the foot of Mount Taygeto. To help in the establishment of Platonism in Florence, Plethon did not just expound the theories of a still unknown Plato who was not fully accepted in Italy, he also opposed Aristotle, who was well known and had been the key philosopher of the Scholastics, opening in this way the panorama of the spirit towards the new decisive horizons of the Renaissance. This was the subject that he developed in the council: "On the differences between Aristotle and Plato". I will not analyse his work here, although there is a very suggestive angle that deserves to be cited, because it inverts the anthropocentric vision towards which Christianity inclines, in order to project it towards its spiritual reality. "We maintain that God has not created human nature for humans as individuals, but individuals for human nature, and human nature for rational nature as a totality." Here "rational nature" would be understood as *Logos*, i.e. that Plethon tends to see our nature guided by and towards a universal Spirit; an idea that we will find in German Idealism and which I still hold on to.

Another of Plethon's important contributions is his theory of the immortality of the soul, whose origin he does not attribute to Plato but to an earlier tradition that begins with Zoroaster, is followed by Hermes and is expressed in the Eleusinian and Orphic Mysteries and continued by the seven sages of Hellenic antiquity. Plethon is busy establishing a kind of genealogy of the spirits who have maintained this correct tradition. In this genealogy there is no Christian name, i.e Plethon proposes a new tradition, showing thus the freedom of spirit that would characterize the Renaissance. Whether this genealogy is correct or not is not up for discussion here; what is decisive is that Plethon observes entire reality as a process of spiritualization or as a progressive establishment of the Spirit, manifest in the wise men of his lineage. This lineage continues, as expected in Plethon, with the Neo-Platonists who incorporate the Chaldean Oracles, as these are the revelations of the Greek gods, in particular that of Apollo, the god of light. "All things descend from fire" says the oracle, in whose words we seem to hear Heraclitus. In Plethon's version of these Oracles, there is a "Father of all things", the "Holy Fire"; his sons are Psyche who can be read as the Universal Soul, and Physis who can be read as Nature. The tendency to see all reality in a pantheist way is manifest. And in this union Eros is the *unitive* factor (using my terminology).

For Plethon the soul has been always immortal. Before descending in the human body and after leaving it, it returns to the primordial and Eternal Fire. This means that the soul becomes One with Divinity, Zeus, participates in the One and returns to Him. It is worth remembering that the Emperor Julian was an enthusiast of this tradition, but he has simplistically and pejoratively been seen just as a "sun worshipper," but he has his reasons. He believed in a Solar Trinity: the Sun as Spirit, or the Good (like Plato); the sun as the Soul of the world, or Helios; and the physical Sun whose light penetrates all, or Zeus. On the death of Julian, this tradition which had reached the high point of the Empire is only continued by wise men until Plethon.

Ficino

"This was anticipated by Plato, who told King Dionysus that there would be a time after many generations when the mysteries of theology would be purified by penetrating discussions, the way gold is purified by fire. This time has truly arrived, Bessarion" (*Letter nº 13 to Bessarion, the Greek*) (Ficino's letters quoted below have been taken from Shepheard-Walwin, London).

Ficino lived fully in the *Quatrocento,* when the spirit of the Renaissance found its maximum expression in all orders. He was the spokesman of its philosophy; although, as was normal amongst the *intelligentsia* of the age, it covered other knowledge's, like the art of correspondence, calligraphy, and music, as he played wonderfully the lyre. For Ficino, discipline in all orders was essential for spiritual life and, like Pythagoras, he was vegetarian and preferred uncooked food.

Being an early philosopher and the best exponent of the spirit of the Renaissance, he exercised the most influence while this spirit was alive. Ficino translated Plotinus and the complete works of Plato for the first time in the West. Later he became more distant and almost disappeared but this is no reason to believe that he was a minor figure; the present criteria to judge the greatness of men seems to me to be essentially poor and wrong compared with that of the Renaissance which had the most respect for our philosopher. "Everything that comes from you is good, all that you think is right, thus all that you write is useful and a pleasure for me." (*Letter nº 33 from Lorenzo de Medici*)

Following a basic Hellenic tradition, Ficino searches for equilibrium in the heavens and in man, in the divine and human Order. It is enough to remember a suggestive title of one of his works: *De Vita Coelitus Comparanda* (How to order life in keeping with the heavens). This language reminds one of another wise man of antiquity who Ficino did not know about: Confucius. Both undoubtedly spoke of the same reality, of an Order which man had to understand in order to live in it in keeping with himself and with his fellow beings. En *De Amore,* Ficino says: "no one on earth is a true man, because we are separated from God; we are separated from our Idea, which is our form." But this Idea is realizable: "It is love that can lead us, through a life of devotion, to this form." Integrating both realities, he says: "We first love God in our things, in order to love the things of God". "Loving God we love ourselves".

The purpose or objective of man is to return to his divine origin. In *The Christian Religion* he says: "Divine Providence does not allow any part of the World at any time (beyond the Christian area and age) to be without religion although the rituals may vary. The *Brihadaranyaka Upanishad,* expresses itself in a similar way when it says: "Offer sacrifices to this god or the other one, each god is His manifestation, as He is all gods." Ficino looked for a unity between Christian religion and Greek philosophy, but with equal rights, one was not at the service of the other, but, as a philosopher, at the service of what he took for truth.

Ficino distinguishes between the body, spirit and soul, the spirit is the intermediary between the other two and is fed by the "divine mysteries of theology" (*Letter n° 5*); as in Plotinus it is the spirit that *travels.* "There seem to be three kinds of good for mortals, those of the soul, the pleasures of the body and external objects". "The first of these is secure and permanent; the other two are transitory and mortal". "Our Plato, the master and guide of all the philosophers, called this virtue of the soul knowledge. He maintained that wisdom was the understanding of the divine" (*Thaetetus 176*), (*Letter n° 51.*)

That Ficino was convinced about the Unity of Reality, is manifest in various passages of his work. In one of his letters (*n° 39*) addressed to his most intimate friend G. Cavalcanti, he says: "The intelligible light who is God (who he calls "The mind of minds, and the light of lights"), forms the transparent substance of the intellect as soon as the latter becomes silent; I would say that it gives this substance its own form, which is the divine, and through this form to all intelligible objects."

In a subsequent letter (*n° 42*) he maintains a "principle of unity in all things, that he (Plato) appropriately called the One in itself. He also affirmed that in all things there is a truth that is the light of the One in itself, the light of God that is in all minds and forms". Even if he declares himself against Averroes who maintains "that all men share the same intellect, through which each man understands what others understand" (*Letter n° 40*), through which it is inferred that for Ficino the unity of the mind is only in its substance.

Ficino's God is Plato's God: "God or, in other words, Zeus, the patron of hospitality, the protector of friends, he who sustains life, venerated in all times by Plato and honoured by Socrates"... (*Letter N° 51*) And (*in letter n° 43*) commenting on Plato's Timeous, he not only equates the Demiurge with God but also the model used by him to give a form to the Universe: "This model can be none other than God himself". And he adds later: "It is for this reason, says Plato in the same book, that the divine mind due to the power of its thought has created with its own substance so many forms in this world as it has seen ideas in itself". In this it is similar to Hinduism, as God does not create from something external to Him, from nothing, but *from its own substance*, like Brahman; defining thus the essence of monist pantheism.

In the letter n° 4 he establishes a *Theological Dialogue between God and the Soul:* "I have read in the Works of our Plato that the divine reveals itself through purity in life before verbal teachings". In a language similar to that of the *Bhagavad Gita*, God tells the soul "I am in you because you are in me. If you were not in me you would not be in yourself, actually, in no way would you be". We also seem to hear Plotinus: "I am the very unity. Stop the movement and diversity and you will surely reach me". And even in a Buddhist language he affirms: "Shake off the matter and leave the rest." Ficino concludes categorically affirming monism: "Through love and understanding, beyond intellect, you ascend to life itself, to pure existence, to the absolute Being". As the reader will see, my point of view here entirely confirms that of the Florentine thinker.

In Ficino there is no lack of psychological penetration: "We are very miserly while spending money and we are completely extravagant while spending time. How many can you name who recognize the poverty of the soul? Everyone believes that they abound in wisdom but lack of money. (*Letter nº 58*) And (in *letter nº 59*): "As we falsely practise the virtues but truly the vices, it is not surprising that in the best of cases we will end up falsely happy and sincerely miserable." As in Plato, Aristotle and Hinduism (also in my conception, see *The Roots of Moral*) happiness depends on virtues.

Like Plato and Plotinus, Ficino searches for the ascent of the soul towards Divinity, which culminates in an experience, in life, in Unity. Besides, the fundamental duty of man would be this quest; which I agree with entirely for the reasons that I will later put forward. But this experience is not enough for Ficino, he wants it to be there forever; hence his interest in *demonstrating* the immortality of the soul, with which he concerns himself in the *Platonic Theology*. Ficino is well guided and we can aver that he has had a transcendental intuition, but the fact that it is not enough for him makes us doubt the penetration and totality of his monist experience. As we saw earlier in his categorical affirmation, he doesn't mean it for himself, but while proving the difficulty of the majority of mortals in reaching this experience he proposes the theory of the immortality of the *individual soul,* the demonstration of which is a product of inferences and obviously not of experiences, as we are dealing with a projection in the beyond. This is a fundamental error, as by not abandoning the *individual perspective* the eternal is subjected to time. In this way Renaissance individualism achieves a transcendent dimension. Since Christianity never overcame this dualist perspective, the arguments of Ficino were a perfect fit on which to base its theory of personal salvation; the immortality of the soul was declared a dogma 13 years after his death, some fifteen centuries after that of Jesus. This is another oblique adaptation of Hellenic thought, as for Plato the soul is not born with the body, it is eternal like Hinduism, precisely because it was never born and all living beings participate in it.

The widespread notion of "platonic love", as a relation that implies carnal contact, that we do not find in Plato, is probably Ficino's contribution, as he understands it as the link between two human beings who want to share the intimate desire of reaching God; without falling foul of any kind of puritanism.

The art of the Renaissance (which I hope to deal with in *The Roots of Art*), put so much emphasis on human beings because it saw in them both the immortal and the divine side; it could be said that they came across as demi-gods. In the words of Ficino: "He (man) can become God, instead of just a man contemplating the divine, through human beauty" (*Letter n° 42*). This experience common to artists and thinkers of the Renaissance seems to me to be indispensable in order to clearly understand the Hellenic legacy. The dignity of man thus took on a metaphysical basis through art. For Ficino the function of art was to remember, through its representations, the divine origin of the soul. Botticelli's *Spring and The Birth of Venus* were commissioned by Lorenzo de Medici, and not only supervised but also directed by Ficino. They undoubtedly represented the Renaissance of the Hellenic spirit.

The Spirit of the Renaissance

"When the shadows have dispersed, our descendants will be able to see with all clarity and reencounter the roads of the past" (Petrarch).

One can only understand cultural movements if one sees in them the movements of the spirit, and the historical periods if one considers the spirit of the age. And by the latter I do not understand (like Hegel) the concept that defines them, but the *experience of that spirit.* In order to achieve this harmony a prior condition is that the inheritors of that culture shift their spirit to the same *plane of understanding* and to the same *level of consciousness* that was possessed by the creators of those inherited riches, as this will allow them to *see* in the same way. This does not mean that they should repeat the same ideas and art, but what has been said: *the same perspective* that should be applied to new techniques, new knowledge, and new circumstances.

I believe that all serious and unprejudiced scholars will agree that what happened in Greece was the response of a highly elevated spirit. So what was produced in the Renaissance was fundamentally the adoption of that elevated perspective. This allowed one to recognize its dark medieval past showing him the luminous Hellenic landscape. One tends to believe that it was the discovery of the classical treatises that generated the movement, but agreeing with the same an authority like E. Brehier argues: "It was less the discovery of new texts than the way in which they were read." "The same works of Cicero were interpreted and applied in a radically different way by

Ambrosio rather than by Erasmus." (*Intr. Renac.*)

For what has been said, the Renaissance seems to me to be a very correct word, as it made no reference to a cultural legacy (which is what those who have seen the matter from afar think) it sought to continue the Hellenic way of thinking, and to give it rebirth from the same spirit. Following this idea, Brehier insists: "The Renaissance has nothing to do with an influence but with the re-adoption (*reprise*) of an intuition, not a tradition". (Cited by F. Mora, *Renac.*) We know however that an intuition is not willingly readopted, so it is necessary to explain why it reappears. I believe that my theory of perspectives can also explain this. When the perspective of an age determines the ways of seeing and thinking about it, when individuals with their own criteria are dissatisfied with the ideas and values that they consider obsolete, when they see that they do not respond to the ideas that compel their spirits to look for their plenitude, they set out in search of a perspective that allows them to widen their gaze; if they come across a creative past, they will again experience reality in the same way; similar intuitions are derived from the same perspective.

Of course, unfortunately the spirit does not always heed these examples, most of the time it falls down, for this reason we must pay attention to the luminous ages when the spirit obeys higher motives and reunites with them in its ascendant path towards its destiny. The return of the spirit to the sources of life, takes place from time to time in history, this approach to the *Universal Consciousness*, which is the Creative itself, generates the periods of apogee, the distance to the perigee (see *The Spirit in History*). Of course, the closeness is relative and takes place only in certain individuals who express their experience in different ways. These can be isolated and even ignored in periods of decadence, while in those of apogee we encounter notable men in time and space. It has to be pointed out that creative periods do not happen only through the appearance of geniuses or wise men, but also through the support of patrons and the cultural infrastructure given by the government, in which freedom of expression plays an important role.

It is feasible that in the Medieval age there were isolated individuals (Eckhart is an example), but besides lacking support and being persecuted, they could not manifest themselves sufficiently to generate a creative movement; these circumstances could only lead to obscurity. But in spite of these dark ages, we see in the spirit a tendency to abandon distraction and alienation that the periods of decadence imply and to itself when circumstances are favourable. Nothing is more natural than the reencounter of the spirit with Nature, although the eternal vices of man might keep him occupied and worried about the in-transcendental.

My theory of the shifts of the spirit, which was born of the observation of the internal movements of the spirit, was seen to be revelatory when dealing with periods when there was an undoubted awakening of the soul. In keeping with this, the spirit oscillates between personal or animal inclinations and the altruist tendencies that expand it towards its plenitude: in the periods of perigee the first predominate, in those of apogee, the second.

Only superior man is capable of making conscious altruist incitements and applying them. Even common man is not completely insensitive and he can admire creative or heroic man; which shows that in some corner of the soul he feels the impulse to transcend his individuality. The concept of altruism, which is shown to be evident in the case of heroism, is not limited to the latter or to the moral; it extend to the arts, to philosophy and religion, as these disciplines respond to the unitive forces or faculties. The (true) artist is not looking for personal interest; art pushes him to transcend itself. The philosopher should transcend himself to accept truth in itself; the religious man, the true one, procures his integration with Divinity which is nothing but Unity.

The Renaissance was not only influenced by pagan thinkers, but their wisdom was recognised in its totality, they were not seen as mere instruments to sustain Christian doctrine or as apologetics, but as they were in themselves. Far from condemning them (as we had seen in the Middle Ages which saw them only as pagan) they were elevated to the highest dignity of the spirit, to that of the wise men. In this way Galeottus Martius maintained that "he who works according to the intimate and innate law of his consciousness goes to the heavens, whichever race he might belong to." (Cited by Burckhardt, *The Spirit. Renai.* p. 391), and for this reason he would have been condemned to the furnace if his ex-disciple Pope Sixtus IV had not intervened in an opportune manner. Christianity was not the only path to salvation and knowledge during the Renaissance; the opening of the spirit is a notable characteristic of this period which is in sharp contrast to the preceding age. Poggio says of the first Humanist philosopher: "Lorenzo Valla condemns the physics of Aristotle, he finds the Latin of Boecio barbarous, he destroys religion, professes heretic ideas, disdains the Bible... And he has even declared that the Christian religion does not rest on proofs but on beliefs that try to be superior to all proof!" And Valla was not persecuted for this.

The Renaissance (the rebirth) was concerned with all spirit in general. Greek knowledge did not arise to oppose Christianity but to fill the great and numerous lacunae that the latter had left in the spiritual and cultural order. Neither was the rebirth of man in opposition to Divinity but the search for equilibrium between both. Only by understanding this can one understand the true spirit of Humanism.

Renaissance and Middle Ages

A series of events and circumstances make the Renaissance different from the medieval past; I will mention some that seem decisive to me: Culture stops being the monopoly of the clergy and almost anyone with time and interest has access to it. Moreover, even if all educated people knew Latin, this was no longer indispensable and it was rapidly and progressively being replaced by Tuscan as a language, which would soon be spoken and read throughout Italy. Dante whose fame had spread beyond the peninsula started this trend and it was continued by Petrarch who became equally popular, and in the XVth century writers found a wide public throughout all social classes. The invention of the printing press in this age made the texts evidently accessible to a wider number of readers. The same social classes also tended to coalesce due to other social factors. "Of cardinal importance was the harmony of nobles and the bourgeoisie from the XIIth century," from then on "leisure and entertainment became common, and the world view of the castle in the fort became essentially obsolete" (J. Burckhardt, *The Spirit Renai.*).

Cities had broken down the walls that had cloistered them during the Middle Ages, now city states emerged. But what had changed within was the concept or ideal of nobility. Legacy began to be of relative importance; relative to the capacities of the inheritor. In this way, Poggio, in his dialogue *De la nobleza* concludes that there is no other nobility besides personal merit (cit. by Burckhardt), in total agreement with Hellenic tradition. And this was so, as there were condottieri (leaders) of humble origin, like the Sforza, who reached the highest rungs of the nobility, by dint of their merit and intrinsic capabilities. I see in this (and I am surprised that I have not come across this fact in the authors that I have consulted) a rebirth of the Roman spirit, where even if the birth right had its influence, what decided the career of the notables were their personal aptitudes; and thus there were generals, governors and even Caesars whose illustrious birth had not worked in their favour. Another fact brought to the fore was the rise of women and their equality with men, especially in cultural aspects; a fact that marks a clear contrast with the medieval tradition in which women had been decidedly undervalued; probably it was believed that they carried the stigma of sin, they had something of the diabolic in them like the rest of nature, and for this they began to be seen almost as animals, (to the extent that a Council of the Church considered whether women had a soul or not.)

It is common to see historians and especially philosophers adopt an *a priori* attitude when they study the Renaissance depending on their religious convictions, which puts them in favour of or against Christianity. The undeniable opening up of notable Renaissance scholars to paganism has given rise to the tendency to counterpoise Greek gods to the Christian god, but this attitude distances one from the true understanding of the Renaissance spirit, that tended towards integration. The opposition between paganism and Christianity in the pre and post Renaissance period really misses this point. For the Renaissance man what was important was not the commitment to the one or the other, but a search for oneself, the expression of one's own inspiration, and here there was no such contradiction. And it is in this way that Christian apologetics ends in the Renaissance, not because it was born a pagan apologetics, but because it had lost meaning.

"If we want to learn the history of thought and knowledge in the western Latin Middle Ages, we should, above all, realize that it had its basis in Roman antiquity and not in the Greek." (Kristeller, *Renaissance Thought and its Sources*). It is important to remember this when one contrasts the spirit of the Middle Ages with the Renaissance because the sources that made this possible were Greek in their primary aspect. Here we touch upon a point that has given rise to many controversies, and it dates to the time of the origin of the Renaissance. Christian writers, who wish to attribute to themselves the achievements of the *Quatrocento*, push back the origin of the Renaissance to the late Middle Ages. E. Gilson in *Humanisme médieval et Renaissance*, pretends that not only humanism but also individualism that are highlighted as the characteristics of the Renaissance were present in the Middle Ages; through a vain and pretentious attempt to prove individualism through a love story of this period (Abelard and Heloise). There have also been those who have tried to find the origins of the Renaissance in Islamic Andalucía, like M. R. Garaudy after he married a Muslim woman.

But if we leave aside these versions inspired more by beliefs and personal desires than in reality, we observe the phenomenon as it was and not as we want it to be, we see that the spirit of the Renaissance only became manifest in the XVth century. It is true that in Petrarch we already find all the elements of Humanism, but, apart from the fact that one swallow does not make a summer, as the father of logic reminds us, it is necessary to keep in mind that the *estudia humanitatis* in its original sense revolved only around literature and rhetoric for which the already existing Latin texts of the Middle Ages were enough, while it was only in the XVth century that art and philosophy were incorporated and they gave a completely new dimension to the spirit, and only then can we speak of the Renaissance. This means that Humanism and the Renaissance do not exactly overlap; the former precedes the latter by a century. And this art and philosophy were of Greek origin, this means that they used sources other than those used by Dante, Petrarch and all those who came before the XVth century. It was in this century that the Greek spirit was introduced; it was the Renaissance of this spirit that generated this period. I do not think it can be maintained that before the XVth century there was an art comparable to this period, but it is argued that there was a Greek philosophy. There was, it is true, a Greek philosophy the Aristotelian, but it would be restricting the Greek spirit too much if we limit it to the work of Aristotle, which although monumental and encyclopaedic is not enough to reveal the Hellenic spirit. On the other hand, and this is even more important, Aristotle and Greek philosophy in general were studied not in the light of the Greek spirit but in the light of Christianity, and they were opposed to the former in so many ways. What stands out most especially in the Middle Ages was the lack of creativity, or the faculty of taking ideas from the Spirit itself. As this capacity was lacking, a characteristic of the Medieval Ages is the imitation, adaptation, and interpretation of all that had already been created.

In any case, my intention is not to demarcate historical periods in broad brush strokes but to show the spirit of the Renaissance, because as we begin to see clearly, our own spirit is awakened. It is undeniable that since the XIIth century there had been a slow awakening in Europe, as evidenced by the Gothic cathedrals, Dante and Petrarch, and there are retrograde medieval symptoms during the Renaissance and even later. But if we nuance the profile of the spirit of the Renaissance it will be very diluted and confused. In order to highlight it with clarity we need Greek lenses, which are really the artists and enlightened men of that period took recourse to in that period.

The Universal Spirit in the Renaissance

Besides the recovery of man's dignity, the greatest

achievement of the Renaissance was the incorporation of Nature in the Spirit which includes the Greek gods who were an inseparable part of it. In the Middle Ages the sacred was concentrated in the cemeteries, the churches and particular places consecrated by the Church. We cannot but suspect in this attitude the well-known interest of this institution to be the indispensable mediator between man and Divinity, in order to be sure of its earthly power. Be that as it may, the rejection of Christianity by Nature is well known, and it is what alienated man from Nature. Of course, outside the demarcated area were the profane and the abode of the devil as it was referred to. The sacred, thus was reduced to a small part of the World. The devotion and care in the construction of great Gothic cathedrals should not surprise us; all religious and artistic spirit was concentrated in them. The result, from an architectural point of view, is the most polished and elevated achieved by Christianity, but, as I said, there was a whole World without Spirit. By rediscovering the Greek spirit, the Renaissance reintegrated it breaking with the narrow framework of the sacred which medieval Christianity had subjected it to. But the Church instead of incorporating this universalization of the Spirit, as an answer to the Reformation, returned, like the latter, to the medieval vision, having never fully understood the great rediscovery of the Renaissance. Because if the spirit of this age is sought to be understood, it should be made clear that rediscovery was its great intuition, its great experience and it has been the latter that has opened and expanded its spirit and illuminated its work without any precedent but the Greek spirit. Because, it should be well understood, without a spirit open to the infinite capable of integrating man in all, that transmutation would not have taken place, nor would that art have been expressed. The *uomo universale*, proclaimed then by poets, philosophers and artists, is not a simple expression of this yearning or a baseless idea; it is the product of a *unitive experience* disseminated in the *quatrocento*. Official Christianity, that had lost contact with the Spirit did does not incorporate the great Idea of the Renaissance, however the latter was not extinguished, like embers covered by the ashes of history, it had come alive in spirits open to universality.

If one considers the Renaissance poor in the field of philosophy one ignores the very resources of philosophy; it is not the great systems that make philosophy. These, in fact, tend to petrify the spirit; the *Summa Theologica* is a clear example. What truly makes philosophy is the opening of the spirit, its reencounter with the Origin, with the Creative itself. And this is what happened in the Renaissance. In the Birth (Greece) and in the rebirth (Renaissance in Italy) man is born again, he finds himself naked before the world which he discovers and which he marvels at, and he answers to no other authority other than to his own experiments and thought. When men become believers, they stop creating; for this reason the Middle Ages could not be creative.

The aristocracy in the Church

That the Church during the Renaissance was prey to all kinds of excesses is of no surprise to anyone who has followed its history. From the beginning notoriously erred on the side of Caesar than on the side of God. It is just puritanical to unfairly judge the Church when its high prelates gave in to lust, which really did not harm to anyone (perhaps apart from a Christian point of view, although this is a contradiction because they "ex cathedra" decided what was Christian and what was not.) The persecutions, tortures, killings and religious wars that took place during the entire Middle Ages were far more pernicious because they affected third parties, and thousands of them. The more power the Church acquired, the more it adopted the

Roman spirit, except that from the latter it was inclined to adopt what offered the most pleasure. Cardinal Rialto celebrated ostentatious and orgiastic feasts in his palace of the Saturnalia in honour of Saturn in the Roman way. These celebrations in the classical Roman context had nothing decadent about them (they were on the upswing during the times of Augustus), but we cannot say the same in a Christian context. Nevertheless, from a historical point of view, which is noteworthy, it reveals itself as one more expression of the renaissance of the classical spirit. Italian nobility identified with the latter, except that it was slightly contradictory when dealing with prelates. In fact they had little that was Christian about them.

It was of undoubted merit in some important Church prelates that they participated and even cooperated as patrons in the Renaissance, but these offices were an inseparable part of the status that they enjoyed in the aristocracy. They lived like aristocrats with their palaces and the attendant luxury. This meant that their participation in the Renaissance had little or nothing of the Christian spirit, hence a critique of the Reformation. But the Reformist did not know how to understand the spirit of the Renaissance, i.e. the artistic, poetic, philosophical and Greek spirit in general, they only observed with the narrow vision of the Christian spirit which was the spirit of the Middle Ages. In other words it was the aristocracy who participated and cooperated in the Renaissance, not the rest of the Church, which boycotted it in the way it had always done regarding anything creative that escaped its narrow schemes, and with particular viciousness in the field of religion, leave alone in the field of the sciences and of philosophy.

The Middle Ages were the result of the imposition of a status quo, which led to stagnation in all orders even in the religious sphere. The Renaissance broke these rigid schemes, it found a way out and opened itself to the world of the spirit and matter, to the *Universus*; the spirit finds and expresses its liberty, its creativity. The Italian aristocracy knew how to understand and feel this, but perforce it had to leave Christianity behind.

Humanism, Renaissance and Reformation

In his "Discourse on the Dignity of Man", written around 1486, the Florentine Pico della Mirandola, tells us that man is the only creature who with his free will can decide on Nature and his destiny. But, he adds, it is through the *adequate exercise* of this faculty that he can attain the state of the angels. "It is rightly for this reason that man has been considered and judged as a miracle and a really marvellous creature". Two messages emerge from this: On the one hand the excellence of our species is exalted, as the new humanists never tire of reminding us, and on the other hand, man, thanks to the correct use of his faculties can achive to the state of the angels, i.e. his divine nature, in the words of Plato, the latter a probable inspiration for Pico. It is clear that this humanist does not point to an individual perspective but to its transcendence by developing the spiritual potential of man. So what I have been trying to maintain is confirmed now, in the Renaissance there was a return to man, something necessary as he had been annihilated in the Middle Ages, but once he was reaffirmed in himself, he recovered his powers and voluntarily chose a transcendent destiny.

The free interpretation of the Scriptures, proposed by the Reformation, is a continuation of this idea of free will, its most positive aspect. This implied the separation of the central power exercised by the Church; a proposal that was the motor of this movement as it mobilised the princes to adopt it. The Reformation soon fell into religious determinism (taken to its highest limits by Calvin), that would become the opposite of Humanist ideals as it annulled precisely man's free will.

The merit of the Renaissance was not that it had rejected religion in order to establish a profane world, but that it *had sacralised the earthly world*, it had rediscovered in man and in Nature its divine dimension and it had reintegrated it in the same. It had not rejected religion, but the Christian religion was not sufficient for it and for this reason it took recourse to another religion, the Greek, which was part of the Western cultural tradition. And principally because this religion had the vital element that it needed; as is well known, the Greek gods did not live in the other world but in this one, in the Olympus, in the rivers, in the forests in the sea and in the air, exhibited in art with perfection and profusion.

Reformation and Counter Reformation

The Reformation was a rebirth of the Christian tradition, a resurgence of the Semitic spirit, a reaction against the Renaissance of the Greco-Roman tradition. Faced with the idea of freedom expressed in different ways by the Renaissance, the Reformation, with a perverse secret sense of the destruction of the creative spirit, unearthed the virus that it needed to make itself ill: salvation through faith and predestination; with the Reformers reason became unnecessary and freedom an illusion. All the texts that had been recovered and translated in the Renaissance became dead again, only one book was necessary. When the Western spirit spread its wings, these Reformists found a way to clip them, and as if this was not enough, the Church betraying the freedom of spirit in which the Renaissance had grown, returned to the medieval schema and even further back to the Old Testament. Both, the Reformation and the Counter Reformation were desertions of the spirit in its path of ascension, an abandoning of its free search towards its Destiny.

What the Reformists never managed to see nor understand was the change in spirit of the Italian nobility of the Renaissance, in which the high prelates of the Church actively participated. What was positive in them, which was nothing but their need for life, art and freedom in the spirit of the new age, was considered negative by the Reformists. Because, and this must be clear, the reformers were not innovators but conservatives; as a result their spirit was medieval, retrograde. And this is the retrograde spirit that boycotted the Renaissance. Unfortunately this spirit was not only outside Italy. One of the mechanisms of power that had taken the Church to such heights, the Inquisition, continued functioning in the Renaissance. And this was a fatal trap into which the Church itself would fall, dragging down a major part of the Renaissance movement. Once more, the very force of the human spirit that needed only to be free to fully manifest the Spirit was not comprehended.

The Church did not believe in this power. It had never believed in the very power of Jesus' teachings that were preached only with this power, and neither did it believe in the spirit of the Renaissance. It was never enthused enough to free itself from this diabolic instrument of power, which was the worm that would consume it from within. The Renaissance was fundamentally on the right path until Luther appeared and turned everything back. In view of this, Leon X, Medici, at the head of a Church imbued with the very spirit of the Renaissance, thought it necessary to use his temporal power to excommunicate Luther. He erred as a Christian and as a Renaissance man. If the Church had sacrificed itself in the name of the Christian spirit of love and non-violence and the Renaissance spirit of freedom of creative expression, it would have been born again and ahead of its times, but once again it chose the temporal power. The Counter Reformation would only change the name of the Inquisition. Instead of ridding itself of this anti-Christian, anti-Renaissance, anti-religious and in general anti-spiritual instrument it would support the "Holy" Office. This was its own slow, unfortunately very slow, death sentence; The West would have to wait until Napoleon for the end of this monstrous institution.

Very rightly says Nietzsche: "The Renaissance was the transmutation of Christian values, the no holds barred attempt appealing to all instincts, and genius, for taking all contrary values, aristocratic values to their plenitude. What happened? A German monk called Luther came to Rome. This monk afflicted by all the rancorous instincts of the failed priest, revolted in Rome against the Renaissance... Instead of understanding, filled with the deepest gratitude, for the tremendous thing that had happened: the challenge to Christianity in its own heartland, he only knew how to extract sustenance for his own hatred from this spectacle. Luther denounced the corruption of the Papacy, when the opposite was there for all to see, or rather that the earlier construct, the original sin of Christianity was that it did not occupy the pontifical throne. Rather life, the triumph of life; the full throated yes to all sublime, beautiful and audacious things. And Luther restored the Church, by attacking it."

We have seen how Lorenzo Valla professed heretical ideas and even despised the Bible, yet in spite of that, the Cardinal of Cusa recommended him to the Pope. This example gives us an idea of the freedom of expression that reigned in the *quatrocento*, an indispensable circumstance for the Italian miracle, just as the condemnation of Bruno illustrates the nefarious transformation of the Church as a result of the Counter Reformation.

Giordano Bruno

The spirit of the Renaissance was still alive in the second

half of the XVIth century during the life of Giordano Bruno. A natural philosopher, his thought was insistently directed towards the explanation of the All. He knew the latest advances in science and, following the Platonic tradition, used the intellect as well as the highest sentiments as a medium. Thus, for the union with God, the final objective of the spirit, the soul is led by love. However, this objective is not attainable in life, hence for him divine love, that is opposed to vulgar love, is accompanied by the negative sentiment of suffering. It is understandable that he called this love, that appeals to the highest virtues but which is condemned to failure, the heroic love. (Kristeller, *Bruno*) But this existentialist sentiment did not detain the march of our philosopher who continued to search for universal answers.

As is usually the case with Platonists, his vision was manifestly pantheistic. The universe is a "holy, sacred and venerable animal" where one single substance resides, the Soul of the world that generates and gathers around it the atoms of its composition. Being the body of the divinity this organism, is as infinite as the latter, and not created in a single moment but recreates itself endlessly. Even if there are in it "countless individuals, all is one, and knowing this unity is the objective of all philosophy" (*Della causa, principio e uno IV*).

Bruno had a very special vision of Divinity. Since it is the substance of the Universe, and all things and beings are manifestations of it, the other means to reveal it is by knowing Nature, which is its image. According to me, the God of Bruno is like an absolute transcendent, as what animates beings and penetrates all things is the Soul of the world, and he who creates it, the efficient cause, is the *universal understanding.* As the reader will see this last fecund idea announces a central idea of my thought.

Plato, whose trajectory is followed by Bruno, had talked

in his most mysterious book of a Demiurge. But in some way the latter, although not as extreme or as definite as the Christian creator, was external to the Universe. In Bruno's vision nothing was external, everything took place within a single reality in which there were innumerable and untiring creators: the demons, meaning not the perverse Satan and his minions, but minor gods, angels and ethereal beings in general. Since I do not see the need to personalise or embody, although impalpably, the forces that act in the Universe, I will not linger on the magical world of Bruno. Just as the Demiurge proliferates in demons, the Platonic sage divides it into different magi who establish particular relations with all.

Just as there is no centre in Bruno's universe, there is no particular point of view in his vision, but an "eye that sees in itself all things because it is all things" (*De Imaginum*), certainly a divine vision in which there is neither subject nor object neither above nor below, etc. Bruno tries to locate his mind in the infinite space which is the substance of all things, in such a way that *the understanding* that underlies the Universe, underlies his own; his mind reflects the former.

Bruno does not "imagine" other inhabited worlds, he is a philosopher, and he concludes that they exist. For him there is an infinite unity full of emptiness and matter, but the One is not nothingness and the other inert and only receptive, rather they are animate, for which reason if there is life in this sector of the Universe, there should be in others. "We are not saying that the emptiness is simply nothingness, but everything that does not present a sensible resistance". "In this way we can say that there is an infinite, an ethereal and immense region in which there are innumerable and infinite bodies similar to the Earth, the Moon and the Sun" (*El infinito Universo. Dial. II*). "In it we find infinite bodies, similar to this one, and none is more in the centre of the Universe than the others, because it has neither a centre nor margins." (*Op. Cit. Dial. III*) Although there are fixed centres "Around which the suns the planets, the lands, the waters revolve, as we see these seven planets revolving around our neighbouring sun." (*Op. Cit.*) This was the first time that a philosopher applied Copernicus' theory.

Bruno and imagination

Like all who have transcended speculative faculties, Bruno warned that they are incapable of provoking a transcendence of the spirit. Once attained by other means, Bruno assumed that all those who think and even imagine, respond directly to his new vision, and their inconsistencies derive from here. Something similar happened to Plotinus, although in a more measured way. Once more I think it necessary to return to the mental mechanisms expressed in my *Psychosophy*: Once a transcendental or essential perspective is reached, all the senses and faculties become more perceptive, more subtle, and this is observed through the numerous nuances that earlier went unnoticed and through the connections that the mind establishes among them. In fact, the senses and faculties are now under a new unifying light, the unitive faculties have now gained priority. But this does not in any way signify that what the subject thinks or imagines in a direct and uninterrupted manner responds to this essential perspective. In fact it is extremely difficult to think without there being a shift in the spirit towards the speculative faculties with the subsequent alienation with respect to the essential perspective. Truthfully speaking I must confess to the reader that in all my writings my greatest effort has been not only to think, but to extricate the spirit from the said perspective, from its original unitive source, let alone the imagination! I do not believe it possible to establish a direct link between such diverse faculties. I am far from disqualifying imagination for this reason, on the contrary, I believe that the great myths, for which I have great respect, were born with the indirect link that the imagination made with the Transcendent, but in this case we are not talking about philosophy, but of religion, literature or folklore.

For Bruno imagination was precisely the ideal faculty to fill the breach left by reason, which is located between the celestial and the earthly, between the unchangeable and the changeable, in the very light of the infinite creative emptiness of all phenomena. Bruno pretended that his understanding was like the eye of the universe where everything is related, and it is the imagination that establishes the links. In fact, once this perspective is attained, all reality is reflected in the mirror of the mind, but the human mind, not the divine, is multiple too.

Knowing that there is a fundamental Unity it is only necessary to establish links in its multiple manifestations, and it is up to the magi, for Bruno, to carry out this task. Nevertheless, for him a magus could be a philosopher, a religious man an artist, a doctor, etc., but he should be in contact with the very sources of life and he must work in keeping with them. "In the first place the magi are equivalent to the wise man" (*De magia e de vinculis in genere*) "If one considers it in absolute terms, one has to understand in its most noble and principal significance", that is, like a wise man. "When philosophers use it amongst themselves, then magi means a wise man with the power of acting" (*Op. Cit.*); this power would differentiate it from the theoretical philosopher. "In the second place (as we imagine it today) the magi is equivalent to the maker of marvels" (*Op. Cit.*). Bruno distinguishes ten classes of magi, and then he warns us against the magician's apprentices: "Although no kind of magic is unworthy of being known (...) it is convenient to keep it away from the crowds and the profane and miserable ordinary people as there is nothing so good that the impious, sacrilegious and evil human species cannot turn into something pernicious before making it useful" (*Op. Cit.*) with which I entirely agree.

Even if Bruno in *Of Magic* seems to be "beating around the bush", he keeps his philosophical roots intact as expressed in "*Della causa, principio e uno*": "The magi have an axiom that God has an influence on the gods and the latter on the stars" and in this way successively on a descending scale till the animal. There then takes place the ascending scale: "The animal ascends to the soul through the senses" he passes through the stars, like Plotinus, in order to reach, like the latter, "the Soul of the world or the Spirit of the Universe, and through the latter the contemplation of Unity simple, optimal, maximum, incorporeal, absolute and self-sufficient" (*Op. Cit.*); no doubt the highest aspiration of the soul.

Another idea that we can recover from this work so full of entangled branches, is that of light: "All the light that there is in lower things comes to them from higher things". "The light is spread and penetrates till the deepest shadow" (...) "These do not understand nor by pass nor do they equal the light" (*Op. Cit.*) If we change the terms, light for Good, and shadows for evil or ignorance, we will observe that Bruno followed a Socratic principle that all Platonism would adopt, including the writer of these lines: Evil does not exist on its own but due to ignorance, due to an absence of Good; shadows grow longer due to the lack of light, as *universal understanding is expressed as light;* showing with it his transcendental experience.

Bruno, conclusion

In three central ideas my thought overlaps with that of Bruno: Thanks to the Soul of the Universe life is possible; thanks to universal understanding (Consciousness) this life has intelligence; both penetrate to the atoms of matter that having an infinite field of action has infinite possibilities of realization; the Universe is a continuous and limitless work of art. Even if these possibilities depend on the potential of matter, since the soul of the world "is found everywhere it does not act in the same way everywhere, because it is not supplied with a matter that is equally available." (*De magia*) For me, and I believe for Bruno, matter has no end nor reason of being, it is simply infinite possibilities, but man, who can know his origin, has a destiny, whose realization depends on him. For Bruno the Universe is full of signs, of ciphers, as Jaspers will call it, which reveal the underlying spirit. As for Hindus, matter and also our mind are of a divine nature;: "We have the doctrine of not searching for the Divinity outside of ourselves, we have it next to us, or as I say, within ourselves." (*2° Presentation in Oxford*). Matter is thus made animate and full of life, spiritualized.

Bruno takes a fundamental step that differentiates him from Plato and Plotinus who in some way deny or minimise this world in the name of another. Bruno does not want to leave it, he wants to integrate it or integrate himself in it; I completely adhere to this. He affirms, by the way, that "what constitutes multiplicity in things is not being, it is not reality, but what the surface of the thing appears (...)" (*Dialogue 5, 138*) This in no way implies the sacrifice of one reality to the benefit of another.

To my understanding, it would be an error to judge these authors for their discrepancies, as they agree on the essentials. The last thing that occurs to the Greek is the denial of this concrete reality, and idealism is of a pure Hellenic brand. I believe that my theory of perspectives explains the small dissensions. We can attribute the mistakes in which these philosophers have fallen to the identification of the mind with reality, which is very natural in this ideology. What had to be distinguished were the different faculties and to calculate their potential and reach. Unifying the spirit and nature has been their common program, the fruit of one single transcendental intuition. But the spirit expresses itself on different levels, from its most pure and essential state until its most concrete manifestations with nuances that have to be highlighted. Even if I disagree on small points, my proposal is to make constructive criticism, consistent in highlighting the common points and not the differences. What is of interest to all is learning from the geniuses, of these "divine and saintly men". Demonstrating their disagreements is much easier as for this it is not necessary to see more than the words; this negative criticism benefits nobody and leaves man in the same condition, in the same stage of fundamental ignorance.

With his universal vision Bruno tried to clear the field of religion and put an end to the discord that tore apart his age, but he accused the Reformists of having caused them, the Catholics of being fanatics and enemies of nature and Judaism for having a blood thirsty and jealous god; a very correct but dangerous critique for his age. Bruno was a true reformer with creative ideas, unlike Luther who merely wanted to move around the same obsolete pieces.

When a philosopher like Bruno adopted the new perspective offered by Copernicus, the whole Universe was transformed, as well as man's situation within it. In fact, the question was not about the improvement of the geocentric but also that of the anthropocentric position. Although Western man is still at an infantile stage in this project (The Hindu more because of his philosophy than for his science finds himself at a more mature stage), the bases for this change in perspective are given by Bruno. He leaves this our planet floating in an infinite space where there exist other worlds, with their suns and planets inhabited like our own. These worlds are in movement, only the whole of the Universe in which a centre is indiscernible, remains unchanged, (*Op. Cit.*) It can be understood that the narrow Biblical vision of the world, as well its anthropocentric vision remain annulled. The Church's interest in condemning him to the furnace if he did not retract can also be understood; but he did not do so, he died heroically sustaining his ideas. Once more the natural evolution of the spirit was truncated. Does the reader understand the magnitude of this crime, the damage that it means for a civilization to kill the spirits destined to animate it?

It is worth remembering that Bruno recovered the thought of the oldest Greek philosophers. In fact, Anaximander and Anaximenes affirmed the existence of multiple worlds that are incessantly renewed within an eternal infinity. Besides his philosophical achievements, exact sciences have proved that Bruno had all the reason in the world on his side regarding three points: the earth actually revolves around the sun; there is no centre nor privileged place in the cosmos; there are numerous planets like ours revolving around the other suns; today we can count thousands of them only in our galaxy and we know that there are millions of galaxies. I believe that these figures demonstrate by themselves the egocentric, anthropocentric and geocentric perspectives, derived from the Judeo Christian belief that Nature has been made for man; an absurdity to which some philosophers like Hegel have adhered to, making scientists laugh derisively.

Spinoza

The book of this author which I will be commenting on is *Ethics Demonstrated in a Geometrical Order, Divided in Five Parts.* (Note: I have followed Charles Appuhn's translation in French. Spinoza devotes two thirds of this book to the *Affections* that I have translated as Emotions or Passions, as the case may be. I have kept the capital letters that I imagine must exist in the original, such as Nature, Body, Soul, Love, etc.) The very title suggests to us the scientific intentions of the author and that it was a very special work. Spinoza takes up the line of thought of Renaissance pantheism especially that of Giordano Bruno. Even if he was not burnt for this, he was excluded and mercilessly persecuted by Jews and Christians, incapable of understanding him or tolerating original ideas about the Bible; although both preached charity. It is very common for those who have not perceived God to persecute those who have perceived him. Indeed his *Ethics* was published after his death for fear of reprisals.

When we talked of Platonists and Aristotelians in the beginning of this *Quest*, we distinguish two perspectives: those that induce the Transcendent from concrete reality, and those that deduce from the causes of this reality. Spinoza's position is categorical: referring to the former he says: "I think that they have not observed the required order to philosophize. Instead of having considered the nature of God before all things, as it comes before knowledge and Nature, they have believed that in the order of knowledge, this was the last, and that things, called the objects of the senses, come before" (*II prop. 10 note*), with which I am in complete agreement, besides, I believe that all true philosophy should begin in this way.

What he takes expressly from Descartes is the method; however he is no more Cartesian than this, even if he shows a dogmatic faith in the method, which I think often complicates the understanding of his thought instead of clarifying it. In his *Ethics* (*II prop. 7*) he categorically affirms that "the order and connection of the ideas are the same as the order and connection of things;" with which he enunciates Hegel's dogma that "the rational is the real," which is serious, as it makes reality dependant on the order of ideas and not vice versa; hence *the geometric order* that he follows in his work.

But Spinoza, like Bruno is fundamentally an idealist, he sees the finite in the infinite, the reality of the senses in God or the substance of the world. "God is singular, i.e. in Nature there is not more than one single substance and this is infinite." (*I prop. 14*) God is the first cause but he is not the personal Biblical god; it seems to him that belief in this god and in the creation of the world according to Genesis cannot even be conceived philosophically.

Spinoza sees Nature from this perspective, as a prolongation or an extension of God, as an attribute of the same, and thus he does not see two realities but one: Nature is also God (*Deus sive Natura*) God or Nature, as he expresses it. "Everything that is, is in God, and without God nothing can exist nor be conceived." (*I prop. 15*) "I understand by substance that which is in itself and what is conceived by itself" (*I def. 3*) this definition is correct in the first part; the second is not really incorrect, but since there cannot be an experience of it, it is the product of a supposition, an inference. This is a small but effective trap that idealists have fallen in: it is one thing to have the experience of (what we can call God), and another to know his will, how he became or wanted to be; this nuance gives his God a certain personal character.

Spinoza does not conceive a substance without its existence. "Existence belongs to the nature of a substance, its definition necessarily has to contain the existence, thus its existence derives from the same definition." (*I prop. 8*) Its definition is derived from this premise.

Spinoza's idea of God excludes all imperfections, it contains absolute perfection, for this reason he discards all doubts relative to its existence. In this way the existence of God is proved. The approach but not the proof seems correct to me, as we can effectively have the experience of perfect order; although I would not call it God in order to avoid a series of misunderstandings and even contradictions, as his God does not become clear and distinct, and hence true. When he says: "By God I understand an absolutely infinite God, i.e. a substance that has infinite attributes, each one of which expresses an eternal and infinite essence;" Bruno also would agree with this.

For Spinoza divine nature has two ways of being or of manifesting itself, one like *Natura naturans*, which is God in itself and the other like *Natura naturata*, which is what we understand by Nature. In the latter it finds two ways of being or attributes of divinity which are perceptible to human understanding: the bodies of living beings are attributes of divinity by extension, and their minds are its attributes like thought. We see that he visualizes the universe like an organism with a mind and body: "the whole of Nature is a single individual, whose parts, i.e. all bodies, vary in infinity of ways, without any change in the Individual like a whole." (*II prop. 13 note*) When I read that finite minds are the ways of divinity as an attribute of thought, I believe that I am finding *universal Consciousness*, but Spinoza has other ideas, he cannot find in human mind specific thoughts of a divine origin, he is interested in describing the understanding of God.

For him, human understanding has little or nothing in common with the divine: "God's understanding is a cause of the essence as well as the existence of our understanding, and thus the understanding of God (...) it differs from our understanding with respect to essence as well as existence, and he cannot agree on anything with this." (*I prop. 17 note*) This is disappointing because we cannot understand the divine mind, and neither does our philosopher understand this, and thus we do not know what the origin of his idea of God is. It even seems illogical as being the cause of an essence and existence of our understanding, we could have a connection with divine understanding. By establishing this disconnection it is clear that what he might say about God is a result of inferences and thus only of a relative value. Here my philosophy follows a very different path, as it maintains that all understanding in the spiritual order has its origin in the Essence, i.e. in the universal Consciousness, and this connection can be confirmed in all our elevated and unitive thoughts.

In the same way, without knowing the will of God, as he ignores his understanding, he infers that "There is nothing neither given nor contingent in the nature of things, all things are determined by divine nature in order to exist and work in a certain way" (*I prop. 29*). This determinism with a certain Calvinist hue is entirely gratuitous, it does not obey any experience, it is an attribute that he grants to God: "For no other reason can it be said that something is contingent except in relation to our lack of knowledge" (*I prop. 33, esc.*). He simply supposes and accepts it dogmatically as happens with all determinisms. However, "things have not been produced by God in some other way or through some other order than the manner and order in which they have been produced" (*I prop. 33*).

What is clear is that for Spinoza the freedom of man

is an illusion: "Men believe that they are free because they are conscious of their volitions and desires, and because they do not think nor dream the causes which they are forced to want and desire." (*I Apen.*) But he is not referring here to the lack of knowledge in relation to knowledge of the divine mind, which is fundamental to my philosophy, but to the ignorance of divine designs and the laws of nature, that neither he nor the human being know of. There undoubtedly persist the remains of the old God which decidedly do not fit within his scheme, even if he tries sometimes to maintain a divine perspective, very opposed to the homocentric Judeo Christian perspective; for example he is far from believing that nature has been created for man. It is enough for Spinoza to explain the efficient causes, he does not postulate nor does he believe in the final causes, nature does not have an objective; final causes are fabricated by man. Like Bergson, he ignores final causes and applies himself to the first causes.

"From what has been said it clearly follows that God has produced things in complete perfection," because they come from "a nature that is perfect at its highest point." (*I prop. 33 note*) However for Spinoza, God's perfection does not include an absolute will or an arbitrary freedom, he thus very logically says that God cannot make a triangle not correspond to its angles. He emphasise this in his Appendix: "everything has been predetermined by God, but not of course by the freedom of his will (for his pleasure) but due to the absolute nature of God." "men usually imagine that all things of nature like man himself work towards a goal and they even think that God himself directs everything towards a predetermined goal; they thus say in effect that God has done all for man, in order that the latter give him glory" in this way – he later insists – "they have invented various ways to pay homage to God in order to be loved by him above all others, so that He lead all nature for the benefit of their blind desires and insatiable greed." (*Op. cit.*) "This prejudice – he continues – became superstition and grew deep roots in the soul." And later he expresses his surprise on seeing that this prejudice continues in spite of the catastrophes and illnesses that affect the good as well as the bad. As such, all those who believe in the will of God over the happenings in this world "they have taken refuge in the shelter of ignorance." (*Op. cit.*) In this long appendix, that I have abridged, Spinoza openly expresses himself against a Biblical anthropocentric vision; he had his reasons for postponing the publication of this book until after his death. Finally he himself poses the inevitable question: "If all things come forth from nature's need for a perfect God, where do the imperfections of nature come from? The perfection of things should be valued only by its nature and power."

On knowledge of the Soul

It is natural for those who have had a transcendental intuition to try to explain that other stage of consciousness by developing a theory of the knowledge of the mind; Spinoza is no exception. In the second part of his *Ethics* he develops a theory of knowledge, but not so much of the world of the senses as that of the mind, or the Soul as he calls it, of the ways of knowing the human being. I find there a similarity with my own theory of the mind, although Spinoza has a peculiar way of seeing the matter because he never forgets the dependence of the mind on the body. Just as there is dependence between God and Nature there is also dependence between the Soul and the Body of living beings. But there is a kind of inversion, as even if God cannot create the world as a whim, the latter depends on the former. God is the first cause; nature with all beings is an extension of Him. While living beings have a dependency relation with their bodies, different species think and feel in a similar manner because they have a similar body, they have a physical structure that determines their minds: "The Soul does not know itself, except when it perceives the affections of the Body." (*II prop. 21 note*) Besides, "The human Soul, when it perceives the common order of Nature does not have sufficient knowledge of it, nor even of its own body or that of foreign bodies, but just a confused and mutilated knowledge." (*II 29 cor.*) This is so because men do not depend on their essence but on the causes and effects that take place in the common order of nature that depend on other causes and effects, and this is so until infinity.

In this view there is an enormous difference between the human and divine mind. God is perfect, while man has an imperfect body on which his mind depends. This is not one of the easier features of Spinoza. The Souls or minds of living beings are also an attribute of God in the form of thought and their bodies are also that in the form of an extension; all Nature is an attribute of God as an extension. "All the Souls constitute the eternal understanding and the infinity of God." (*V prop. 40 note*) Although he does not say so, it can be inferred that God also uses human being's thoughts; this inference will lead Hegel to a fundamental point in his system.

In his *Ethics* Spinoza distinguishes three types or genres of knowledge. Some interpreters talk of levels of knowledge; I personally prefer to follow the language of Spinoza, because even if there is some similarity with my theory of the knowledge of the mind, there is, as we will see, a radically different posture or vision. Suffice to say that it has nothing to do with the *levels of consciousness* that I put forward, because these refer to intrinsic changes of the subject, while for Spinoza knowledge is fundamentally external; this position actually determines his philosophy.

The knowledge of the first genre is what common man has in his daily life, in which he works in reaction to external stimuli, in this sense he adopts a passive attitude; it is not active in the sense of being intelligent or creative. If we remember that for Spinoza human minds (and that of other species) are ideas of their bodies, we will see the human mind here at its most elemental level, as a bodily reaction to the world of the senses, with a minimum of rational reflection. It is the useful knowledge for survival. Through this knowledge all things useful for life are known. It is what I have called *utilitarian knowledge*, even if I include here the knowledge of the second genre. But Spinoza wants to differentiate this elementary level, in which ideas are not clear but vague and uncertain. In this state "the mind does not have suitable but a confused knowledge of itself, because "it is externally determined by fortuitous circumstances to contemplate this or that." (*II prep. 29 note*) In sum, it is the *opinion* of which Plato spoke. False ideas are derived from this imprecise knowledge, as "falsity consists in the privation of knowledge, which is involved in unsuitable, mutilated and confused ideas." (*II prop. 25*)

The knowledge of the second genre, responds to ideas rationally or logically related. These allow for independence with respect to things, they are not passive ideas. "By suitable idea I understand an idea as it is considered in itself, without relation to the object." (*II def. 4*) This does not mean that they are independent of the body; Spinoza insists on this dependence, but even so the human being can have common ideas that are clear and distinct because all bodies coincide in some way, for this reason they can be perceived by all; he also calls them "common notions." It is this independence with respect to the reality of feeling which makes him fall, according to me, into the dogma that the ideas so conceived are true: "He who has a true idea knows at the same time that he has a true idea and cannot doubt it." (*II prop. 43*) Spinoza undoubtedly thinks of mathematics and geometry but extends these ideas to nature, i.e. he confuses the exact sciences with those of nature and man. For this reason he expresses himself in a *geometric mode*, and he believes the latter is inexorable and incontrovertible. We should not blame only him for this false step, even today countless naturalists, sociologists and psychologists fall into the same trap.

In the knowledge of the third genre Spinoza seems to change perspective: Given that "everything is in God and is conceived by God, from what follows that we can deduce a great number of consequences that we know suitably well and thus form a third genre of knowledge." (*II prop. 47 note*) Nevertheless there is no change of radical perspective. According to me, in his case there has been an isolated transcendental intuition that does not let him change the order of his knowledge, his method.

There is thus another way of knowing: "All the ideas considered in their relation with God are true." (*II prop. 22*) This means that if things are seen in their essence, knowledge is certain. Thus, "a suitable and perfect idea is given in God as he constitutes the essence of our Soul, and thus this idea is true." (*II prop. 24 dem.*) Besides, he affirms that "All ideas are in God, and considered in relation to God they are true; for this reason there are no unsuitable or confused ideas unless they are considered in relation with the singular soul of someone." (*II prop. 26*) Although Spinoza does not speak of perspectives, as is usual in my theory of knowledge, it is evident that he is talking of two ways of seeing, one is suitable, the other not. For this reason "Falsity consists in a privation of the knowledge that envelops unsuitable ideas i.e. those that are mutilated and confused." (*II prop. 35*) i.e. true ideas exist but they lie enclosed, *covered,* and it depends how we see them so that they be *discovered.*

Spinoza does not abandon his naturalist vision and

consequently the intimate relation between body and soul which, in my opinion, complicates the understanding of his propositions. But if we closely follow its development we will see how the soul keeps liberating itself from the body, although he might not express it in this way. In the Appendix of the first part we saw how the supposed freedom of man was mocked, but in the last part of the book the demonstration of freedom, though not of the individual but of the Soul, is expressly shown due to the power over the passions. Here the title of his work as ethics takes on meaning and of the highest order as he is dealing with transcendental morality. "Here I will deal with the power of the soul, i.e. of reason and the empire exercised on all passions in order to reduce them and govern them." (*Pref.*) "The soul can work in such a way that all the affections of the body, i.e. all the images of things refer to the idea of God. (*V prop. 14*) He takes this opportunity to clarify his idea of God, because if man has to overcome his passions he should also free God from the same. "He who loves God should not make an effort to make God love him too." (*V prop. 19*) as with this effort he would be wanting God not to be as he is, i.e. impersonal.

It has been observed that Spinoza's morality is very close to that of the Stoics, as it tends towards a state of tranquillity and equilibrium (*ataraxia*), I would add that it is very epicurean, in the way that it sees pleasure linked to good and evil linked to pain: "By good I understand all kinds of joy and all that fills our desires. By evil I understand all that generates Sadness and all that frustrates our intentions." (*III prop. 39 note*) But beyond these particular tendencies and its habitual naturalist vision, it tends towards a total integration: men "can desire nothing better for the conservation of their being than being in agreement, in such a way that the Souls and Bodies of all are composed of in some way one soul and one body." (*IV prop. 18*) Of course, given our human condition these aspirations of desires are utopian, but notice the common objective that involves a higher realization that unites all men in one single soul and body.

Later Spinoza shows with clarity two basic forms of knowledge: "Things are known in two ways: either we conceive of their existence in relation to a determinate time and space, or we see them as contained in God (...) in the second way we conceive of them under the form of the eternal." (*Prop. 29*) I believe that the concepts of time and space that he has not used before are fundamental in establishing the ways of knowing. These concepts, as we will see, will be basic for knowledge from Kant onwards; Spinoza does not say more than has already been said, but he has given the key which will be helpful to the former. "To conceive of things – he continues – under a kind of eternity (*sub specie aeternitatis*) is to conceive of them as real beings through the essence of God who covers existence as well as our soul." (*V prop. 30*)

In the fifth part of his Ethics, he undoubtedly revisits his initial inspiration and sees the essence of the matter. When speaking of the soul, he recognizes that there is a part that remains after death, and here I completely agree with his manner of posing the issue, that involves the theory of knowledge of the mind, leaving its essential side linked to the Eternal, and to God: "it seems that our Soul, and the way that it knows, is an eternal mode of thought and which is ended by another eternal mode of thought and henceforth to the infinite, in such a way that all together constitute the eternal understanding in the infinite of God." (*V prop. 50 note*) From here is derived that "the external part of the soul is the understanding." (*Cor.*) Here he has hit the target as regards the essence of the Soul and of Nature; it is this vision that we must keep as a reference and example.

This true understanding comes from the third genre of

knowledge: "This third genre of knowledge depends on the soul as its formal cause, as the soul is also eternal." (*V prop. 31*) "From this genre of knowledge is born the contentment of the soul and the highest it can attain, the highest form of happiness that accompanies the idea of God." (*V prop. 32*) More than closeness here, we see an integration of the soul with God, which is what Spinoza calls *intellectual Love*.

As the mind (Soul) for Spinoza is one with the body it is expected that with the death of the latter, the former will also perish; and he says this: "It can only be said of our Soul that it endure, and its existence can only be defined for a certain period of time, as it supposes the actual existence of the body" (*Prop. 23, note*), but in the same proposal he affirms that "The human Soul cannot be absolutely destroyed with the human body, there is a *part* of it that continues being eternal." And this he maintains (supposedly) by experience: "we feel and we know that we are eternal" (*Prop. 23*). And thus we can conclude that *in its essence* the mind *continues* being eternal, and in its conception we can infer that it was always so, that it is not born, as in Plato and Hinduism; although he does not say so.

Here we see Spinoza contemplating the eternal, expressing the liberty of the Soul and in its highest state which is the Beatitude, which as we know is a mystic state. In this state he expresses the culmination of his ethics: "Beatitude consists of the love for God." "And the more it opens up (*s'épanuit*, a beautiful French expression has no Spanish or English equivalent) the Soul in this divine love or this beatitude, the greater is its power over the passions." (*V prop. 42*) But at the same time he expresses an inversion of knowledge which is intrinsic to the one who has had a transcendental experience: "This opening (épanouissement) is not obtained by the diminishing of our sensual appetites, but on the contrary it is the opening (of the soul) that makes possible the diminishing of our sensual appetites." (*Op. cit.*) And he finally shows the union of the understanding, of the soul with his moral consciousness: "Beatitude is not the price of virtue but virtue itself." (*Op. cit.*)

Spinoza, conclusion

Spinoza's language is not easy to follow. Added to the difficulty of his method, there lies the manner in which he has structured or edited his work, as if they were theorems that contained the premises that have to be demonstrated, to which are added constant references or "quotations" of the author from other sections of the same book which makes its reading even more difficult. It does not help that at times he displays his thought from the second genre of knowledge and others (less often) from the third genre. This being the case I will use my own language in this commentary.

Many will think that Spinoza's morals are very narrow, and they will feel the same when they reads my ethics in *The Roots of Morality*, because he does not apply himself like Aristotle to defining the vices and virtues nor does he stop to give useful advice. His moral is not preceptive, like me he stakes his understanding on the soul, taking for granted that once achieved, the correct action is necessarily derived. He does not talk about levels of consciousness, as I prefer to do in my ethics, but of different states of the soul, very different to the state of most mortals. There is a notable similarity with Buddhism in this radical difference between the wise and the ignorant, and this because both know that there is an abyss between he who has perceived God or the Nature of the Buddha and he who has not had this experience. Although Spinoza seems to feel a certain disdain for the ignorant, the common man, the unfortunate (and other similar epithets that he uses) while Buddhism shows compassion for them.

We saw Spinoza's aspiration that the souls and the bodies become "a single soul and a single body." This aspiration should be highlighted because it expresses, although in abbreviated form how his pantheist monism encompasses all his morality. On this point my vision essentially overlaps because, as I have expressed in *The Roots of Morality, there is no moral base firmer than the realization that we are all One.*

We saw that even Spinoza asks himself: "If all things follow from the need of the nature of a perfect God, where do the imperfections of nature come from?" Spinoza believes he has an answer by emphasizing that Nature should not be seen in keeping with human interests, and we agree with this, but this is just one part of the matter. From what has been said it follows that Nature does not have a purpose that can be understood by a finite understanding, it is men who manufacture final causes. Although the ignorance that we humans suffer from is not an answer, the question still exists; the imperfection of the world is still inexplicable and the ontological situation of the *Natura naturata* is not clear as we do not know the limits that separate it from Nature as God. However, there is not a total identification, Spinoza understand by *Natura naturata* the infinite substance that *underlies* Nature.

I believe that Spinoza comes closer to my theory of perspectives which I would like to clarify since I consider it very important. It is evident that a transcendental intuition has inspired all his vision, there is not a true change of perspective in him but a change of vision from the same perspective. It is one thing to see nature *in* God and another *from* God. This should be clearer further on when I will elaborate on my theory of perspectives. Suffice it to say at this point that the difference is decisive; but I still insist that he sees in the correct direction and the heart of the matter.

It could be said that Spinoza's error lies in his method, but this would be a simplification as his choice is due to other reasons. Our philosopher has undoubtedly perceived the Unity of Reality but his experience is transitory since he is dealing with an intuition, even if it is enough for him to persist with his idea. The latter gives him another perspective, but actually it is not him, or the centre of consciousness which has changed perspective, but only his manner of posing reality, his philosophy; his ontology has changed but he has not changed ontologically; it is not enough to think in order to be. This will be clearer to the reader when he reads later about my idealism. Spinoza's correct intuitions and failings become clearer in the light of these mental mechanisms. His intuition shows him through experience that there is a higher way of knowledge that allows him to intuit the Eternal, hence he realizes that the most correct way of seeing the world is *sub specie aeternitatis*; which is very correct. Unfortunately he cannot maintain this vision which would correspond to what I have called the *essential perspective*; hence the error in using the geometric method.

Spinoza retains his transcendental idea, but after his experience he descends to his individual perspective and in unison with his usual ways of thinking. Not, of course, to the knowledge of the first degree which is vague and confusing, but to the second that makes him adopt the geometric or scientific method. Since God is Nature, the method adopted by the sciences seems the most suitable for him; and from this he will develop his entire vision of Nature, of living beings, of man, of society, and a good part of his philosophy. Thus the *Natura naturans* obeys in good measure a transcendental perspective and is expressed from this, while the *Natura naturata* responds to its individual perspective and is developed as any naturalist would do (albeit from his desk, without carrying out field work and research that seem to wear out the latter), abjuring any link with the Transcendent.

The two *Natura* are united by his original intuition, but in the development of the *naturata*, and of the world of the senses, we do not find signs of the *naturans*, these remain merely an idea beyond the horizon; the Transcendent remains as such. I do not wish to deny the *scientific* value of his reflections on nature, man included, but by being linked or delinked to the Transcendent only by an idea, their value as philosophy strictly speaking or as I see it, is scarce. While dealing with *Natura naturans* we saw the heights they reach. Doubtlessly with his intuition he had found a rich treasure and the pearls that he had brought out from the same are of great value because they point to the existence of that Reality that inspires and excite the seekers of ideas-realities.

I do not mean to imply by the title of this chapter that the matter is ended. Spinoza's *Propositions* is a project that is still to be realized. We should not remain only with the words and consider it as static knowledge; the reader of the idealists can take for granted that there is always *something* more. It is easy to declare oneself a follower of Spinoza and to say that Nature is God, but this is not exactly Spinoza's vision, which begins and ends with God. These are two ways of looking at the same thing, but different ways of seeing and understanding; both are pantheisms but different. This will become clearer when I explain monist pantheism. If the spirit of the reader opens up to the idea that Nature is sacred, Spinoza's project will have fulfilled its objective. Without the correct understanding of the *third genre of knowledge*, this fulfilment will not become effective; and it is not *easy,* he himself recognizes at the end of his work: "If the path that I have shown seems very difficult, it can still be achieved. Of course that which is found so rarely ought to be difficult." "All that is excellent (*beau*) is as difficult as it is rare."

The Quest in the Enlightenment

The Enlightenment was a cultural and spiritual movement during one of the deepest crises in Western culture when all values, beliefs and institutions were questioned. However unusual the particular development of Kant, a critical philosophy was an inevitable consequence; human knowledge and even reason had to be challenged. But, as the Enlightenment corresponded to a period of transition, thought did not offer anything finished, definitive or absolute; a kind of intellectual bureaucracy was necessary to reorder the whole. So great was the need that the most important thinkers of France, for the first time in history, set out to elaborate an Encyclopaedia, in which each concept had a new meaning; naturally it was condemned by the Church. Although Rousseau's conception was different from that of Voltaire, man began to be seen with new eyes. A cultural rupture, with the resultant reordering and criticism, was needed at all levels in order to liberate the spirit bound by concepts, beliefs and obsolete traditions, facing a new horizon open to creativity. Thanks to the Enlightenment thinkers, those of Romanticism found themselves faced with this wide open horizon in which they could freely develop their faculties. It is true that the Romanticism of artists would react against the rationalism of the Enlightenment and oppose sentiment to reason, but it was the latter that disposed of the rubble of the past, for man to act without thinking of it and instead concern himself with his own present, with the new problems of his time.

The Enlightenment had paved the way for a new rebirth in its most decisive aspect, it had awoken the Hellenic spirit: freedom of thought, creed and expression, philosophic and scientific interest within a corresponding aesthetic framework, from which Neoclassicism is derived, which naturally clashed with the absolutist monopoly of the Church. An inevitable coalition took place with the French Revolution. The Church possessed more than 10% of the France's territory, spread out, of course, through the cities and most productive areas; with incalculable economic benefits. If to this we add the political power and predominance in the field of education, it can be understood why it had to be done away with. The Enlightenment had proposed the return of the Greco Roman cults and had made overtures to Indic religions, although by reaction and projection, as continues to happen amongst those who ignore these religions, there were also enlightened people who proposed the extermination of all religions. We know that the revolutionary Convention wanted to replace the Christian cult with that of the goddess of Reason and changed the name of Nôtre Dame of Paris to the Temple of Reason and Freedom. As was expected with this new civilizing project, the obstinate Christians adopted the same posture as with the Roman project 1500 years before. Nevertheless, the Revolution, like all revolutions, committed too many excesses and betrayed in several fundamental points the ideals of the Enlightenment for which Voltaire had fought so hard.

We have been taught that the Enlightenment brought about the French Revolution. Yes and No. It made a push for it, but other forces found a place for it other than that proposed by the enlightened. These forces being underlying currents were closer to the masses, and brought power to the new adepts and took fanaticism to an extreme. Freedom yes, fraternity, of course, but not equality; this killed the great political aspiration of those thinkers: the government of the enlightened. Voltaire firmly believed in it and spent a good part of his life in this task; he never believed, as anyone with a fine psychology and historical knowledge could, in the government of the people. (Voltaire deserves more explanations that I will give in *The Roots of Morality*)

Kant

It is very interesting to return to Kant because the fundamental premises in his thought and structures are indisputable; I am referring to his pure ideas, to his *a priori* concepts. But Kant is obstinate in not searching for their causes; it is enough for him that they are firm foundations for the knowledge of man and his earthly circumstances, the tangible world. This means, that once having reached his pure ideas, and indisputably genius intuition, he refracts his spirit in them in order to apply them to phenomenal reality; he ascends with his intuition to the *a priori* forms, and descends to analyse them with his discernment and an exemplary rigor. If you remember my theory of the psyche (illustrated in a scheme in my *Psychosophy*), you will verify that Kant uses the mechanism of reason that I have divided into *intellect,* which is the creative aspect of it as it feeds on intuitions, termed as reason by Kant as it has access to *a priori* forms, and *discernment,* in charge of establishing relations between the said intuitions and the phenomenal, of analysing and speculating on them; Kant does this marvellously. He did not ignore other planes of understanding, such as sentiments, and the internal or unconscious, but he ignored the *central, vital or unitive plane,* which in my conception is the real path towards the Transcendent. This prevented him from perceiving *ideas in themselves* of the Good and the Beautiful of which Plato talked about, even if he intuited the pure ideas "of reason", the forms of time and space that are the recourses of reason for the comprehension of Nature.

Everything coordinates perfectly so that within this system there is nothing to object regarding Kant, far from it, humanity should expresses its recognition, but within this system everything is enclosed in phenomenal reality; Kant errs only due to his limitations. Being necessary to overcome these, this is what the idealists tried to do, with their successes and failures, but so many were their wrong choices that they brought discredit to the whole attempt; although there were other ways of recovering Kant as Schopenhauer did and as we will do.

Time and space, as *a priori* principles necessary for the knowledge of the sensible world, are Kant's great discovery and there can be no objection to this, on the contrary these principles will remain forever established. Even if we can accept these forms as pure ideas as they transcend reason, they are, as we will see, between the Transcendent and the phenomenal. The closeness to the latter makes Kant treads firm ground with his reason, but the same does not happen when he ventures in the Transcendent properly speaking, which he barely reaches with his intuition and explains only badly with his reason, but the same does not happen when he ventures in the Transcendent properly speaking. Thus, in his first *Critique*, Kant was in his element, but the higher he raised his gaze, the further away did the panorama present itself, and in his second and third Critique, when he fixed his gaze on the supra-sensory, it can be observed that he does not see clearly, and for this reason his arguments are even more vague.

Even today there are those who seek in Kant a platform from which to jump to the Transcendent, but they will perforce slip on it, just like Kant. Because the latter's interest was not discovering intelligible realities, but giving a basis to the knowledge of the sensible world. He expresses it thus: "The principal task of reason lies in distinguishing the sensory from the intelligible world, thus indicating the understanding of its own limits" (*Metaphysics of Customs* III). And "the concept of an intelligible world is no more than a point of view that reason is obliged to take from outside the phenomena in order to think of itself as practice" (*Op. cit.*) To this objective he adapts his method: "I seem to have chosen in this writing (*Op. cit.*) the most adequate method, which is that of going analytically from common knowledge to the determination of the supreme principle of it, in order to later return synthetically from the verification of this principle and the origins of it, to common knowledge, where it finds its use". His interest is not in finding the Good, like Plato, but "a supreme principle of morality" (*Op. cit*). Kant looks, albeit from a great height, down; when he wants to look directly and unidirectional upwards, he sees only ideas, not realities. Hence the sad conclusion at the end of his *Met. Cust.*: "The idea of a pure intelligible world remains a usable and permitted idea for the establishment of a rational faith". This is a contradiction, as the moment when reason cedes its place to faith it ceases to be rational. He throws this last dart into the void.

In the Transcendent he definitely does not see clearly. The Beautiful and the Good can be defined in their application to the sensory reality, but he does not know how to resolve the very important ideas of freedom, happiness and God. "Freedom is only an idea of reason" (*Met. Cost.* III) "Freedom is a pure idea whose objective reality cannot be demonstrated in any way by natural laws nor through any possible experience" "It cannot be conceived of nor can it be known, it is only valid as a necessary supposition of reason" (*Op. cit.*). From a vital point of view, I cannot imagine a poorer definition; he treats it almost as a material object. Searching for freedom as an objective reality is absurd, while as we shall see, as a *unitive experience* it acquires its full meaning. We can make the same objection to his idea of happiness which he defines as "the state of a rational being in the world, such that in the totality of existence everything proceeds according to his will and desire" (*Crit. Pure Reason*, 224). In the first place this being cannot be human, so happiness would be denied to it, secondly, this outward projection, which nurtures greed, is the opposite direction to happiness which is an inner path to liberation, that implies detachment; here Kant is completely disoriented to the point of being inconsistent (something unusual in him) with his morality.

If Kant proves the limitations of reason, precisely for the supra-sensory, how does it occur to him to postulate the possible existence of a rational God? Evidently it does not occur to him to think of another way of being and understanding the Essence of the World. In Kant reason goes as far as it should go. It is in human beings that reason fulfils his mission. If God were rational he would show his limits, besides he would be worldly, as reason is made to respond to the needs the world generates; so needed God would be, like all humans, desirous, anxious and alienated from the essential, i.e. from Himself. Kant definitely does not see the defects of reason, its psychological limitations, and the impediments it generates.

In the same way, if in the highest strata of the spirit, Kant found a lack of intention or purpose: "The moral or categorical imperative maintains: I should work in this or that way absolutely on regardless of what I want" (*Met. Cost.* II) And also in his aesthetics: "Delight in the beautiful is the only selfless and free satisfaction as there is no interest, neither in the senses nor in reason" (*Crit. Judg.* 5). Why did it occur to him to think that at an even higher level "Someone" had to have an intention? Couldn't God be an artist?

As I see it and using my terminology, Kant undoubtedly

had intuitions that allowed him to access pure ideas, to his *a priori* genial forms. His high level of consciousness allowed him to establish his spirit in *altruistic consciousness*, from which those intuitions are much more accessible, but he always maintained his *individual perspective* from which he looked at reality; it is for this reason that he refracted the spirit in the intelligible world in order to apply it in the sensible. He did not have a displacement of the spirit enough to change his perspective, in order to look from the Intelligible at the World, although he looked at it with ideas that he extracted from it. He was at the doors of perception but he did not enter, he got the ideas he needed and returned satisfied because this allowed him to explain phenomena. Thanks to this, however, he has left us the stre intelligent, solid and original theory of knowledge ever imagined by man.

Kant shows with probity a fundamental principle of reason and of all theories of knowledge: the unity of apperception that converges in the *I* (self), and the subsequent leap from it to the soul, i.e. from the empirical ego to a substantial subject, as well as the unity of the World, i.e. the idea of the unity of all phenomenal reality, and the idea of God as a being that conjoins all perfections, which constitute the central ideas of his *Critique of Practical Reason*. These ideas, which he calls transcendental, are the result of a natural mechanism of reason that tends towards the realization of these synthesis *a priori:* "the task of reason is to produce a systematic unity in all the empirical operations of understanding, in the same way that understanding unifies the multiplicity of phenomena by means of concepts and puts them under empirical laws." (*Critique of Pure Reason 692*) Although this faculty limits it to reason and the said transcendental ideas only have a regulatory function, they are not verifiable realities.

According to me, all the faculties of man, not just

intellect, but also sentiments and in particular intuition, are capable of transcending reason, and tend to Unity because this is its very Nature. This unitive capacity of the human mind Kant discovers in reason, but as it adheres to the limits of discernment, i.e. to its speculative faculties, it could only reach these *a priori* transcendental ideas, which are, rightly speaking, midway between the world of the senses and the Transcendent, which in reality is (transcendent) to these speculative faculties; hence he does not believe in intellectual or transcendental intuitions. Hegel obeys the same mental mechanism. These transcendental Ideas are not innate for Kant. In my conception, however, they are so as they are a product of the same substance of *unified consciousness* that the human being intuits in his inner being. As we will see later, God is a personification of the Unity; he is the unitive factor *par excellence* expressing the very centre of consciousness. Unity comprehends the transcendental ego, the unity of Nature and God; fundamental ideas for Kant and for humanity. It is not God who makes Unity, but Unity to God. The pure Idea-Reality is Unity, not God.

The historical vision of Kant

What we invariably observe in Kant, is a systematic split in man himself and between man and the Transcendent. Curiously before his attempt to reach the Transcendent, the *noumenal* with his *Practical Reason,* he writes his *Idea for a Universal History in a Cosmopolitan Sense,* in which he outlines a philosophy of history. At the beginning of the work he tells us: "Whatever be the concept that in a metaphysical plane, we may have of free will, their phenomenal manifestations, human actions are determined, as well as other natural phenomena, by the general laws of Nature".

The split cannot be clearer. The metaphysical plane seems reduced to concepts and disconnected from human actions that are determined by the laws of Nature. Unlike Plato, there is not even participation here. Then, we should ask à quoi bon la *methaphisique?* But it turns out that Nature is not blind, in fact it possesses intelligence, and rather we humans are too blind to see its purpose. We should deduce this by ourselves, because here Kant plunges us, without any introduction or basis on to another figure: an intelligent Nature independent of Divinity, which makes us think of the Samkhya philosophy of India which would have been fascinating for him to know. "Man in particular and people in general do not imagine that when they pursue their own talent for themselves or in mutually opposed pursuits, they inadvertently follow a common thread: the intention of Nature, which they ignore." (In Spinoza, the reader might remember, we find the same belief).

We cannot avoid thinking of the root of one Hegel's most important ideas who had only to change the concept of Nature by the universal Spirit, as well as the resource of seeing its intention behind reality. The truth is that for someone as mentally ordered as Kant, human history is presented as incomprehensible chaos. "There is no other outlet – he tells us sadly – for the philosopher, as he cannot imagine the existence of any rational purpose in men and in their whole game, other than trying to discover in the contradictory course of human things, the intention of Nature, so that by using this, it is possible to trace a history of similar creatures who proceed without any plan". (*Op. cit.*) The plan is thus outlined by Nature, even if in the same it is foreseen that happiness and perfection have to be sought by man. The latter is inclined to be lazy and is motivated by the desire for honours, power and goods, but these vices are necessary as they push him in the aforesaid direction as (in agreement with Heraclitus) "the medium that Nature uses to achieve the development of all dispositions is antagonism". Kant, (and this also occurred to Hegel) ends up justifying in some way the gravest consequences of antagonism: he will talk of "the historical-universal function of evil".

Without vanity and the insatiable desire to possess or of control "all the excellent natural dispositions of man would eternally sleep." Here is suggested the mechanism of natural selection and survival of the fittest: "As happens with the trees of the forest, when they try to snatch from others air and sunlight, they try to look for them up above and in this way they grow upright". The spirit of liberalism, with competition as the driving force is well enunciated. But all this has a happy ending in spite of the victims: *a grand federation of nations, a cosmopolitan or world civil state.* (*Op. cit.*) All this seems to me to be untenable: A disorder that tends towards order, a selfishness that leads to unity, and a struggle that ends up in peace. I believe in the opposite. Theories like these only indefinitely justify the deferment of the said end.

The teleology's that tend to justify in some way the present evil seem nefarious to me. Evil must end here and now at least in myself, in each one of us, because evil is bad now and always, not bad "for the time being". We have to avoid the present day victims, not only for themselves (who are generally "others") but because we should be good now. Each one should achieve his integrity in this life; this is the best way to sow (the necessary kindness) for future societies. I should plant an example today so that it flourishes tomorrow. Observe history and you will see that what remains of men and the ruin of civilizations are the exemplary men due to their virtue. Kant, of course, does not fall into Marx's grotesque error of searching for and pointing out the victims and justifying their sacrifice; we can only blame him for his theoretical error, although it might have paved the way for later ideology. In another work that he writes a little later *The presumed beginning of human history*, he insists on the need for antagonism directly referring to war. Given the "level of culture in which humanity still finds itself, war continues to be an inescapable way to go towards it (to freedom), and only – God knows when – after having achieved a complete culture could it be healthy and even possible to have perpetual peace". But then he undoubtedly kindles the fire of the present day and postpones peace to an uncertain future. This is of course very dangerous for the present when all the means to destroy the planet exist. With these conditions the "categorical imperative" is peace, here and now and from now on.

Kant, in some way, believes in the designs of Nature, which he calls providence, and he resolves the matter in his own way as he will do with God: "But if we have to suppose that Nature does not proceed without a plan or an objective, that idea could be useful". In this genius we also find the seeds of pragmatism. And in the last subject he dealt with in this book he says: "A philosophical essay that tries to construct the universal history in keeping with a plan of Nature, we should not just consider it possible, but it is also necessary that we think of its propelling effect" And he added: "It seems to be a happening which is a little strange and even incongruous to try to conceive a history in keeping with how the world should run if one clung to reasonable finalities; it seems – he concludes with a premonition – that the result would be something like a novel". Hegel listens to this message and feels that he is the chosen one to "conceive a history according to an idea", and he works silently for many years without worrying that his work could seem to be a novel.

There is a principle in Kant (the second principle in his *Idea for a Universal History*) to which we should pay particular attention, because it will become very important in Hegel who will pass it on to Marx, and it will become the underlying principle of all modern ideology. Kant says: "Those natural dispositions that in men point to the use of reason should be completely developed in the species and not in individuals". He has this opinion because "each man would have to live for a disproportionate length of time in order to understand how to use to perfection all his natural dispositions". Without trying to deny the infrastructure that a relatively organised society provides for individuals, we cannot go so far as to invert values and give priority to the species above the individuals. I see in this a kind of fiction that reason leads to. The species is an idea, a universal, not something truly real. There are individuals, who make up the species, but the latter does not exist in itself, and thus can only develop badly if it does not develop earlier in individuals. It is of course of no interest to me to enter in vain scholastic discussion over terms, but I notice that behind this inversion there lays hidden alienation. I think that the individual is indebted to society and to the species, but his first duty is to develop the natural faculties in his person, otherwise he could only comply badly with his neighbour.

For the rest, I categorically affirm that the individual can develop all his decisive potential, mainly which allows him to achieve his freedom and the knowledge of the Transcendent which were unrealizable for Kant, and as a result, the knowledge of his place in the cosmos and his mission in society. Hope placed in the future of humanity and in the cooperation of mankind in this future is very laudable, but we should not lose sight of the first and decisive objective of man, of each one of us here, in this present life, which is to achieve this knowledge, freedom and integration. The species, the State and the interaction of the States in a cosmopolitan society will be the result of the level of consciousness achieved by citizens. This idea of humanity sounds good to the ear, but it also has its negative side that, in keeping with the way it is used, implies the negation of the individual. The intelligent, the creative side of man are the individuals, thanks to them humanity is something. The massification of contemporary man is also a consequence of these generalizing doctrines in which the State and the society have a point of view on man's place; and it is for this reason that his creative faculties lie dormant.

Why do I insist on Kant since I definitively do not agree with him? because since Kant has covered all the possibilities of the *individual perspective*, that is to say, of the speculative faculties, he is an indispensable reference for my project to be understood.

I have said that the trinity: I-discernment-memory, constitute a closed system in which the human spirit is found, and for this reason I have started believing that reality is the way this system presents to it. What Kant did was to minutely go over this system and like an excellent surveyor of thought he established its limits. This map of the mind has great value for all lovers of knowledge. It does not just involve Kant, as his work is finished, neither does it mean doing away with his work, even though unfortunately these are the positions generally adopted, but of overcoming this trinity, this closed system, this perspective, in order to liberate the spirit.

With Kant there is a detour in the path of knowledge, another direction is taken, another path that is directed towards the way of knowing, the method that precedes the object. With this he managed to clear a forest of sterile trees that had reached till the sky. Since the Renaissance, scientific knowledge has been sought and a method has been necessary. Descartes notices this and methodically begins his reflections, but he had his shortcomings, in his mechanism the inner workings were not always in tandem, but he united them according to his beliefs; by doing so he continued to make the same mistakes of scholasticism.

What Kant does is to put aside belief and adjust to the demands of reason that obeyed principles that bound the inner mechanisms together; he had discovered an instrument of knowledge that functioned with precision. This, of course, disgusted and continues to disgust all those who want to put their beliefs before knowledge, but what is laid down by Kant is irreversible. With Kant we are witness to the funeral of Thomas Aquinas; all those who do not believe in life did not come to the funeral, i.e., they did not read nor did they understand the genius of Koenigsberg. One can believe in God, but there are no reasons to do so, there is an undeniable force that projects the imagination towards the Transcendent, but it is so precisely because it transcends reason. For this reason the Kantian mechanism functions to perfection while it clings to the world of the senses. His *Critique of Pure Reason* remains firm, but his other critiques directed towards spiritual reality do not achieve their objective; there we see his rigid mechanism slip on an ethereal element.

Kant taught us to use reason when necessary, but thinkers after him almost without exception have believed that it is necessary to continue to think in the same way, since emanating from his work is the idea that reason is not suitable for understanding spiritual reality; it being necessary thereafter to find other paths of knowledge and other mediums applicable to this reality.

On its moral and its aesthetic I invite the reader to consult my work in *The Roots of Morality* and *The Roots of Art.*

The Quest in Romanticism

The sincere, effective and exhaustive search of Kant to put forward the objectives of knowledge that cannot be demonstrated as truths is a landmark in the history of Western thought. In a strictly philosophical way, although without directly attacking them, and without proposing to do so, in an attitude similar to that which Darwin would adopt with his scientific method, Kant definitively discards from the field of knowledge the rational premises of dogmatic religions and demonstrates the dogmatisms of reason in philosophy.

With these elements the German idealists try to end with the subject-object reality, to find a unity that is higher than that which covers them, which takes them to a higher plane, to a self-consciousness in which apperception is unified; in the words of Schelling, from an "absolute I", which "in no way can become an object."

Here, intentionally again, this vehicle of knowledge collides head on with religious dualism and places itself on the side of religious monism, which is and has been the constant aspiration of Hinduism and Buddhism and will be sustained by my philosophy laying emphasis not so much on logic as much as on the means and mechanisms that lead to this self-consciousness. And it will do so, precisely, in order to escape from the planes of reason that enclose it and alienate the spirit from a unifying and all-encompassing consciousness that I have called *universal Consciousness.*

The line of idealism that I am trying to underline is

clearly defined by an attitude that gives pre-eminence to consciousness over the object of knowledge, and for common ends, in particular the search for Unity. But a difference in the means has to be highlighted because it determines the mode of seeing the ends and interpreting the relation of the One with men and the World.

In Plato, Plotinus and Porphyry there is an insistence on the need for an inner search, for a discovery of the soul, followed by a growth of the spirit through the means of moral and even ascetic practices which give these doctrines a religious profile. While the German idealists were well instructed in theology, they never considered these practices as necessary for attaining their objective, which is unfortunate as they would have greatly cleared their vision and understanding. We can barely imagine the philosophies these powerful intellectuals would have forged imbued with a direct and clear vision of the Spirit. Conscious of this, by re- appropriating the line of idealism I have considered it indispensable to not only incorporate the said practices, but also investigate the psychic mechanisms that they lead to and the spiritual consequences that are provoked. These are psycho-philosophical investigations that are developed in my *Psychosophy*.

Fichte

Already in Fichte's "*Fundamental Propositions of Philosophy*" we find an *I* (self) that "poses" (and imposes) its own being and a Non-*I* that opposes it, and where it presupposes a will or intention behind Consciousness. And even before this it presupposes that this I is pure activity. The non-I is Nature. These propositions or presuppositions will be the premises on which his philosophy will construct itself.

Fichte like Descartes, projects himself externally without much ado, he only detects the pure or transcendental I in the activity of objectification; in this he makes it an objective for a subject. The transcendental *I* of Fichte is an infinite activity, but this is just a transposition if not a projection of the individual *I,* even if Fichte intuits a transcendental not an individual *I,* besides from there onwards the two I's intermix. In other words, the transcendental original intuition of Fichte is right, but later, instead of searching deeper with this *I,* he takes this I for the absolute I, which is not there, and thus he begins to think with the individual *I* as if it were the absolute. I believe that the same occurs to the other two German idealists. I mean that, on reflecting on the absolute *I* they anthropomorphise it. In my experience the intentions of the absolute cannot be known, so we should be careful with the projections of our reasons.

There is no doubt that Fichte rapidly exteriorizes the spirit as for him the consciousness of oneself requires the existence of the other; a Non-*I* is the first reality that the *I* find. And this is what effectively happens with the individual *I,* but not with the absolute *I.* This is also evident when he maintains that the absolute *I* search for its freedom through morality; as if the "Absolute" had still to end its own realization.

When he sees that consciousness of himself demands the existence of the Non *I,* he is undoubtedly making a transposition of the Kantian theory according to which Nature generates permanent opposition, as this confrontation is necessary for the spirit in its growth towards its liberation. Kant as well as Fichte project this liberation in a very far off future; for Kant it would be the realization of humanity, for Fichte of the absolute I. In my conception this realization is that of the spirit of man as an individual, an aspiration that can be actualized in life as it was for Kant it is an ideal project for humanity.

When Fichte maintains that the non – I is a necessary condition for the consciousness of oneself, he is evidently projecting his individual consciousness, he is speaking of the human condition. The same will occur to Hegel. For there to be a consciousness – he opines – the subject as well as the object should exist; here we see the spirit of Fichte centred in discernment, not in an absolute consciousness.

All this indicates that Fichte had a relative experience of the Absolute, as when the latter reveals itself as it is, in-itself, it does not show itself as desiring to be, but in being; what is experienced is the Being not the desire to be. This desiring to be is another transposition of Kant, the ought to be is again a human not a divine project. Man finds himself in a World in which he faces oppositions as it is a World that he has not created, he himself is created without his will, however, this does not happen with the Divinity as the latter does not create in order to find contradiction or opposition.

In keeping with my perception there exists a *vital force* that is translated into all forms of life and this implies the necessity of *survival.* It can be said with Fichte that this force is the same as that of freedom, but in man and in all living things, the sphere of need and freedom are contradictory. However the force of life is not the same as the need imposed by Nature. Fichte does not strictly speak of a vital but of a natural force that tends towards satisfaction, of natural and material needs, and the latter often inevitably offers resistance to the unfolding of the human spirit. And in the reduction of that resistance to the minimum lies the effort or moral understanding, that is, the moral action that liberates my spirit, at least from these bonds. This is part of man's program towards his realization as a moral being, although, of course, it is not all. Without knowledge of his destiny through intuitions and experiences, the project would be truncated; however many sacrifices occur. I believe that Fichte in his desire to unify all, in order to prove his absolute idealism forces and violates phenomenal reality.

This reality and the soul of men are full of dualities and contradictions which cannot be overcome by searching for reasonable explanations or logical justifications within a prior ideology. If it were so easy to know the Absolute and establish a relation between man and this Absolute, thereby reducing man to his logical consequences, humanity would have been liberated for some time now. The human soul is much more complex than this and is far from being resolved by reasons. Natural impulses and drives are too strong and real to be reduced to a logical unity prior to its existence and, we know from Freud, very often reasons obey unconscious motivations that reason completely ignores. And this is something that rationalism and philosophical idealism, and perhaps we could include all Western philosophy, should learn once and for all, that for the spirit to achieve its totality, the Absolute, *all* the human faculties are necessary.

Reason ignores this logic. Though our idealists lived in the middle of Romanticism and greatly ignored sentiment, they arranged all the showcases of the World with only reason. And although I appreciate and admire the capacity of discernment of these philosophers, I have no doubt that it is much more difficult to know and harmonise the other planes of understanding than to construct these philosophical systems; for the simplest reason that logic does not affect us. Thus Fichte observes pointedly: "from a transcendental point of view my being is constituted by a single impulse"... "If I consider myself as an object, determined by the laws of sensible intuition and discursive thought, then my own impulse becomes a natural impulse, as I am nature. If on the contrary, I consider myself as a subject, the impulse would be of a purely spiritual nature". (*Op. cit.*) This is correct, but this does not impede that "I consider myself as an object" and obey the forces of Nature when the latter are put into action.

Fichte however has a solution for this, and it is obedience to moral consciousness. This makes me believe that Fichte had a clear experience of his moral consciousness, hence the certitude that the latter provides "the immediate consciousness of our duty". However, it is surprising that Fichte, on referring to this consciousness, defines it *only* as a sentiment since he correctly judges as he uses the plane of the intellect as well as that of the sentiments, he intuits and feels it, that is, he has a *unitive experience,* and in this intelligence of moral consciousness, he finds the key for the Transcendent. Kant as well as Fichte intuited that it was found through moral consciousness, but they had no confidence in a knowledge that was not clear to their discernment with which they tried to tenaciously understand moral consciousness as well as the *noumenal.* Fichte, very correctly, leaped out of discernment and saw in "immediate sentiment" a harmonious relation between the empirical I and the absolute I. Nevertheless, since it is a kind of unfinished ethical project, it does not guarantee, according to me, an infallible moral certitude.

In keeping with my experience moral consciousness is fed from *universal moral Consciousness,* which is not a project but something finished, perfect, always in Order. These two consciousnesses are one in the final instance. In the moral project of the absolute I, we notice the projection of the empirical I that Fichte makes in the former, in which he shows his lack of direct knowledge of the Absolute at which he arrives through induction. If the moral realization of this is a project, it will be so for the absolute I; of course Fichte inverts this order making of the project a universal matter, a desire of infinite will, in which men would be the actors.

We see that the idea of Nature as a necessary opposition of the moral realization of man, had been shown by Kant in a minor and brief work, *Idea of a Universal History for a Cosmopolitan Purpose*, and this is the idea that Fichte will take in order to give it a universal dimension. Now it will be the absolute I that needs the confrontation with the sensory world for its own realization. It can be inferred that the idea is not the product of Fichte's personal experience but a gigantic enlargement of an idea on which Kant had not laid much stress; on a humble human level whose final objective would be "a great federation of nations" in a historic future. Nevertheless, in another brief essay (of some ten pages) *"Speculative Beginning of Human History"*, which is nothing more than a vague sketch (I mean without his usual critical bases) he says: "The fourth and last stage of reason that elevates men much above the society of animals, consisted in man understanding that he was the genuine finality of Nature". This nefarious idea, this cosmic anthropocentrism whose origin is found in Genesis, will be taken by Fichte and Hegel to make sense of their philosophies. The fact that Kant was not very convinced of this idea is proved by the fact that he refers, in a note to the work which we earlier referred to, the "inhabitants of other planets" and "our neighbours in the Cosmos", which Fichte and Hegel had forgotten as they reduced their vision to a planetary plane, depriving it of universality. For Fichte, in that stage of his thought, as well as for Kant, religion is a medium towards moral realization, but in his personal evolution these concepts will be inverted.

Fichte had begun to philosophize from a young age. His philosophy had three points of support: The intuition of the transcendental I (in the sense that we have seen), the experience (intuition) of the moral consciousness, and the structural idea of his system, an absolute idealism. But in his adulthood this scheme is insufficient. Although he does not renounce his earlier work, he realizes (in my believe, as he does not confess to it) what we had observed: that the structure of absolute idealism imposed limits on a wider vision. The ghost of Kant reappears to him; the *noumenal*, that he believed he had overcome during his youth with a simple recourse, it begins to seem transcendent to him. His first intuition, the *I*, that he called absolute is not enough, he warns, in order to explain the Transcendent, that he will call the infinite or infinite reality that underlies all the finite. Professors of philosophy will tend to see in this change in Fichte a waning of his philosophy because it is not entirely consistent with his earlier thought, but truths make up philosophies, and what makes the philosopher is not his interest in presenting to us a well formed package of ideas, but his incessant search for the unconditional Truth.

The way I understand it, and in my language, Fichte warns (and this should be taken as a conscious realization), that in consciousness everything is representation, there is nothing real, there is any being. As this consciousness seems to understand as much of the finite I as much as the absolute I, it desists from the latter as it does not manage to perceive this Being that intuits. If earlier the transcendental I was represented to it as a pure activity, he sees now the infinite reality as an infinite will, which is quite similar, but it seems to be more like an intelligence, and he even calls it *infinite reason*. (We will see the dimension that Schopenhauer gives to the concepts of representation and will). But like before, this will or infinite reason is still not conscious, it becomes conscious through human consciousness, even if it remains transcendent, in the World the only consciousness is the human. But then what is the *raison d'être* of this Being? Establishing *moral order in the World*. "He creates the world in our consciousness of what and why the call of duty is deployed, the feelings of harmony, intuition and the laws of thought" (*The Mission of Man*). We observe that he does not abandon the concept of Kantian duty, but now it is not the fruit of a rational imperative, it now has a metaphysical premise; although it cannot be demonstrated if we adjust to Kant's scheme.

Fichte's religion

In this philosophical process we should see a parallel transformation in the soul of the philosopher. And he takes this transformation in a direction contrary to that of his youth, from moral to religious consciousness. A progressive interest in religion is awakened in him. It is not surprising to hear him later say that the absolute being is the Divine being, God. Fichte has his own God and even his own religion, and thus instead of adapting to the Christian doctrine, in *The Doctrine of Religion* he attempts to identify the Verb creator with the Absolute being; meaning that his search and his message are also religious. And a sincere and rational searcher will also find that Fichte´s God is much more consistent and credible than that of the Old Testament.

Contemporary man has to reconsider his vision of Divinity and his relation with it. He cannot continue with the well-known alternative of believing or not believing, of having faith in a dogma established by the Church and save himself, or not having it and condemn himself, he has to learn and think and feel for himself, as Kant said in the context of the Enlightenment. And this is what these thinkers were doing, opening doors, smoothing the path of man towards God, of consciousness towards totality. It does not occur to Fichte to postulate a Divinity with all the attributes of perfection in order to explain the reason of being of all beings, keeping as "mysteries" the contradictions that derive from them, as this postulate, that obeys an expression of desire is a very puerile recourse to be admitted in the kingdom of philosophy. Fichte's merit is that he distances himself completely from this recourse in order to consider in philosophical terms the relation of the Transcendent with the World through the facts received in his consciousness.

With Fichte we are face to face with the God of the philosophers, and in this fundamental point he stands out in comparison to Schelling and Hegel who since they adapted to the official religion made concessions which disfigured their philosophies. Fichte never abandoned his philosophical positions, something that should be underlined, and which I am also interested in highlighting as I agree with him on crucial points. Fichte undoubtedly has an intellectual intuition of *the universal moral Order*, this itself and his logic make him discard the existence of a personal God. If it were like this, he maintains, he would be limited, as any substance, to time and space and he would be finite, perishable, and his attributes would not be divine but those that things have; this is incontrovertible for all lovers of truth: a personal God is a contradiction in terms. In Christian theology the contradiction is evident: On the one hand it is said that God is a person, on the other that he is omnipresent; the persona implies finitude, the omnipresence implies infinitude. If this is explained as a "mystery", nothing is explained. The recourse of *constructing* God by applying to him all the attributes of perfection is also not valid either.

Fichte's intuition and his logic converge in a Unity: God and the moral order are one and the same; although as I pointed out, by using the concept of God, he slips at times into duality, affirming that God is the one who orders the order. It is reasonable to suppose that someone has to order, but with this he insinuates that he is "behind" with a desire and a will, with which he anthropomorphises him and alienates us from direct experience; in our desire to intellectually understand we forget the Kantian principle etched in stone which we tend to ignore: discernment is on *this* side of reality. From discernment we tend to inevitably anthropomorphise the *noumenic*; the reader will understand my need to highlight the use we make of the different *planes of understanding.*

But in the final analysis Fichte clings to his perception of the *universal moral order*, so that for him religion reaches up to there, "any belief in a divinity that adds something more to the concept of moral order, will be a product of the imagination and superstition" (*Private Papers*). The faith that had been put in religion should be applied in the transcendent moral order. Although in my message I systematically defend the replacement of faith by experience, this appeal to faith in something real seems to me in the practical order, although not conclusive, edifying, as I consider fundamental that in his process of evolution man feels he is participating in a *Universal Moral Order* (See *The Evolution of the Spirit*).

In *The Path towards a Holy Life or the Doctrine of Religion* we see in the very title and throughout the work, that Fichte has reached another level of consciousness in which he perceives with even more clarity the religious consciousness towards which he directs the content of his moral consciousness. We see that his individual consciousness goes on disappearing as his *unitive consciousness* expresses itself. For this reason the *I* disappear from his language and it will be replaced by the absolute Being: God. On abandoning his concept of the absolute *I*, that earlier was confused with his individual *I*, the latter is distanced: The Being, the Absolute, has the courage to admit it, it is unknowable for the human being, but the spirit is not divided, individual consciousness, as in Plato, "is an image of the divine." The Divinity, on its part, is unified with Nature: "the content of the divine consciousness is the World." Fichte is experiencing a pantheism in which he ends up identifying God with life: "the Being and life are one and the same".

It is necessary to understand the nuances in which the spirit of our philosopher displaces itself, not accepting the Christian doctrine which establishes an irreconcilable trinity between God, Nature and man. We are faced with a more inspired conception, at the level of a higher consciousness; we are witnessing a marvellous process of integration of the human being in the *Universus*. Every aspirant to the said project of integration will do well to pay attention to this process. In his *Doctrine of Religion*, philosophy and religion are reconciled. Fichte has suffered a transformation in his consciousness; it is this that allows him to perceive divine Consciousness in the World, and human consciousness as a reflection of the divine. At this point he observes with clarity that a life that seeks satisfaction of the natural forces is wrong, because he himself has left behind that life which is now represented to him as unreal, virtual, while he experiences as true the life oriented to reaching the eternal. This language is fully religious, and not that of a dogmatic believer but of someone who nurtures himself from his own experience. If the language of these last writings can seem less philosophical, it should be realized that it has been chosen by a philosopher who expresses himself in the best way that his knowledge allows him to.

Schelling

It is well known that Schelling has different proposals that at times become contradictory. This, together with his abstruse language makes him difficult to follow. I keep my doubts to myself, because the abstruse language, so common amongst the thinkers of the XXth century, is due more to a lack of clarity of vision than to the complexity of his thought,. When the view is clear, the map that is drawn should also be so. In the case of Schelling it is perhaps justifiable since he frequents high and difficult peaks (where our contemporary thinkers never reached, where it is easy to take the wrong path and get lost. Commentators have differentiated between three to five periods in his thought. But it is my intention to follow the constants that distinguish them, in particular his project of integrating Nature in itself as well as in the Spirit, in a total reality. As we will see, the different phases of Schelling can be explained by the perspective that his spirit adopts in each one of them, and we can benefit from all of them except when they are contradictory and exclusive. We get the impression that for Schelling philosophical activity consisted more in maintaining the flow from the tap of creativity than in filling glasses; it is thus indispensable to make a choice between them.

Philosophy of Nature

Without any doubt it is in his Philosophy of Nature that Schelling shows his originality, I mean, his own vision, his penetration and philosophical genius, therefore I will mainly attend to these.

We see that for Fichte, and later for Bergson, Nature constitutes an obstacle for the free development of the Spirit. For Schelling Nature is not a mechanism, but an organic whole, that far from opposing the absolute *I*, tends like the latter to indefinitely extend itself. Nature itself, even if made up of contrary elements, find equilibrium when they collide, which reminds us of Heraclitus, and is moved by a vital force. In his vision, as in that of so many with a pantheistic inclination, the Universe is an organism, which I take as a correct form of representation, not just because it does not go against the sciences, but because this implies an integration of the phenomenal, that which today we would call ecological, including a common spiritual element that Schelling calls the Soul (*On the World Soul*). (This magnificent idea, which we find in Plotinus, probably had its origin in Hinduism. Max Müller sourly recalls that Schelling had never returned some recently translated Upanishads that he had lent him). In order to explain the Organism, Schelling proposes a higher or speculative physics that should search for its foundation in the theological model that the philosopher finds in Nature. But surprisingly for Schelling the Soul of the World is not an intelligent spirit, though (as was God for Kant) it offers a useful hypothesis of speculative physics for explaining the universal organism.

In its development, Nature follows a dialectic process in which the opposites find a synthesis that will subsequently also find their opposite, and so on successively. Hegel, although he does not recognise it, will use this dynamic in order to apply it to his philosophy of history. In fact, Schelling had already advanced this idea dear to Hegel: the self-development of the absolute consciousness, not only in Nature but also in history (*System of Transcendental Idealism*). In his search, always directed to integrate reality, Schelling conceives the concept of the Absolute where Nature and Spirit, object and subject fuse in a Unity. There is no doubt that Schelling had a *transcendental intuition* thanks to which the Absolute is shown as immutable, always identical, without diminishing or changing its nature in its infinite manifestations (*Presentation of my System*).

Schelling acutely perceives that the Spirit possesses a *natural principle* that inevitably makes it become Nature, for which he cannot remain as a pure spiritual Being. In my idea, the human spirit (although at this level of consciousness it would be incorrect to call it human), can leap ahead and experience the pure Spirit in itself, which transcends Nature, from whose perspective he sees the Spirit spreading across the World, becoming an inseparable part of the same. I must confess that I do not perceive the said *natural principle*, however, since it fits so well in my idea, I tend to accept it as a reality.

Another of Schelling's great contributions is the incorporation of art into the knowledge of the Absolute. Without any hesitation I agree with him that art, in fact, has the virtue of recognizing the Spirit in Nature and in this way reveals the Absolute; the artist can recognize and express the eternal and perceive the unity in the multiple. The artists and ideologues of Romanticism joyfully subscribed to this vision; I believe it was mainly this that made him the philosopher of the movement. Schelling also sees in the artist the capacity of unifying the subjective with the objective. I could agree with this, but I prefer to talk of the *unitive*, because one is dealing with a direct vision of unity rather than a convergence between those opposites. But my intention is not to entangle the reader with concepts, but to clear the air; since they are visions that superimpose and coincide. It is in his *Philosophy of Art*, which I have commented in *The Roots of Art*, that Schelling reaches his highest level.

Although Fichte and Schelling might not have used this terminology, the incorporation of faculties other than reason and faith, which I have called *unitive,* that were overspent with use is one of their invaluable merits; the former were the ethical, the latter the aesthetic. Moral philosophy and the philosophy of art are indispensable mediums to reach the Transcendent; the ignorance of the latter is what makes the modern epistemologist reduce knowledge to the horizon of reason.

The Romantic philosophers do not seem to notice at what point the displacements of their spirits make them adopt different perspectives or visions. The direct perception of the Absolute is fundamentally the product of a *unitive perspective* or vision, while the development of Nature or human history inevitably takes one to an objective vision. Hegel adheres to the latter and thus to his reason, while Fichte and Schelling alternate between one perspective and another. I believe it is very important to have a clear position of the spirit when formulating a theory of knowledge. The case of Schelling illustrates well this play of perspectives. In the period that we could call unitive (accepted as a *system of identity*), Schelling has no doubt that he is seeing Nature integrate itself in the Spirit, that he is talking of the essence of Reality, but later he feels the need to explain the process followed by Nature and man, for which he adopts an objective perspective, which is necessary in order to observe the said process that develops in time and space, but which distances and alienates him from unity, and takes him to a dualist vision; in which, in the process of thinking, and here lies the trap of reason, he gradually falls, until his final alienation.

The problem here is that he renounces the identity he had intuited in his earlier system. However, he visualizes Nature as an evolution that goes from the inorganic to the organic state and from here to the spiritual; nature increasingly gains consciousness until it reaches freedom in man. This seems plausible to me. Sri Aurobindo (see my commentary on him in *The Evolution of the Spirit*), reaches a similar conclusion, except that this mystic philosopher does not forget the Spirit, while Schelling at this level seems to have forgotten it, for what reason we do know not.

Schelling affirmed (in his *Foundations for a Philosophy of Nature*), that in its first phase the Absolute objectivises itself in an ideal Nature, in a universal model. We will see later, when talking about *primary manifestations*, how much truth is enshrined in this affirmation, which is a pure expression of idealism. We can, then, agree with Schelling that the Absolute is objectivised in Nature, but in a second phase it is made subjective. Here we must tread with care and observe the displacements of the spirit, because this subjectivity does not now obey the original perspective, but the individual consciousness of man who has been alienated from the former, from its Essence. In the same way Schelling infers a third phase in which the Absolute returns to its original unity, but he does not seem to notice that it is the human spirit which aspires to its origin, while the Absolute, since it is so, remains immutable. In Hegel the universal Spirit and the human spirit will take up a common search, but both authors commit the same mistake of adapting the universal Spirit, what is transcendental to reason.

I do not share the anthropocentric inclination that involves all Nature in human designs. For my part I consider it useful to think that the Organism is made of minor organisms, like galaxies and, within these, stellar systems, this would allow us to naturally visualize our system like a solar organism, as we know the dependent relation of our planet's life with the shining star. In my view, Nature is not there "for" the spirit to develop, (besides it is impossible to know the endgame of Nature), but it is the medium, (and we know this pragmatically) in which the spirit develops. Nature, as Schelling says clearly, knows itself by the spirit, but it is imbued with the spirit and it is in the measure that we recognise its impregnation that it acquires meaning; i.e. as the real becomes ideal. When the phenomenal becomes *noumenal*, transcendent, Unity becomes real; then Nature has completed its mission.

Since the framework of Nature is infinite in time and space, and the infinite is a concept that cannot be apprehended by the human being, hypothesizing on its destiny is to leave the field of knowledge and to enter into that of fantasy. Within this field countless theories can be wagered whose value of knowledge will always be doubtful. We can only be assured that Nature contains the Spirit and tends towards Him.

The fact that the human being has achieved the greatest knowledge on this planet, could lead us to believe that within this context Nature was guided towards the creation of our species an idea suggested by Kant, but we know that our solar system is an insignificant point within Nature, other beings, in other solar systems could with equal validity use the same argument, and thus we would not be sustaining a universal argument.

Since my philosophy adheres to the knowledge of certitudes, it does not speak of the teleology of Nature, but of a teleology of man within it, which is the knowledge of its own essence, which is the Essence of Nature. After the realization of this knowledge or destiny, if at any time he achieves it as a species, only the expression of the same remains, i.e. his natural expression within the moral aesthetic and spiritual Order in general. We can infer this from the example of enlightened individual men.

Schelling's Intuition

It is undeniable that in his philosophy of Nature, Schelling overcomes the subject object dilemma; Nature and Spirit will be manifestations of the Absolute. He glimpses this and the Unity that underlies his manifestation through an intellectual intuition, but does not manage to change his perspective, for this reason he maintains that the Spirit can only be recognised in the becoming, he does not see the *Spirit in Itself*, and he denies that it can be seen in this way. There is no mistake in his vision but short-sightedness; he needed to make a leap towards the Transcendent in order to see from It how overflows into Nature. He intuits that the subject-object identity takes place in the Spirit, but since he cannot remain in the (perspective of the) Spirit, he acknowledges Him in its manifestations; without observing that in this way he places his nucleus of consciousness in the becoming. This means that he finds a plausible rational response, but not a vital and integral solution, he does not identify with the Transcendent, and he does not find liberation.

His intuition, however, leads him to delineate a new project of evolution: There is an unconscious force that functions in Nature, that becomes manifest in man like a process of self-consciousness that tends to reach and realize the Spirit as such. Schelling correctly notes that in this process of self-consciousness the spirit tends towards freedom, but he does not conceive of the latter as an experience, rather it occurs to him to identify the latter with death, when it is precisely the very Source of Life; which once again shows that he cannot see from the other side of reality.

For Schelling the original "idea" is unconscious but it tends to generate a progressive consciousness. To my understanding, this posture is an inversion of Platonic idealism, which is derived from a lack of perception of the idea or of *ideas in themselves*. If it is seen as Schelling sees it, from a rational perspective, it will appear as "unconscious" because it does not have a structure or way of being rational, but reason is not the paradigm of the conscious, it is a recourse of man, a limited faculty suitable for the concrete reality and for practical ends. If it were reasoning the pure Consciousness would cease to be, as would God, if He were to exist as a rational being. In its conception it is similar to that of Hegel for whom the Idea also had a dark background which human reason had to complete with its light; and this is so because they do not see light in itself.

Schelling realizes that in this process of self-consciousness there is an opposite force that identifies with "reflection", by which he understands egocentric thought, which takes over the weight of animal nature. In this he shows a psychological penetration that Hegel lacked.

Schelling observes sharply that there is an egocentric vision that the philosopher should avoid. I believe that we could clear the scene from my angle of vision: this reflection is born from discernment that is intimately linked to the *I*, and that imposes on it an egocentric vision. But even if this is the basic mechanism of most mortals, a change of perspective, generated by a leap in the level of consciousness, can make discernment and the said reflection come to the service of more elevated ends that transcend personal interest; this takes place from the *mediate unitive consciousness* (see my *Psychosophy.*)

When I speak of the knowledge of the Absolute "in itself" I do not mean that it exists autonomously independent of my consciousness, but that it is the way it is and not determined by my individual consciousness that is seen from it in absolute identity with consciousness. Even Schelling speaks, in his *System of Philosophy*, of "a true in Itself that falls in the point of in-difference of the subjective and the objective". For Schelling "the *I* sacrifices its own individuality for its own act", however, the matter is not resolved with an act of will of the *I*, imposing itself as a working hypothesis but through the natural disappearance of the same.

What I observe time and again in Schelling is a rational *tour de force*, even, if he intuits that he should transcend reason in order to reach the Absolute. And it is precisely in this effort that he shows his weakness, and from then on he forces the Spirit to manifest itself in the becoming, the One to reveal itself in the Other. And this weakness or lack of clarity in vision becomes manifest when he distances himself from these transcendent realities in order to adapt his philosophy to religion, when he inserts the idea of God which seems unnecessary to me. And he commits the grave error (Hegel too), of wanting to see behind the Transcendent, when he still has not seen the latter with clarity. Then the question is posed: "What does God want when he creates the World?" With this he personalises Him and supposes that there has to be a Creator behind Nature. "He wants to be himself, reveal himself to himself, be the Other than himself". But since Schelling does not want to leave his pantheism, he says that the World is the exterior side of God. We can agree or not, but if there is no way to prove the existence of God (Kant), it will be less so for His Creation. Matter, he maintains, would be the unconscious side of God who even though separate Nature from Him, He tries to again attract it making matter conscious. This double process is very much in keeping with my thought but Schelling stays on this side of reality, which makes him postulate a God on the other side, when it was going so well with the impersonal Spirit.

In his search for unity Schelling starts with some of Fichte's premises, but he gradually advances overcoming the latter's duality that he applies to reality: that of the *I* and the non *I*. Why – he asks in his search – should the Non *I* not also be the same as the *I*? Observe the agility of his spirit in this that leads him to a complete change of perspective that allows him to see an interaction and in this integration. In this manner he establishes a dialectic process between Nature and Spirit. In this process he recognises an unconscious force that increasingly becomes conscious until it reaches man, who either participates or is an actor in a history of self-consciousness and is part of the evolutionary process of Nature that is forming, becoming complex and expanding in multiple directions obeying a force similar to Bergson's *vital élan*.

In these points that I have summed up from the *Philosophy of Nature*, I agree with Schelling (and with Bergson; see my commentary on the latter in *The Evolution of the Spirit*). Schelling however continues to use his old terminology which according to me complicates and diverts the matter; I am referring to the concepts of the *I* and of the subject and object. Thus the Spirit should be the Object for itself, even if it is originally not an Object but the absolute Subject for which everything is the Object, as if the Spirit were thinking in these dualist terms. And since Nature and Spirit are one single reality and the former is permanent productivity, the Spirit will also be so; and here he adds that the Spirit realizes Itself in the progressive realization of men, through the self-consciousness of the free men.

This will be a central idea of Hegel's thought, even though he will never recognize the plagiarism, and he will make both incur in what we could call *cosmic subjectivism,* as it is not man who would become conscious of his approach to the universal Spirit, as can be imagined, but the reverse. This error springs from the beginning with an *I*, which however universal, obeys an individual point of view. There can be a pan-psyche from the point of view of the universal Spirit, but not from the human point of view; Hegel will construct his entire system from this erroneous premise; he does not discover the Absolute, he constructs it. I have the repeated impression that Hegel has borrowed his great ideas from Schelling, who had experienced the Transcendent and got his ideas from there. Hegel, frankly speaking, heard the church bells ring but did not know their provenance; he then not only invented church bells but a whole cathedral, not with his intuitions but with his discernment.

Schelling's Religion

Schelling could not explain Unity nor the evolution of Nature, and so he abandoned his earlier position thus committing in my opinion, a grave error. Here there is a limitation of the spirit that finds itself at this point at the vertex of Reality. Thus, instead of recognizing that it is an absolute perspective from which the spirit can shift towards other perspectives, that are closer to Nature, he takes his spirit without warning closer to his own individuality and reason where he finds appropriate concepts but to express another reality now. And in this way he slips into the becoming, from whose perspective Unity disappears and duality reappears, in which Nature, as if it were looking to spiritualize itself changes from being an inorganic to an organic matter and from the organism to the spirit in order to reach the human being. We can only notice here an inversion and an anthropomorphic view of reality in which the Spirit has the human being as the objective and no vice versa. Here it is not clear whether there is a force that pushes Nature, as he thought in its earlier period, nor a force of attraction, and thus we do not know why Nature works in this way. He intuits, however, that the aspiration of the human spirit is towards freedom, and with this I agree.

At this stage in life, Schelling seems to be lost, and thus he takes the old recourse of faith, to which he applies his discernment and not his creative intellect to justify the supposedly "revealed" Scriptures. It is difficult to say at which point Schelling, in his desire to be the most recognized thinker of his age, gives in to his vision of religion and moves towards Christianity. But since this is something that we cannot know, perhaps it is futile to raise the issue. What is certain is that his philosophy degenerates perceptibly when it tries to level with established religion. The personalization of God, an idea that was perhaps born as a result of his opposition to Hegel's Idea, who, for Schelling, represents negative philosophy while his own represents the positive, leads him to lose his initial lofty state where the Absolute reigned supreme. It is well known that the competition with Hegel became an obsession for him and after the former's death, he was appointed professor in Berlin, where they gave him charge of the philosophy of religion so that he could rectify Hegel's philosophy, which even though it never did a disservice to Christianity, had nothing orthodox about it. Schelling had become another instrument of official religion.

Thus, God manifests himself in time and space and concretely in the person of Jesus, in Judea; and finally in the Christian myth that he calls revelation in opposition to the earlier mythology. We see that he does not talk through his own perception or "revelation", he accepts what he has inherited; as a philosopher he was finished. He managed to get the recognition of his contemporaries, but lost his historical mission of transforming, reinterpreting and above all reanimating the religious consciousness which was languishing in the West. Schelling and Hegel, commit the double mistake of trying to adapt their philosophy to Christianity. What is curious about the matter is that both of them disparage their philosophy in the name of an objective that they never achieve because even with their adaptations they were too far from the Orthodox Christianity which never accepted them.

At this point of his doctrine, Schelling changes his concept of the Absolute, which will now not be the subject-object identity of the Spirit and Nature, but only the Spirit. In this way Nature, the finite, detaches itself (it was detached from an uncertain past), from the Absolute and *falls* into... sin. Nevertheless, from that moment the finite begins to reincorporate itself in the Absolute; and this will be the history of humanity. With this change Schelling does not only betray his earlier philosophy but also the Romanticism of which he had become the leader philosopher. Now it is not Nature that is part of the Absolute, abandoning this pantheism that had brought nature to the forefront, he moves it to a second plane. This would not be so serious if he had not introduced the idea of "sin", the murky idea with which Christianity has sullied all life. This sinister cloud that had darkened the Medieval Age hovers over a Nature that shone with an aesthetic glow. With this concession from Schelling the hope of liberation from the burdens of Christianity is once again lost. The ode to life and joy that was Romanticism is transformed once more into a lament, an ode to death. Nietzsche was completely right in accusing Christianity of this burden.

By trying to adapt his philosophy to religion, Schelling takes the only religion that he really knows and adopts its myths, that of creation and the fall. But since this religion is dualist by definition, he has to divide the Unity from the Absolute, and this is his "fall" as a philosopher. He commits the grave "sin" of adapting his philosophy to these myths, thus inverting the order of things and the order of knowledge to the point of disintegrating his system.

Schelling correctly notes that mythology has unconscious roots, but instead of seeing a process in the inner psychic life of man, as in my philosophy (see my *Parallel Civilizations*) for him it is a stage in the inner life of God. The latter is in a stage of development, as it is for Hegel; although it is not easy to understand how a perfect being could be so. Neither, of course, that a personal being be infinite. Schelling has these contradictions and others as he keeps adapting to Christianity. Thus, the Revelation, that for him of course is a higher stage than mythology (as if Christianity was not replete with this), is not produced as in my conception due to the plane of understanding used and to a certain level of consciousness of the individual who receives it, but due to an act of the will of God, who does so in a fixed time and place for the first time in the person of Jesus of Galilee. We should presuppose that Schelling completely ignored the fact that the Vedas in India, written fifteen hundred years before Christ, was also considered a divine revelation. The Koran later claims the same right and it is difficult to believe that Schelling could have ignored that as well. Of course one cannot make an interpretation of the universal Being reducing his manifestations to a single culture, this means that He cannot be seen from a provincial point of view.

By coming closer to Christianity, Schelling goes farther away from the Absolute, to the point of gratuitously, illogically and dogmatically affirming that "the absolute I is the Son of God", for this reason "we will celebrate the incarnation as a man of God"; in this way he concludes his *Bruno*. I don't think it was worthwhile to sacrifice his philosophy in order to accommodate it to a mythology; a grave error that will have given him some passing privileges, but which will make him stumble as a philosopher. He, who had all the gifts to leave us a perennial philosophy, would be dragged along by a secular weakness. How many times have we seen great spirits hollowed out by the small cracks of the soul!

Schelling's change of direction in his last years can be compared to the desertion of an outstanding soldier during the thick of battle who seeks refuge in a secure outpost. When he had reached the highest point of idealism from which he could have thrown his spear forward, he let it fall and stepped back to look for support in an obsolete doctrine, as the French Revolution had noisily proved in the life of the author. Since I have found this spear of idealism thrown on the ground, although covered with the dust of so much sterile philosophy accumulated over one and half centuries, I have taken the liberty to pick it up in the conviction that with it I can continue the march of idealism towards its destiny.

Schelling's change of direction is seen as a particularly conspicuous paradox, however much he protested against "the scandal" that philosophy offered when each philosopher presumed truths that were opposed to others, when he himself was capable of generating such disparate philosophies that seem to come from different thinkers. Even the language he uses is different. I think that when he was an adult even he would have been shocked at the dogmatic language he used as an old man. (For example: "*The miracle* of the gracious revelation of the *mystery* of the divine being", in *Philosophy of Mythology*). And the "scandal" was ever greater than he imagined: While Schelling aged in creativity, A. Comte published his *Course of Positive Philosophy*, in which the last "age of the world" imagined by Schelling, that of revealed religion, was displaced by Comte to a primitive stage and overcome by the man of positive spirit, similarly Marx maintained that religion constituted an illusory world created by man in his alienation of the sole reality.

The fissure through which this great spirit filtered itself also elevated the ego as usually happens: the competition between Hegel and him that led him to search for an outdated "positive philosophy", and his aspiration of recovering the sceptre of "official philosopher", that had been taken away from him by Hegel. This low aspiration made him fall and lose perspective. But I am far from censoring Schelling for these inconsistencies, on the contrary, I have done everything possible to highlight his creativity and rescue his correct assessments. We have to reflect on the unity that he intuited in his most lucid moments:

"In all of us there resides a secret marvellous power in order to *liberate us from the changes of time*, to remind us of our secret individuality away from externals, and thus we discover the eternal without transformation. This manner of showing us to ourselves is the truest *personal experience* on which the supra sensual world depends as we all know. This representation shows us for the first time the *real existence* before which everything other *only seems to be*. Different from any other representation for its *perfect freedom*, while all the other representations are limited, overwhelmed by the weight of the object. This intellectual representation occurs when the object stops being such, when retreating in ourselves, the image emerges as self-perceived. At that moment we eliminate time and the duration of time, we are no longer in time and *the very eternity is in us*." (*Philosophical Letters upon Dogmatism and Criticism*) The italics are mine in order to highlight that all the elements of a *transcendental intuition* are present: elimination of time, perception of the eternal, in front of which concrete reality seems to disappear and the spirit flies free.

Hegel

As with Medieval Age, the reader can skip this chapter, since Hegel, like Christianity, is outside the quest that we are looking for.

Two reasons have led me to leave Hegel outside the scope of this work: firstly, I have already dealt with him in *The Evolution of the Spirit*, secondly Hegel is not part of the line of idealism that we are following, which coherently searches for consistent consciousness in the progressive integration of the Spirit with Nature; this integration depends fundamentally on an inner growth that leads to an elevated level of consciousness. Hegel simply ignores this growth and the need for it; he believes that everything can be resolve with reason without going through these vexations. As do Fichte and Schelling, it is true, but they repose faith in intellectual intuition as another road towards the same end. Not so Hegel, who is determined to pave the way of history with his discernment which he uses like an elephant of the spirit, bulldozing all obstacles, in its path without concerning himself with the amount of historical material that is tossed, nor and above all, with its victims.

Hegel also betrays the other form of idealism that we have pointed out, the moral that is projected as hope in an ideal. But if there are no high ideals that maintain the spirit in an ascending dynamic, the spirit, like a physical law, descends and falls into some of the well-known human vices; hence the importance of this form of idealism. This is a force, a positive energy that activates our virtues, but since it is not necessarily a product of knowledge, it can bring with it vices that the enthusiastic subject will end up excusing in the name of his ideals. Hegel has no future for the human being, his entire history is based on the universal Spirit, there is no moral imperative, nor ideal, but only an Idea that uses man for its own purpose. His history teaches us only that things are as they had to be. Here there is no outlet, no liberation, except for his Idea.

Hegel starts from a premise laden with scepticism that he accepts without demur: "the real world is as it should be", (chap. "*The historical motors*" (101-104, *La Raison dans l'Histoire*): "History shows itself to be the altar on which the well-being of people, the wisdom of the States and the virtue of individuals have been sacrificed". In it, "the passions, the objectives with a particular interest, the satisfaction of self-love, are the greatest power". "The natural force of passion is more connected with human nature than the long and artificial learning of the sense of order and moderation, of law and morality". Thus, "in order to tolerate (this spectacle of history), we tell ourselves: it has been like this; it is destiny; nothing can be changed". "We have started our reflections with these considerations". But he does not direct these to search for solutions but "in order to know for whom and to what end these immense sacrifices have been made". "We do not want to see more than the means in the service of which" (they have been realized), "the true result of universal history"; is the latter's its preoccupation and task. There is nothing exemplary here, not even an education for our future. The only winner is the universal Spirit. He tells us nothing about what we can learn from Him, as he unconsciously manifests himself through an astuteness to achieve his goals.

Hegel does not discover truths, he constructs them, and even God has to adjust himself to his construction. In talking of the State this procedure becomes more manifest. The State does not just provide facilities "Man owes everything he is to the State. All his bravery, all spiritual reality is only because of the State." (*136*) Did he think, for example that Jesus who lived in a village and who would be executed by the heads of that village, owed everything to this State? Did he wonder as to how many distanced themselves from the State in order to improve their spirituality? He did not, for it is in this that he finds the Truth: "Truth is the unity of subjective will and general will" which happens in the State. What does a scientific discovery like the theory of relativity, for example or artistic creation have to do with general will? Nothing. He also constructs ethical truth in a similar manner: The State is the real and existent ethical life, as it is the unity of the subjective want and general and essential and want". What do loyalty, prudence, courage; all the virtues that emanate from one's intimate being have to do with the State? And in this way, after constructing with reasons that escape reality and clash with common sense, Hegel brings the same Idea in order to divinize the State: "What the State has of divine, is the Idea as it exists on earth." "The States and individuals offer to us figures in which we should study the manifestations of the spirit" (*139*). As if the State was not an entity governed by leaders who most of the time are power hungry and look for their own benefit and have no idea of Hegel's Idea nor that of any universal Spirit. Of course, the latter is manifested unconsciously; another dogma in which we should believe in order to follow him. And as if this were not enough, just as he was taught in theology school he puts the Christian dogma, including the belief in the son of God and the superiority of this religion over all others, without bothering to learn about other doctrines which he vilifies and delegitimises in the manner of some local parish priest.

As I have noted elsewhere, dogma is the closure of the spirit in external faculties. Once the spirit is closed it does not seek verification in experience but its confirmation in discernment, which is a submissive subject, with the task of finding data, reasons, excuses etc. in order to "prove" the "truth" of faith. This is the mechanism used by apologetics and which should be included within Sophism. The only difference, in favour of Greek sophism is that this was a conscious technique in which the Sophist tried to demonstrate any "truth". We have the example of the Greek Sophist invited by the Roman Senate who received an ovation from the patricians for the demonstration he had made, but the next day he went and showed that the truth he had shown was false. "This is Sophistry", he exclaimed. The senators who had believed the first demonstration felt they had been scorned and had him exiled. That is the difference. The believer, the typical Scholastic, has the ingenuity to believe the reasons that he produces in order to sustain the faith in which he believes; something that is invalid from a philosophical point of view.

This is what Hegel does with his own Idea which he "demonstrates" with his discernment until he is completely enclosed within it like an autistic person. He talks to us of a universal reality, it is true, but all of it takes place within a bubble in his mind. In this kind of scholasticism we have a monumental example of how a mind can be enclosed and lost in discernment. What is surprising is that this happens after Kant, who hadn't seen the said psychological mechanisms but knew well the leaps in the air and the resultant blows of Scholasticism.

Hegel had suffered a Christian education; one has to accept his dogmas as if they were the Word of God. The basic dogma is that the real is rational; the next dogma is that the reasons of the author are the rational ones. The rest is well structured, undoubtedly, but if we take out the dogmas and apply common sense, his system falls like a house of cards. And we should do so, because philosophy is the love for knowledge, not the obsession to discern; without the light of philosophy, thought seekers will be directionless however much they reason. And if the philosophers, who are the ones who have to show us our destiny, are directionless, even the State will be adrift in the current of history. Hegel "logically" ends up justifying all history, including its countless aberrations, as "this great mass of desires, interests and activities constitute the instruments and means used by the Spirit of the World."

Following the spirit and Christian recourse of submission, Hegel urges us to obey Providence, the intentions of which are only understood by great men, who are not the wise men or moralists but men of State. In Hegel there is alienation with respect to Nature and even with respect to divinity as they mean nothing to him and he does not receive any inspiration from them, he thus alienates the Spirit and alienates us from the latter. Nature is a soulless field, just as in Christianity, where the human spirit develops for the benefit of the universal Spirit; and reality is thus entirely inverted. Hegel betrays those of the Renaissance and the Romantics by subtracting the Soul that these had conferred to Nature.

The entire effort to discover the Spirit of Nature from Plato to Schelling is wasted. After centuries of disdain for Nature, the Renaissance reverts this trend, there is a rediscovery of the beauty of the world, and the Beautiful is intuited in it. In Rousseau, that was a source of inspiration for the romantics, we find this trend. This entire effort of the integration of man in Nature is ruined by Hegel. History develops thus at the margin of all morality, what triumphs is the current generated by the majority made up of individuals who pursue selfish interests. In reality, individuals do not count in history it is the will of people that triumphs. This idea, which will be central in Communism, not only clashes with the evidence of the contribution of the geniuses in it, but also ignores the importance of the exemplary life of superior individuals, of its heroes. In Greece, in particular, epic and dramatic literature is inspired in exemplary men due to their virtues. In this way, literature and art have been decisive in Hellenic culture and in a most real and effective way this has contributed to the inner growth of these people allowing them to achieve the highest strata of the spirit. To ignore this is to ignore the most decisive in psychology, education and history.

Hegel, who has the spirit of scholasticism in his veins, wants to demonstrate not only that Providence exists, what would be for him "incomplete knowledge", but also the way it functions, as "the Spirit is its act, it is only what it does... (*Phil. of Law, 343*) "it makes the world, where it is alienated, in order to become more complete, to a higher degree of knowledge" (*Op. cit.*) That the Spirit of the world is alienated and evolves, seems to us to be too human, now, that it depends on our history it is already an inflation of man (of Hegel) on a universal scale. "History (...) is the necessary development of moments of Reason, of its consciousness of itself and its liberty; it is the explanation of the realization of the universal Spirit (*Op. cit. 342*) The later explanation continues adjusting to the discernment of Hegel: the spirit goes through different peoples to whom it keeps giving "its greatest achievements and glory" (*Op. cit. 345*) "The dominant people in the history of the world have as their mission the fulfilment of the evolutionary process of the consciousness of the Spirit of the world". This is another Christian trait, a missionary attitude that justifies its imposition, since "he is the representative of the spirit of the world; the spirit of other peoples are without a law, like those whose time has passed and do not count anymore in history" (*Op. Cit. 347*).

My vision of the spirit of peoples in history is very different: When a civilization is very settled in its tradition and has a philosophical, religious, artistic and moral storehouse, with which it organizes its society, its science, its laws and the systems of government, i.e. when a civilization proper has been established, the spirit remains forever in this people, as it has all the spiritual resources to be reborn after the catastrophes that accompany history. This is the case of the three greatest civilizations that our planet has produced: the Hellenic, the Indic and the Chinese whose rebirths and resurgences prove my theory. Everything seems to indicate that the Spirit still has a task to fulfill and is again preparing its residence in the Far East.

There is a certain parallelism in the mental process that Jesus and Hegel followed. These two acted like dispensers of ideas that would be taken up by more concrete minds like Paul and Marx, and later by the Church or Lenin, Stalin and Mao who will apply these ideals *manu militari*, making of them an instrument of political and economic power. The example illustrates how the same idea is seen and applied in a different way in keeping with the shifts and residences of the spirit in the mind of each one of them, in such a way that the idea follows a progressively dogmatic and earthly descendant path, until it lands in the spirits of politicians and those who are ambitious for power whose egocentric perspective is opposed to the creators of original ideas.

I have always suspected that Hegel took his Idea from Schelling. Maybe he had a transcendental intuition, but this was not enough, it was in any case an isolated fact, a ray of light that illuminated his discernment and later shut down; but it was sufficient to give force to his discernment with which he began to construct his system. He did not later receive other intuitions (although he did take other ideas from Schelling), in order to continue lighting his path, he followed only with his reason believing that this was his light. In this way his philosophy was structuring and growing, disconnected now from the universal Spirit, it was distancing and taking different paths from the original inspiration. Hegel was alienated from the Spirit with his reason; so his philosophy did not respond to Reality. There is no experience for him, everything is inference. It constructs from here, from the concrete, to the beyond, the spiritual. For this reason the spirit is made of acts and from the acts, human history, is *induced.* This *shift of the centre of consciousness*, this *inversion in perspective* is extremely important in the history of thought and as a result in the history of the West. His perspective would be the same as that of Feuerbach, for whom it is man who creates God and for Marx, who just had to remove out the Spirit from the scene to be alone with matter and with all the baggage of Hegel, in order to establish the lowest philosophy that our species could conceive of. This is the fundamental reason why I have not included Hegel among the idealists that I have chosen, because they begin from some experience of the Essence of the World from which they deduce reality, their perspective is diametrically opposed to his; since it is this *essential perspective* which is the objective of this search that concerns us.

The dialectics of history

The historicist vision of Hegel, whose origins are Judeo-Christian, places him in the antipode of the *unitive* vision maintained by *universal idealism.* By making of an ideal

Being the greatest protagonist of history, he aligns himself amongst the idealists, but alienates himself from the human spirit; although there are many who by not paying attention to their own alienation, and that of Hegel, elevate him to the pedestal of idealism. In the best of cases it is another kind of idealism, based on discernment, which does not see more than facts and concepts, and distances and alienates itself from the unitive consciousness, and hence from the creative intuition, from cyclical vision and finally from Unity. Since Hegel cannot see this in its immediacy, he projects and develops reality in history, and since he does not find sense in human history of itself, as he himself confesses, he projects it onto an ideal being. And this has a lot of moral idealism, and he unsurprisingly adapts his philosophical idealism to this bud of theology. However, this God of Hegel was of no use to the Christians or to anyone, it was no more than a cloud created with his logic which the currents of history, following the new trends, would soon dissipate. And more seriously, with the heavens made bereft of gods, only matter and human history remained: In fact, with materialism, exteriorization and alienation would be complete and the spirit would achieve its perigee; and since then we have lived in a spiritual darkness.

We should understand this once and for all: history in general has lacked and will be devoid of meaning until man understands its Unity. It is not history that makes unity, but Unity that makes history. Those who have made history fecund are the idealists whose inspiration and aspiration is Unity, be they mystic philosophers or artists, and some exceptional visionaries who have seen in them the future of humanity.

Although I might have differences with Hegel as regards his interpretation of the historic moments with which he wove his dialectics, I agree with him that human history is dialectically developed. But where I find the greatest discrepancy is in the origin or the impulse behind the said dialectic, in fact I find myself at the opposite end of the spectrum: while Hegel thinks it is the way that the universal Spirit expresses itself and imposes this model in history, I maintain that what makes men act by reaction take opposite sides and what leads them to exclusive dualisms and to extremes, is *incipient reason*, and the last thing that occurs to me is to think that the universal Spirit is still in this mental stage. The truth is that the Spirit of Hegel is far from being universal; it obeys a Biblical tradition that is egocentric at first and consequently geocentric and anthropocentric. It might or might not revolve around the sun, this planet continues being the centre of the universe, and like all its living beings, it is stupid material at the service of man. This primitive and provincial vision does not correspond to the size of the universe. This is the reality: "The human being is a kind of advanced monkey, who lives on a small planet that revolves around a mediocre star." (Stephen Hawkins). In my work I have never looked to scientists for support, but it is interesting that I entirely agree in this respect with the vision of the most notable scientist of our age; and it is conducive for philosophy and the sciences to come to terms with each other. Three centuries before Hegel, Giordano Bruno was closer to this vision, but he was condemned because he did not adjust to the narrow point of view of Genesis.

Thus the dialectics of history, far from being the result of an elevated and inevitable Reason, are the product of a poor reason that still governs the human being, incapable of appreciating nuances, of avoiding dogmas, of maintaining equilibrium. They also belong to the clan of incipient reason those who search for reasons for themselves and not for "truth in itself." The man of spirit, on the contrary, has the *spirit located relatively or totally in his central or unitive Consciousness,* which is what allows him to articulate all his faculties in equilibrium. This perspective allows him to *observe the intentions* of his internal plane, his desires and fears, weigh them in the balance of his moral consciousness and make up his mind in keeping with this balance. *This concert of faculties is the generator of the zone of psychic and moral equilibrium.*

The universal Spirit, perceptible from the central or unitive Consciousness, inspires the just means, the equilibrium in thought and action. The alienation of man from this centre, takes him to extremes. This means that man has effectively taken this dialectical rhythm due to his own foolishness and he will continue to do so until he understands this principle that our doctrine maintains. Of course, the process of harmonious interaction that takes the spirit to the *zone of equilibrium* should be realized in a gradual manner, in such a way that the gap between the extremes is slowly filled. There will always be a dialectical evolution, it is true, but the less distance there lies between these extremes, the more man will avoid falling into them, history will be less forced and suffering will be reduced.

Idealism and Philosophy of History

The necessary character that underlies all the actions of man and of his history, probably influenced by Calvinist determinism, that we find in Kant and in the idealists, apparently explain the sense of history. Finding sense in a process without sense is highly noteworthy, but when we think of it at length, we begin to doubt its worth. In the first place the destiny of man is always uncertain, enough for us to not believe that it *has* to fulfill itself in some way, unless we introduce a dogma that we have to accept; and this is what Hegel does by imposing the identity of the real with the rational, although it is known that the recourse of the dogma is not very philosophical. On the other hand, even when we accept its explanations as sufficient, this determinism would only explain the "destiny of humanity", a concept that is too abstract to explain a reality as tangible as human life. Before fulfillment, at the end of time, as distant as it is uncertain, how can the humanity that we see today be explained? It will be said that it has lived for only a moment in the process that is only explained by the result. But it is not so, for if we consider the thousands of years that have passed and that will pass, we will see that "the moment" is everything. And how is the immense majority of humanity which has, precisely, made history explained? But as long as we continue with this abstract term, which is apparently all encompassing, we will not see the reality of the matter. "Humanity" is made up of men and women, each one of whom also has a destiny and also has a personal life that is inalienable. Should we alienate our single life in the name of a hypothetical social future? And what kind of society would this be? Who would be the winner in the struggle for supremacy?

If there is no explanation for me, for each one of us living beings, what is the value of this explanation that projects the sense of this life that we are living, far beyond our deaths, to the end of time? This Providence that only sees the final result and ignores the millions sacrificed for countless generations, seems to me to be a monstrous divinity that looks impassively over the heights of the horizon while the necessary victims for the initial purpose fall at its feet. We cannot accept this *intention* of Providence (let alone speak of the delirious Calvinist vision), nor of any explanation of history congruent with it. It is pathetic and nefarious to look at history like a battlefield in which victims are unimportant in view of the hypothetic final victory of the final survivors.

My philosophy of history sees each being as a whole, since each life is a totality. And this is not another generalizing abstraction; it is something that each one of us can experience. My discipline proves moreover that on a higher plane, consciousness covers all totality. To kill a human being is to finish off a totality. This teaching seems to me to be much more practical (moral) and decisive as compared to those teleology's that alienate us from our present reality and debase it.

Universal history like each individual history, has no other destiny other than the one man gives to it. If I want to end my particular history, I do so now; I decide my own destiny. But by this I do not in any way wish to imply that my life and the lives of others have no meaning or that this is capriciously decided. Absolutely not, because as soon as I think that I can end my life this minute, I see that I will not be able to do so, a vital force compels me to continue writing and acting and makes me feel like a participant creator of human destiny; a force of aesthetic attraction stops me from abandoning the beauty of this world. These energies perceived with complete clarity by my religious, ethical and aesthetic faculties give meaning to my life, they provide me with a destiny. Here in synthesis is my answer: developing these faculties, awakening consciousness until these forces become evident. Once is achieved, human destiny shows itself with as much evidence as tangible reality, but with much greater vehemence. As can be seen this is not an *ex cathedra* demonstration of a destiny that only the philosopher and Providence know about, and which the rest of the mortals, whether they want to or not, should carry out, but a teaching, an education, so that everyone can be participants informants and volunteers of this common project that is history.

Man is entirely free in his final decision and he can, as is evident through the shades and nuances of his past, realize his most arbitrary, unbelievable and irrational whims. In these contemporary times when history can be abruptly terminated with a single mistake, it is absolutely indispensable to put an end to these romantic utopias that allow and even justify all errors, in the belief that man's destiny has to be fulfilled whatever he might do. If he makes a small mistake, he does not fulfill his destiny, if he errs greatly, he fails as a species. To avoid this failure, which would be a monumental tragedy, through which man would show his ignorance of all past tragedies, it is necessary that he know its origin and his destiny, not at the end of time but here and now.

Idealism, conclusion

By dealing with the German idealists, it has been my intention to superimpose my vision onto that of theirs so that their commonalities become more visible, in order to ratify the truths that underlie them. However much we differ, the reader will be able to verify that the similarities must have had their origin in the same reality that inspires not just us but all living beings, hence the importance of recognizing it in some way. It is true that imagination and rational development took these thinkers very far, and for this reason they have been attacked, but those who have simply disqualified them have also sinned through excess; they should have taken into account that if these authors ventured afar, it is because something forcefully pushed them along. We philosophers are discoverers not inventors. This is that *something* that I am interested in recovering, that inspirational element, before those concrete doctrines that are a consequence and superstructure.

The experience left to us by German idealism is like a great artificial firework display. We marvel and are attracted to it and elevated and start believing that this is the only reality, but in the end we remain in the original darkness, with the same stars, with the same unresolved transcendental problems. The initial fire had something of the real, its intuitions were true, its aspirations were legitimate, but philosophy is a science besides being an art, and has to leave us something more than sensations and reasons. It is not that they did not have reasons, they had them in excess, but if the reasons were not real, of what use were they?

In the attempt to unify object and subject, Spirit and Nature, following the most genuine Hellenic tradition, we find the immense merit of German idealism. This marks an indispensable landmark in understanding the spirit of the West that make a necessary link to recognise the orthodoxy of our thought, the referential line that idealism has traced from the Pre Socratics until today. By *integrating* Nature, and thus man and history in one single Reality, which had been divided by Christianity, idealism takes us out of that *universal alienation* in which Nature and life were reduced to painful means for apparently "another" life while this life could not arrive at its full meaning nor reach plenitude.

It is not completely mistaken to incorporate the Spirit in the becoming and thus assimilate it to Nature, but this is only one part of reality, an aspect of the Spirit, that leads one to an insufficient pantheism, in which the Transcendent is excluded because the Spirit in itself is not perceived, it is only intuited from *outside*. *Pantheism* takes on its full meaning when it is seen from the perspective of the Spirit, as from there it can be seen how it overflows into Nature, life, the mind and the heart, in such a way that our consciousness and existence take on full meaning.

Following Hellenic orthodoxy and rectifying the errors of past idealism, in my philosophy and transcendental psychology, i.e., my *Psychosophy*, I feel I have arrived at a felicitous conclusion in this millenarian search. Of course, this does not mean the end of the task of the universal Spirit, as Hegel wished, or the end of thought, but on the contrary, the beginning of a new way of seeing and understanding the *Universus* in which we live.

The Romanticism of artists

An error which philosophy professors and even some philosophers are prone to commit, is that of interpreting the spirit of an age by its philosophy, as if the latter, when it speaks of the essence of things, expresses better the essence of that spirit. There are periods, and of no less importance, like the Renaissance and Romanticism, in which philosophy lies in the shadow of literature and the arts.

Eighteenth century philosophies tried to reach the Transcendent, but reason was resorted to precisely because religious sentiment had declined. It was a grave mistake trying to fit so much space into such a small recipient but it was understandable because unlike religious sentiment, rationalism was not in such decline. For this reason German idealists even though they had an élan that corresponded to the highest aspirations of Romanticism, used reason when sentiment was scarce, although this was not the case with musicians, poets and artists in general.

Romanticism should be considered as another Renaissance of the spirit, and in this way like the Birth of the spirit of the West in Greece, it was fundamentally artistic; besides its very ideologues were men of literature. The philosophers sailed along the shores of the principal currents, only Schelling waded deep into the water with his philosophy of Nature, and he later lost direction and was adrift. Hegel was an adherent of Romanticism only when he was young, later as we saw, he betrayed it in the name of an extreme rationalism. Nothing was more contrary to the spirit of Romanticism, which was inspired in sentiments, imagination, intuition and lack of confidence in reason; Hegel only believed in the latter and mocked the others. What is more, Romanticism can also be defined as a reaction against rationalism.

The immense contribution of Romanticism is that of having rediscovered Nature, just as the Renaissance rediscovered man, both were discovered and expressed to perfection by the Hellenics. But just as the Renaissance did not express a mere individualism, even though it was considered as having done so, Romanticism did not express a mere realism, Nature was imbued with the Spirit, as has evidently been proven by its art and philosophy, in which the Idea of the universal Spirit that governs the human and universal Order reappears.

Since the elevated sentiments that characterize this movement correspond better to the field of ethics and aesthetics, I will develop this theme in *The Roots of Morality* and in *The Roots of Art.* I am taking only a significant sample from there, as probably nothing better expresses the spirit of Romanticism at its peak than F. von Schiller's *Ode to Joy,* (*An die Freude*). Beethoven must have surely thought so, and for this reason he incorporated it in the last movement of his final symphony, in which the said spirit reaches its apotheosis. I am retrieving some paragraphs here:

"Happiness, beautiful spark of the gods, daughter of Eliseus! Drunk with ardour we penetrate your sanctuary, celestial goddess!" "All beings drink joy in the heart of Nature." Joyful, like the stars that roam the great celestial spaces, go forth on your journey, happily like the hero towards victory." "Don't you see the world, the Absolute?" "Oh World do you not see your origin? Search for it over the canopy of stars!" "Embrace yourselves numerous creatures!" "Brothers!, over the star studded canopy there has to live the *Universal Mind.*"

Schopenhauer

What makes a real philosopher is his unconditional service to the truth. Curiously, even though this is a service that every philosopher should render, very few have been consistent in this objective. In no way do I mean by this that they were not great thinkers, but that they are less reliable, as they let themselves be carried away by beliefs that they adjusted to their feelings, either to their character, or to their own reason, that made them create systems to which the truths had to adjust to. With them we have to be more astute, as "the shrewdness of reason" has no limits; besides, the startling speculative capacity that some have, makes us follow them through the longest and most intricate paths of the spirit, for which we need time and patience besides astuteness.

I believe that Schopenhauer is Kant's most worthy disciple. This is something we should not forget: his dignity as a philosopher, i.e. his submission to truth as he perceived it and his coherence as regards the principles of reason. He has the virtue of presenting life to the naked and making us face the world as it is represented, i.e., without all the impediments implied by the usual baggage of preconceived ideas, latent and inherited beliefs and optimistic inclinations to justify the human condition and to make our miserable existence more tolerable. Lamentably and inevitably, life is as it is and not as we would like it to be. Of course, the great majority lives by illusions, to such an extent that if they are not realized in this world it ends up believing that they will be able to in “the other”, and thus there are so many “believers”.

The true philosopher (as there are many metaphysical illusionists and masters of utopias), firstly avoids illusions and distractions. But disqualifying Schopenhauer for his pessimistic conclusions has been a serious mistake, either due to these ideas and beliefs, optimistic aspirations, or the aforesaid illusions and distractions. One of these professors of philosophy who Schopenhauer could not digest (we will talk about them), ends a little book about our author by saying that its conclusions are “finally the logical price for having substituted the rational premises of the world for an irrational and impulsive essence”. This gentleman starts from the gratuitous belief that the said essence should be rational, i.e., an anthropomorphic being; he already has an *a priori* opinion on how it has to be the essence of the world. Does the reader understand what I have been saying?

I will soon clarify these and other points, because far from disqualifying an eminent thinker like Schopenhauer, I intend to correct him in order to incorporate his rich legacy and redirect the philosophy often perverted and hampered by scholars, who as I mentioned are ignorant of their situation and perception. Schopenhauer clearly says to this effect: “There is nothing more difficult for man than to understand the problem of metaphysics when since childhood an anticipated solution has been imposed on him, as the point of departure of all sincere philosophy is the profound conviction of the truth of Socrates: I only know that I know nothing”. “The accusation that is hurled against metaphysics of having made little progress through the centuries, is rejected keeping in mind that no other science has developed under such constant oppression. In all (European) countries it has been used as an alibi and persecuted by the dominant religion, that finding itself with the monopoly of metaphysical knowledge considered it a bad weed". And with these words he ends his first book of *The World as Will and Representation*: "A system of philosophy has no measure of its value other than truth. Philosophy is essentially the science of the world: the world is its problem; it is its only concern and it leaves the gods in peace, but in return it also asks that it be left in peace." These kinds of appreciations make Schopenhauer's work very edifying reading, because the great philosophers are those who teach us how to see, not how to believe.

I have not included Schopenhauer among the Romantics because his thought emerges when the Romantic spirit was in decadence, but it would be a mistake to attune his figure to that movement and to declare him decadent. We find him depressed, it is true, but due to other external and internal circumstances; his spirit, closed in its individual perspective, felt the anguish of life and set out on a new search: the situation of man in the world. According to me, the concerns of Schopenhauer are completely existentialist; although he maintains a strong tie with the Transcendent, and it is in relation to the latter that the measure of a philosopher is taken.

The World as Will

At the beginning of his main work *The World as a Will and Representation*, Schopenhauer traces out the guiding motives behind his thought that seem impeccable to me: "The main difference between all these representations is that they are intuitive or abstract. The latter is constituted by a class of representations, the concepts". He calls the capacity to produce these reason which is exclusive to man. "The intuitive ones cover the entire visible world, the so called experience, together with the conditions of their possibility". These are the *a priori* forms of time and space laid down by Kant, of whom he insists he is a follower.

The distinction between intuitive and speculative or

conceptual capacity seems to me to be indispensable from the start (*The Return to the Sources*). It also seemed so to Bergson who I have written about in (*The Evolution of the Spirit*). But the first decisive step was taken by Kant, who by reducing the field of reason to phenomenal reality put philosophy on track once and for always. Schopenhauer knows this: "He who does not know about Kant's philosophy is in a state of innocence; a captive of that infantile and ingenuous realism in which we are all born and which will make us ready for everything except philosophy". In fact, when one reads it "one is shorn of all illusions and sees things in other perspectives." (*Pref.* 2° Ed.) Not just Christian thinkers who adjusted reason to dogma fell victim to these illusions, but also the believers in reason itself who attributed to it metaphysical powers that it did not have. Of course, an exit had to be found not for reason but for philosophy, and this lay in intuition. The idealists who preceded Schopenhauer instead of searching for another outlet wanted to overflow the framework established by Kant through reason, hence this commotion with all the symptoms of a derailment that came about.

Schopenhauer doubtlessly shows sincerity and seriousness in his research when he returns to Kantian premises, to which he adds his theory of intuition, which even though it opens a door is still captive to that structure. In fact, on the one hand he continues with the subject-object duality, that Schelling had tried to overcome by all means within his reach, and on the other hand his intuition as in Kant, only transcends the phenomenal in order to find a cause that explains it; two aspects that signify retrogression with respect to idealism. I had seen the need to delink the faculty of intuition from the speculative faculties, but for this I consider it illustrative to separate the same reason into discernment and intellect, since the latter has the capacity to intuit the Transcendent, when the spirit reaches a high level of consciousness. (See my *Psychosophy*), a capacity that Schopenhauer as well as Kant *a priori* deny, i.e. without having investigated the necessary conditions for its actualization.

Man has the very natural tendency of projecting his way of being and thinking on the other. "A thief believes everyone steals", as the saying goes. It is impossible to determine how much this posture has created misunderstanding amongst men. And this same thing has been done with the Cause of the universe. In this way man has imagined a personal God, jealous, wrathful, and vengeful, protector of his people. A little more refined vision has brought him out of the vices and has projected the attributes of perfection in him, something not entirely wrong but it includes reason, will and intention. The number of contradictions that this has generated given the undeniable evil in this world is not sufficient to believe that the Cause could be entirely different. We find this change of attitude in Schopenhauer, who adapts his thought to reality, at least in the way he visualizes it. I think we find in Schopenhauer for the first time an irrational but not a mad Cause distant from the principles of reason. Kant could have arrived at this conclusion as the *noumenal* escaped this faculty but it never occurred to him to try out paths other than that of reason. Schopenhauer concludes that the premises of the world are an unconscious life force that he calls the Will which signifies a giant leap towards the truth of *noumenal* reality.

However, after his intuition, Schopenhauer returns to phenomenal reality in which he wants to demonstrate with his reason the relation of dependence of this reality with respect to the Will, which is valid, but these are still just inductions that do not reach the *noumenal*. I believe that his vision of *noumenal* as well as *phenomenal* reality comes to him from a transcendental intuition, because the latter produces a shift of the spirit towards more spiritual regions and a resultant distancing of external faculties making him see the world as unreal. In my first work I said that one would rarely find a poet who had not expressed this way of seeing, and Buddhism tacitly declares that "the world being as it is, resembles a dream". This is what occurred to Schopenhauer, a distancing from the objective world, that leads him to perceive of it as "a mere representation," with a strong dose of unreality, as illusion (*Maya*); for this same reason he searches for a transcendent support. But lamentably he searches more for a support for the physical than the spiritual order. His Will, in effect, is an energy that tries to explain the priorities of matter, the physic-chemical ones (like gravitation), of plants, of animals and of man. He barely concerns himself of the Will in itself, his preoccupation lies in explaining its relation with the objective world of representations. He declares explicitly: the Himself, the Will, is unknowable; we can only recognize it from its expressions. This lack of knowledge of the Himself does not allow him to see the virtues it possesses and its sacred aspect. By saying this I do not want to jump into religion, or to a religious explanation of the matter, but rather place myself on a basis of experience, truth and philosophy.

Schopenhauer has two points of departure: the first is *the world as representation*, which seems right to me and from which fruitful conclusions can ensue, and the second is *the world as Will*, which seems partial and which should end as a negative vision of reality, even though in the development we find many fecund thoughts. Schopenhauer wants to begin with an immediate reality: "my body and my will are the same thing", except that the "will is the *a priori* knowledge of the body and the *a posteriori* knowledge of the will". (*The World,* II, 18). "The concept of will (...) comes from the very fount of the immediate consciousness of the individual, in which he recognizes himself immediately in its essence" (*Op. cit. 22*). He then projects this transcendent will in itself and makes it the essence of the world that manifests itself in the latter as energy and necessity, as a blind creative force, as an instinct of life.

Using the terminology of German idealists, Schopenhauer says, that the Will "objectifies itself", this seems to indicate that it becomes an object for a subject, which is inappropriate, it seems more correct to say that it emanates, just as the sun projects its light thanks to which life is possible. While there is a subject, a separated demiurge, there are remnants of a personal God or an anthropomorphic vision that derives from the dualistic vision of discernment. For Schopenhauer the whole world is objective, he begins by separating consciousness from the world; it is not surprising that the "Will" also works in the same way. It should be noted that our faculties are also an objectification of Will, but in Schopenhauer there is an unbridgeable gap. Will seems to be of a different nature, hence the disconnection.

While speaking about the instinct of animals and the functions of the body which we are conscious of, he says of Will that it is like a "creative instinct that is externalized" (*The World* II, 23). A little later he includes plant life "with respect to its essence as plant", and, as is to be expected, he extends it "to all those forces that in Nature work according to general and unchangeable laws" to the "phenomena of the inorganic world", like the force of gravity. In conclusion, Will "constitutes the being in itself of all the things of the universe and the exclusive nucleus of all phenomena (*Op cit.*)

I believe that Schopenhauer, like all idealist philosophers has had an original transcendental intuition, which he denies. The fact that, like Hegel, he does not admit to it reveals that the very intuition has passed by unnoticed, which also indicates that they have the spirit centred in their individual consciousness, accustomed to depending on discernment, on which they base their reflections; even though the psychological depth of Schopenhauer allows him to investigate the internal planes of knowledge.

This adherence to reason (discernment) entails serious negative consequences that our philosophers seem to ignore. Firstly the limits imposed by reason. The most unfortunate case is that of Kant, who knew how to mark them out with precision, but in spite of his privileged talent he did not know how to overcome them. Another quite usual and no less harmful consequence is that they continue creating their system; they are committed to what has been said, like spiders that restrict their life to within their web.

I differ radically with Schopenhauer in that, for him, the thing in itself is not an object of knowledge for him, but only as regards its manifestation as a representation or phenomenon. For me, Consciousness in itself is the most indubitable and imposing experience that the spirit can register.

The World as belief

I would not say that the external world is just a belief; Jacobi's position has been correctly rejected by Schopenhauer. Reality cannot really be reduced to an article of faith. Nevertheless this belief which is not a direct experience, but a conclusion or an abstraction, constitutes a valuable aspect of knowledge. Not only scientific knowledge but also our daily life depend on this belief, we take for granted that the world outside exists and that when we open the door of our house we will encounter not an infinite abyss but the street, the alley and normal reality; we believe in a fixed reality, determined by the concepts that we keep in our memory and this faculty exists for this reason. Jacobi is also conscious of this belief. However not so the immense majority, their belief becomes reality in daily life, hence it uses memory more than the creative faculties that have the gift of seeing things in another way.

The realization that external reality depends on our beliefs about it is a good antidote for materialism. From a strictly philosophical point of view, materialism is savagery, it disconnects itself from the spirit and this is unthinkable when one reasons well and in a consistent manner. It had barely made its appearance when Schopenhauer said: "Materialism was born dead, as it disconnects itself from the subject and the forms of knowledge" (the forms of Kant). "There is no object without the subject; this principle makes materialism impossible" (*The World.* I,7). Schopenhauer clearly observes that the antidote for materialism is not spiritualism as is superficially thought in general. "Spiritualism affirms that the subject is independent of matter", "it consists of admitting outside matter another substance." (*Appendix* I) It is thus only apparent and a false cure for materialism, whose sole cure is idealism" (*Op. cit.*) Although Schopenhauer's objective is not unity, he notices and rejects the duality of spiritualism, his solution, correct to my mind, is the world as representation.

The virtue of adapting to reality, at least as he sees it, leads Schopenhauer to discard all theology that had been the death knell for the philosophy of the idealists that preceded him. With him the concept of God disappears and the first reality is expressed in terms amenable to philosophy, an indispensable inversion awaited for centuries. It is true that the I, the Idea etc. had been talked about, but the shadow of divinity fell on them at some point in time. With Schopenhauer there are no traces of inherited beliefs or of anything non-philosophical. And so sincere is he in his search that instead of a happy ending, he is led to a disappointing idea of life. Of course, the *mal du siècle* was already being felt; the seeds of existentialism had begun to grow.

Although Schopenhauer begins his work (*The World as a Will*) with the immediate intuition of the Will, like Descartes he does so with a methodical principle. Without hesitation he sees the need to differentiate intuitions from reason (it is no coincidence that my ideas overlap with his at this point), later to pass on to representations. It is as if he wanted to postpone his determining intuition, as it is only in the second book that he speaks of Will and, curiously, only later in the third book does he explain the mechanism of his thought that I will reproduce, because in it he reveals what I understand as transcendental intuition. Schopenhauer never abandons the subject-object scheme, which repeatedly muddles his demonstration, nevertheless the attentive reader will note that when there is reference to the "pure subject", he is speaking of a spirit that has transcended the subject to a perspective that would correspond in general terms to the consciousness that I have called unitive.

In this singular chapter he warns (*The World*, III, 34) "the reader will be surprised by what I am saying" if he does not follow this minute analysis. He says: "When man, elevates himself from the ordinary to consider things through reason, he does not limit himself to searching for the relations between them (...) when he does not investigate where, when, why and for what they exist, but only what things are; when he does not give himself up to abstract thought, to the concepts of reason, but concentrates all the force of the spirit in the *intuitive vision*, getting completely absorbed in it, and when he fills his consciousness with the tranquil contemplation of all natural objects (...) losing himself in them, or rather losing himself in the *pure subject*, in such a way that the object seems to be alone, without the being that perceives it, and when the subject cannot be separated from the very perception (...) what is known is not a particular thing, but the idea, the *eternal form*, the immediate objectivity of the Will; and for this reason he who gives himself over to this intuition is not an individual, as the latter has lost himself in the intuitive act, but a *pure subject of knowledge, above the will, passion and time*". I have highlighted these statements in italics as they are noteworthy for their wide ranging implications.

I believe that by changing the order followed by Schopenhauer and by exposing his experience and way of seeing, the reader will understand this philosophy more clearly. Apart from this, as was to be expected, he will use these same arguments based on that experience to elaborate his aesthetics that could have aspired to transcendence if an immanent philosophy had not been imposed from the beginning. Unfortunately that experience for him is temporary and is only sometimes useful for escaping the oppressive force of Will that governs his conception of the World. He defines his Idea in this way: "We have given to that essence, common to all phenomena the name of the manifestation in which the Will shows itself to be clearer". With this word we designate "that which through one of its facets at least is infinitely better known to us and more familiar than everything else". (*The World* II, XXV) With this he implicitly admits that there is another side, the thing in itself that he does not perceive.

I believe that Schopenhauer has discovered a great truth; his Will is an indisputable energy manifest in Nature. But his vision is reduced to what we can call the descendent aspect of one of the essential forces of creation, reproduction and reordering, i.e. of life itself even if he tries to establish a direct relation between the Will and the World, in this way for example, gravity would obey what has been necessarily laid out by it. I tend to believe that the relation of the energies of a subtle spiritual order would be indirect with respect to those phenomena that would be generated *a posteriori* due to their gradual interrelation in space and time. By establishing a direct relation, Schopenhauer enters the field of sciences, and I leave the scientists to judge him in this respect.

Schopenhauer views the world as a necessity, but it is not only this, he stopped considering it in its ascendant aspect as a biological and spiritual evolution (although he quotes Lamarck and not Darwin). (The reader will see this point developed in *The Evolution of the Spirit*). Our author does not see the cyclical aspect of life, neither does he perceive the other essential forces that spread over the world and fill consciousness; I refer to the *primary manifestations*, that I will later elaborate on whose ascendant aspects elevate the spirit and rescue it from the sordid daily world, from the weight of matter, from the vices that our bodies cling to without which life, in Schopenhauer's view, is a misery. But we should not deceive ourselves by disqualifying his philosophy, because as I said, he has discovered a great truth that shows us the cruel reality, the sad human condition in which we live. At first sight the reader will think it a strange proposition, but the latter draws on an old belief. The Christian god actually has the will to force us into the same situation, with the aggravating factor that by knowing and wanting it to be so, he is guilty of it. The Will of our philosopher is not like this, even if he falls into another determinism, he reduces the task of the main creator to a necessary unconscious force, to whom we can reproach nothing; it would be like getting angry with the force of gravity.

Our author has the courage and the intelligence to see life as it presents itself, because we must recognise that those who confront life head on are rare exceptions, most spend their time juggling balls in the air, veering between one illusion and the next in the search for pleasures to alleviate the disappointments. There are very few who "want to get to the bottom of the true nature of things and life. This question is the only one that interests the intelligence, the pure subject of knowledge emancipated from all intentions of the Will" (*The World.* III, XXXIV).

The internal circumstances of Schopenhauer

Schopenhauer also expresses a transcendental idealism, but with a sickly pessimism. The bright fireworks of Schelling and Hegel were already being extinguished. Schopenhauer shows us that they were artifice and brings us back to the hard reality of life. I believe that the descent leading to Existentialism was necessary. The disease is the same: lack of hope, the perspective of nothingness, the disappearance of the unitive and integrating factor, called God. But Schopenhauer still has a transcendental vision, the spirit has still not yet descended sufficiently to alienate itself from the essence and fall into existence, nor so low so as to drag itself into materialism.

In my appraisal, Schopenhauer does not have a clear vision of *noumenal* reality in itself; he himself confesses this, and all the deficiencies of his system are due to this shortcoming. Firstly, we can only know the Will through its manifestations, especially the will to live, although in this case it would be more correct to say to survive, as we are dealing with a mere struggle where selfishness rules supreme; where Darwin is assimilated. My critique of this (in *The Evolution of the Spirit*) is applicable especially to Schopenhauer, as life is, as we will soon see something else altogether.

Schopenhauer is weighed down by life, he suffers it, and he does not perceive the positive aspects of the Transcendent: the good, order and all that it justifies, gives sense to life and makes it happy. For him happiness is "essentially negative", it is nothing but the "freedom from pain, the overcoming of need", "the end of desire". As it can be observed, the language seems Buddhist, but there is no way out for him, there is no Nirvana, there is no transcendence (see my study on Buddhism in *The Evolution of the Spirit*); the tedium, the boredom and the *spleen* are deep in his soul, and this is heightened as there is no post mortem outlet: "in reality before us there is just nothingness". He is naturally on the brink of suicide; he only discards the idea because he sees it as a triumph of the Will, to which he does not want to submit his spirit; the essence of his philosophy is once more the search for freedom.

The World as representation

It would be incorrect to ignore Schopenhauer's aesthetics, these being a fundamental part of his philosophy, of his *World as Representation.* I will however be brief because I will elaborate on this in *The Roots of Art.* In fact, it is through aesthetic contemplation, an indispensable step or medium in art, that this thinker finds an outlet or solution within his philosophy which has Will as its unavoidable context weighing heavily on our lives.

I believe that what is decisive in his thought, as happens with the greatest thinkers, is the intervention of intuition, which does not happen to him just by having it, he warns that it is another faculty and, precisely that which is the most indispensable for the knowledge of ideas. It is not surprising that he reproaches Kant for not having clearly established the difference between abstract and intuitive knowledge. Thanks to this intuition and the separation that he observes between the faculties, he notes that all the relations reason lays down in order to attend to the material needs in this world, including scientific knowledge, obey a *relative knowledge* which is at the margin of the ideas finally excluded; ideas, of course, in the Platonic sense.

Knowledge of these ideas implies overcoming the principle of reason and in this way escaping the tentacles of Will. This happens when the subject is attracted and absorbed, through aesthetic contemplation and disappears in such a way that subject and object (as in Schelling) become one single reality. In this experience a kind of transformation takes place in the observer who thus becomes a "pure subject of knowledge", while the object reveals to him the idea of the same, its eternal form. But in contrast to Schelling who stubbornly remains in an ideal world, Schopenhauer does not forget his human situation subject to the incessant urgings of the Will. It is only in this state of contemplation by not establishing any rational relation, as intuition is immediate and there is no mediation of reason, that the subject is freed of the same and of Will.

Other factors besides the aesthetic intervene here, I am referring to morals and to states of mind, so connected to the human condition that the penetrating psychology of our philosopher cannot but observe. In this state of rapture the individual is bereft of pain (and I would add of desire and fear) and of the anguish that accompanies daily life. Aesthetic contemplation, as he rightly observes, generates a state of peace in the subject similar to that experienced by the Stoics who called it *ataraxia*. The sum of this aesthetic and moral experience, reality seen and felt in this way would be for him the *World as Representation*.

This experience, he maintains, carries the conviction that the knowing subject is the bulwark of the world and of all objective existence; the subject perceives nature as a prolongation or an accident of his own being. In my opinion he gets entrapped into a tangled web spun by the mind, into which Berkeley had also fallen, which can be defined as subjective idealism; the most elementary amongst idealisms, and also the weakest. In spite of this subjectivism our philosopher pretends to be dealing with another *I*, that has had a radical transformation, and for this reason believes that he is speaking the same language of the Upanishads, the subject, he maintains, is the world, "You are That."

In my opinion our philosopher has not quite come this far. The Upanishads speak of a definitive liberation; he speaks of a temporary phase that soon makes him captive of a Will that implacably continues to drag all in its path. And this is because he does not definitively abandon the subject. His own language reveals this; the subject, although he might call it "the pure subject of knowledge," is always there. From his subjective idealism he contemplates nature, he says then that as the latter is eternal, he is also this way; which contradicts his later affirmation that after death only nothingness remains, as we know that Nature and all beings in it are perishable.

In spite of these errors, we should recognise that Schopenhauer was well positioned on the path of intuition and had the merits we have highlighted. He was not on the wrong path, he just did not reach its conclusion; intuitions, that have borne the best fruits in Western thinkers are not enough. All that Schopenhauer says is true... from his perspective, and this comes from the medium of the current of life; this current is Will. The definitive solution requires more than just intuition, which is a *unitive experience* capable of transporting the spirit to a higher perspective, of carrying it to the banks of life from which one can see it flowing impassively, as did Heraclitus; I refer to a state of absolute contemplation. Schopenhauer would argue that the state is temporary, and so it is, if the spirit identifies with the body, but not with the *other consciousness* that awakens with this state; here the spirit knows that it is swimming in other waters, not those that become, but the eternal.

Ascending and descending life

The intrinsic problem with this Will is that far from being the most elevated amongst us and amongst creation, it is an elementary force linked to the I and to the survival of our body, and thus instead of elevating us, fixing and determining us in a being from which we want to emerge from a situation that we want to overcome, and a form of thinking that we would want to transcend. We can do none of this because the Will determines that we bear all this with stoicism. "From the time that the consciousness of the I or subjectivity, or in other words the Will recovers its predominance, a new level of discontent and agitation is produced in us, the discontent comes from us recovering the feeling of corporality (i.e., of the organism that is itself the Will) and the agitation, because the will through the mediation of intelligence fills our consciousness with desires, emotions, passions and cares". (*The World,* III, XXX). We can only momentarily escape from this situation through aesthetic contemplation that allows us to "eliminate the will of consciousness", sublimate the external world and make our personality disappear, hence (notice the psychological penetration of this philosopher) "all pain derives from the Will that is the *I*" (*Op. cit*).

What is despairing of the matter is that life, if is seen like this, raw and naked, be it the work of "the Will" or not, i.e. even letting it go, it is effectively the way our philosopher proposes. The problem is how to extricate oneself from this agonizing situation. The solution that he proposes, deriving from what has been said, is aesthetic contemplation, with which he expresses a belief accepted by the ideologues of romanticism who were literati and artists.

Bergson's élan vital (on which I have commented in *The Evolution of the Spirit*), is an advance with respect to Schopenhauer's Will since it becomes clear that the first

Motor is of a spiritual nature, while in the latter it seems excessively to be like physical energy, even if the human mind responds to it, it does so as a biological influence from which the spirit can temporarily escape through the medium of aesthetic contemplation and asceticism. Although I cannot agree with Bergson when he says that "The élan is over, it has been given once and for all", which seems to me to be an atavism inherited from the Old Testament; vital experience precisely reveals to us a constant energy always revitalised and present. The concept of energy refers to physical forces, but I should insist on its spiritual nature that has a direct effect on the mind of human beings as an individuation or prolongation of the same Nature as consciousness.

This energy is nothing strange for the human spirit; on the contrary, it is in its very essence. However, we should recognize that even if it is the same energy, it has two directions, one descending, which is the process of individuation (where the Will of Schopenhauer is exhausted), and the other ascending, which is the process of unification or transcending. The former is the will of individual life, indispensable for life to be possible, whose extreme is selfishness, even if the circumstances of the individual, the other lives force the spirit to overcome that extreme: life in society already forms part of the ascendant ladder and involves a sacrifice of the individual. Although we are still in the terrain of survival, weighed down by biological necessities, a consciousness higher than the individual continues developing, and this is the social consciousness that has made civilizations possible; the fact that only some peoples have acquired it (and only a part of its members), indicates that humanity is still in this stage.

The relation with other beings, as in the case of other *unitive energies,* like love that bring us closer to the neighbour increase the *altruist consciousness*. The latter clarifies to us the virtues, which as we know are the antidote to the vices and they free us from the heavy burden of selfishness. As we increase our level of consciousness, we can see individual consciousness from a clearer perspective, i.e. our I, the reasons that we bring forth to justify our selfish activities, in order to get us pleasures, etc., while at the same time the spiritual panorama becomes more tangible, more real. All this paves the way to the Transcendent. The spirit starts detaching itself from matter and starts recognizing the *ascendants* and integrating *forces* that are *unitive.* If it manages to settle in this stage and maintain itself perceptive, it will be in a very stable state of contemplation with a spirit already liberated from the interferences of the *I* or of its individual consciousness, and it will be in a condition to perceive the *primary manifestations of the Essence*, i.e. of having transcendental intuitions. The authors we have commented on have used this in varying ways, even if I notice that as soon as they reach them, they refract their spirit into themselves in order to apply them to human matters. Nothing wrong with this and very natural, and yet all elevated spirits have sought their inspiration in the said intuitions of the Transcendent, for this reason they are exemplary and will continue to be reference points for humanity. But the road ahead does not end here, a little further on we will see the invisible rungs of the ladder, but we cannot reach them in one leap; for this reason I have deemed it necessary to trace this ascent from the beginning.

The tragedy of Schopenhauer and the philosophers

I have found in Schopenhauer the legitimate legacy of Kant, and as will be seen, I have my reasons for trying to be a beneficiary of this rich idealist tradition. Although I really do not know to what extend this was necessary as the riches I had received from Plato were enough for me.

But this talk of legacies always distorts reality, the reality of the philosopher I mean. Those who roam searching and connecting cultural legacies are the scholars who have found philosophies in books. Schopenhauer has talked about them, and I would like to take up the theme again, not to demolish them like he did but with the desire to clarify, as always.

The true philosopher does not find the eternal problems of philosophy in books but in Nature, the reason of life and its correlate death, happiness and freedom, need and anguish, the infinite that precedes and succeeds us, etc., he finds them in life. Of course, all of us search for ourselves in these subjects, but we do not react to them in the same way. The great majority ignore them, their interest is centred on the most pressing and immediate things in life; is still in the *stage of survival*. In an intermediate stage are those who feel a curiosity for philosophical problems and become professional at it. They are interested in connections and cultural legacies, the history of thought, but they are also worried about survival, thus they live off their profession, "*of philosophy*"; the philosopher as Schopenhauer distinguished well, lives *for* philosophy. But unlike this author I do not feel any disdain for the professionals of thought, except when they arrogate privilege to themselves, abusing their power to dismiss, minimise or disdain the work of the philosopher, when the latter is not part of the framework that they have made for philosophy. This same abuse is heaped on artists by art critics who are not artists; and we need not mention the way mystics have suffered at the hands of priests. What the critic should understand about art, philosophy and religion is that the true artist, philosopher and religious person (the mystic) see the world in a singular and unpredictable way as if for the first time. This is what Plato referred to as the experience of amazement of the philosopher.

The problem that derives from the philosophy professors, against whom Schopenhauer inveighed, they are in the end codifying by establishing doctrines, static ways of interpreting that they pass on to students, and this is nothing more than accumulative knowledge. This is one part of philosophy, but the objective of the latter, as I understand it, is *to transform the aspirant* bringing him closer to the world of ideas in themselves, from where concepts and doctrines emanate. Philosophy, in fact is dynamic, dialectic, maieutic, finally a quest. It is not, as Socrates warned, the knowledge of the virtues of this or that subject or act, but "the real character through which all pious things are pious." (*Eutifron*) And the same happens with "the virtues which, although they are many and of all kinds, have one and the same form due to which they are virtues." (*Mennon*) How can judge this transcendental vision who does not have it? The philosopher stands before the critic or the academic as before a judge who has all the codes which, nevertheless, do not include the particular case he is judging. What he will do if it is just, will be not to condemn the author but rectify the codes; if he is unjust and arbitrary, he will condemn him. And this has happened many times in history and keeps happening; I myself have suffered it.

Nature is presented to the philosopher, the artist or to the mystic like an open book; this is what Campanella said, who suffered terribly from the cruelty and insidiousness of those who learnt philosophy from books made of paper which they took to be incontrovertible truth. Even Jesus suffered them before the Gospels where written; later the whole reality was adapted to these books and he who did not follow this model was condemned. Jesus forgave; the scholars who interpreted him however burnt thousands of books and the people who did not conform to "their" books. The professionals of thought are arrogant because they aspire to be something, the philosopher, like the artist or the mystic does not want to be, being happens to him; he has not chosen it, a higher force compels him, he is a victim; hence his passion. He can do nothing else in life, he is urged on to respond to his disquiets before life finishes off with him. As can be seen, I am not an apologist for the philosopher; I am only narrating his tragedy, which means taking charge of the tragedy that implies existence. Everything is overwhelming for him: time seems vertiginous, space is an immense abyss, and injustice is a universal damage.

The Cosmic Vision in America

Although we would not be able to define it like a transcendental monism, since we are not dealing with philosophers like Spinoza, but of visionary poets, the movement that took place in the New World and especially in the United States, an obvious prolongation of the spirit of the Renaissance and Romanticism, deserves a mention. It's most important thinker was Emerson who was undoubtedly influenced by Schelling, as is clear from the title of his book *The Spirit of Nature* which came to be a kind of manifesto.

His proposition was a return to the contemplation of Nature; he believed that the fundamental answers lay therein more than in the study of the authors of the past: "Why grope around in the decay of the past?" "The sun also shines today." "If man has to be alone, he should look at the stars." "Nature never has a vulgar appearance." Far from it, the inspiration that it engenders is uplifting. "It could be said that the atmosphere has been made transparent with this intention: offer to men in celestial bodies, the perpetual presence of the sublime."

The concept of God is in Emerson, but not as something separated from nature nor from himself, and in this union he seems to find the roots of the moral: "Standing on the bare earth, the air caressing my face and facing infinite space, all mean selfishness is diluted. I become a transparent ocular globe; I am nothing, I see all; the currents of the universal being envelop me; I am a part of God." The unity of spirit and nature that so moved Schelling, is also his experience:

"Nature always has the colors of the spirit." "Philosophically considered, the universe is made up of Nature and the Soul."

He experiences the perception of Unity like an aesthetic phenomenon: "Nature is a sea of forms fundamentally similar and even unitary. A leaf, a ray of sun, a landscape, the ocean, exercise an analogous effect on the spirit. What is common to all of them, is that perfection and harmony, it is beauty." "The measure of beauty is given by the entire gamut of natural forms, by the totality of nature; the Italians expressed this when they defined beauty as *il piú nell' uno* (the multiple in one)." We see that he echoes the pantheism of the Renaissance and Romanticism and probably even the Hinduism that he came into contact with in England, the objective of which was always the search for *Unity in Multiplicity*. And, in keeping with this doctrine, he speaks of a universal Soul. "Man is conscious of a universal Soul which is within or behind his individual life, where the essences of Justice, Truth, Love, Liberty emerge and shine like in the firmament." In this last part he conforms to my philosophy in which we find that the paradigmatic virtues emanate from the Spirit or universal Consciousness.

This once again confirms my theory of the superimposition of the ideas of the authors, which obeys more the place of the spirit in some part of the mind than a cultural legacy. Without denying the influence that the latter can exercise, it is interesting to know the mechanism that consists in awakening this zone of the spirit, and thus generates a common perspective and not the desire for imitation. We find a clear example in Walt Whitman, Emerson's successor, who evidently has a similar perspective, but it would be unjust and even absurd to say that he "imitates" him. Like so many other pantheists, they share a cosmic vision; Emerson called it *cosmic optimism.*

This vision included a *natural religion* and a *natural*

ethics divorced from the Church, from its dogmas and from the Old Testament in general, including its arbitrary and vengeful God, and, especially, the original sin; this left man a participant of Creation and his soul united with the universal Soul. This line of thought extended to the other extreme of America: the project of the Argentine José Ingenieros is that of *A Moral Without Dogmas*, which although it loses its universal dimension, is an interesting option for the sceptics of the Transcendent.

Summary of the shifts of the spirit

Greece

History in the west has made Greece its exemplary point of reference and I hope this trend continues as I wish to contribute to it; the enlightened ones in the West have never hesitated to use the treasury of Athens in their search for the most precious gems of their culture. Pericles's pretention that Athens was "the school of Greece," has greatly surpassed its aspirations, it has been the school of Western civilization and now with globalization it is expected that it will be the school of humanity. I am not implying, I hasten to clarify, that contemporary Western civilization should become an example, but only that Athens be a school to other cultures, and also that exemplary periods of other cultures, especially India and China be of use to the West.

Greece is exemplary not only because of its virtues but also because it highlighted the vices. In the treasure of Athens, as in the histories of pirates, we find snakes and other vermin, but these are in sharp contrast with its gems and they serve as a model for us. The Greek genius created and practiced all forms of government, its philosophers developed all kinds of thought, its mythology roamed the most recondite labyrinths of the mind and, using this baggage its dramatists sublimated exemplary tragedies that are based on the eternal struggle of the virtues against human passions, which its artists expressed in the most pure, refined and elevating manner. An energetic and aesthetic people *par excellence* made of life an art and of art the most essential of life: such is Greek tragedy.

The Greeks knew of these contrasts and their interrelation, and these constitute the essence of life purposefully expressed perforce left for later generations as models to follow. And they were so conscious of this that they created not just "one more" philosophy, but a model which they would follow and which as followers we continue to use, for they searched for prototypes not just in history but also in eternal principles. All this and more, as I have excluded the first historians, mathematicians, geometricians, chemists, doctors, astrologers and scientists in general, because they represent an aspect a little external to the spirit, and do not express the most intrinsic and revelatory for the human being, although something of undoubted value. To all this we must add the *freedom of spirit*, which (as we have seen in *The Spirit of History*), accompanies all the ages of growth, that allowed for the widening of the arc of creative possibilities until they had covered the whole spectrum of human alternatives.

My theory on the shifts of the spirit and the perspectives that derive from there can help us in understanding the subject in all its depth. In order to arrive at the vision of the Greeks we should reach the perspective that allows us to see the unified world and remain in it participating in the *universal Order*. Our idea of the world differs greatly from the Greek, it is wider and more defined, but it is "objective" or alien and thus does not allow us to integrate ourselves in the said *Order*. The Greek order will seem to us a product of the imagination to the point of being unreal, but the fact is that it had the virtue of integrating consciousness into the Whole, i.e. of maintaining it unified. Not in an absolute manner, for this one needs to place the spirit in the very Transcendent, as I have pointed out, but sufficiently enough to achieve this vitality and creativity that made the

Greek miracle possible.

Balanced and surrounded by equilibrium the Greeks had prepared the necessary conditions for creation. I am persuaded that its astonishing creativity in all orders was the product of *a spirit centred at a high level of consciousness*. Its moral integrity, its capacity for altruism, thanks to which they did not hesitate in sacrificing their lives, not only to save their city, but also to prove to themselves their capacity for courage, which was the result of un unconditional heroic sense of life; its need for beauty, the product of an elevated aesthetic sense of life; its profound understanding of the psyche expressed in its myths, in its religion and literature, and, to crown it all, its indisputable philosophical capacity, which is proof of the aforesaid shift of the spirit towards what I have called *unitive consciousness*, that duly comprehends the moral, aesthetic religious and philosophical consciousness. When this shift takes place, I insist, an intrinsic change in man happens; and every human being should aspire to this.

It is necessary to constantly speculate about what would have become of our civilization if we had been bequeathed all our Greek heritage, as it is well known that only a small part has passed on to us. It can be argued that these conjectures are pointless as what has been lost is unrecoverable, but I do not believe this as I am speaking not only of a cultural but a fundamentally spiritual heritage. What I wish for is that the importance of that birth and of the need to be born again be realized, as what contemporary man can create and inscribe with his technology and all his external possibilities is unimaginable, if he were to have his centre of consciousness centred and elevated like the Greeks.

I would like to clarify that when I refer to a centred people I do not mean it in an absolute way; we have seen that this state is the legacy of strange and isolated individuals. In the case of the Greeks I would like to say that the spirit moves with regularity within a *zone of equilibrium*, which is possible thanks to an elevated level of consciousness and is exceptional in any society. The Greeks undoubtedly had a special instinct in maintaining this equilibrium, but this should be understood, the said attempt was and is a product of an eminent perspective that allows one to intuit and choose the right means without needing an experience of the extremes which, as explained earlier, is the result of an incipient reason.

Rome

The Roman has his spirit located in the external utilitarian faculties, from which he gets the most advantage: he is practical, ordered, hardworking, an organizer in his public and private life. He is not alienated from his unitive faculties amongst which his moral is the most important, although it is in the latter that he seeks support for his practicality. The other unitive faculties are not shown to him directly, they seem to reach him second hand, for this he generally takes recourse to the Greek genius which he tries to imitate. The admiration and respect the cultured Romans had for the Greeks shows an intimate affinity, and proof of this is the adoption of their gods, their aesthetic tastes, their philosophy, nonetheless, a distance separated them from these sources, or from the Creative itself. This is confirmed by the fact that their thinkers as if restrained, did not venture to fly in the metaphysical heights. So, in vain we will search in Cicero's or Seneca's philosophical treatises for something more than a moral; their perspective leads them to incline towards the practical aspects of life. The Roman did not find time for leisure, which is where philosophy finds fertile soil; they were an active people *par excellence* and they looked for solutions in action, not in contemplation. I believe that the limitless expansion of

Rome responded to this situation of the spirit; even if the intellectuals most imbued with the Hellenic spirit or the most centred and balanced such as Pliny the Young and even Adrian, were aware that it was necessary to avoid this extreme that concluded by breaking up the empire.

Medieval Age

During medieval times when Christianity was predominant, the spirit, following the tradition of the Old Testament, affirmed itself in its individual or egocentric perspective and projected itself onto an ideal that could not be satisfied, but which due to this reason inclined towards hope and took refuge in faith, considered cardinal virtues by Paul of Tarsus who invented this mechanism. It is from this perspective that the believer tries to realize his project of personal salvation, which in my opinion is a contradiction in terms and implies a doubtful moral situation, as all altruism is directed towards a personal benefit; the final objective is egocentric.

During medieval times, the Western spirit was apparently interiorized but actually externalised, projected onto another imagined reality, alienated from its humanity and from Nature, completely decentralised; hence the manifest contradictions between the two worlds, the earthly and the spiritual, between which the spirit shifted from one extreme to the other: religious fanaticism, the desire for power at all cost, cruelty in the name of love and other clear symptoms of madness kept man alienated from unitive faculties that remained dormant for eight centuries. The lack of creativity in all orders is explained by the alienation of the spirit with respect to the Creative.

Christianity has been and is a moral idealism in spite of all the attempts at making it a philosophical idealism. The attempt to invert this order leads to its failure as a philosophy, and we have seen that in this order the real is knowledge and not belief. When a belief is projected in an ideal that cannot be experienced and more so when it contradicts the experience, as in the case of a good and just god unmoved by millions of insistent prayers and who allows evil, injustice and suffering to proliferate, it generates doubts in the meanderings of the consciousness that are sought to be overcome with a self-imposed faith. The dogmatic presupposition, in keeping with the revealed texts, that others had this religious experience in a remote past, results in the same mechanisms. This self-imposition of faith leads to fanaticism, while intolerance and the desire to impose on the other the same faith which is so difficult for the believer himself to maintain, generates internal and external violence. And when violence enters consciousness, the latter fragments and all manner of vices penetrate through the fissures.

Renaissance

Humanity and Nature were rediscovered by the Renaissance. It can be said that the seed of individualism was sown at that time, but, as I explained when dealing with this age, at that time it was indispensable for man to regain his place in the World and achieve an equilibrium that generated that movement, as *the spirit had again centred itself in the Creative*. We also find in it the seeds of rationalism that would spirit shift towards the external planes of reason, i.e. discernment, from which matter shows itself to be clearer but the spirit more diffuse.

Romanticism

As we know, Romanticism reacted against rationalism and its cold and objective manner of seeing the World and rediscovered the value of sentiments. *The romantic spirit shifts to the animated plane of the sentiments* and as happens in the origin of the great cultural movements (see *The Spirit in History*), it does so at the highest levels of consciousness, and then continues declining from the most elevated sentiments to the level of emotions, to then reduce to individual consciousness; this decadence finally killed the romantic spirit.

From Romanticism onwards the spirit in the West has fallen off the cliff of externalization and individualization. This means that the spirit or the centre of consciousness has shifted towards its external faculties in detriment to the internal faculties from which it has ended up alienated. The decadence of philosophy, religion, moral, aesthetics and sentiments is explained by this alienation; selfishness, the cult of the personality, the attachment to matter, the belief in external or material solutions are explained in the same way. The shift of the spirit implies a change of perspective that makes us see and believe from the point of view of our alienation.

The Enlightenment and Romanticism were new rebirths of the Hellenic spirit, but the latter was to be the swan song of that spirit. Positivism, Communism, a progeny of Christianity and capitalism, the child of materialism, contaminated the atmosphere in such a way that Venus does not emerge in each spring to revive our consciousness as she used to do during Hellenic times.

Our times in the light of the past

Since the objective of this work is the search of the spirit within the parameters of idealism, I could have disregarded the philosophies after Schopenhauer. In keeping with my psychosophy, I will briefly comment on them in order to highlight the position of the spirit and the perspectives adopted by modern thinkers in the West who have distanced us from the high peaks of thought.

The human being has the latent intuition that there exists a higher reality distinct from the one he lives through every day. But, due to the erroneous location of the spirit, the aforesaid higher reality is shown to be transcendent, i.e. as alien, diffuse and remote, distant and so unreachable that he imagines it belonging to another world; hence the success of religious doctrines that project this reality beyond the threshold of death. We can imagine that the theorists who sustain these doctrines so out of ignorance of the aforementioned mental mechanisms, even if we suspect that their profitability should incline them to maintain them. This ignorance is the product of the same alienation of the spirit and since it cannot evidence reality it believe in it; hence the recourse to faith. Man also intuits the difficulty of the project; he knows or suspects that his fears, desires, and his passions in general constitute tremendous obstacles on the path towards this knowledge, and thus he tends towards the belief that he will acquire that knowledge freely or with very little effort through the singular effort of dying. The fact is that this belief, often transformed into faith has been held by millions of people over the centuries.

Now, the loss of this faith has generated a crisis of values within which new currents of thought have emerged. Unfortunately the failure of the vehicle of faith was that it did not lead us to look for spiritual reality through more fruitful paths, but to a skepticism that took the spirit to opposite extremes. The present crisis of values has been fundamentally provoked by the alienation of Western man from his moral consciousness and his moral premises. The fall of Christianity that had monopolized morals and which involved a series of beliefs in myths that are no longer relevant also contributed to this; and thus in its fall religion dragged along morals and in a predictable dialectic, Western man after having abandoned the spirit turned towards matter.

The *process of exteriorization* will determine materialism and the process of individuation will do so for existentialism.

Both involve alienation of spiritual reality: the first will believe that reality is made up only of things, the latter when it wants to transcend that reality finds nothing: the spirit shines by its absence. Contemporary man is alienated from himself but he cannot realize this consciously as he is unconscious of its essence, for this reason he destroys the environment in which he lives, the air he breathes, the water he drinks. As he is estranged from that medium and exteriorized, he only sees matter and thinks with his external faculties that are suitable only for things; this is what happened to Marx.

For Marx "History is the continuous transformation of human nature," and we could agree with this, but he later develops an economic theory of history, in which he presumes that the productive forces are capable of changing our nature. His erroneous vision, product of his *exteriorization*, leads him to see man from the outside; therefore it is enough to change Nature and society in order to transform the former. Marxism tries to help man by denying the individual. This vision which is already a contradiction, as he views societies as if they were made up of replaceable and inanimate pieces (a psychopathic vision par excellence), has contributed to the contemporary "culture" of masses, a very strong opium that keeps people in a daze.

In any case, Marxism could not be a solution because it is imbued with the Judeo-Christian spirit which had already shown itself to be unsuitable for our civilization: Both spirits refer us to Genesis, which Marx believed was so distant from his "scientific" method. In fact, one of the most dangerous premises of Genesis is adopted by Marx with the greatest naturalness: Nature, including all living beings, has been created for man, for this reason one just has to transform it for the benefit of our species in particular (here too there are clear psychopathic traits). The project has the same roots: Ezra, considered by some historians as the real founder of Judaism had already put forward the idea: "If the world had really been created for us why are we not in possession of the world?" (Oesterley, cit. Toynbee XIV, 42).

The result of this egocentric vision has naturally been fatal for the planet, and if we do not change our perspective, there will be no ecological project that can be effective. Partaking of the same Judeo-Christian spirit, the similarities with the Marxist project are manifold: the dogma of the truth of the doctrine; the lack of tolerance bordering on fanaticism; its messianism; its perspective of the oppressed; its promise of an idealized future in which "the last will be the first;" the program of recruitment through a populist politics that appeals to the masses, to quantity and not to quality, to the politics of action, to militancy, to free equality at the expense of merit, and, of course, the justification of violence to achieve these objectives, as these are the most "just". And, in order to complete the relation, Marxism is also a moral idealism that opposes itself to philosophical idealism, distracting us too from this elevated design. Besides, Marx revived the Semitic spirit that was fading away in Western civilization. Marx is the modern Luther who repeats the same story boycotting the Renaissance of the Hellenic spirit that time and again struggles to manifest itself in Western culture.

Marxism has become obsolete because it could not respond to a moral idealism that was equally badly posed. The materialist vision of the world is embedded in the mind of contemporary man, and not only in the West, it has spread throughout Russia, China and Japan, and to some degree to the rest of the planet. The situation is serious. It is more so because it involves an alienation of the human being from its essence and its true centre of consciousness. We can agree with Marx on the importance of overcoming the stage of necessity, but we are faced with the same obstacle: the externalization of man leads him to search for external solutions. Man's endeavour to improve his material conditions is very meritorious, but material growth is horizontal; even though it might manufacture planes and rockets, with this he does nothing more than to enlarge the human anthill, I mean that it does not take him out of the animal state.

My project is similar in to that of the authors that we have seen. Who stretch back through history, it tends towards an internal change and is vertical and ascendant. This means that the conditions for this change were already there 2600 years ago, when men used candles and lanterns and walked on foot or on horseback as proved by the Buddha, Lao Tse, the Upanishads, the Pre Socratics and the geniuses of tragedy. (On this crucial moment in the history of humanity see *The Spirit in History*). Within the project of these wise men was all that man needed to overcome th*e animal state. All material progress is nothing more than dispensable superstructure, and all this can collapse* if the foundations are shaky, and the bases are the human mind; the whole human anthill and the realization of our species depend on our mental equilibrium and on our level of consciousness.

Faced with collective de-spiritualization (there are particular exceptions like Bergson's case), caused by the heavy weight of materialism, the human spirit attempts a new recourse, a new hope directed towards existence, without noticing that this dialectic movement is also a consequence of the alienation of the spirit from its Essence.

Perhaps everyone should be an existentialist at some point in their lives, I was once and I considered it indispensable and edifying, as we cannot avoid giving a sense to our existence, but this is a stage in our life, an adolescent stage. An adult thinker should overcome this puerile stage, as it is the inevitable design of philosophy to search for the Absolute. This is not a dogma; it is unavoidable because from an individual perspective there cannot be an agreement between men. It is not enough to find a reason for our existence, and as we cannot pretend that this reason be valid for all, it is insufficient for all society.

In the conception of Pico della Mirandola's of man, as a "compendium and epilogue of the universe", we can see the beginning of the individual perspective that will grow in crescendo until existentialism, but we should differentiate the beginning from the end. Pico, and the Renaissance in general, speak of the "man" *as a point of equilibrium in the universe* in which he should extend his spirit, while the Existentialists start from the "individual" who, alienated from the universe, feels "thrown" into it like a "foreigner" faced with life and death. There is no sentiment more opposed to the Renaissance (and every period of growth), than anguish, this is a product of the closing of the spirit, while in the Renaissance there is pure opening and thus optimism.

The answer is a synthesis between essence and existence, a proposal that we could call *vital idealism.* This synthesis is not an eclectic or even voluntary solution but the consequence of a *unitive experience that finds essence in existence.* We find the most intense and authentic moments of existence when forgetting time we live our present, as it is in the present where our Essence resides. This means that the more intensely we live, the more we approach our Essence, and the more we feed our existence with our Essence, our life becomes more authentic and real. The authentic life that the existentialists so emphatically proclaimed is found in this integration. There is no pre-eminence of the existence over essence nor vice versa, there is Unity, and the latter is not an abstract postulate. *This spontaneous experiencing, thinking, feeling and acting from its essence defines the fulfilled, unitive human being.*

Undoubtedly in the XXth century, when men in the West were faced with the catastrophes of the two wars, they needed to discover themselves and their individual roots. They needed a sincere consciousness, independent of the beliefs that the catastrophes had generated. In the second half of the XXth century, existentialism began to be abandoned, but individual perspective was never abandoned, the puerile stage in which the spirit had fallen was never overcome. Hence this entire play of words and adolescent caprices called post-modernism that left the soul even emptier than its predecessor, whose search was more sincere, authentic and necessary. Post-modernism was not so and history could have omitted it.

The problem, according to me, is that we continue to favor reason which is all modern philosophy has done, especially that which is used in the development of complex epistemologies that ending by enclosing it in a vicious circle. And amongst these there are those who are attempting to show the sciences their path, as they move autonomously with freedom and swiftness, and they do not really need this “philosophy”.

Plotinus had warned us: “The greatest of difficulties for the knowledge of the One consists in the fact that we do not reach Him through science or through the intellect but through a presence that is superior to science. The soul is not absolutely one when it apprehends the scientific mode; because science is a discourse and the discourse means multiplicity.” In my language, I would change two words: presence through experience and discourse through discernment. The last sentence will be read like this: because science is the product of discernment and discernment involves multiplicity. The modern epistemologists have not understood this warning.

In keeping with this great visionary I would say today

1700 years later: Every inductive epistemology is destined to end in uncertainty, i.e. to failure. For this reason my project consists of tracing the ascendant paths of the spirit in order to prepare the conditions which allow it to achieve through intuitions, available only in the higher strata of the spirit or, better still, experiences of the final Reality, from which the relation with the multiple and human world can be deduced. The surest path towards the said Reality is levelled by self-knowledge, which goes hand in hand with the moral. For this it can be said that there is no better epistemology than the moral, and, thus, all epistemology that is not concerned with the moral, ignores the mediums as well as the objectives of philosophy.

The actual efficacy of the sciences is due to the fact that suitable faculties are being used for the knowledge of the phenomenal; the failure of modern philosophies is due to the fact that our thinkers are using the same faculties as the scientists. This makes them misunderstand the *noumenal* as they are ever concerned about explaining the phenomenal; as they can tell us little about the former and as the sciences are solely concerned with this, their task is useless and sterile.

The sciences are marvelously fulfilling their role, while philosophy which should be preceding them to show them the way, by following the methods and using the faculties of the former has lost its way (and its time) and has fallen behind. In this way the sciences and technology are vertiginous, and extend everywhere directionless. This would not have happened if philosophy had not forgotten its specific function which is to make man wiser as its etymology makes explicit. And the times urge philosophy on to this function, as without direction the sciences and technology constitute a threat, and it could be the greatest that man has confronted in his history. When philosophy attended to its specific function, every educated person was inspired by it, today it has become a specialization that only concerns a select group of intellectuals.

As we have seen that which leads Hegel to look for an explanation and also a salvation in a universal Being and not in the human being, is his absolute skepticism with respect to our nature: "history reveals itself to us like an altar on which the welfare of peoples and the virtues of individuals have been sacrificed." The reader, each and every one of us, should consider the cause of the skepticism in so many thinkers who have studied and judged Western lamentable history. I should confess to the reader that I share this skepticism, if we consider man as he is and has been. My philosophy, however, considers him as he could be, better yet, the way he truly is having reached his plenitude, because the truth is that the human being has not yet reached adulthood, he is on the path of evolution.

I have faith in my project because my experience has led me to confirm that it is possible to transform our nature, not in an absolute manner, of course, but sufficiently in order to give a direction to our existence and to history. I am not offering a promise but only a remedy that I believe is efficacious and I am not presenting it as a novelty as the struggle of good against evil is as old as our species; it is just another way of presenting this millenarian project of overcoming and transformation, always aborted by the same vices used to distort the moral, political, economic, religious and philosophic projects.

Everything depends on how we look at history in order to understand it and give it a direction. If we look at it *unitively*, i.e. from the perspective that I have called essential, history is presented as a search, usually unconscious, of the man of universal Consciousness; it is this philosophical vision that we have been following. But given the alienation of the man of this Consciousness and the consequent ignorance of that force that moves it, history presents itself as a succession of man's leaps from one illusion to another; and this when he is motivated by an ideal; most of the time it is merely moved by selfish or animal desires. Seen from this perspective, i.e. objectively and anthropologically, the human being is decidedly historical, he depends on his cultural and material circumstances, but from the essential perspective, these are not decisive situations, as what motivates him is transcends history. The idealist, who has transcendent references, cannot define himself as a historical being; he only depends on history as the means he uses, just as the artist uses the tools that he finds in his epoch. Historicists should consider these points of view.

We should recognize that the weighing scales of history, in spite of some particular sporadic triumphs of the good, incline towards evil. The weight resides in the quantity, as the majority is ignorant of its moral consciousness and myopic and deaf to the elevating motivations that proceed from the Transcendent; even when it tries to escape daily banality through music or through religion, it inclines towards its most elemental aspects: popular (not folkloric) music that puts one to sleep, and the religions that offer illusions, such as hope after death, or magical solutions like miracles in general.

The struggle against evil has always been the work of a small minority, hence it is heroic. The selfish man does not want to understand the altruist; small men cannot understand great men. They will always project their egocentric vision and will attribute selfish intentions to their projects and works and will always believe that they harbour a personal interest. They cannot understand the spiritual pleasure that consists in overcoming the animal state of man and freely opening up to the *Universus*.

I truthfully believe that it is very difficult to reverse this situation. But there is a moral and transcendent imperative as well as a latent hope, based on a patent truth, which compels me to point out the correct path. The latter however cannot be followed or even seen from the individual perspective. This is what has been determining human history and impelling man to repeat his defects without intrinsically evolving as happens to other species. The reason, I will once again state, is nothing more than an un instrument that, at the service of the egocentric perspective can only transform the external circumstances of our species without producing any transformation in its substance.

The distinction between unitive and accumulative knowledge that my theory of knowledge establishes may contain the key to the present situation. While the spirit sleeps for lack of the first, it continues its accelerated march producing the means thanks to the second. This has generated a vicious circle, as accumulative knowledge tends to send the unitive spirit to sleep due to lack of use and to keep it distracted with incessant inventions of amenities and comforts. The danger of this vicious circle fundamentally consists in the fact that without the unitive knowledge, which depends on philosophy, religion, the arts and the moral, which are the faculties that provide the ends, man finds himself without direction. The only ideal that occurs to him towards which he himself can go is material progress. It is through this that he will seek his happiness and peace, which being the domain of unitive faculties, he will never find them.

In fact all modern societies are led forward through faith and hope in an earthly future of promise, in which they can realize their internal spiritual goals, with material external means which are two irreducible elements. This faith and hope are maintained by consumer societies that educate consumers in the belief that amenities and comforts are the genuine road to happiness. Since money is used to obtain these, the key for the human being lies here and not in knowledge. Materialism has triumphed, not so much for the apparatus it has produced, but because it has become a faith and a hope. It will be understood that with such low ideals, selfishness and ambition and their correlates such as insecurity and dissatisfaction will increase. If to this lamentable internal state we add the destruction that material progress demands, and the growing needs generated by the incessant increase of the population that keeps our species in an eternal state of survival, misunderstanding between people and nations will be inevitable. It is very difficult to be optimistic in such a situation. Only a spiritual realization can break this vicious circle and avoid the foreseeable catastrophe; my proposal could be an efficient means for this.

Religious experience and knowledge

This should be clear: all definite or verifiable knowledge of a religious matter is born of a religious experience and does not differ in the essential when the latter is achieved. But there are different levels of understanding in keeping with the level of consciousness reached. This means that the differences of interpretation do not make the object of knowledge different as it is unchangeable, and so one who enters in direct contact with it will find the same asall those who have reached it. The differences keep growing as the spirits keep distancing themselves from the object, as they depend on the clarity of vision. This clarity, unfortunately, is not related to the reasoning capacity, this is another mechanism of the mind, another faculty. Besides, reason is usually more developed in thinkers who have not had to spend years meditating and contemplating, which are necessary means for the mystic, and thus it is viable that they know how to express what they have seen with difficulty better than those who have seen with clarity.

Added to this is the fact that what the latter has seen is very difficult to explain. Because of this it is rare that a mystic also be a philosopher, in the history of Western thought I know very few who have seen and clearly expressed what they have experienced.

There have been numerous philosophers and each one has had an opinion (not knowledge as Plato would say) on the matter. There have also been those who have been so myopic or distant from the religious "object" that they have denied his existence (Marx) or they have thought that it is the product of a neurosis (Freud). In the history of Western thought we have all the nuances that stretch from the knowledge of this "object" to the total ignorance of the same, the entire spectrum from light to darkness, and each one has used a multitude of reasons to show their point of view.

Lamentably there are few who admit that they are speaking from a "point of view", and even fewer those who are ready to concede that they are not seeing the said "object" with clarity. Kant seems an exemplary exception to this rule. If all thinkers recognized their limitations, as he did, philosophy would be more respected as dependable knowledge. But it has not been so, and the most recognised philosophies have been those which are the best structured, not the best based on solid ground.

There is no definite knowledge of what will happen to us after death. Philosophy in a strict sense ends there but not philosophical speculation if its level of uncertainty is recognized. Although it is not certain that this will happen, he who has reached the Transcendent has the natural conviction, born of the present experience, that his spirit has been diluted in the universal Spirit, he knows that he is One with the Consciousness of the world. But for the rest, the great majority, destiny is shown to be more uncertain. Two theories prevail: One maintains that souls are either condemned to suffer eternal fire or enjoy the contemplation of God. This conception, particularly Semitic, maintains duality even in the "other world", and this presents various grave drawbacks, the principal one being that it disqualifies the spirit impeding its greatest aspiration and maximum experience in life: its Unity. The other theory besides affirming the latter believes in reincarnation. This has the great advantage of always remitting us to life until the final liberation. Here life is not condemnable nor is there condemnation after it. The spirit has countless possibilities of improving its situation, of evolving: life is an eternal spirit and as there is no hell, the spirit always has the possibility of achieving its destiny. If one does not believe in one or the other, there is a third, which is our proposal: to have this experience in the only life in which we are sure we will live: this one.

Eastern and Western perspectives

After covering the history of thought and sentiment in the East and West, this is my conclusion: The disparate and heterogeneous history of the West is a consequence of the lack of direct perception of the Transcendent. And the similarity that we find in the Far East, particularly in Hinduism and Buddhism, far from being, as Hegel said, a lack of dynamism or creativity, is the natural result of a clearer vision of the Transcendent, i.e. what it has of the "repetitive" is due to the constant convergence of the individual spirits in the universal Spirit.

My experience confirms that this is not just an opinion, it is reiterated throughout my work in which both cultures have converged and to which they have contributed. But on entering these two worlds of thought my spirit invariably adopts different perspectives; which the reader will now know how to differentiate. When I enter the Western world I find the individual perspective, and it is from this perspective that the thinker wants to elevate his spirit, using isolated intuitions with which he infers the reality on high. It is with his discernment that he establishes the relations that he needs in order to explain the world below, the surface of which he is familiar with. In the Eastern, Buddhist, Hindu or Taoist world, if I do not place my spirit in an adequate perspective, I will simply not understand what they speak of or the space through which I weave my way, but as soon as I adopt the right perspective, the clouds disappear and I clearly see the material and spiritual realities. We can say that these philosophies-religions not only hit the target but view reality from the target; this is the *essential perspective* to which I have tried to bring the spirit of the reader. I have written all my work from this perspective and these philosophies become transparent from this perspective. I believe that this is the most pertinent thing a Westerner can do for the understanding of the Eastern spirit.

While following the trajectory of thought of the most lucid spirits of the West, we have seen that they tend to converge on a common objective which is Unity, which since it is absolute, tries to unify external or material reality and the internal or the spiritual. I believe that what I have called *universal Consciousness* is the sought after point of convergence. Already in possession of this knowledge (although it will be clear that rational comprehension is not sufficient), I would like to relate my thought with the Monist philosophies-religions of Buddhism and Vedanta. I believe I have referred to them sufficiently in *The Evolution of the Spirit*, to which I direct the interested reader, but it would be idle not to insist on clarifying this very important issue.

In the Far East, this search has been more consistent and homogenous for the simple reason that this idea was clearer, the spirit of the philosophers has been closer to the Spirit, their consciousness never managed to alienate itself from universal Consciousness. Political and historical reasons also contributed to it. They never had political-religious organizations that dogmatically imposed a faith in opposition to other beliefs, and thus the spirit and history could follow a *natural development in an atmosphere of freedom*, an indispensable factor for all spiritual and material evolution. They had as many wars as the West, but these were not religious wars. India only knew and suffered this catastrophe with the Muslim invasion, but this could only destroy its temples, it could not reach the spirits. The fact that orthodoxy has been established by those who have had the experience of the Absolute is of the greatest importance and decisive, because from them partiality, dogma, violence, etc., could never have taken place since they are inspired by absolute paradigms.

For these reasons monism has been a constant in the Far East. Within it there have been different schools, but those which have marked orthodoxy, through their own moral and philosophical strength, have never been opposed to religion. For this reason, before orthodoxy, it would be more correct to speak of a principal current, of a permanent reference generated and maintained by its notable mystics and thinkers who have been confirming their experience through the experience of their ancestors who modifying them with nuances up to the present day. One of the last philosophers and mystics who deserve special recognition is Aurobindo, on whom I commented in the aforementioned work, but who will now be useful to me in order to lay down the comparison.

The central current or orthodoxy of Hinduism and Buddhism has been that of a radical monism in which true reality is entirely spiritual. Material reality is taken as a product of Maya, which is like a veil that covers the Reality or Brahman. This veil is produced by our mind in a state of ignorance. Now I do not share the extreme notion that this Reality is singular and the world non-existent, and neither did Aurobindo, who made efforts to incorporate material reality in the tradition of Vedanta. As I have explained, I do not believe that either Shankara or Mahayana Buddhism denied the existence of the universe, of Buddha himself and of human beings; although his theories seem to confirm it. Their interest, to my way of thinking, is to lead the human spirit to the experience of the Absolute; it is nothing but a radical methodology. If nothing less than the existence of the universe is at stake (on a theoretical plane, of course) what is truly important is the psychic reality in which two realities are contrasted: ignorance and wisdom; this is the crux. He who perceives only a concrete reality is ignorant, he who perceives Brahman, the absolute, attains wisdom.

In *Origin and Destiny of Man* I wrote about the origin of man as a rational being when he becomes conscious of his individuality, his *I*, from which he develops his reason and accumulates what he has learnt in his memory. From then on our species distances itself from other species which it manages to dominate, it can organize itself in societies and it seems to progressively improve until society, as we know it today, is formed. Our history, if we can forget the atrocities committed, is shown to be positive, but this is just one part of reality. Various mythologies speak of a *fall* of man in his origin, of a descent of the soul at a moment when it seems we start to be different from the other species. Even Aurobindo in the XXth century speaks of a descent of the divine state to the human, and when they asked one of his contemporaries, Ramana Maharishi, another enlightened soul, what he thought of original sin, he answered that he had his own vision of the matter, that "the sin began with the first thought," that is to say, with the I and in the identification of the I with the body. This means that where we humans believe that our progress begins, it is on the contrary, the start of our ignorance and errors.

I wanted to clarify this, because without any idea of Ramana's position, it is easy to say that he is against reason, progress, etc., but we always come to the same problem, that of the ignorance of reality that transcends reason. I believe that my theory of perspectives can throw light on this matter. When viewed from the individual perspective, it will only be understood with difficulty; for this reason the objective of this entire treatise is the improvement of this perspective. Ramana Maharishi, like so many other mystics has simply remained in universal Consciousness from which this whole world is presented as a chaos, a turbulence, a struggle of warring, ambitions, a bunch of banalities; we cannot reproach his attitude. I consider it entirely legitimate to remain in that state of beatitude that besides this serves as an incentive to perceptive spirits. But there are other postures, other ways of spreading the message through philosophy, or art for example. For Ramana, who followed Shankara, only unity exists in Brahman, for common man only the multiplicity of the world exists. We cannot opt for one or the other as if the two perspectives were equal, we should not ever forget that the *essential perspective* comprehends the individual; this is the abysmal difference, only he who sees from the *universal Consciousness* gets to choose. I believe that the correct interpretation of these mystics consists in the acceptance of their teachings without any a priori emphasis on the presumed denial of concrete reality; a posteriori, after having attained that knowledge one will be in a condition of deciding what to do with the world and history.

Personally I do not believe it necessary to sustain the non-existence of concrete reality, because this leads to erroneous interpretations by those who see only one side of reality, but I accept the theory of Maya that leads to seeing this world as illusion, as it is an effective means of approaching Reality. In the *unitive experience of the Absolute*, the individual spirit and material reality are effectively absorbed in the Spirit, however the human condition does not allow for definitive establishment in this state, there is a return, but with another perspective; this perspective, it will be understood, is the human matter par excellence.

Of Buddhism and Hinduism

Diverse historical, cultural, religious and philosophical

factors have made the West mature enough to be able to receive the project of a Spirit or universal Consciousness like the one proposed by my philosophy. But as I am conscious that this discipline's approach is strictly philosophical, restricted to a small intellectual group and due to my natural inclination to be isolated, it will not reach a wider public nor will it produce a decisive change in history, thus I have decided to cooperate with Buddhism and Hinduism opening channels in order to churn their waters in our culture (See *The Evolution of the Spirit*). Since these disciplines are essentially similar, I believe that their confluence in the West can greatly contribute to this supreme and immense project of preparing the spirits in order to direct them towards the knowledge and experience of their own consciousness. Besides, even though my philosophy has demonstrated the means towards this end, the praxis of these means needs the supervision and guidance of competent teachers that these traditions can provide.

Christianity has demonstrated its obsolescence, and the immense gap it has left behind after annihilating the native religions of so many people, European, American, African and others, needs to be filled. The intelligent people in the West are accustomed to scientific rigour and philosophical reasoning, and Christianity cannot respond to these needs. Christianity is marginal in contemporary mentality because it bases its faith in church imposed dogmas, and the infallibility of these dogmas is due to presumed revelations, to the Church's own self-declared authority. Beyond these doctrinal aspects, its inefficiency has also been proven. In the West the *intelligentsia* is irreligious; it lives oblivious to spiritual life. This is an extreme reaction that has created a general skepticism that has spread over all religions and over the concept of religion in general, and this is serious because there ensues an emptiness in souls that needs to be filled by religions that have been active and dynamic and shown themselves to be capable of integrating the scientific, rational and philosophical demands of the contemporary world. Since Buddhism and Hinduism are in fact based on experience, and do not have a pretended "scientific" idea of the creation of the world, together with their capacity of renewal without need of contradiction or even justification, as their *Dharma* is completely spiritual, these doctrines can be welcomed by every rational, intelligent and demanding person who is concerned with the future of our species. We can also add that their disinterest in politics, economics and power in general; their clear objective in contributing to the mitigation of the suffering of the other, without looking for their own benefits; their projection on to all living beings; their protection of the species and the planet are features of these religions.

We should not forget that we Indo-Europeans share more than just linguistic common roots, which are not negligible as they are modes of expression of a common mentality; but we also have other cultural and spiritual aspects as similar mythologies and common ethics. I believe, for the reasons laid out and for many others that I will later expound on in *Parallel Civilizations*, these doctrines could fill the religious gap and thus revive the human spirit in its totality, that in general the idealists have tried to resurrect so many times in history; in reality all the rebirths that we have had in our culture, have tried to do so. Buddhism and Hinduism can revive our spirit for the simple reason that they are alive and in force and because they are expressions of the most elevated idealism.

However it should be clear that my intent is not to merely import these religious-philosophies as a dogma of the faith, although the opening of the mind towards them can in no way be pernicious, on the contrary, they will contribute to the awakening of the present spirit as well as the Hellenic spirit. I believe that these roots are sufficient to allow Western and Eastern civilizations to grow naturally and vigorously, as they have borne fruits whenever they have been allowed to grow.

My Idealism

"Wisdom is one single thing: the knowledge of the Intelligence that governs all things." *Heraclitus.*

Vital Philosophy = Integral Idealism

In my entire work I have tried to express paths, with their obstacles and the ways to overcome them, which lead to the last stage of the spirit: the Transcendent. There the spirit finds its home, consciousness finds peace. But human consciousness cannot remain in a state of rapture in its purest condition, the spirit is refracted in Consciousness, it penetrates spatial and temporal reality, and observes more unitively than objectively the evolution of living beings, the pitiful march of man towards his Destiny, its knows that human history has to continue its march, in joy and sadness, leaving at times its footprints of blood; and nobody has more consciousness of this than one who sees from this transcendent perspective.

My philosophy points to the Transcendent, but this does not mean that it is directed towards an objective beyond life, but to the plenitude of the same that is achieved in the Unity of the spirit and Nature. It does not pursue an abstract and unachievable ideal, but a *vital experience.* Fichte rightly said "one doesn't learn philosophy, one learns to philosophize", I would add that one learns to philosophize when one learns how to live. Not, of course, when "one manages things" in order to live, which is something that anyone can achieve and which does not have any moral requisite, but to live in Life, i.e. in Totality, in the *Universus*, integrated in inner and outer reality. It is from this *essential perspective* that we truly philosophize, because we move in freedom, within the limits of Reality and the demands of reason and nurtured with pure sentiments, in keeping with the evidence of our vital experiences.

Of course my development does not finally explain particular historical facts rather it concerns itself with the essential currents of history, of the spirit underlying them and of man's constant search that animates and nurtures daily activities. History can be understood as a succession of concrete facts, but this only shows us what man has constructed (and destroyed) regarding the material and external aspects of his activity revealing to us solely one part of the human being. Of course, historical facts are not only explained by the movements of the spirit, they are definitively the result of its interrelation with matter what generates its struggle for survival, that in turn awakens the passions that take man along uncharted roads alien to his destiny; this is the human condition that history continues to weave. And this framework is so dense, multiple and complex that it leads to the concealment of the fundamental threads spanning his origin to his destiny. Rediscovering them and exposing them to the light of the eternal Consciousness of the world is the function of the philosophy of history.

My thought as a system

I have maintained that my thought constitutes a *synthetic system*. I will try to clarify succinctly what I understand by these two concepts that are constantly varying until they lose their original meaning, as inevitably happens when they fall in the hands of different thinkers.

My system is synthetic in the sense that it expresses a totality integrated in a synthesis. Using Kantian language it can be said that this synthesis is pure, as it is not empirical but *a priori*, but it would also be *a priori* to the forms of time and space; the synthesis takes place in the *Transcendent* strictly speaking, it entirely transcends reason.

In principle I adopt the Greek concept of *system* as understood by the Stoics to be *order*. The order of my thought, like all orders, derives from an *Order* that is of an intelligible or transcendent nature that in turn is a *primary manifestation of the Essence or of the One*. This Order is perceived through *transcendental unitive experiences* (to which I will refer later) which show how Order overflows and is overturned in the *Universus*, i.e. in all spiritual and material reality. This Order then extends to Nature, but the latter does not faithfully respond nor does it correspond with the original order, as the Stoics and many later thinkers believed whose extreme we find in Leibniz.

All beings register instances of Order and try to adjust to them, but do so in keeping with their nature and potential; hence their conscious and unconscious intention of perfecting themselves. In the kingdom of the spirit we do not live entirely in agreement with the said Order, this is clear in the human spirit, which although it tries to perfect itself is decidedly imperfect and full of contradictions.

From what has been expressed it can be derived that by system I understand the extension of the said emanation of Order in the spirit of the philosopher who in their attempt at interpreting the *Universus* extends themselves along the different branches or disciplines of philosophy such as psychology, ethics, aesthetics and the theory of knowledge, all of them transcendental as they enmesh with metaphysics the roots of which are the *primary manifestations* that feeding off the Essence of the world, the One or universal Consciousness. The said branches have to grow naturally, always expressing their origin, I must add, never letting go of the sap. These disciplines try to manifest their origin, they never try to *construct it*, they never turn into themselves in order to close the system being an open one, the branches extend freely and indefinitely without contravening, as far as possible, the demands of reason. They never deviate in order to adapt to it, rather it is reason that should submissively adapt to reality, as it is nothing more than an instrument and not always the most adequate. Besides, my system remains at the periphery of logic, in the sense that it does not want to *demonstrate* anything with inferences, syllogisms of even through dialectics, as my objective is metaphysical and in this field as Kant, the master of reason has demonstrated, logic has shown itself to be insufficient and often false. Showing and not demonstrating is the objective of the system. In this sense it assimilates the arts; it could be said that this system would be the art of showing the reality of the *Universus*.

As can be seen, the method is deductive, never inductive, as it always conserves the path from the universal to the particular, from the one to the many; the only return that it procures, and this is its final objective, is that of the human spirit to its origin, however only exhibiting its manifestations in nature and its mind in order to attract it, to induce it; only in this sense would it be inductive.

Knowledge emanates from Unity

If my philosophy is well understood, it will be clear why I say that man tends towards unity. Through this generally unconscious intent, he seeks to relate things, as when he unifies quantities, with numbers as well as forms, like the geometrical, the triangle, the circle etc. He also finds more subtle ways, as in poetry in which he relates similar things, like a bird and an arrow, a leaf in the wind with a butterfly, etc. These figures have beauty, which is a higher inspiration as it does not have a practical mission and tends towards the heights. Religion also uses images and ideas in order to find a unity and explanation in a multiple world: the personal god that creates and governs the universe is also an attempt at unification, even if it remains a simplification. In all these attempts man creates unities that are useful in acquiring knowledge even if everything seems to indicate that he ignores the last goal, which is precisely the one that pushes him to unify, and that allows him to survive while he carries out his search, using these partial unities or truths for practical ends. He uses a similar mechanism when his entire knowledge converges on the knowing subject in an arbitrary unity, which is the *I* or the ego; that is also another simplification. This mechanism (simplified here also for easier comprehension) is what a normal man uses, i.e. he who has realized his individuality but not his universality. Now, beyond the normal consciousness that creates relative and partial relations, amongst which we should include scientific projects, however useful they might be, as they are the product of the same individual consciousness, there is another consciousness that located in Unity, generates another *perspective* that I have called *essential* because it views from the Essence itself. The entire quest of man in the final instance is directed towards this objective, all idealist philosophies point towards it; my entire philosophy tries to clear the paths that lead to this goal.

I believe that my philosophy can reopen the problem of the *universals* as it places them between the two extremes of realism and conceptualism. It is realist in the sense that it affirms the existence of a Unity from which are derived the primary manifestations which are real energies and which act in Nature and in the mind. The latter uses this unity, which it unconsciously intuits, as a reference in order to extract universal concepts. From these manifestations are derived the forms of time and space that allow one to think

(Kant). Thanks to the intuition of the immutable, an idea is formed of the mutable, the multiple is deduced from the One and from the latter the partial unities, as a species, genre, kingdom or any other universal. Universal laws are possible thanks to the same reference, as Unity integrates all reality. Besides, the desire to integrate is born of the mind's need to reintegrate itself in Unity. All knowledge is relation, all relation is integration. The arts pursue the same objective: the relations that the poet establishes, although not rational, integrate reality, the painter integrates it in painting, the sculptor searches for the essence in their model because they compare it (unconsciously) with the perfect, the One, who is Beauty in itself. In the harmonious relation of nature that the musician establishes there is integration and also the manifestation of the integration of things; and this is Unity: absolute integration.

My idealism and the perspectives

My proposal of re-establishing idealism can only be embarked upon from a more elevated perspective than that sustained by the last idealism. We cannot base ourselves in the latter because we will fall in the same manner as the spirit fell after Schopenhauer, but we can begin with a common principle that I consider unsurpassable: Only consciousness is immediately given to us. However, it is necessary to pose a prior question here: Does my consciousness have the correct perspective? It seems our philosophers never posed this question, except perhaps Plato who did not begin with this principle. We can agree with Schopenhauer and say: "all that we know is a phenomenon of consciousness" due to which "the objective world does not exist except as representation" (*The World* Ap. I, 1), but here too we find the same doubt. So the error lies in starting from the perspective of the individual consciousness. There is a task that comes before philosophizing, which is that of investigating our own consciousness, recognizing its nature, its potential, its ascending and descending tendencies, its capacity for displacement, the places to which it is displaced, discovering the *planes of understanding and the levels of consciousness*. As an old oracle observed, one has *to know oneself*, as this is the knowing subject, that is not one entity where the *I* faces the world and in which the latter is represented, but also a multiple and complex interior world that is very difficult to know due to its shifting nature and to all the reasons we have for not wanting to discover it,.

Firstly one has to achieve a *level of consciousness* in which we are certain that this is the final rung, the perspective from which before we see the world we can see our mind clearly; in fact we are dealing with a consciousness that comprehends both, that views the world and the representations with equal objectivity. When Schopenhauer refers, especially when speaking about the capacity of the artist, to a "perfect objectivity", I believe that he intuits the consciousness that I have called *unitive*.

Since my theory of perspectives plays an important role in my philosophy and the concept of *perspectivism* obeys a very different and essentially opposite vision, I will try to lay down the differences. Even if *perspectivism* naturally admits that some know more than others, it tacitly or latently assumes that human beings find themselves on an equal plane of consciousness, in such a way that each one can contribute to a total knowledge. Ortega y Gasset expresses it in this way: "Juxtaposing the particular visions of all the complete and absolute truth can be woven"; this would be "the sum of all of them". Ortega refers to a type of knowledge that finds its validity in the multiple and empirical world, but I greatly fear that it is invalid for achieving the Absolute, as it cannot overcome the relative. The sum of all the perspectives obtained will not give us the total knowledge as Ortega wished, but a confused mass of differing opinions grouped together and impossible to evaluate; this democratic and hypothetical solution is unrealizable in practice and unsustainable in theory, it would really be the opposite of knowledge properly speaking. The perspectives to which I am referring in their ascendant path lead to a unifying summit, to the Unity itself where individual perspectives and all relativism disappear. While *perspectivism* is lateral, my theory of perspectives is vertical, ascendant, and presupposes an intrinsic transformation of the observer.

Disparity in philosophy

To Schelling the discrepancies, divergences and sectarianism that we find in the history of thought seemed "scandalous", and rightly so, as they have caused a lot of discouragement, skepticism and, more seriously, the fall in prestige of philosophy. If this is the "mother of sciences", and this is perhaps the only thing on which all philosophers agree, it will be understood how disastrous the matter is.

In view of this situation there have been sincere attempts at conciliation. "The syncretism, which is affirmed by the conformity of philosophical thought with itself, is considered by Horn as the true result of the history of philosophy." (cit. Brehier *Intr. Hist. Filos.*). Justus Lipsius thinks that "There is no more than one sect in which we can securely inscribe ourselves: the eclectic sect" as "alien to all factions it will easily become the companion of truth" (*Op. cit*). Every attempt at conciliation is entirely laudable, but I do not believe that real truths can emerge from either syncretism or eclecticism, rather the margins will be diluted and the content will become imprecise.

My proposal, as I mentioned at the beginning of this work in the chapter on *The Origin of Ideas*, is to highlight the *superposition of common ideas* of writers despite being from different doctrines. Wherever there is an overlap of thought amongst philosophers, there is also a commingling of experiences that point to common truths. It is significant that we have not even been able to agree about the *raison d'être* of philosophy itself. We would apparently all agree with Plato that what makes a philosopher is a love of truth, but the interpretations have been so diverse that this agreement can be doubted. If we were to adjust the idea a little more towards that of Aristotle and say that it consists of the search for the first principles, and identify these with the truth, we would have a framework of reference. The most notable Western thinkers have persistently agreed with the intuition that these first principles have to be found in Unity. Thus we have a framework of reference and a tradition that delineates orthodoxy of the purest Hellenic model, which is what I adhere to, not dogmatically, of course, but it is the richest vein we have found in our culture. In no way does this mean that we are limited only to this (that would be a dogma) as the spiritual and cultural discoveries of the Far East can also greatly benefit us.

In my opinion, belief in the power and reach of reason has been abused to a great extent in the West, which has pretended to replace the imprecise knowledge derived from isolated intuitions of the Transcendent, and therefore fills the gap that lies between it and Nature and man. We are not denying the effort and inventiveness implied by philosophical systems, but if these structures do not correspond with the first principles, they do not increase, however great they may be for our knowledge, since these thinkers teach us how to think and not to how see. It is here that we can benefit from the knowledge techniques used in India, which are directed towards the experience of the Transcendent through a prior and necessary transformation of the aspirant. I will never tire of insisting on this preparation, as the understanding of my own philosophy depends on it, as do Plato and Plotinus who also insisted on it. This ought to be laid down once and for all; it is *after this experience* that reason can be applied in the *noumenal* plane in an edifying manner. Inductive reasoning is sterile on that plane, as Kant had warned.

Reason, faith and experience

There are two fundamental reasons why Western man has abandoned God; he is right on one count, wrong on the other. He was right when he put away the God of Christianity because this story did not respond to the needs of the spirit. In the other he erred, not through a decision but due to ignorance, ignorance of the historical process, that was unconsciously produced, and of the Transcendent, who he identified with the divinity which he had renounced. He never understood nor does contemporary man understand that Divinity has a very important role to play: that of the *unifying archetype Idea* of a *unitive factor par excellence in the Universus*, in which all transcendental intuitions are inspired and towards which they are directed, which nurture the religious sentiment which is also a way to the Transcendent. The *universal Consciousness* fulfils these functions marvelously well; even if there are multitudes who need a personal god, various gods or special saints in which they can materialize their vague intuitions of the supra sensible. This process of going from faith to knowledge will be long, and we should be tolerant, even with those who were not so when they wanted to impose their faith.

To my understanding and my taste, the West has abused the field of the philosophy of discernment, as if this faculty were the most ideal and fruitful, to the detriment of other faculties that are much more so in my opinion. This emphasis and confidence in the speculative faculties increased with the achievements of the exact sciences, which produced a kind of inversion as from then on philosophy followed in their steps, producing a sadness similar to what we feel when we see adults trying to imitate young people; which curiously is a typical sign of decadence in societies.

In the West something similar also happened with faith in the religious field, as if there were no other means in this terrain for their objectives. Of course, the Church had interests created for it, but it is surprising that the philosophers did not warn of the limitations of the method. The fact is that in Western culture there has been and continues to be a millenarian controversy between these two specializations: reason *versus* faith, a vicious circle that has caused a lamentable delay in our understanding. In both cases what has surprisingly not occurred to the philosophers is to appeal to experience, not of course in the scientific way but to the direct and immediate experience of the spirit of its object: the Transcendent; there are other paths to understanding that are more encompassing, integrating, complete and suitable. The philosopher needs poetry more than geometry, he needs to love before he can reason, to expand the spirit before dividing it into pieces, to live before thinking about life, he needs in sum: *spiritual experience.*

Religion does not only have goals in common with philosophy, but also the means that they should share. A dose of religiosity, in the sense of a contemplative life, necessary for the filtering of ideas, and of asceticism, in prudent measure, with the objective of purifying and dematerializing the spirit, is a complement of great value for the philosopher, while the religious man should accept the exigencies of reason and not "sacrifice the intellect" in the name of dogmas that he is not ready to question. The fortunate and edifying convergence of these disciplines, has allowed for the highest peaks of the spirit to be scaled in

India. Conscious of the benefits of this interaction, my own discipline is directed to the development of an *experimental knowledge of the Transcendent.*

Unitive Consciousness and knowledge

In my *Scheme of Mind* (see this chapter in my *Psychosophy*) it will be seen that even if they super impose themselves, philosophical consciousness is displaced towards the plane of the intellect and religious consciousness towards that of the sentiments, since if this is the inclination of the spirit of the latter, from this perspective it will reclaim an object to which it can apply its sentiments such as love, devotion, fear, submission, etc. However if it projects itself towards the plane of the intellect it will see its path smoothened towards a depersonalized object. It will be understood that what is decisive here is the clear vision of the displacements of the spirit and the capacity to move it with freedom. Bradley rightly said that the concept of God is a demand of the religious consciousness, whereas from the philosophical point of view the need is to see it as Absolute; even if instead of an exigency, I see it as an inclination of which the spirit should be conscious.

In the first instance it will seem, at least to the philosopher, that the philosophical side is superior because it projects itself towards Unity, and practice confirms this opinion, however, the highest and purest stage of religious consciousness also overcomes the personal vision of the *I*, and does not then project its sentiments on a personal god, but so to speak, as if it were the latter, flows his sentiments over all beings, since his spirit refracts itself in the Absolute and projects itself in Nature; it looks, thinks and feels *from its universal Consciousness; it is this perspective that I have called essential.*

But we should be prudent and adhere strictly to experience in order to not fall into what psychoanalysts call the inflation of the personality. In the refraction mentioned the spirit follows a *process of unitive individuation*, this means that when it returns to its finite state, it is a spirit psychically and morally integrated with the *Universus* because it conserves its unitive vision; even though what is discerned will be limited to its human faculties and act within the spatial–temporal limits of its particular animal body. It knows that thanks to his change of perspective it has exchanged an egocentric vision for a universal one, and an *ontological transformation* has taken place in him, that in mythical terminology would correspond to a transfiguration, and in initiatory language to a renaissance (rebirth). Its faculties will be elevated, its senses sharpened more, Nature will seem more luminous, but it will be stuck on planet Earth and in the moment of action it will be subject to the human condition.

Although in earlier works I have explained this process of unification and unitive individuation, I wanted to make clear these paths of the spirit. Just as Kant marked out the limits of knowledge from the individual perspective or that of discernment, limits that have been transgressed with impunity time and again, as if the genius of Köenisberg did not exist, but which I have personally accepted and also taken as an indispensable reference, I feel the need to *establish the limits of the spirit from the essential perspective*, which even if transgressed, will not be so because my lack of clarity lends itself to this.

Intuitions and vital experiences

As Bergson had observed, all notable philosophers, especially the idealists, start from a basic intellectual intuition, which I call transcendental. For those who have not experience this it is usual (and natural, given human psychology), that they feel angry with talk of a "privileged" intuition, they prefer philosophies that are within the reach of all. But neither I nor anyone is guilty that Nature is like this, everything that is excellent is exceptional: the giant pearls, the diamonds of great purity, and the remarkable Ideas. And just as there is no dearth of "critics" of philosophies, who since they are not philosophers, are uncomfortable with the recourse of *transcendental intuitions*, there will be many critics of my *unitive experiences*, because they are not within the reach of all. But this democratic reasoning goes beyond natural, philosophical and historical reality, and this is serious in philosophy. Intuitions and experiences are indisputable facts that have inspired all the great discoveries of man and history demonstrates that there have been very few philosophers. I have no doubt that all great philosophy has been born of a vision of the Transcendent, proof of this is that the fundamental themes of philosophy, freedom, happiness, Order, love, the origin of life, are precisely the very content of the Transcendent.

Those who have not had an intuition of the Transcendent, ignore its implications. I have explained my theory of the shifts of the spirit, that an ascent of this not only grants more clarity of perception, but also a greater integration of oneself and the World. The reason is simple: the complete apperception of the Transcendent (*total unitive experience*), is the consummation of all virtues, the harmonious integration of all faculties, in particular that of the intellect and the sentiments (vital experience), it is the realization of the eternal aspiration of man's unconditional freedom and happiness. As the spirit approaches this experience, through intellectual intuitions and elevated sentiments it will participate in the plenitude of life.

Schelling's affirmation that the objective of philosophy is the Absolute is derived from his experience and he confirms it when he clarifies that it can only be achieved through intellectual intuition and not through reason.

This has had and continues to have great consequences in the history of philosophy, and it should be assumed so by anyone who has not had the said intuitions. And we should not forget that the great majority who concern themselves with philosophy, i.e. those who teach, transmit, comment, criticize and write histories of philosophy have not had these intuitions. This makes them incline towards those who they can understand and follow their reasoning. This explains the passion of so many intellectuals for Hegel and, symptomatically the inclination of the philosophers for Schelling, in spite of the latter's lack of clarity, meanderings and contradictions.

In the philosophies that we have seen, the immense creative power of intuitions has been proven, but also its limitations. I am convinced that *experiences* can lead us to other stages of knowledge. Within my limitations I have provided the means so that *unitive experiences* present themselves, but I do not ignore the difficulties of obtaining psychic and moral equilibrium, nor the interest and will required for this. If the experiences are strange it is because men with the necessary virtues are strange. What is unacceptable from a philosophical point of view is the "grace of revelation" and the appeal to faith in it. In keeping with my understanding, religious experience is no different from the philosophical; everything depends on the plane of understanding used. "Grace" is an *a posteriori* premise of those who *believe* in a god *alien* to the consciousness, without realizing the level of alienation that this implies. This belief has led to many mistakes. For this reason Schelling hastened to clarify that his intuitions were not "mystical privileged experiences".

Here there is no privilege as there is no external god who grants it, as it is the result of the aforementioned integration. If the path of sentiments is more exalted, the sentiment of the sacred will become more patent, if the path of the intellect, the doors of the transcendent will open, but here there is no *revelation*, but a discovery. Everything happens within the Consciousness, there is no heteronomy. But, once more, we should be careful to not inflate our individual consciousness believing in its unlimited autonomy, as there is none like this; on the contrary, it is very limited and replete with weights and obstacles that the ego ceaselessly interposes. I am speaking of *another* consciousness that annihilates the former, of a unitive knowledge, which is in no case subjective. For this reason belief in a god to whom we owe submission, renunciation and the sacrifice of our ego, has been shown to be effective; it can even take us to the doors of the Transcendent, but it does not open them for us to enter and contemplate the World from the inside.

In *vital experience* it is not only the thought that transcends but the whole spirit of the subject, which thus stops being such. And this happens because there is an integration of all the faculties as all of them are unified, in such a way that the individual spirit mingles with the universal Spirit becoming *one single Consciousness*. This is the *first principle* not just of philosophy but of all reality. The fundamental aspect of this *total unitive experience* is that the subject does not disappear as abstraction, but in reality, the body of the subject remains individualized and the spirit recognizes this individuality, but it knows that it is essentially spirit; it has suffered a radical, *ontological transformation* giving it another perspective with which to see the world and its own individuality. The said transformation makes of this individual a *moral being* because as Fichte rightly intuited, there is *a moral universal Order* that Fichte identifies with the Divinity: "The divine is the moral order". He also rightly believed in the moral finality of human existence and in the development of consciousness towards this end. The *unitive experience* takes the spirit towards this realization; it stops being a project and an aspiration and becomes an act.

Needless to say, this transformation requires a *praxis of moral purification* the aforesaid integration of all the faculties. In any case the said integration is not achieved with the will nor with reason, it is the product of successive *conscious realizations* in which all faculties join together. This *unitive integrated knowledge* allows the whole spirit to shift until it reaches a level where there are no isolated intuitions of the Transcendent, but a direct vision, a continuous experience of the same.

In my philosophy the *plane of central understanding*, i.e. where the spirit is centred, is not that of the intellect, nor that of the sentiments, but that of the *vital*, which includes a substrata of both. Here one does not just intellectualize nor feel but experience, one both knows and feels Life, and the individual lives integrated in it. It begins from a state of contemplation, but not of objects as subject, but experiencing its integrity. The nucleus of consciousness is the nucleus of Life. From its *essential perspective* it experiences life overflowing from its Essence; and one, as an individual, is part of this universal waterfall, which flows over time and space. It is the plenitude of life here and now.

While we are centred, Life is ever present, though due to our animal condition we cannot remain in an absolute state of contemplation. It is the other side of life that alienates and disintegrates it is the state of survival that leads us to attend to the particulars and particularize us. Knowing that there on the calm bank we can find the peace of contemplation, we should not let ourselves be dragged along by the current of the quotidian more than is necessary. Vices are born from the pleasure of being dragged along by it; virtues by our inclination to come out of it. Only when we are full of virtues can we exist in the current of daily life, even with pleasure, without falling into vice.

The experience of the spirit

I have not explicitly confessed this experience for many reasons. In the first place, because one is dealing with the abode of the *Sacred* itself, and I feel it is a desecration to talk about such intimate subjects. This strange and profound feeling of respect for the Sacred made the Orphic and other similar teachings "mysteries" reserved for the "initiated" who participated in an "esoteric" knowledge. If this reserve was considered necessary then, it is much more so in the present when the communication media, charlatans, fraudulence, bad taste, vulgarity, lack of respect and the impostors have invaded everything, including all that should be "esoteric", hence this pseudo-spiritual *mélange* which is today called "esotericism", a witches cauldron for opportunists and false gurus, who disguised as wise men search for fame and money, thus propagating ignorance in the guise of the spiritual; unfortunately this happens at a stage in history when nothing is more urgent than intellectual and moral seriousness. It is for this crucial reason that makes me express this knowledge within the domains of philosophy.

Why make such an intimate and private knowledge esoteric during such decadent times? Firstly I did not choose to be born in this time and place; at least in my knowledge. Secondly, I have spent more than 30 years trying to lead the spirits towards this experience through my writings, without too many results. Without doubt the most efficient means is the direct transmission from teacher to disciple practiced by Hindus and Buddhists, but I have not had the time nor the patience for this. Thirdly, because I am at the end of my life and it would be a waste to take this knowledge with me to a reality where silence reigns, since I myself have lamented the fact that the Greek mysteries have been forgotten.

The danger lies in the fact that if final answers are given, then this is pre-digested food so to speak, and nourishes nobody; what nourishes is the process of assimilation that each one should undertake. *Unitive knowledge* consists of precisely this, in the harmonious integration of the consciousness, a product of the slow filtering of experiences. For this reason I have differentiated it from accumulative knowledge, because this is external, like clothing, and this is what the *I* invariably uses, he dresses himself up in ideas and beliefs that change his appearance but do not produce an intrinsic transformation. Without the said internal labour, my philosophy cannot be understood. I confess that I do not know what will happen to my philosophy, I ignore its destiny; there are always unforeseen historical variables, like natural or social catastrophes, that lead to unexpected realizations.

This experience includes all the faculties, the intellect and sentiments which are in complete agreement, for this reason I have called it a *vital experience* that happens, as I said, when there is a total integration of the faculties, only possible when there is no interference from the sentiments or from the unconscious, or from dreams. This requires a prolonged process of self-knowledge in which moral consciousness plays a first order role and a contemplative life is indispensable. But these are just mechanisms, the means that need a driving force, an incentive, and this is the sincere constant, and if necessary a vehement interest, in searching for definitive and indisputable answers without appealing to beliefs. It is when the spirit is found clean and unperturbed and stretched to its limits, that it ruptures the sphere of individual consciousness, the nucleus of which is the I and its content: reason and memory. This experience is not just spiritual, it manifests itself in the organism in the most dramatic and undoubted manner.

In *The Return to the Sources* I have related the process followed by the spirit, its search, its doubts and some prior experiences on the different planes of knowledge including the internal or subconscious plane, as the mind continues integrating and unifying itself until it finds its original Unity. When the spirit pushes reason to its limits, it either returns to discernment, as in the case of Kant; or is obliged to transcend it.

In my case this leap towards the Transcendent took place after an intense search for answers that reason did not provide; the infinite was present but I was searching for an idea that made up my reason; these same ideas impeded the outcome. What lay beyond everything? was finally the question that unraveled the spirit. I did not have a rational answer; my spirit escaped my body through the higher and central part of my mind expressing itself as an intense light and a deep noise, like a tremor in my brain. My spirit and that light were only one entity, they projected themselves towards the infinite but not in a straight in a but circular line around the All; it could be said that it was a universal encirclement, however it was around a limitless light that was All and which made the World disappear; all Reality was contained in that light. I do not know how much time this absence from Nature lasted because the spirit had definitely transcended time, space and matter; it had found immutable Unity.

After this encirclement the spirit in the form of light returned to my body through the same orifice in the brain vertically crossing my body. When it entered my body I experienced the latter like a stranger, as if the spirit could well have descended into another's being, but it had done so in my body and I felt I was in strange attire, as if in a scuba diver's outfit in which I could observe my own breathing.

When I saw the external reality everything was in Order, and this happened because *empty space had more presence* than the things that it had ordered, the Spirit was more real than matter; everything was well. Matter was charged, impregnated with the luminosity of the Spirit; the Beautiful was perched on the World; everything took on life as if this impregnation had given a Soul to Nature, everything was animated with Life. The spiritual light illuminated and revealed another Consciousness, it gave the spirit another dimension, and it discovered another reality, from which concrete reality is shown to be less real and secondary, as an expression of the first Reality.

By observing the animation of Nature, the spirit was slowly becoming conscious of time and space, but these would not be the same as it observed them from another perspective, not from the point of view of the I, the individual, but from outside of it; a perspective I have called essential, from which the spirit contemplates the becoming.

I confess that I have only once experienced the disappearance of the World wherein it became nothing more than light. However, since then, when I concentrate on the light that penetrates my mind, or when I contemplate the empty space in Nature, that is accompanied by a sound like that of crystals, which is internal and not from the ear, the Spirit becomes more patent than matter, and Nature again becomes alive in the aforesaid manner and recovers its beauty and plenitude.

At that time (I was 42 years old), I felt a strong pressure in the centre of the upper part of my head, where the ray of light entered without any intention on my part, and everything around lit up, not, of course, through my volition. For two years I did not entirely regain my discernment, during which I did not dream but could control the images that appeared on the internal plane (see *On the Control of Dreams*, in *Psychosophy*). I believe much more time would have lapsed, maybe even the rest of my life, distant from this faculty so connected to the *I*, to time and to space, if I had not made the effort of writing, which inevitably involves the intervention of discernment. I believe that by expressing these ideas, by philosophizing, I have to a great extent lost a state of permanent happiness and plenitude. But, as I have explained elsewhere, we are not only ourselves, we are also part of humanity, and as such a project towards Unity.

These experiences lead me to conclude that there is a *pure Consciousness* which is expressed as light, which would be the Absolute. This light extends over Nature, it draws it in and envelops and encompasses it; this intelligence transcends reason and evolution. Consciousness is unified, it is the *universal Consciousness.* The human spirit cannot remain in that state of absolute contemplation, but conscious of that transcendent reality, *it keeps its essential perspective* from which it sees, hears, thinks and lives in the becoming; it is installed in the *unitive consciousness.* It will be understood that from this primary and primordial reality which flows over all beings, I have extracted what I have called *primary manifestations*, which are not hypothesis but reality undoubtedly experienced. And not by a subject, as the latter is the first to disappear.

In this process the moral plays an important and indispensable role, as in my case I had even to revisit the mischievous escapades of childhood. This should be well understood: all guilt, however minimal, generates a turbulence that prevents us from seeing clearly into the depths of our conscience; like a well into which we drop a stone that muddies the surface whenever we want to see the bottom. In other words, an exhaustive moral purification and a mainly contemplative life is necessary, as each action in which our moral has been in play should be reflected in the conscience until it is seen with complete clarity.

Actions are not only resolved with thoughts, both need a sincere and persistent examination of the conscience. All rational justification, which is the mechanism that usually issues from our immoral acts, however minuscule they may be, I repeat, generate an impediment which will remain until it is questioned and resolved, not in keeping with our I but with our moral consciousness.

Not everything is resolved with transcendental intuitions or mystic experiences. Without a firm, healthy and purified moral consciousness, they would be like artificial fireworks which are extinguished and fall lifeless to the ground after a brief period of splendour; nor can we rely on faith, which has nothing to do with experience.

The spirit accedes to another consciousness, that it immediately recognizes as superior, for its purity, height and amplitude and above all because it is found liberated from the *I*, with all its beliefs, memories and daily problems; it transcends the multiple world, it finds itself in the Unity, its Consciousness is One, it is unified in the *Universus*, it lives free and integrated. This unconditional Freedom naturally generates unconditional Happiness.

It is the plenitude of Life, not only mine, but of all the living. I believe that this experience is what the Buddhists call the *samadhi* of Emptiness. The aesthetic experience of the artist, the astonishment *vis a vis* the life of the poet, the sentiment of *the sacred* of the religious, the perception of the Absolute of the philosopher; these are all intuitions of this Reality.

On its return to multiplicity, i.e. to the habitual external faculties, the spirit finds itself estranged and it is difficult for it to adapt to reason and it must pass through a period of adaptation; the problem is that it does not want to adapt to it. My mind needed some two years to find equilibrium between the two consciousnesses, the unified and the individual, until it found it in an intermediate consciousness which I have called *unitive consciousness,* which I have considered the correct one for the human being in which without losing its *essential perspective,* it can attend to its bodily needs.

In the beginning I wanted to write these experiences but I could not do so without losing the said perspective; this forced me to write in a concise, spontaneous manner in the form of maxims so characteristic of the language of the mystics, that did not satisfy me but which I could not avoid, because as soon as I discerned, my spirit shifted and even alienated itself from the Sources, to which in order to return, it had to enter into a *state of absolute contemplation.* Fortunately I could do so as I lived far away on a mountain in a kind of paradise, next to a forest where the spirit found itself in its element.

It is by observing these comings and goings of the spirit that I have been forging my theory of the shifts of the spirit and the perspectives that it acquired on different planes and levels; as it is the spirit that contemplates its movements on its way, it is not the I that looks at the spirit, but vice versa; it is this that makes self-knowledge possible. I tried to express all this in a rational language, but when I later read it I found it too abstruse and unintelligible. I noted that it spoke of psychology, of ethics, of aesthetics, of the different domains of philosophy; I decided then to adjust myself to the demands of this discipline, in the conviction that it would be accessible in this way to religious people as well as to intellectuals.

In my first book, *The Return to the Sources*, my effort to adjust to reason can be evidenced in the language used that seems at times to be written by two people, and, in fact I felt obliged to establish a dialogue with my "inner voice". The difficulty lies in adapting reason to the Sources, and not vice versa, without giving in to beliefs, presuppositions, ideas or additions that do not correspond to experience, without falling into the traps of sophism, literature, and even the logical necessities that require a system of thought; finally without losing sight of the *essential perspective*, in order to deduce without ever inducing; hence my insistence in establishing the spirit in the Sources before practicing philosophy. This should be clear and clearly laid down: we are not dealing here with strange mental states, with "visions," but of a radical and positive change in man, as all the virtues emanate from the said Sources, they make us better or as the Greeks said, more beautiful.

In this maximum experience the spirit proves that its essence is light, and that the essence of biological reality is also light. This leads me to conclude that the spirit manifests itself as light generating the elements or atomic corpuscles necessary for life and particular spirits that are prolongations of this Essence. And in this way we see in space a myriad of suns capable of generating life and particular spirits.

I insist that I do not perceive a rational Will wanting a concrete result, but only an expansion of the Spirit that becomes matter. I also insist that it is not a material force blind to the matters of the spirit; it is imbued with the *primary manifestations* from which virtues emanate that express the way of being of the Universal Spirit, the *Origin and Destiny* of particular spirits; that in turn can become conscious of the primordial Spirit.

This should be clear as far as possible: we are not dealing with a "personal" experience; the experience takes place precisely because the person disappears. Who has the experience then? This is a question to which only experience can respond. All that the individual spirit has done is to liberate itself from the *I* with which it finds its freedom. All that it has done is to empty the mind for the Spirit to fill it, in such a way that it can see with the eyes and hear with the ears of a particular body. Is this what the universal Spirit does, contemplate with the senses of the living beings? This is asked *a posteriori* by reason. But the experience of the Spirit is present. The empty mind is not only what is in the mind, Emptiness, the Mind extends itself, it penetrates and fills all things, it is the Soul of all that is living, it is the *vital élan,* it is Life itself, the very conscious, it is the unity of the consciousness, it is the *universal Consciousness.* There is thus nothing transcendent, everything is immanent. But, on the other hand, there is the human condition; for the spirit cannot remain in that absolute state and returns to its individuality.

From what I read or know of this experience in others, it is normal for it to last only a few moments, enough to greatly transform the subject, it will now no longer be the same, and will know that there is another reality and that the Transcendent exists. But, apart from exceptions, and although they will now not see the world in the same way, these instants are not enough to produce a radical change of perspective, for they will return to their individual perspective and begin to reason from it. The experience in these cases is similar to an intuition. If it is of a sentimental kind and its access path has been the *plane of the sentiments,* we will have the case of the mystics who will seek a religious interpretation, if it is of a rational type and has used the *plane of the intuitions,* a philosophical explanation will be searched for. Plotinus confesses that he had had this experience four times; hence the penetration of his thought. But we are still not faced with a radical change of perspective, it is as if our philosophers did not notice the need for a radical change and rushed into explaining and developing what had happened; this is the case of the idealists that we have seen, as also that of Bergson, whose *vital élan* is, undoubtedly the product of a *creative intuition.*

Schelling saw the need for a change of perspective, but it was more the "adoption" of an absolute perspective from his individual perspective than a real change, due to which he could not maintain himself in it; hence his "fall".

My proposal is to persevere in the *search for an essential perspective,* until the spirit is ensconced in it. For this, one has to leave the reasons in parenthesis and apply oneself to a constant praxis that includes a contemplative life. The guidance of an experienced teacher is advisable. Buddhism and Hinduism have developed specific techniques for this purpose. An experienced teacher knows how to lead one to this experience and it is precisely when it takes place that he is most needed in order to avoid a fall; it is what the Buddhists call "sealing" the knowledge. What is sought is the overcoming of this transient sentiment or intuition, and to achieve an enduring and stable experience that can be repeated when desired and that would include both; not due to the will of the I, but as explained, generating the conditions conducive for it. In this way the spirit *seals* its knowledge. It will return to its human condition, it will experience how it shifts from unity to multiplicity, how it enters vertiginously in time and space where it will be living, but it will not lose its *essential perspective,* it will have lost its *individual perspective*, even if for its survival it knows how to recover it, but without alienating itself in it. Because herein lies the matter: man is alienated from his Essence, and decentred in his consciousness; he who is centred in his Consciousness and sees from his Essence, knows this for a fact. This is the *unitive man,* he who the human being has been searching for from the Origin.

Universal Consciousness

"It could be said that one single person has written all the books in the world; such central unity is in them that there are undeniably the work of a single all-knowing master."

Emerson

The First Principle

The first principle is not the transcendental *I* but the experience of existence. I could say of *my* existence, but by "my" I would not understand my body but a spirit (to give it a name) unreachable through reason, where my experience and the World converge. This spirit expresses itself in absolute repose, in peace. *The fundamental and primary experience is that of a free spirit.* When identified with the *I,* it stops being experienced, ipso facto, as free, because this I implies the limitations of time and space, due to which it becomes a subject of a species, a historical man. The spirit cannot, like Fichte's transcendental I, become an object of (individual) consciousness because it is the eye of consciousness itself. By projecting it outside and transforming it through this action into an object, I shift the spirit towards the external planes of knowledge with which I place it within *phenomenal* reality, from which the World represents itself to me as Kant saw it, and the *noumenal* reality appears to me to be transcendent, *as a thing in itself.*

Unquestionably immediate is consciousness and it presents itself with such evidence that it needs no demonstration. It is the first principle; it is the condition for all other knowledge that will necessarily be *a posteriori*. Thought, sentiment and will are actions of consciousness. If I say "I think" besides activating my consciousness, I am implying an *I*, which is something that reason has constructed and defined *a posteriori*. And if to the *I think* I add *therefore* I put discernment into action, which is always mediate; and thus we will be far from the first principle. The first principle should be axiomatic, an axiom that we may experience in a natural and immediate way.

As I have observed in my earliest writings, precisely as a consequence of the experiences that I related in the earlier chapter: "as soon as we think we transform reality into an abstraction, it stops being what it is in order to *become* an abstraction. When I myself am the object of thought, the consequence will be understood. When I think of myself, I stop being what I am, I annihilate myself with the thought, I transform myself from a reality into a concept. The *I* is a conclusion, an idea, not an existent. Since we can establish between both a relation that we can prove many times, we will conclude that there exists an *I* who thought, imagined, etc. but it is precisely here that the unreality in which we are living begins, the mirror of the world of concepts, when we begin to live with refractions and thus dualities. It is not a matter of demonstrating our existence with symbols, but of living our existence, and for this the mirror that does not let us penetrate the present and live it has to be eliminated. When dealing with something as vital as our own existence, demonstrations are not enough: one has to perceive oneself existing." (*I think, therefore... The Return to the Sources*)

"We thus object to the Cartesian principle that remits us to our individual perspective and then to our world of abstractions. In our understanding, the principle of a philosophy cannot be a product, something constructed or elaborated, but, on the contrary, something simple and solid as a cornerstone. Philosophy would be the development of what is evident to us precisely for its simplicity and unity. An authentic principle should not need proof or demonstration because it should be so unequivocal that it does not need it. If the principle is preceded by a then or therefore it is not a principle, but a result. I do not exist because I think, first and foremost I experience myself living; or, better, *there is an experience of life that precedes my thought.*" (*Op. cit.*)

Is it the first absolute principle, or the principle of the particular knowledge of each one? Both, but in order to understand this we should overcome particular knowledge and not just this but also the I to which this knowledge is referred, i.e. understand this from a consciousness other than the habitual. It is in fact the same consciousness, but from a perspective that comprehends the individual, which is an individuation of the former. But we will not commit the well-known mistake of beginning with our *I* and trying to extend it to all ends of the Universe. If we begin with the particular and go towards the universal, we would *induce* reality and this would limit us to the phenomenal and our knowledge would be relative. Only a change of consciousness or perspective allows us to *deduce* reality. And for this we need to apply a method of knowledge that is neither subjective nor objective, that allows us to continue integrating not just external but also internal reality, to use our faculties to know and to know ourselves, in order to feel and to feel ourselves; for this reason I have called these faculties, *unitives.*

In a revelatory passage (I do not remember where and thus I have to express it in my terminology) Kant observes that for there to be an intuition there should be a consciousness in which the intuition is refracted, a consciousness of that truth. But from this observation he does not extract positive conclusions, as it is very rich in potential. Actually where do so many philosophers get their transcendental ideas? Could it not be from another consciousness? And if this is so, what is needed is to awaken. Hence my theory of the *levels and shifts of consciousness* that has as its final objective *Consciousness in itself.*

The first principle cannot be in the current of the becoming, as we do not arrive at it through inference but through an experience of the Immutable, it is Consciousness in itself. Time and space are not only the forms that condition knowledge but also the conditions for the existence of Nature; the two indispensable coordinates for reality; the two undoubted and necessarily infinite expressions of the Absolute. The symbol that represents the infinite, (*8*) a creation undoubtedly due to a genial intuition, encloses the key of the matter: Unity takes place where the becoming meets the immutable, consciousness is stopped and it is observed how the becoming is poured into it and at the same time flows over Nature.

My philosophy locates the universal Consciousness in the centre of Reality, which is at the centre of man's consciousness, and, in all probability, of all living beings.

For Kant the forms of time and space are the *a priori* indispensable conditions for all empirical knowledge. This is unquestionable and it has an unprecedented permanent and universal value. But we are not yet in the first principles, which are *noumenal*, transcendent. Here is the first principle of knowledge: *the Unity of consciousness is the a priori of all knowledge*, including the forms of time and space.

Universal Consciousness 2

Everything in this World, the large and the small, the near and the far, the ugly and the beautiful is reduced to consciousness. All that is known is because consciousness has reached and covered it. He who has no consciousness is dead and the World is dead to him. We attain consciousness in as much as we know the one who knows, ourselves and the external world. And the latter is of little use to us if it is not reflected in our consciousness, in such a way that it makes us reflect on our situation in the World.

To say that universal Consciousness existed before I took consciousness of it, is legitimate as a belief, but it is an inference, not a direct expression of experience. This shows us that it is eternal, but this eternity is not in time, but in an absolute present. This experience, however, is not "mine" but that of the universal Consciousness, my individual consciousness is submerged and dilutes itself in the former, and thus coming up to the surface it knows that *universal Consciousness is the nucleus and essence of the mind.*

If I keep strictly to experience, I could not say that universal Consciousness precedes the existence of my consciousness. Some clarifications are necessary: when my consciousness is in universal Consciousness, it is at one with it and looks from it (*essential perspective*), it knows that it is now not individual consciousness, which it is now not "mine", it knows itself to be transcendent. This experience can be called mystic as the Idea of Divinity derives from it. But the spirit can assiduously return to universal Consciousness and know it sufficiently well in order to reflect on it philosophically, establishing a nourishing conversation with individual consciousness and distinguish what belongs to one and what to the other. This dialogue develops in an intermediary consciousness that I have called *unitive.*

I remember that there exist two realities in Taoism and Confucianism, the sky and the earth, and man finds himself in the middle. I infer without effort that Lao-Tse and Confucius had their spirit's in unitive consciousness. Their philosophies confirm this as they speak of a universal Order that they call Tao, which derives from the said

Consciousness and which I have classified as a "primary expression" of it or of a universal Spirit. Man in equilibrium is centred in a *unitive consciousness*, he is found, like Hermes, between the men and the gods (in all mythologies there exists an intermediary being).

I am convinced that all gods derive from the universal Spirit, the variants are results of different intuitions that man has and that he processes *a posteriori*, with his other faculties, in particular his internal or subconscious plane, prolific in the production of myths. This in no way means that these gods are false, on the contrary, they are part of the truth, and they make man participate in the play of the Spirit in Nature. Mythology is religion expressed as art; in fact all true art is inspired by the Transcendent. With this reference the artist creates their literature, sculpture and painting. (see *The Roots of Art*) Whether they believe in one god or in many does not make a great difference; as long as they believe in a personal divinity, they still have not experienced the universal Spirit.

Of course, if one has a prolonged and repeated experience, the concept of universal Consciousness will be concluded, but men in general have to continue with the gods of religion, since they are far from experiencing and understanding the God of the philosophers. But, it should be clear, religion is derived from experience, it is of little import if the subject has had the intuition of this or that divinity; this is and should be for him real, because it moves him. Belief and faith in one or more gods can stimulate us some part of the way (though in most cases, is merely a passive and comfortable attitude through which without effort or search we adopt the divinities that have been beneficial to us), but later, in the final and steep path they are a serious impediment as the spirit has to search for the truth free and without preconceived ideas; this attitude leads him to the God of the philosophers.

Universal Consciousness 3

We can take consciousness of our universality the way we have done with our individuality, our mind is as prepared for the multiple as it is for the One; it is indispensable that this truth be believed in order to direct the spirit towards the experience of Unity. This should not surprise us as we live within the two realities, why should we not be prepared for both? Of course, there is a epistemological, psychological and philosophical priority in general, the One comprehends the multiple, but from the latter the former is not understood. One perspective is more elevated than the other, it corresponds to a more advanced stage of man; our knowledge and the history of man should be directed towards the former.

I believe that the biological evolution of beings should be linked to spiritual evolution, and the latter happens through realizations of the stages of consciousness. Universal Consciousness sows consciousness in beings that continue to grow in spirit through their incipient bodies. Consciousness does not do so voluntarily because if it did it would stop being pure Consciousness, but emanates the spirit that inspires individual consciousness. The Greek muses were to be the mythical representation of that experience.

Universal Consciousness is not only a "fact of consciousness" as life emanates from it. This *vital impulse* is spiritual and is full of the said inspiration and attraction; it is imbued with its Essence. I believe that the key to existence is in these elements; from which the primacy of the Essence over existence is inferred.

Universal Consciousness is not a postulation, it is a total and undeniable *unitive vital experience*, and once acquired it is easily accessible; my system emanates from it. This can have personal expressions or characteristics, but it cannot essentially differ from the view of those who have seen from it; and I call this true knowledge.

We have a Consciousness which is already in the World, that is One with Nature, but as the I is a creation of discernment, we then translate, we discern that First Reality, and transform it into a concept which is a record that we keep in a box: memory. This may be useful, but it is already an archive, not Reality. For this reason it would be more convenient to not say that consciousness *Is*. Now, there is no doubt that this Consciousness makes beings be, it is that which gives them their being, thanks to it things are; for this reason it is the Being and Essence of all beings.

Everything indicates that this is the original Consciousness of man, before its individuation. The present experience makes us infer that this is how it was in the past, when we were one with the World, as it was with other animals; but, as happens to human beings apart from rare exceptions, they are not conscious of that Consciousness. Man is only conscious of his individual Consciousness but not of (his) universal Consciousness, for which he yearns as if it were a lost home, and thus it is easy to infer that the repeated myths of "the fall" come from the process of individuation that has made him feel guilty about his egocentric consciousness, that seeks utilities for the subject, that looks at the World *for himself,* in detriment to the vision of Reality *in itself.* The fact that it is not conscious of this and the process that it has followed reveals alienation. These myths remember the moment, which could have lasted many centuries, in which the spirit shifted from its "divine" to its human Consciousness. It will be understood that these myths are a religious recourse, as the latent objective of all religions is to reestablish the spirit in "divine" reality. But if we are not alienated from all, we can perceive the attraction and the force the spirit feels on returning to its original state. This attraction, impulse or force is obviously the generator of myth, but there are recourses other than the religious such as psychological and epistemological which go to the root of the matter, without needing to use the fruits of imagination. The myth of "original sin", if we interpret it in this way, can have meaning, but this does not justify that these fruits should be taken as reality, prioritizing the metaphor over reality. (About this see *Origin and Destiny of Man*).

Since my philosophy is based on experience and the latter comes from the first causes, I would be unfaithful to my own method if I were to search for a Will or some Being that generated them from behind elsewhere; this would be to make of the causes the effects of some presupposition or some inference. Besides I note that if I were to do this, I would be adapting that purely spiritual reality to the human being's way of seeing from his individual perspective, i.e. I would be replacing that *essential perspective* for another one that does not correspond to that reality.

The truth is that he who has seen Reality clearly does not need to see "behind" it because he knows that he has reached, as Plotinus said, "the end of the journey", there is nothing nor can there ever be anything after Unity. This is the cycle of the Spirit, this is its *Origin*, and its *Destiny*. But this end is also a principle as the spirit who has known the Source of Life, returns filled with this sublime inspiration and propagates this knowledge contributing to a universal program imbuing all with that Spirit. It cooperates in this way in establishing the cyclical dynamic of Life which will be so much more enduring, stable and harmonious when it adjusts to the said *universal unitive forces*.

When the spirit penetrates the Absolute he will be found in an infinite Emptiness. This Emptiness is definitely beyond the limits of the Universe, but I do not mean that the spirit travels as far as there, as time and space are absent, but that it should reach its own Essence, which is also that of the World; as soon as it turns its gaze it perceives the World as One with It. Is when it penetrate time and space, happening when it shifts its spirit from its *unified consciousness* to its discernment, that it finds a multiple reality. But it knows that this is not another reality, as this same Emptiness, this same Essence is among things and in things testifying its Unity. The duality of spirit and matter derives from the discernment with which the *I* has identified alienating itself from the Unity, it is the perspective of the spirit when it is immersed in the current of the becoming and is dragged along with it.

We saw that liberty implies a prior transcendence. The spirit that has known this does not suffer a total "fall" but it follows a *process of unitive individuation*, which if fully conscious of its shifts and experiences does not allow one to arrive at an egocentric perspective, but will shift to a *zone of equilibrium* that I have called *unitive consciousness*. It knows its freedom, and also its Unity, through which it will exercise its freedom with the intention to integrate, as knowing that in its Essence it is One the last thing it wants is to disintegrate. The great moral and social consequences of this *unitive man* are easy to infer.

Although the difference is only one of grade (this is my opinion in agreement with Darwin, see *The Evolution of the Spirit*), thanks to its greater consciousness, man has achieved more liberty than that of other species, but is too identified with its *I* in order to experience its freedom. The spirit is free because it begins by being unconditional freedom; it conditions itself by becoming matter. Man is conditioned as long as he identifies with matter and free in as long as he recognizes himself as spirit.

Universal Consciousness 4

When the spirit becomes One with universal Consciousness it sees how the latter is manifested overflowing into Nature.

It is thus pure Spirit that imbues it acting slowly over it, as long as the matter is receptive and sensitive to these subtle influences. All things have been adapting to the natural medium and to these influences which however subtle are indispensable as they contain the spirit of life, the force of growth, expansion and perfection, with all the time in the world. If, thanks to an order, integration and comprehension of this process, universal Consciousness is understood, *unitive*, creative and integrative forces will be found, and they are appreciated in a state of absolute contemplation. If the spirit that has reached this realization wants to create, a very natural reaction, as it is lodged in the Creative itself, it will use its human faculties to do so. This is the human condition (in its finest expression).

I completely agree with Plotinus when he affirms that "all that which has reached the stage of perfection", has to engender (E. III, 8, 10). It is only natural that the Creative, create, but, as I said earlier, it does not directly create but generates an energy that incites order and unity, the harmonious relation between things, the establishment of order and unity. I dare to infer that the concentration and relation of the elements of the atom, of the latter with others, the formation of cells and bodies, respond to the said energy. But matter cannot realize its ultimate objective as in its concentration and expansion it produces shocks and disintegration, even though, curiously, it returns to search for order and integration.

We can verify that there exist two forces in the universe, one tends to expansion and reproduction, and the other tends to integration and unification. We should not be surprised to find these two tendencies in the psyche of man: the extroverted and introverted. If one thinks a little one can believe that life consists of the expansive part, but this opinion responds to the perspective of the extrovert, and inversely the introvert will tend towards the concentration and unification; the mystic is probably the one who has taken this tendency to its final consequences, and it will be very difficult to find an extroverted mystic. The perception of Life is precisely in the *sector of equilibrium* between these two forces, the art of living should be inspired from the harmony that is derived from them. The Greeks, supreme masters of this equilibrium, took this art to its perfection, and they taught us that all extremes are dangerous. If history is observed it will be seen that it fluctuates between extroverted periods like the present one and introverted epochs, and the periods of growth take place when there is equilibrium between both. (See *The Spirit in History*).

As we possess a mind that is in line with or is made in keeping with all reality, the latter can also be revealed through an interior path, i.e. by knowing the mind, but this self-knowledge is practiced by few, as it belongs to a higher stage in man than that attained by the common herd who are still rooted in a state of survival. The human being as a species is in transit between the stage of survival and the unitive stage that can lead him to transcend the former and transcend himself. It is in the *unitive experience* of the Spirit incessantly penetrating all Nature as a vital force where Unity resides. Unity is found in the Source of Life.

The *total unitive experience* allows the spirit to penetrate the present where the Eternal resides, which is so because it transcends time and space, it is the Transcendent, it is the pure Consciousness and the Absolute. When the spirit penetrates Nature after this experience, it finds itself in an integrated All. The individual perspective is born of the ignorance of that state and exists as long as the spirit identifies itself with its *I* and the identifications of the *I*, its body, its family, its race, etc. and, of course, with all the ideas that it has of its personality, constituting a whole world of abstractions, a reality seen from a perspective that is not false but partial, erroneous and disintegrated. It is from this individual perspective that the idea of the subject is born which finds itself with "external" objects. All the sciences start from this vision, and try to understand the world, following the innate impulse of man to reintegrate, as well as the philosophers to unite, of mystics to liberate themselves and to follow the path contrary to the one followed by man in their individuation.

I have spoken of the transcendent and the immanent, of the spirit and matter, of universal and individual Consciousness, but these are nothing more than ways of understanding, perspectives of the spirit that in the final instance is One single Reality: the Unity of Consciousness. The universal Consciousness is immanent to the *Universus*. The Transcendent is as I have said only for certain accumulative and speculative faculties i.e. to reason, to certain perspectives of the spirit; when the latter reaches the Transcendent, it stops being so, it becomes immanent, and so the spirit, which is the universal Spirit, experiments itself overflowing into the *Universus*. Therefore *all beings participate in this Spirit, in this Consciousness*, they only perceive it in keeping with their individual faculties, according to their potentialities, but everything has a life and consciousness; hence the intelligence of the flowers (Maeterlinck), the instinct of the animals, and man's intuition. The universe is multiple and is one in essence; the mind is also one and multiple. *There is nothing external to matter, there is nothing outside the spirit, the Universus is One.*

God and universal Consciousness

It should be clear that in my conception of Reality there is no creator God behind Nature and man. If I have used the concept of God in my earlier works, it has been in order to change this idea, but I greatly fear that in order to achieve this objective (as the idea of a personal deity is very rooted in the West), I might have inadvertently aided in the misunderstanding of my philosophy. Hence I no longer use this concept.

God and universal Consciousness are useful concepts as they serve as exemplary references, but there is a great difference between them, and though God has always been merely a concept, universal Consciousness stops being so in order to be *Consciousness of itself.* Beyond this, there is a descent of the spirit to the external and dual faculties. It is the first Reality, it is the Creative itself, everything derives from it. It is from its intuition that the concept of God is derived; this is a derivative and not the first principle.

The need to assign to a God the attributes of a first principle together with the desire to have an object of devotion and to make it more amenable to reason, has generated the personal god of religious people. Universal Consciousness is so great, so pure, so exemplary, and so sacred (it is in reality *the sacred* itself) that it awakens the feeling of devotion, but there is a miscarriage when this sentiment is filled with the idea that derives from the same. With this knowledge the philosopher adheres to experience itself.

I am convinced, after having compared my experience with that of the mystics that I found in studies of comparative religions, that he who has always been referred to as God is a product of an intuition of the universal Consciousness. The identification is naturally born of its similarities, but it is necessary to clarify these concepts well, as to God has been attributed qualities that are not always born of experience, on the other hand what I have called universal Consciousness strictly adheres to it and to the demands of philosophy, which I have never sacrificed in the name of a belief or doctrine. The fundamental similarity is that both are transcendent, i.e. they do not come from individual consciousness, from an *I.* As long as the spirit identifies with its individual consciousness it will experience universal Consciousness as external and alien.

We could call God universal Consciousness but since we have experience of the latter and an idea of the former, we would obscure its understanding. I believe that this is what the Hindus call Brahman, and the Buddhists call the consciousness of the Buddha, in order to avoid all personalization and abandon the concept of Atman or universal Soul. Although we might refer to the God of the philosophers, i.e. delinked from all myths or religious traditions, and although we might stay far away from a personal Divinity, the idea of God implies a postulate, a someone who is behind the material and spiritual reality, i.e. behind our experience, and this idea denaturalizes Reality as the latter is One; the experience is immediate, and God is presented as mediate which generates a duality and thus an alienation of the spirit from itself and its own Consciousness. This in itself is serious, now if the personal God is proclaimed as the final reality, the duality that it involves becomes an obstacle in the realization of our Destiny; the hindrance that this imposition of God might have signified in the West can be gauged. And if to this God we add a myth and personalize it to the point of assigning a Son incarnated as man, we completely alienate our spirit, we disqualify it from all experience and we oblige it to replace this for a belief. Needless to say the stages of a personal god, belief and myth are more accessible to the multitudes, and thus it is understandable that they are more popular.

Descartes approaches this divine reality when he affirms that if we possess the idea of perfection it is because perfection exists. But this logic is not sustainable, as in the same way we could say that if we had the idea of an absolutely evil being, the latter exists, and we could also think that he himself is all powerful, etc. and we could have a Devil as omnipotent as God. Leibniz commits a similar error when he says that if God is possible, he exists, but everything is possible beyond our understanding. Here perceptions is what is important before thinking and believing. And all of us have the desire for perfection to a greater or lesser degree, *the experience of the aspiration to perfection*, and then the latter exists. This is the "demonstration" that we would use if it were necessary. The same can be said of our aspiration towards Unity (when we are in order) as Unity is perfection itself.

I see no need to postulate an intelligent God to explain the sense of the universe, not even as a moral premise, as Kant believed, that leads to a "practical faith" of very weak philosophical basis. An intelligent God is anthropomorphism in various senses. Firstly, it is difficult not to refer in this way to a personal divinity, whose place in the universe (or outside it) is very difficult to establish. Secondly, the projection of resolving difficulties through discernment is obvious. Thirdly, expecting "others" to indicate to us the path or the direction to be taken is puerile. The postulation of a God is unnecessary and is presented as a "third party in discord" in the unity of subject and object. The myth of a God creating Nature in times past disfigures reality and weakens our understanding.

Of course, I have no explanation for the reason of the *Universus*, but this rational demand denaturalizes the matter as it forces the spirit to once again fall into a human perspective. universal Consciousness simply Is. This Absolute, that is completely sufficient from an essential perspective, is not so for the individual, because the latter, who is not, wants to be; and for this he uses his reason, in order to help him in this endless design.

The religious path

Possibly what is most difficult to understand, at least for

spirits locked up in the external plane (discernment), is what has been called sentiment (which is not just that, as it derives from a certain perception or a latent intuition from an individual perspective), of the sacred that undoubtedly derives from the magnificence of the Spirit, its brilliant transparency, which surpasses all understanding and breaks rational schemes, hence its "miraculous" aspect.

It is very important to awaken this sentiment generally provided through the devotional path. But the latter suffers from intrinsic problems that we should highlight. Firstly, it generates a duality between the devotee subject and the object or divinity that impedes the subject from transcending with its whole spirit or being in order to achieve a total unitive experience, in keeping with a belief or, in the best of cases, with isolated intuitions of what remain transcendent. And from this perspective the almost inevitable tendency is that of anthropomorphizing the object or divinity.

Faith is a leap in the dark that involves a multitude of additional beliefs to fill this vacuum, and many possibilities to be drowned in it. The danger is obvious, we can bet our whole life on an uncertain destiny; "sufficient reason" to leave faith out of all philosophical projects. My project is spiritual experience and, in keeping with it my ethics and theology are pragmatic. With correct behavior man frees himself from interferences, obstacles and mental clutter, and in this way purifies his spirit integrating it in the *Universus*. When he achieves a total integration he has realized his destiny. As can be seen, the gods are unnecessary for this entire process. The reward is the realization that implies transcendental knowledge, unconditional liberty and untold happiness. There is no punishment, unless one includes the hell of ignorance, subject to fear, wants and base passions in general, in this life.

But this should be clear: Man's destiny lies in achieving Unity (see my *Origin and Destiny of Man*), nourishing oneself through virtues and expressing them and thus contributing to the universal Order. In this way all paths that lead to this end are edifying. It is enough to say that the belief in one God and the exclusion of another is a grave mistake, and if to this we add the imposition of our creed or doctrine on another, we ostensibly show our ignorance of the matter, as we have not even extracted the virtues that derive from knowledge and we are expressing our personal vices, our personal egocentric vision. In this case the morality of an atheist based on common sense is of more value as long as he is not entrapped in the opposite extreme of atheistic fanaticism. *The real path is that of the ethical*, which smoothens out with virtues and distances us from our egocentric vision, and each and every one has to make this path and cover it alone. (See *The Roots of Morality*) The doctrines are nothing more than signs along the path, which we have all the right to doubt and we will do well to adapt them to our experience and criteria in order to exercise our understanding.

The primary manifestations

Time and space are not only the conditions for knowledge, but also the conditions for the existence of beings. They are found between two realities, on the border of the Transcendent and Nature, they are the infrastructure of the Universe. Universal scientific laws will throw light on this infrastructure.

The primary manifestations of universal Consciousness come before the forms of time and space: *Order* in itself, as an ordering energy; *Good* in itself, as an aspiration towards the perfection of action; *Love* it itself as an integrating energy; *Life* in itself which is the energy of life; *Beauty* in itself, which is the aspiration towards the perfection of forms; and the *intuition-instinct* that is its intelligent manifestation. These are the guiding principles of everything that exists, all of them emanate from Unity and make creation possible and maintain it; all things tend, according to their possibilities, towards Unity, which is perfect Order, the Absolute.

All the intuitions of universal matters are refracted in Unity, and are inspired in its perfection, in its total Order, in its exemplary integration, harmony, correspondence and, naturally, uniformity. The Good and the Beautiful emanate from Unity, which illuminate moral and aesthetic consciousness; man extracts his moral, his ideals of justice and his sciences from the perception of Order; Love makes him integrate it harmoniously; his *vital élan* moves him to live. I am speaking of the most essential, decisive and intimate elements of human nature, which for this reason I have called *primary manifestations of the Essence or universal Consciousness.*

Firstly the Good and the Beautiful, Love and Order are the *a priori ideas* indispensable for knowledge in general, without them we would have no capacity for judgment, they are the references without which we would not know which road to take; they are like the compass of reason. We only have to reflect to see that they are in each decisive and ascendant choice; because, of course, capricious and descendent choices seem to lack these parameters. All morality would be impossible without the Idea of *Good*, all art without the *Beautiful*, all relation without *Love*, all sciences without *Order* in our mind and without the premise that there is an order in Nature. God and the religions would be inconceivable without the attributes that these ideas suggest to us. But these are not just ideas that occur to us, (those who think so lightly this way surely forget to think why they occur to us) they move us and they push us to act, they are forces that are acting in Nature, they accompany life and advance it in its ascendant path.

The *intuition-instinct* is, in a manner of speaking in order to make it clearer for human understanding, the intelligent manifestation of universal Consciousness, but it is *a priori* to all intelligence, it is the pristine aspect, essential to it. I believe that other animals' instincts have the same origin, except that they cannot process them like human intelligence, i.e. they cannot apply reason to them. Intuition puts us in direct contact with the *Creative* itself, for this reason it is the creative aspect of intelligence, that can *a posteriori* construct around original intuition, but this construction obeys another mental mechanism that I have called accumulative knowledge, while the former, like all primary manifestations, is *unitive*.

The human being ignores the origin of his intuitions because it is not he who creates them, they come to him, and he receives them from the *universal Consciousness*. The same happens with the rest of the animals with instinct; it is for this reason that we humans ignore from where they get this kind of intelligence, which at times seems more ingenious than ours.

The difference, in any case, between intuition and instinct, as well as between human intelligence and that of other animals, is not radically different, as Darwin has highlighted, there is only a difference of degree, which are just degrees of understanding and, above all that which establishes the greatest difference, the capacity of processing, of discerning. We know that higher mammals are in an intermediate stage, which has allowed some like dogs to partly understand human language and live with us. (See *Origin and Destiny of Man*) And not just this, they are kind and are capable of loving in their own way, sometimes in a more diaphanous and spontaneous manner than man and of expressing altruism to the point of giving their life for their master. With this I want to indicate that they do not just perceive the primary manifestation of Intuition, but also that of Love, a supreme faculty that tends to temper anger and selfishness and to establish harmonious relations between beings, besides projecting the spirit beyond the body in an ascending direction towards the unity of all beings. The aesthetic sense shown by birds especially by some, when they attract their partners with their beauty expanding its wings and with their songs, makes us think that they are inspired by the *Beautiful* in their own way, i.e. their "instinct" reaches the *Transcendent.*

Only thirty years ago I considered love a clear example of the primary manifestations, since I was convinced that we had all experienced it; I have now lost this conviction. But if the reader has not been unfortunate enough to feel this lack and has sensed the hand of Aphrodite in their soul, they will know what I am talking about. The effects of love, sung and expressed by the arts by the most receptive individuals since the days of yore have always been the same, there has only been a variation in degree and intensity. The beloved feels possessed by this feeling that distances him from the utilitarian side of life, which appears to him to be useless, even feeling revulsion towards it as for everything profane. He rejects personal interest, it would seem to him a crime against humanity and against his nature to do the slightest evil, he truly desires to do good, he wants to be generous, he wants to maintain the harmony that he experiences, he doesn't want to be distracted; he has become contemplative. The material loses importance and value and even reality. Nature is presented to him like a dream, he feels something sacred in it, as if his past life had been a mistake and now makes sense; something intangible but which is experienced as something more real than mere things, that moves and shakes him; what he wants to do is to love. He wants to escape from the routine, to travel, to go to the other side, towards the new and the unknown. He really has the urge to fly with his beloved, not in a metallic apparatus, he prefers a magic carpet. In fact everything is filled with magic; everything seems more luminous and beautiful. He now sees how the sunlight penetrates the leaves of trees, the flowers and birds take on a life and seem to be saying something. He feels inspired and would like to write beautiful things like a poet.

So in philosophical language he has perceived in some way the primary manifestation of universal Consciousness like Love, a unitive force *par excellence*, that spiritualizes the *Universus* and thus his particular consciousness, but which in a certain way has transcended it. It has shifted its spirit or nucleus of consciousness towards *altruistic consciousness*; hence his desire to do well, to go beyond himself. In his shift he has brought the Good and Beautiful together, hence his perception of the beauty of things. He perceives Order, hence his fear of a bad arrangement. Love emanates from universal Consciousness and impregnates all consciousness and all things.

The primary manifestations of universal Consciousness are spiritual and existent and overflow on to the Universus and by extending over all spiritual reality they are in the human mind and for this reason they are paradigmatic par excellence, i.e. they are obligatory and priority references and *a priori* to all human thought and action. They are *a priori* to all moral idealism and they are the sources of the same. Man does not create moral, aesthetic, religious or philosophical ideals; he interprets them according to his understanding and imitates them.

These *primary Ideas* are the causes of our ascendant thoughts and actions, they inspire us and attract us to think and act well, beautifully, and in a friendly and ordered manner. The principle of causality will not have the mechanical rigour here of things, it is subtle, as corresponds to the spiritual nature of these manifestations, but decisive in the elevated aspects of our mental faculties; our aspirations and ideals, penetrating intuitions and profound experiences that are nourished by them.

We have the most evident experience of the existence of primary manifestations in ourselves,: our desire to live, to live in order, of doing good, our inclination towards the beautiful. It will be said that human beings break this rule very often, I do not deny this but the statistic is not a good parameter for this knowledge. Our species is in an evolutionary process, if it had already achieved its objective no philosophy would be necessary. But this is a fact that can be proved: the more we know ourselves, the more elevated we are, the more knowledge we have, the closer we are to these parameters, and we see them more clearly and identify with them. All of us distinguish with our innate capacities, the good from the evil, the beautiful from the ugly, and we do not feel right if we do wrong. Have we asked ourselves why? Why do we call as wise the men who express virtues, admire them and consider them exemplary? Do we not consider the ones who best understand the order of things as geniuses? Where do love and the pleasure of living in harmony come to us from? Where does the artist get his inspiration from, and why are we entranced by the work of art and all that is beautiful?

The primary manifestations are the indispensable references for all ascendant knowledge. They are elementary forces that are expressed as energy in matter, as instinct in animals and as instinct, sentiment and intelligence in higher mammals. The final knowledge is Consciousness of these forces that flow over the World. A clear example is the effect of Order understood as practical reason, like a moral applied in society. It is no coincidence that all those who intuit that Reality, such as mystics feel compelled to preach and establish a moral order. These forces are behind all knowledge that tends towards Unity, establishing relations between things and beings, scientific and judicial laws, or through more spiritual and harmonious paths like fine music and poetry, that are directly inspired in the Sources and for this reason are more inspirational. Have we asked the need for music to be harmonious; what leads the poet to establish relations that transcend logic but which, precisely for this reason, transport the soul towards the higher levels of the spirit?

The ultimate objective, the Unity that is absolute Order, can only be realized by the spirit, and this is not an inference but an experience, that can be realized by any sensitive person with a capacity to love beyond particular objects or people. Various philosophers have observed that Love is a universal force. For Plato it is "a great and admirable god who extends his power over all in the human as well as divine order" (*Symposium* 186) "in such a way that the whole is connected with itself" (*Simposium* 203). Are we not speaking about the same unitive energies? They are impalpable forces that work on the most subtle and light elements, leaving Nature free to create in keeping with its potential.

The disorder that exists in the world is due to the imperfection of matter. It is not that the latter is "bad", pernicious or diabolic (as has been believed) it is simply concretization, materialization. Nature is not composed of objects that constitute an obstacle to the spirit, as Bergson and others believe, it is an Organism that does what it can to be and to subsist, as all mortals like us do. Evil is born when there is consciousness and intelligence is applied to personal survival in detriment to other beings, and it is a product of alienation with respect to primary manifestations. Goodness, beauty and all the virtues tend to overcome the individual perspective because they aspire to transcendence. The primary manifestations contain the virtues that we have in consciousness; they are like rays of light of universal Consciousness that illuminate each and every one of the spirits in the Universe. All knowledge is possible thanks to transcendental intuitions (although unconscious for the immense majority), of the said manifestations, applied to the understanding of particulars. The more universal knowledge is, the more it approaches Unity. Scientific knowledge would not be possible without the intuition of the Order that underlies things and its relations, and that of course is in the spirit of man, in his universal Consciousness. Societies would not be possible without the integrating unitive energy of love. Life is viable because a vital force pushes it and attracts it to unconditional Life. The evolution of the species obeys subtle but decisive spiritual forces towards perfection and this is the pure Spirit that mobilizes it, it does not put them in movement but inspires them and attracts them through unconscious levels.

A *moral universal Order can be intuited*; Taoism, Buddhism and Hinduism take it as a premise, so do Plato, Fichte in his own way and I in my thoughts, as expressed in *The Roots of Morality*. Almost all men experience a unitive force on a personal plane that we call love and many suspect that it transcends this plane. We all intuit that there is a vital force in action that nurtures our lives. Everyone, at least at some time has been enraptured by the beauty of Nature; the aesthetic phenomenon is capable of transporting us beyond the matter that we contemplate; as Schopenhauer believed. These suspicions and presentiments are absolutely real and can be experienced on higher planes of consciousness. Where do these manifestations come from? From the Essence of the World which is not a postulate as from it we can have immediate consciousness.

About the knowledge of primary manifestations

In my entire work I have constantly tried to awaken universal Consciousness from which one has the undeniable experience of primary manifestations overflowing into the *Universus*. But the history of humanity proves to me that there are few who are seriously predisposed to achieving this objective, and even less so in descending periods like the present when the spirit is attached to external faculties. These same faculties require "concrete proofs", for which I have to change the method if I want to satisfy them and sacrifice the unitive method for the objective, which can be very harmful for the one who misunderstands, who conforms to this, as not only will the subject and object reappear, but I would be feeding these faculties that I had earlier wanted to overcome. Nevertheless I will make the attempt in the hope of awakening disquiets for knowledge that transcend objective knowledge. The attempt is legitimate because there should be no contradiction in the result, only coherence between both methods. Besides, reason has the right to reject all illogical connections, but I must insist that reasons and beliefs are not enough and that they should be used only as incentives for searching a more suitable knowledge of these matters. Objective knowledge, as the reader will remember, establishes a dual connection, in such a way that these manifestations present themselves to us as external, i.e. as something that we can accept or not, that seem to us relatively valid, for certain occasions and that we can keep in our memory to use when we like. That it does not work in this way can be proven throughout history; the *I* has more earthly preferences, more visceral inclinations, which keep men fragmented, with their peers, with the World and with themselves.

Human faculties exist in order to establish connections in the material as well as in the spiritual world. The spiritual faculties that I have called unitive, establish a link with the *universal Consciousness, this is the total link.* Spontaneity in morals is the result of the direct intuition of the vital plane. Unitive knowledge integrates us in such a way that if we take it to the final consequences, it unifies us. From the beginning it incites us to consider things in another manner: the spiritual, that lies dormant in man, who has many "reasons" to maintain himself in this state, it becomes more evident, more accessible, nearer and above all, more intimate. We experience these unitive forces as they are now not intuitions of the subject, they are a part of us as if they were our heartbeats distributed in our blood they reach our tiniest capillaries, I mean, we are filled with them and we see the way they act as primary forces that move us and push us to act, and move other beings according to their spiritual and biological potential. They go with life, they are life itself; I feel that the heart beats through these heartbeats. Everything is filled with the spirit, whose primary manifestations are the decisive ones, not only for life but for the evolution of the species, for the slow process of the evolution of the spirit.

There is no universal Spirit searching for itself, this vision is a projection of an alienated individual spirit, but a search common to all beings who due to their spiritual nature tend to return to their Origin in order to fulfill their Destiny; hence the importance of recognizing and knowing these spiritual energies. When speaking of a Destiny I do not want to imply any kind of determinism nor any kind of Will that would lead to such an objective, I refer to the natural course of things, the free flow of the spirit. So also when I refer to "forces", they should be understood as very subtle and not urgent as they have all the time in the world to adapt to material limitations.

The difficulty is the same as always: the difference in nature between the phenomenal and the *noumenal.*

Schopenhauer's attempt seems to me to be sufficiently legitimate, entirely coherent and irrefutable. As we saw, he devotes an entire volume to establishing the relation between the *principle of life* and its manifestation in Nature. And since this principle is one of the primary manifestations, I take the liberty of incorporating his arguments on that aspect; the other manifestations just have to be "proven".

Philosophy, religion, aesthetics, morality and the sciences derive from the primary manifestations of the Essence; they are different ways of perceiving, interpreting and expressing them. I wish to say that the *spiritual faculties of man are in keeping with the perception of these manifestations*. To my knowledge the reason for the existence of these faculties has not ever been explained, they were simply accepted as something that the human being possesses. In my opinion they exist in order to respond to what is most essential and decisive in life. What is curious is that the *process of individuation* followed by our species has been accompanied by a kind of specialization that has separated the faculties into relatively static compartments. And this is easy to prove, as even if we have access to each one of these faculties this access is limited. Jean Cocteau rightly said that art is accessed through a narrow door through which few can enter. And we could say the same of mystical experience, of philosophical intuition and the perception of a transcendental moral order; although we might know how to appreciate a work of art in some way, we might be moral sometimes and we might have a religious sentiment and we can study philosophy. This "kind of specialization" is due to the centre or faculty adopted by the spirit when it becomes individualized, which is what makes up the *I*, from the perspective of which the subject observes and judges its circumstances. For this reason the vision and contribution of others has been so edifying for our species.

Now if we observe the scheme of the mind that I have designed in *Psychosophy*, it will be seen that as the spirit elevates its level of consciousness, the faculties continue converging and unifying. This is obviously not a simple mechanical curiosity, but a matter of the highest epistemological importance in each and every one of these orders, faculties or disciplines. In fact, elevated aesthetic contemplation leads to the understanding of moral order, philosophical intuition illuminates the religious field and the Good and the Beautiful correspond, Order awakens the sentiment of the sacred and is Beauty in itself. The reason for my insistence on the need to integrate the faculties will be understood, as this generates a reverse process of individuation: the process of unification, which leads to single consciousness, universal Consciousness.

When *Unified Consciousness* extends into the *Universus*, before the spirit discovers time and space, I mean, conserving the essential perspective, it perceives how primary manifestations emanate from Unity.

The reader may have noticed that two of the primary manifestations, the *Good* and the *Beautiful*, were part of the intelligible world for Plato and Plotinus, sometimes they elevated them above this world to the highest stage of the spirit, they even identified with God. If we leave aside the intelligible world with all its complexity, postulated allegorically by Plato, will see that the Ideas and experience overlap. The *primary manifestations*, constitute an immaterial reality of Ideas; a marvellous *Reality* that is neither objective nor subjective, but unitive; an indispensable reference for all objective knowledge, for all artistic creation, for all moral action, for all ethical formulation. This interest in linking the *noumenal* and the *phenomenal* is easily explained as we are obeying our original Nature that incites us to reintegrate ourselves in Unity. In any case, we are not speaking of a "world of ideas" delinked from reality, but on the contrary, thanks to it we can link it; we are talking of *Ideas-Realities*.

Monistic pantheism

We have seen in this work how often a concept of reality like pantheism appears. We find it as a distinctive characteristic in the most flourishing times: the birth (the Greek Naissance), and the rebirths of Renaissance and Romanticism. But we have not dwelt on this concept because its correct comprehension needed a vision that only now we are able to adopt. This vision involves the unity of Spirit and Nature, but we have proved the difficulties that the comprehension of this convergence presents, given the habitual mental composition of man that leads him to see everything in a dual manner (see in this regard *The Conformation of the Psyche in Origin and Destiny of Man*). This is what has led him to develop dualist doctrines and to believe in them, all theisms fall within these categories.

The theism that accepts a personal God, obeys this individual and rational perspective, it is dualist for this reason and no other. It can be inspired by distant intuitions and impassioned feeling, but nothing more, as there is no direct experience of it. When there is, there is neither separation nor distance; Reality is monism. But even within this there is a zone of equilibrium. To say "I am God", as some mystics have done (and there are some who have believed it), is the consistent error in uniting two dualities. Sustaining a personal pan-psychism would be a contrary delirium leading to a monstrous inflation of the ego. Greek mythology, in its usual wisdom, is prolific in examples of the gods punishing such believers.

It is not completely wrong to label pan-psychism as pantheism, but with some additional clarifications:

there are no traces here of any person or the divine, even less of an individual. This means that there is a total transcendence of the subject, so that if one speaks of the "psyche", this would be the Psyche of the World. To incline it towards atheism or theism would be to rationalize it to the point of drawing the spirit from its direct and present experience. Theism like atheism implies a duality, they are its progeny. The Spirit, in effect, is one with Nature, but if we view the Spirit from the latter, we will end up *believing* that it is only matter, we would be only seeing Nature. The Spirit would then be on a second plane, which would bring it closer it to dualism.

Here lies the grave danger of a pantheism badly understood, that we could call Aristotelian at best of cases, or materialist at worst; in the former the universal Spirit is shown as diffuse, it is an abstraction, it disappears in the latter and those that adopt this view find themselves adoring a soulless nature. In these two visions unity is established by reason, i.e. it is artificial; it lacks the unitive factor which is that which gives it certitude.

It is a certain perspective that makes all the difference; one is an individual perspective, which is a belief, the other is that of the Essence itself, which is an *experience.* Without this it is a project, an aspiration born of well-directed intuitions, but which does not end by taking shape, it is for this reason that the concept of pantheism has not been correctly formulated and has not concluded as satisfying. My entire work is directed towards the realization of the said *unified consciousness*, from which the *essential perspective is derived, and it is only from this perspective that pantheism achieves its full meaning.* A Hindu text (Hinduism by definition is monist) expresses the right understanding of the matter: "Brahman is all, but all is not Brahman".

In conclusion: Monistic pantheism is the final and most ultimate "ism" of man, it is the culmination of the human search, and it has reasonably been the constant search of the most enlightened philosophers. But it should be clear: *true pantheism is achieved with the unitive experience of the Transcendent*, where it is not a personal God who is found, but rather the presence of the Sacred, which is not out there, but which floods Consciousness and overflows in Nature; this is my religion.

A point of convergence (Facing Nanda Devi and other giants)

"The mathematical theory of black holes is a subject of great complexity; but its study has convinced me of the basic truth of two old aphorisms: The simple is the seal of the true; beauty is the splendor of truth." S. Chandrasekhar; from his speech when he received the Nobel Prize for Physics.

In earlier works I have laid sufficient emphasis on the fact that the sciences of the spirit do not need any kind of confirmation from the natural sciences as they have different methods as well as a different objective, (using my terminology and theory of knowledge) the former have the unitive and the transcendent, the latter the accumulative and the concrete world which is inevitably relative, and for these objectives they use different faculties, the former use the unitive, and the latter the external (reason at the service of discernment).

Since I think that philosophy should fundamentally or at least as a matter of priority concern itself with the matters of the spirit, i.e. of the first principles as Aristotle thought, I believe that the great error in the history of Western thought has been that it has followed the exact sciences like a child follows its mother, and this has meant an inversion of values with serious consequences, as philosophy has always been the mother of sciences. And it should continue to be so because it does not only respond to the most intimate desires of man and the highest aspirations in the metaphysical order but also in the moral order, which should come before all human action. Ecological disasters, linked to over population, nuclear explosions and unbridled consumption, a consequence of growing human greed, are example enough to validate what has been expressed.

The change came about when the natural sciences, thanks to Newton's genius, expressed well founded universal laws which until then had been a legacy of philosophy, which began to use a scientific method to explain matters of the spirit. Spinoza is a good example. We saw how his intuitions of the Transcendent are mixed and overshadowed by his observations of Nature: at times he uses what I have called an idealist or monist pantheism, at other times an earthly pantheism, visions that obey different perspectives, those of the philosopher and of the scientist.

Although they might not have the same vision as philosophers, all good scientists who observe the firmament and extract from it the laws of the stars, are looking in the same direction with their gadgets; it is there where I see a *point of convergence.*

The man of spirit cannot avoid projecting itself in space and time and this is so because it feels the force and attraction of universal Consciousness. In the simple act of travelling he discovers other sectors of his Mind. This journey is not just in space, his interest in history, or in philosophy adds other perspectives to his spirit in his mind, as all thought and actions of men obey certain perspectives. If we observe the human psyche we will see clearly that the thoughts and feelings that generate beliefs obey perspectives, and as these beliefs originate idealisms and the idealisms lead to action, we see that each one of the periods of history has functioned under one predominant perspective, placing the spirit on a level of understanding and consciousness that determines the period. (See *The Spirit in History*)

Beyond these particular perspectives, there is, as we have seen, an essential perspective, which is the very centre of the Mind, which is unconditional and absolute even if this is only for the philosopher who is concerned with essences and the Absolute. As soon as we enter the material world, we are in the area of the relative, and in this way in the field of particular perspectives. However, universal laws can be made through them in the field of the sciences of Nature. It is possible that Einstein might have used the resource of viewing reality in keeping with different perspectives, in order to discover his theory of relativity. Einstein openly declared that for him God was Nature, just as it was for Spinoza, Schelling and also for me, with the saving graces that I have pointed out; though in the case of Einstein it is viable to assume that it was a conclusion through inference and finally a belief and not a transcendental intuition, i.e. an inversion of perspective. I believe that this juxtaposition of ideas, although some are a result of the investigation of matter and others of the spirit, should be pointed out.

However, the field of the natural sciences applies only to the Universe. My philosophy applies to the *Universus* by which I understand the spiritual world which includes the human psyche and physical world, as the reader now knows. Although it does not try to explain the physical world with the certitude of the natural sciences, I believe that it is interesting to bring these disciplines together so that they complement each other wherever possible. Unity as in the Spirit is not a consequence of juxtaposition and the sum of the spiritual and physical reality, it is a universal Consciousness that covers matter; the essential and absolute perspective is derived from Unity. It is also necessary to clarify that even if my system has used the mechanism of changes in perspective, its decisive method has been that of the unitive, corresponding to spiritual reality. And this method uses the most elevated of sentiments, which are not subjective but unitive, in order to become inspired and elevated; in this it differs completely from the scientific method which is essentially objective and accumulative, in which sentiments do not intervene.

My system has developed in a manner completely independent of even the natural sciences and psychology in general; precisely in the manner that I earlier explained (see my *Psychosophy*) because the method of the latter is fundamentally "scientific", as if the mind were matter, and hence it has not been able to transcend it, while my *psychosophy* has an *Origin and a transcendent Destiny*; it is a philosophy, a metaphysics that is applied to physics. The fundamental error of psychology has been that it has tried to explain the spiritual and the metaphysical including religion as a product of the individual mind; this has led it to psychologism; which is the opposite of philosophy which seeks absolute truths. With this we return to what was said earlier: the sciences are relative, while philosophy is absolute, in the sense that it covers the relative; even if it concerns itself with the two sides of Reality.

I have referred elsewhere to the sign of the infinite as a very fortunate symbolic representation of a transcendental intuition that unifies the changeable and unchangeable reality. At the point of meeting the two circles in the symbol *8* this encounter takes place. But we should not confuse the symbol with reality, this is experience itself. Without trying to make a scientific appreciation here I would like to make a comment that could contribute to the understanding of the matter which as usual is connected to my theory of perspectives. I cannot help but notice an intimate connection between the said experience and the discovery of black holes, which I repeat I will not try to explain but connect.

Unified consciousness experiences the unchangeable. This *unitive experience* is incomprehensible to reason because it is transcendental. From this consciousness the essential or absolute perspective is derived, from which the changeable is experienced as it is absorbed by the unchangeable and converges in it in unison, emanating from the same and flowing from the *Universus*. From this perspective the changeable, the becoming is experienced in another way, it becomes patent in a most vehement I would say alarming manner. In my opinion, based on the aforesaid experiences, there is more a Unity between spirit and matter than a permanent inter relation. The mind, like the universe, is multiplicity as well as totality and it is only logical that it be so.

What the scientist does is rationally explain the phenomena already present in their Mind, in the *Universus*, but they will see them within the limits of reason and their perspective that presents to them a relative, never an absolute, reality. If we apply this theory to black holes, we will see that the scientist has to find the limits within their individual perspective, their rational faculty and their objective method. There will in fact be a moment, when *the hole absorbs not just the matter but also time and space, and with it reason too*; the rest is only apprehended by the unitive, transcendent faculties. I believe that the key to existence lies in black holes, but in keeping with what has been said, it will not be found searching for material elements, however subtle they might be, but for spiritual ones. The key lies in how the spirit, which is pure energy, becomes matter, how the primary manifestations apprehensible with unitive faculties act on what is apprehended with the speculative faculties.

When we become aware of the sidereal figures that

our astrophysicists present to us, the spatial – temporal dimensions, the velocities and forces that are in play in the universe, reaching the limits of the infinite, we cannot avoid a profound recognition on discerning the negligible human condition; everything alive produces vertigo, our deaths are not differentiated from those of insects, all vanity disappears. As we have said, according to Stephen Hawkins "the human being is a kind of improved monkey, who lives on a small planet that revolves around a mediocre star." Everything invites us to transcend this miserable condition.

These black holes in the galaxies show us that there are realities, and not of any lesser importance, that transcend space and time. In keeping with my idea, implicit in my entire vital and unitive philosophy, if this happens in external reality, there should be an equivalent in our mind, a correspondence, I mean, an understanding of the Transcendent; the Cosmos consists of two realities, the material and the spiritual. Nothing of the essential of life is alien to us; though we might be insignificant as matter, we participate in the All.

The cycle of individual life ends with the knowledge (vital experience) of the Transcendent; in the macro-cosmos everything induces one to believe that the same thing happens: the cycle of life of concrete reality, on a universal scale, also ends in the Transcendent.

Universal Consciousness and the Cosmos

Universal Consciousness does not concern itself with anything in particular; for this reason it is universal. It is the Creative itself, it emanates creativity. But, as if it knew that this creativity would not last at all if it were chaotic, it emanates primordial virtues, which are the first manifestations that precede and accompany material creation.

I can only deduce that the Spirit becomes matter,

without losing its being, on the contrary, it expands. The Spirit transforms into stardust, the particles of which are filled with creative virtues; this expansion allows the galaxies to develop on their own as matter, they have their freedom but not their complete independence; matter conserves its spiritual dependence, its tendency to integrate itself, to order itself, to unify itself, to feel these virtues, to acquire consciousness. Since the moment of matter's creation takes place in cosmic time and occurs constantly it cannot be apprehended by the human spirit. The concrete reality that we see on our planet is a much later consequence, very distant from its material origin, but in no way disconnected from the said emanations that are present and active in all that is living.

We can appreciate in the *Universus*, i.e. in the totality of spirit and matter that constitute Reality, a centrifugal force that tends to expand and generate the multiple, and also a centripetal force that tends towards concentration and original unity. Both are emanations of the primordial One, of universal Consciousness. These forces are spiritual in their origin but in their projection they interact with matter. We can observe these forces in the expansion of the stars and in their force of attraction in the cosmos. But since this material aspect of the *Universus* falls in the domain of the natural sciences, we can leave the explanation of this phenomenon to the scientists; we will attend to the spiritual sciences.

Many mythologies speak of an original chaos on which a later order was established; this is not my experience. The original Unity is the absolute Order and on expanding it disintegrates and multiplies, and it is then that chaos *can generate itself.* On becoming matter Consciousness is not now in its Essence, nor is it purely spiritual; nevertheless it projects itself into the whole cosmos and fills it, and thus strictly speaking there are not two realities but one *Universus*.

The first things that emanate from universal Consciousness are the *primary manifestations*, which are unitive and of a spiritual nature, i.e. they tend towards unification and reintegration in the original Unity. From what has been said it is clear that between the manifest centripetal and centrifugal forces in the *Universus*, there has to be an equilibrium that is maintained through contact with the *unitive forces*, if this were not so the chaos would establish itself immediately.

These unitive forces, these primary manifestations of the One are *a priori* the forms of time and space, that reason uses (Kant) in order to understand the material world. The mental faculties that are connected to the concrete world are external, utilitarian or speculative and generate *accumulative knowledge*. These faculties are the mental or spiritual part of the centrifugal force found in the *Universus*, which tends towards expansion and multiplication. They are also a projection of the One, but they are *mediate or secondary manifestations*, already interdependent with matter.

The immediate or primary manifestations are purely spiritual and respond to centripetal forces that tend towards the reabsorption of the *Universus* in its original Unity, they tend to the absolute Order that is found in the Unity of Consciousness. The *Universus*, the spiritual and material whole, I repeat, is thus maintained by the equilibrium of the aforesaid forces; hence man's need to maintain contact with the *unitive faculties*, as disconnection with respect to these, that is alienation, leads to chaos.

The specific function of philosophy and the sciences of the spirit is to stimulate the centripetal forces of the spirit, whose final objective is reabsorption in the Unity of universal Consciousness, where the spirit achieves its freedom, not just from matter but also from its dependant faculties: the utilitarian.

It will be understood how my project differs from philosophies that wanted or tried to be "scientific," as speculative or utilitarian faculties do not respond to this objective of unification and liberation. My proposal is to make philosophy and the sciences of the spirit more independent of the natural sciences, not to oppose them but to complement them in order to establish the necessary equilibrium, in order to maintain coherence in human action.

It is evident that in our times centrifugal forces are so predominant in man that they occupy his mind and his activities. If one considers the aforesaid on alienation and the consequent chaos, it will be admitted that the situation is alarming. For this reason I have insisted on knowledge of the mechanisms of the mind in my theory of knowledge in general, explained in my *Psychosophy*, and in the need to awaken and activate unitive faculties.

The paths of transcendental knowledge, which are unitive, have our unification as their objective i.e. to make us more real. We are real as long as we participate and manifest our Unity; we are universal, because reality is the *Universus*. As individuals we are effectively an illusion. In other words, as we near the ideal, our universal Consciousness, we are real, i.e. *the ideal is the real.* To the common man this could seem to be a play on words by philosophers, but religious beliefs, moral motivations, the urge for justice and to perfect ourselves, to order our ideas, to become better, etc., which are part of the daily routine of normal man, all obey this natural, universal urge to unify us. To give just one example, morality, which is one of the paths of transcendental knowledge, makes us more real, the immoral act disintegrates us, it scatters and alienates us, it launches us into the chaos of the multiple and it leaves us like a meteorite in infinite space.

It will be said that man is a wolf and I completely agree with this just as Hobbes, Kant, Voltaire and all those who have been capable of viewing human history objectively did. But, from where does this wolf derive these spiritual disquiets notwithstanding they might be sporadic and exceptional? He finds the answer if he retraces his spirit towards its Origin. This is not easy as first he has to abandon his wolf, and later integrate all his faculties and spiritualize them, i.e. put all his activities at the service of the spirit. Curiously the appreciation of the ephemeral nature of existence can awaken the other consciousness that lies dormant in the wolf.

As humans, as individuals, we have a particular cycle of life, but this is minimal and because of this reason it never satisfies us. We only need a part of our mind for this task which is reduced to survival; although modern man might have extended this mind and task to many dispensable objectives. This is not wrong, if he knows that he is distracted from the essential. The great majority go through life trying to justify this miserable individual existence, and this is what makes him miserable. It is the attachment and conditioning to our *individual perspective* that keeps us tied to this animal stage; for this reason we continue searching for transient satisfactions, which is not wrong, if we remember that we are merely killing time.

The Spirit beats in our consciousness so that the latter is concentrated or expands and diversifies, thus configuring the whole *spectrum* of the Mind. These two movements of the spirit in opposite directions are necessary for life itself and for the development of living beings, although the immense majority might ignore it. But it is very appropriate for human beings to know this as they are making their own history. When the spirit is concentrated, it approaches its own essence, the Creative, when it expands it creates (inspired by the Creative) and grows as an individual, society or species. Individuals and societies expand in such a way that they forget their systole, i.e. their inner life and they are left with no base and fall apart, and they are projected like fireworks that will fall after having been displayed, and disintegrate.

It is my aim to bring to consciousness this kind of diastole and systole of universal Consciousness in which all beings will participate, the Unity that underlies diversity and plurality, the need to maintain a permanent relation with this Unity which we really are. Conscious of this Unity and harmonious beating of its Soul, man can develop, avoiding the extremes of thesis and antithesis, walking on the *zone of equilibrium*; they will recognize the adequate speed for their creative and dynamic evolution. (See *The Spirit in History*)

There is only plenitude of life in the experience of totality, which is the totality of consciousness; there is only plenitude of love in the experience of Love in itself. It is the apperception of the said emanations in all beings that gives plenitude of life to this existence. The human being is part of universal Consciousness, he is part, consequence and extension of it; hence he has the motivation to create, to love, to order and also to philosophize, which leads to the comprehension of its Origin with which he closes the Cycle of Life and realizes his destiny.

Synthesis of my project

I do not know up to what point the reader has had the patience to follow me on this quest, but beyond the complexities of philosophical language and the differences that may exist among the authors we have seen, there are simple truths in which all agree and that the reader must retain in their memory: a life without love, without kindness and without beauty, that is to say without an aspiration that takes us away from its repetitive, tedious, profane and animal side, without a quest and without the practice of meaningful paradigms, is a life of misery and, in the best of cases, a nightmare. This quest is not the task of idle intellectuals, but of sincere seekers of the reasons for our existence. These Ideas, that can be called Unity, Nirvana, Brahman or the Absolute, project us towards the culminating point of our life, towards our plenitude.

I have presented a philosophical system that should not be interpreted as a fixed system of ideas, but as stimuli in order to awaken the consciousness; everyone can do as they like after this awakening, there will be no great risks and the diversity will be infinite, as is the World that surrounds us.

My philosophy is not born from a hypothesis from which reality is induced; it is a *theoria* in the original Greek sense, an expression of Reality. My proposal can be summed up as follows: a transition from the survival stage to that of living in plenitude, from belief to experience, from the stage of necessity to that of happiness, from the functional to the aesthetic, from the material to the spiritual. My project tries to reverse the process of individuation, externalization and alienation, and replace it with one of internalization and unification. It is a return to ontology, but in no way does it return to already obsolete beliefs, to imaginary realities, but to an experience of the Transcendent, that should not be understood as a distant ideal, but as a vital necessity of the human being, that of finding oneself, of being integrated in the *Universus*.

End of the Search